SOLDIERS & CIVILIANS

Bantam Windstone Books
Ask your bookseller for the books you have missed

SOLDIERS
&
CIVILIANS

Americans at War and at Home

SHORT STORIES

Edited by Tom Jenks

BANTAM BOOKS
TORONTO · NEW YORK · LONDON · SYDNEY · AUCKLAND

SOLDIERS & CIVILIANS
A Bantam Windstone Book / November 1986

This book was published simultaneously in hardcover and trade paperback.

*Windstone and the accompanying logo of a stylized W are trademarks
of Bantam Books, Inc.*

International Creative Management: "The Ghost Soldiers" by Tim O'Brien. First published in *Esquire.* Copyright © 1981 by Tim O'Brien. "Big Bertha Stories" by Bobbie Ann Mason. First published in *Mother Jones.* Copyright © 1985 by Bobbie Ann Mason.

Alfred A. Knopf, Inc.: "Operate and Maintain" from *A Flag for Sunrise* by Robert Stone. Copyright © 1977, 1980, 1981 by Robert Stone.

Brandt & Brandt, Inc.: "Where Pelham Fell" by Bob Shacochis. First published in *Esquire.* Copyright © 1985 by Bob Shacochis.

Stephanie Vaughn and Georges Borchardt, Inc.: "Able, Baker, Charlie, Dog" by Stephanie Vaughn. First published in *The New Yorker.* Copyright © 1977 by Stephanie Vaughn.

Rick DeMarinis: "Under the Wheat" by Rick DeMarinis. First published in *The Iowa Review.* Reprinted in *The Graywolf Annual.* Copyright © 1974 by Rick DeMarinis.

Viking Penguin, Inc.: "On for the Long Haul" from *Greasy Lake and Other Stories* by T. Coraghessan Boyle. First published in *Esquire.* Copyright © 1985 by T. Coraghessan Boyle.

Wallace & Sheil Agency, Inc.: "Human Moments in World War III" by Don DeLillo. First published in *Esquire.* Copyright © 1983 by Don DeLillo.

Library of Congress Cataloging-in-Publication Data

Soldiers & civilians.

1. War stories, American. 2. American fiction—20th
century. I. Jenks, Tom. II. Title: Soldiers and
civilians.
PS648.W34S65 1986 813'.01'08358 86-47574
ISBN 0-553-05180-6
ISBN 0-553-34312-2 (pbk)

Published simultaneously in the United States and Canada

*Bantam Books are published by Bantam Books, Inc. Its trademark, consisting of
the words "Bantam Books" and the portrayal of a rooster, is Registered in U.S.
Patent and Trademark Office and in other countries. Marca Registrada. Bantam
Books, Inc., 666 Fifth Avenue, New York, New York 10103.*

PRINTED IN THE UNITED STATES OF AMERICA

FG   0 9 8 7 6 5 4 3 2 1

For My Father
Edwin Riley Jenks, Cmdr., USN, Ret.

War stories aren't really anything more than stories about people anyway.

—Michael Herr, *Dispatches*

CONTENTS

SOLDIERS & CIVILIANS

INTRODUCTION

It would be tempting but too optimistic to say that the generation that came of age during the 1960s will be remembered most as one that resisted war. We grew up with our fathers' stories of Europe and the Pacific. There was, for instance, in the 1950s a Sunday school teacher who, when prompted, would tell his class how he ran fast across an open field only to be caught by machine gun bullets tracing a path up his right heel, calf, thigh, and hip. He had a limp and the scars to show. His close neighbor, who bore no scars and still served weekends in the reserves, never spoke at all about the war. But sometimes, when he was out, his wife and children would take a small diary from his desk and read. It described longitude and latitude, topography, dates and times, vectors, deployment, dry minutiae of tactic and strategy, which left ample ground for visions of bunkers and mud and death. More frightful was the dawning awareness in children who late discovered they were Jewish and then began to understand their parents' care in disguising the past as a way of preserving the future.

Our history texts were structured and punctuated by the events of the nations' wars, in which American victory and compassion figured more prominently than, for example, the lost War of 1812 or the internment of Japanese-Americans during World War II. As children, most of us knew there were Civil War veterans surviving, and we watched their passing with a sense of wonder and loss. Often, when we played, we wore our fathers' cast-off uniforms and drew on their stories or on stories from books and movies. We fought Japs and Germans, Rebels and Yankees,

1

fought the old wars, killing and being killed. Some of our older brothers had been in Korea. Some of us would go to Vietnam. Soon a high school football star who left to be a pilot would come home paralyzed. A friend who slipped back from Canada for a few days to visit his mother would tell us about the successful use of aliases. A daughter of a prominent man would die while committing an act of terrorism. Others, later, went to Lebanon, Iran, Honduras, Nicaragua, Salvador, on missions of violence and mercy. It seems unlikely we'll ever resist war.

Instead, we bind its wounds, study its lessons, argue its reasons, refine its forms, scaling it to the times. The scale has grown smaller, and infinitely large. We are familiar with terms such as "limited nuclear warfare." We have rapid deployment and peacekeeping forces. We give military aid around the globe and engage in conflicts. Most of us, if asked, would respond that war is a mistake, fundamentally wrong, or immoral. But now, as always, we are poised for war because few of our leaders are fundamentally opposed to it.

This discrepancy between private belief and public action is an ageless conspiracy of human nature. In his *Devil's Dictionary*, Ambrose Bierce defined "War" as "A by-product of the arts of peace" and commented that "The soil of peace is thickly sown with seeds of war." Tolstoy explained it this way:

> Napoleon ordered an army to be raised and go to war. . . . He had the power and so what he ordered was done.
> . . . What is power? Power is the collective will vested in one person. On what condition is the people's will vested in one person? On the condition that that person expresses the will of the whole people. That is, Power is power. In other words, power is a word the meaning of which we do not know.

A glance at the contents page of the collected work of almost any writer in any age reveals the strong influence, if not the absolute chronological and thematic pattern in life, of war. The only other theme as frequent is love, and, from the beginning, as in the *Bible* or *The Illiad*, the two themes have been one. Together, they tell the story of good and evil in the world.

War is in the air—literally—on TV in romantic mini-series about the old wars and in slick fast-paced ads for Army recruitment. Seriousness and patriotism in the newest war movies have replaced the important irony in the war films of twenty years ago. A bestselling Dr. Seuss book treats arms escalation as inevitable, even if foolish, and among children, G.I. Joe, the American Hero, is making a comeback, close behind Luke Skywalker and Voltron, Defender of the Universe.

Our sense of war has grown more and more ethereal, removed from bone and blood, acted out in play and reality with buttons and computers. Children and adults feel deeply, half-consciously most of the time, that war is dangerous but not physically, not really, to *me*, since it happens "out there" inside a video screen. On campus, among older youth, teachers note a confusion or absence of historical sense. Korea blends into Vietnam. Was the last world war I, II, or III?

So far, the end of the twentieth century has been more about style than substance. Popular and political culture in America have shifted so that there is little distinction between left and right, liberal and conservative. In place of causes or beliefs, there are life-styles, fashions, personal statements, individual careers and interests, each fueling the national interest, which is termed vital and understood to be territorial and, above all, economic. American style has everything to do with what's required to maintain it, and where the economy is troubled and patriotism is fashionable, the postures of war can be trendy, especially among a new generation that will not yet have recognized its own mortality.

In one of the old war stories, William Faulkner's "Shall Not Perish," a little boy who wanted to accompany his elder brother to war hears his mother console a townsman over the loss of a son:

> "All men are capable of shame," Mother said. "Just as all men are capable of courage, honor, and sacrifice. And grief, too. It will take time, but they will learn it. It will take more grief than yours and mine, and there will be more. But it will be enough."
>
> "When? When all the young men are dead? What will there be left then worth saving?"
>
> "I know," Mother said. "I know. Our Pete was too young too to have to die."

Spoken by a mother, to a father, about the loss of sons, and overheard by a younger son drawn toward battle, these are words in the deepest current of life, words for the next generation and the next. Within the fears and fashions of most of us who came of age in the 1960s, within all the American talk of human rights, within the "human potential" movement we are now bequeathing to an even more cautiously self-caring 1970s and '80s generation, there lies the thought that as we live so will we grow stronger and better at life. This anthology is dedicated to the effort and to the belief that stories are an ultimate way of understanding the world, of keeping the difficulty and passion of human events most accurately before us, and of continuing the search for coherence and meaning and peace.

The twenty stories collected here are entirely contemporary, but reach back to old wars and anticipate new ones. About half the stories deal directly with war or military life. The other half are civilian, and in them the voice of war is in the background, often very distant as it is in life. Together, these stories present a modern vision of the nature of man and war and of the ways in which martial values influence our lives, even, or perhaps most especially, in times of peace. The authors represented have never limited their work to martial themes, and, in fact, most of them are not known for war writing at all. Rather, they are gathered here through force of storytelling ritual, gathered because there is no one whose life has not been touched by war. Almost every story was recommended by one or more of the authors of another story included in the collection, as well as by friends, who, when asked to suggest a story, responded with titles affirmed by others. And if you listen carefully, you will hear older, familiar voices— Hemingway or Homer or Tolstoy—mingling in the spirit of a new generation that bears witness to war.

The collection opens with Ward Just's "I'm Worried About You," which sounds a note of sadness appropriate to the losses occasioned by the passage of time and history. Don DeLillo's "Human Moments in World War III" closes the book with a meditation on the hope and danger that lie in man's future. At the core of the collection lies Vietnam, as in John Mort's combat story "Tanks" or Larry Heinemann's raw and powerful "Good Morning to You, Lieutenant." Many of the stories—those by Robert Stone, James Salter, Andre Dubus, Breece Pancake, Tim O'Brien, Bob Shacochis, and Stephanie Vaughn—redefine traditional military values: courage, honor, glory, duty, loyalty, discipline, and their dark twins, cowardice, cruelty, horror, shame, and defeat. Others—by John Sayles, Jayne Anne Phillips, Rick DeMarinis, and Bobbie Ann Mason—show the consequences of war. And all of the stories play on themes whose sum is as large as the mystery of our race. Mark Helprin's "North Light" evokes the highest spirit of battle, while Tobias Wolff's "Soldier's Joy" portrays troops disengaged, lonely, and irritable for action. Kathryn Kramer's "Seeds of Conflict" is Swiftian in its satire of the complacent ease with which we often regard the pervasiveness of war, and it is keen in seeing the face of war in family and individual conflicts. In Richard Ford's "Communist," peace and understanding conquer fear, and in T. Coraghessan Boyle's "On for the Long Haul" fear wins.

These stories, if not yet timeless in their vein, are at least among the strongest that our age offers. Their presence here together calls for special thanks to Gary Fisketjon and Guy Martin, whose enthusiasm and encouragement brought refinement to the initial idea, to Reginald Gibbons who has given the example of publishing stories that others would not, to Scott Walker and Pat Strachan for their editorial interest, advice, and support, to Liz Darhansoff for faith, guidance, and knowing when to crack a joke, to my wife Carlton for love, and finally to Deb Futter and Steve Rubin, who listened and carefully brought the stories home.

—TOM JENKS

August, 1985

I'M WORRIED ABOUT YOU

by Ward Just

At Verdun it began to leak rain, staining the concrete of the monument Ossuaire. She insisted on taking a photograph of Marshall and Harry, who stood uncomfortably on the steps in front of the building. They were as gray as the day, dressed in floppy hats and trench coats. French tourists moved around them, apparently oblivious; one old man stood staring at the graves, wiping his eyes. She fiddled with the camera and finally snapped the picture of the men, who looked off to one side, casually, as if they did not know they were being photographed.

Later, the three of them went to the Tranchee des Baionettes, hustling because they were late; Harry had to catch a train. He kept looking at his watch while Marshall and Janine circled the trench. He knew the battlefield well. Look, he said finally, look carefully in there. You can still see their bayonets pointed up. Killed where they stood, buried. See the bayonets?

It was true, the points of the bayonets poked through the soft earth, a grim iron garden. There was also a bent and rusted rifle barrel. It was a memorial to one of the great legends of the first war, members of the 137th Infantry Regiment holding the line, though bombarded and eventually interred by German artillery.

She said, You can't mean that the bodies are still there?

No, Harry said, looking at his watch. They have buried the men in the Ossuaire but left their weapons in place. It's to give you an idea of how it was in the spring of 1916. La Gloire. Mort pour la France. The goddamned French, he said savagely. This place is a monument to death.

Janine stood looking at the trench, shaking her head.

6

We have to go now, Harry said. My train.

I've been waiting for twenty years to see Verdun, Marshall said. I want to see Douaumont, and Fort de Vaux. Then we can go. You won't miss your train.

Inside Fort de Vaux, they stood next to one of the French 75s. On a sunny day there would be a fine clear field of fire. They stood silent a moment, oppressed by the closeness and thickness of the walls and the low ceiling, the dampness and the mass of the gun, silent for sixty-eight years. Fort de Vaux had been taken when the defenders ran out of water and ammunition; later, it was retaken. There was no graffiti on the walls and everything seemed to be as it was then. The rain had turned to a sporadic drizzle, almost a fog. Marshall looked at the fields below and imagined line upon line of German troops. Then he turned to his wife and said, Can you imagine the racket in here when the gun was firing? My God.

She said, I can't forget the old man at the Ossuaire.

At last they were en route to Bar-le-duc, where Harry would catch his train. He had the schedule in his hand and was calculating whether it would be better to go to Metz or to Nancy. They were very late. The road was slippery and Marshall drove slowly, taking no chances; he did not know the road. Harry kept looking at his wristwatch and sighing. He was returning to Paris to have a farewell dinner with a girl. He intended to say good-bye to her at the dinner, and break off their affair.

You can pass that truck, he said.

No, I can't, Marshall said.

Harry said, This is very stressful.

We'll get there in time, Marshall said.

I never should've come, Harry said. I should have stayed in Paris. Then he began to talk about the girl in short sentences, non sequiturs. Marshall only nodded, keeping his eyes on the road. He did not know the girl well; really, he did not understand what had gone wrong except that it was another busted love affair. There was a snapshot in Harry's Paris apartment, the girl in deshabille, sitting on a cocktail table. She was wearing one of Harry's oxford shirts, the shirt unbuttoned all the way down. She was sitting Indian-fashion, leaning forward, her head a little to one side. It was a low glass cocktail table and the photographer was above her, shooting down; the result looked professionally made, grainy and slightly off-focus. It looked like Harry's work. A cigarette hung from her lower lip, the smoke just visible around her head, a goofy smile curling around the cigarette. She held a

champagne flute at an angle so anyone looking at the picture
wanted to cry out, Watch it! You're going to spill your wine! The
whorish effect was comical because the girl was very well groomed,
short hair, fine bones, and a cleft chin: a model's composed face.
She was lovely to look at. It was just a snapshot stuck in a
bookcase but it caught everyone's eye. It made people, men
mostly, smile when they looked at it.

The girl's name was Antoinette and she came from a very old
French family. Her great-grandfather, the viscount, was men-
tioned by Proust as an habitue of the many soirees Chez Verdurin.
Harry said she reminded him of an earlier, happier, more orga-
nized time. She made him laugh. He called her Off-with-my-head-
Antoinette.

He said, I'm worried about her.

Marshall said, We're almost there.

Harry said, As a matter of fact, I think that was the first thing I
said to her in seriousness, the night we met, "I'm worried about
you." I was, too. She didn't look well. She was mixed up with a
bad crowd. And she still is. But the hell with it, it's all in the past,
at my age you're happy for whatever you get, for whatever
duration. And we had a great six months. These women today,
they're too modern for me. But I came in at the end of everything, colonialism, the novel, decent movies, worthy women. And
she's so goddamned young, only thirty-five. I kept telling her that.
And that I couldn't ever be French. I'm an American and I don't
want to be French. The goddamned French. So I'm going to end
it tonight, and put myself out of my misery. Her, too. She had a
right to her own life, don't you think? Can't you hurry it up,
Marsh?

Here we are, Janine said from the rear seat. Bar-le-duc.

You two have been great, Harry said.

Marshall said, Good luck.

His hand on the door handle, Harry turned all the way round
to smile nervously at Janine. His mind was still on Antoinette. He
said, Were you surprised by Verdun.

She smiled back. Surprised is not the word.

He nodded. Well then, did you like it? A lot of people can't
take it. And why should they? It's an ugly place that only a
Frenchman could've designed. All that concrete, those crosses
and the bayonets. But it's something that you have to see, once.
It's where Europe died.

She said, I didn't *like* it, Harry.

He patted her knee with his free hand. You know what I mean, he said, sighing again, looking at his watch and then out the window. They were stopped at a traffic light. He said, This is ridiculous, we'll never make it. I'll have to go to Strasbourg with you. I don't know what'll happen to her, that's the thing. I just want to get it over with.

The train was in the station when they pulled up. Harry opened the door and flew out of the car. Marshall parked, and he and Janine strolled back to the platform. The train was already moving, Harry waving at them from the vestibule of the first-class coach. They watched the train disappear and then they turned and looked at each other. Janine closed her eyes. A great weariness came upon her, and she slumped against Marshall's shoulder. He sensed her mood at once, steering her firmly off the platform and into the waiting room and around the corner to the buffet. They drank one glass of wine and then another, and when at last they were on the road again, Janine realized she was tipsy. Her vision was blurred and she felt exhausted. She put her head back but was unable to nap. The snap of the windshield wipers and the whine of the little car's engine irritated her. Everywhere it was gray and pissing down rain. Dusk was coming on. When Marshall lit a cigarette she turned to him and said sharply, You're smoking too much. Why did we have to go to Verdun?

They did not make Strasbourg that night, choosing instead an auberge in a tiny hillside town near Nancy. It was almost eight-thirty when they arrived. Without a booking, Marshall wanted to secure a room immediately. The auberge was highly recommended, and popular on weekends. But Jan wanted to talk, to clear her head, to breathe deeply, to get the kinks out; really, she was tired of rushing. This was supposed to be a vacation, a *holiday*, their first in three years; it wasn't supposed to be a forced march, or a memorial service for the death of Europe. And Europe wasn't dead, it was only temporarily out of service, for the moment elusive in the darkness—

Your friend Harry, she began.

Our friend, he corrected.

Harry, she said, then didn't finish the sentence. Harry was Harry was Harry was Harry, and if he wanted to believe that Europe was dead, he had the right. She wondered why he hadn't added Europe to the list of things he had come in at the end of. She would listen to it, but she didn't have to believe it. She didn't have to *like* it.

They walked the few feet to the graveyard of the old church, and stood looking over the stones into the valley. It was very dark now and no one was about; light rain obscured the valley, and she wondered if there were a town and farmhouses below, or whether there was only forest. There was no light anywhere, but she heard the sound of rushing water. Something made her turn and she saw a priest glide soundlessly from the side door of the church. Inside were the dim yellow lights of candles; a vigil. She might not have noticed him at all, except the white of his collar glittered in the candlelight. The priest locked the door and moved down the path, picking his way. He was a portly priest, no stranger to the cuisine of Lorraine. He looked over at them, seemed to hesitate, and then went on.

Spooky, she thought. She turned to Marshall to say something, but he was distant. His mood reminded her of Harry on the way to the railway station—sighing, consulting his wristwatch, distracted, worried that he wouldn't catch the train, worried about Antoinette, mixed up with a bad crowd. . . . Marshall stood with his hands plunged into the pockets of his trench coat, looking like a sentry doing disagreeable duty.

It's chilly, Marshall said.

Yes, she said. It's good autumn weather, football weather, but nice, so quiet and dark. Let's walk just a minute more. She took his hand and pulled him along, past the graveyard to the road leading into the valley. There were silent shuttered houses on either side of them, and she wondered if the town were a summer resort, like Edgartown or Welfleet, unoccupied until the summer season. Then she saw a sliver of light behind one of the shutters, a dancing blue fluorescence; television. She turned quickly away.

It's time to get back, he said.

Just a minute more, she pleaded, one minute. She took a step forward. The road sloped down to the right and was lost to view. She wanted to follow it into the valley. She said, Isn't it great to be here? She heard him fumbling in his pocket and then he lit a cigarette, the match flaring, and the smoke hanging in the heavy air. She was looking again into the darkness, listening to the rushing water, and wondering where the road went. His hand was on her arm. She tried not to notice his impatience. She felt somehow that the place was enchanted, and that her own life was entering a new chapter. No one in the world knew where they were.

Jan?

Shhhhh, she said.

He moved close to her and explained that they had to get things settled. He had to speak to the patron to see to the booking here, and get the luggage up to the room—assuming that there was a room—and find out about dinner. It was already close to nine, and the chef was no doubt temperamental. If the chef closed his kitchen down, well then, they'd had it. Also, he had to cancel the booking in Strasbourg. And Harry had made a reservation for them at that restaurant, whatsitsname, and it was important that they cancel that. Two telephone calls.

Gosh, she said. All in one night?

And I want a drink, he said.

All right, she said. Okay.

He said, I hate these details.

She said, Me too.

But we don't want to be stranded, he said.

She said, Do you love me?

Yes, he said.

I love you, too.

He laughed and took her hand, and when they turned around they saw the auberge, its lights rosy and welcoming through the rain. It was like a mirage in the desert, or an advertisement for gastronomic France. A pretty sign, and flowers in pots outside. Wonderful smells came from the kitchen. She suddenly felt very hungry.

They stood for a moment without moving. Marshall smelled escargot, and smiled to himself because escargot meant traditional cooking, heavy, rich sauces and large portions. He hated the delicate nouvelle cuisine.

This town, she said.

What about it? He pitched his cigarette into the street.

She said, It's insecure. It looks dead, doesn't it? Feels dead. An Ossuaire, and I've had enough of Ossuaires. No one's home in this town. Did you notice the priest, so furtive? Listen to the water, there must be a river in the valley. What a strange place this is. What's its name?

But Marshall had forgotten the name of the town.

She said, I'll call it Forlorn.

He said, It's late, that's all.

How did we happen to come here? she asked.

He took her hand and they began to walk. You found it in the *Michelin,* he said.

That's right, she said.

And a good thing we did. Good for you, finding Forlorn. We'd still be on the road, otherwise.

She opened her mouth to say something, then didn't. The odd

thing was, this village in Lorraine reminded her of the town they lived in, an anonymous suburb north of Boston. In the suburb no one moved after dark, and the streets were always silent, blue fluorescence everywhere. They had lived in the same house for three years, and knew no one on their block; it was too much to call it a neighborhood. Of course the shape of their suburban town was familiar; it held no surprises.

The next day they moved on to Strasbourg, and the day after that to an inn at Hirschegg in the Kleinwalsertal. It was a punishing drive, and they stayed at the inn two days, taking a long hike on the second day. The following afternoon they found themselves in Freiburg, where they dropped off the car. After lunch, they visited the cathedral, taking a seat quietly because a son et lumiere was in progress. The narration was in German and they understood very little, so after fifteen minutes they left their seats and padded around the perimeter of the church. Then they left the way they came, by the west porch, the one with the frieze depicting a princely satan leading a procession of virgins; the son et lumiere continued, in hostile incomprehensible German. Outside, in the shadow of the great cathedral, a crowd had gathered around a brightly colored gypsy caravan. Two mute white-faced clowns were shilling for a circus due in Freiburg the next day. Marshall and Jan pressed closer, watching the pantomime. The caravan was filled with animals, and these the clowns introduced one by one. A boar, a goat, a monkey, two hobbled doves, three roosters, a terrier, a black cat, a wee Shetland pony and, finally, rats. One gray rat after another appeared on the steeple of a misshapen cuckoo clock in an alcove in the front of the caravan. The dour clown gathered them up and let them crawl on his shoulders and around his neck. He seemed not to notice his necklace of rats. He put the largest in his shirt pocket, its long snout moving this way and that like a cobra's head. Meanwhile, the goat and the boar nuzzled each other, and the pony sat down with the dog. From its perch on a three-legged stool, the black cat eyed the doves. The monkey moved to the feet of the dour clown and he picked it up roughly, cradling it in his arms; the monkey's odor was pungent, and the rats ceased to move except the shirt-pocket rat, whose snout swayed from side to side, sniffing the monkey. The cheerful clown reached inside the alcove and brought out a cassette, which he punched into the tape deck on the pavement. It was a Mozart concerto, scratchy, badly modulated. The cheerful clown began to hop in time with the music, while his confederate stood to one side, blank-faced, rats motionless on his shoulders.

When the dwarf burst through the little door below the alcove the crowd laughed and cheered. Marshall gaped. The dwarf was the smallest man he had ever seen. He seemed scarcely larger than the monkey, yet he had a beard and heavy, powerful arms. The dwarf pirouetted once and crashed to the pavement, all this without a sound. The crowd cheered again, and the dwarf doffed his derby. The dour clown gave the dwarf a rat, which he placed in the crease of the derby. With a look of disapproval, the other clown shooed the black cat off the stool.

The doves waddled away.

The boar nudged the dog.

The crowd began to chant.

The cavorting dwarf embraced the boar, caressing it, muttering something into its ear, laughing soundlessly, then deftly plucked the gray rat from the crease of its derby and stuffed it violently down the animal's throat—though that may have been an illusionist's sleight-of-hand, it was so sudden and unexpected. The crowd gasped, delighted, then roared its approval. With a malicious grin, the dwarf released the boar and advanced on the Shetland, creeping really, moving on all fours like an ape, his hands scraping the ground. The roosters and the goat backed away and settled under the caravan, alert and wary. The two clowns stood off to one side, bored and weary, as the music ran down, now off-key, sounding more like Kurt Weill than Mozart. A strange nervousness swept the crowd, for no one knew what might come next. The dwarf, sensing this, paused and turned its heavy head left and right, leering, the muscles in its forearms bulging—and in a moment had flung himself into a front flip, landing on the pony's tiny back. He crouched, his cheek touching the shaggy withers, looking for all the world like a professional jockey approaching the starting gate; the dwarf and the pony were in perfect proportion to each other. They looked like toys. The pony moved hesitantly, a step at a time, as if walking through a mine field, its eyes wide and terrified. When the dwarf opened its mouth and howled—the sound seemed scarcely human—the pony flared and stepped crabwise, moving in a circle around the other animals, which remained rigid. The dour clown had moved surreptitiously to the front of the caravan, and now began feeding the rats back into the mouth of the cuckoo clock; show almost over. The dwarf was balancing himself on the pony's back, and now laboriously lifted himself in a handstand, to thunderous applause.

The pony cautiously picked up speed and the other animals
retreated, scuttling under the caravan or into the arms of the
clowns. A single rat remained on the clock's steeple. Still upside
down, the dwarf's eyes were wide open, fixed on a point in the
middle distance. He clenched his hands, digging into the pony's
flesh. The pony shuddered. Then the dwarf began to do something else, one-handed, and Marshall turned away.

He said, Jesus Christ.

Jan said, I think we are very far into Europe.

And with that, the great bells of the cathedral began to toll.

Marshall was sleeping badly. He would wake up at two or three
o'clock in the morning, the room cool but his body slick with
sweat. It always took him a moment to remember where he was,
whether this was Hirschegg or Nuremberg. The first few nights he
thought he was coming down with something, the flu perhaps,
but after a week he put it down to nerves, a kind of unease that
he could neither define nor suppress. He would lay awake for
three hours, then fall asleep and snap to punctually at nine. He
had two books in his bag, one a book of history and the other a
novel. The history book was dense, and he began with that after
an hour's sleeplessness. The preface to it was a lovely thing, the
historian's memories of conversations with friends. He mentioned
one particular friend, and the many conversations sitting beneath
cedar trees at Souget, his friend's house in the Jura. Marshall was
beguiled by the preface, so rigorous and civilized, and whenever
he thought about the horrors of war he thought not about young
children with their lives ahead of them but about the two old
men, two of the most learned men in Europe, sitting beneath
cedars on the lawn of a house in the Jura, trading memories.

The book of history was so demanding that after thirty minutes
Marshall would put it aside, twenty pages read, and turn to the
novel. This was the novel about old Sartoris. He tried to enter the
life of the page, the lines of type that always reminded him of
the formation of infantry regiments of the nineteenth century. He
allowed the lines of type to advance, and to overwhelm him. It
was necessary for him to open himself to any possibility, to enter
fully into the spirit of the transaction. He allowed himself to feel
the heat and fragrance of the deep South, in order to come to
know the novel's characters, and the great burden of the past.
These were characters who seemed to have no future. They were
in chains to the past, moored as securely as any vessel in a
swift-running river. At the end of the hour, Marshall realized that

he was not understanding what he was reading. He parsed the page a word at a time, the words not windows but mirrors, and the story not the novelist's but his own. Old Sartoris receded, and finally disappeared. Only the lines of type remained, motionless.

When he put the book aside and turned to look out the window, it was dawn, gray and uninviting; cloud cover shrouded western Europe. His body was dry and he pulled the covers up, fearful of a chill; his nose was cold and his feet numb, and his mind thick with sleeplessness, though he knew he had been dozing while he read. Perhaps he only dreamed the business about the two old men sitting under cedar trees, reminiscing. Outside, traffic began to move. He heard the clang of a trolley's bell and, far off, the hoot of an ambulance, eine kleine nachtmusik. Except it was not night, it was dawn, six o'clock by his watch. He heard Jan turn and sigh in the next bed, then mutter something in German. Amused, he raised his head to look at her, concealed in the covers; her face was hidden but her familiar hair was sprayed carelessly on the pillow. She knew no German, and in his muddled state he wondered if somehow he had wandered into the wrong room. Wrong room, wrong fraulein. He looked out the window again and decided to take a long morning's walk while she slept. His clothes were slung over the chair across the room. He could stroll to the square and have a cup of coffee and watch the city wake up, read the *Herald-Tribune* and catch up on the ball scores and the campaign, connect again to American time. But it was very gray; the streets were desolate. Turning over, Marshall fell asleep.

In Berlin they found a gallery that specialized in the German expressionists. They bought four posters, two by Beckmann, two by Grosz. The posters were exceptionally cheap, so on a spree they bought an Otto Dix lithograph also. They spent two exhilarating hours in the gallery, wishing they had ten thousand dollars to spend instead of two hundred. How thin and flimsy and self-indulgent the American moderns seemed beside the pre-war Germans. A little bit perverse, she thought, bringing these Germans to their quaint Boston suburb. Beckmann's thick black lines, Grosz's pig-faced capitalists, Dix's oppressed masses. But it was a way of retaining something of Europe, and especially of Germany, which had come to mean so much to both of them: a way to measure themselves, and their own time, and their own country.

On the street again, the posters and the Dix secure in a

cardboard tube, they walked up the Kurfurstendamm to their hotel. The street was thick with youngsters, teenagers of every nationality. A city of children, he thought. A curt cabdriver had told them they were mostly young men avoiding the draft in Holland, Scandinavia, France, and the United States. Divided Berlin was the gathering place of the youth of all nations, so eager to evade their responsibilities. Drugs were cheap and plentiful. There was no discipline in Berlin. Marshall said, There is no draft in the United States. The United States is not at war. Ach, the driver said, is that so? No military service at all? Then why are there so many American young in Berlin?

Marshall had no answer to that.

Jan tugged at his arm as they walked up the great glitzy boulevard, brilliant with light. For their last night in Germany, she thought they should ignore the tyrannical *Guide Michelin*. They should trust to instinct, find a place that looked cheerful and not too expensive, and tuck into it for a feast. She tapped him on the shoulder with the tube, grinning. Their luck had turned, how else to explain finding the gallery with its trove of German expressionists.

She led the way, past the sidewalk troubadours, off the Kurfurstendamm, to a small noisy restaurant. They ordered a bottle of wine, sausages and sauerkraut, specialties of the house. She was animated, talking about the first afternoon at Verdun, the drive to Bar-le-duc, and later that night, in the town she named Forlorn. Some of the details had gotten out of hand, but all in all they had done well. Perhaps in the future they would plan a real itinerary, not leave quite so much to chance. But it was difficult, travelling in a strange country, not knowing the language or the customs.

She said, The other night you were muttering in German.

He laughed. I was? So were you.

In your sleep, she said. You talked and talked.

I wonder what I was saying? he said.

The sausages and sauerkraut arrived, and they began to eat. He was trying to remember the clowns in the square at Freiburg, and the exact sequence in which the animals appeared. She was silent, her head bent over her plate. He said, What a menagerie! Narrative by the Brothers Grimm. Grosz could have done something with the clowns and the dwarf on the pony's back. He said, You were right when you said we were very far into Europe. Marshall signalled for another bottle of wine, then noticed that Jan wasn't eating.

He said, Is something wrong?

She said, The sauerkraut reminds me of my mother. She made such good sauerkraut, it was just the best sauerkraut, my mom's. Sorry.

She was crying. He leaned across the table to touch her hand and she looked at him, biting her lip, trying and failing to smile. Her hand was hot and damp. The noise rose around them, and they drew closer; it was as if they were in a cocoon, wrapped in hostile foreign voices. He murmured something to her, but she didn't hear. He said, You are my one and only. She made a little ambiguous gesture with her hand, pushing at her food with a fork. He filled her glass with wine and she raised it, toasting him, and drained it, every drop. Presently she began to eat and then, impulsively, leaned across the table, closed her eyes, and kissed him.

At the Cafe Einstein, where they went for a drink after dinner, she was pensive again, inspecting the room, scrutinizing the intellectuals. Conversation around them was low and intense. They were served cognac by a sullen Asian in black tie. Marshall wondered if he was Vietnamese; his English was flawless, idiomatic American. She said, I'm sorry I was so mean to Harry. I didn't understand his life, the way he lives, what he has to cope with. He said he was an American and couldn't ever be anything else, but I'm not so sure. I think I understand him better now. This has been such an experience for me. I'll never forget it, ever. I feel as if we've been in Germany for a hundred years. I feel pushed back in time. I find myself remembering the strangest things, old emotions, memories. What was it that Harry said about Germany, that I didn't believe?

Marshall looked up and shook his head. He didn't remember.

She said, This is the place where all modern history begins, he said.

They were to meet Harry at his apartment, then go on to dinner. But driving in from the airport, Marshall had a sudden inspiration. It was afternoon in Paris, the trees turning and the weather warm. The French strolled hand in hand, animated, dressed in summer colors. He leaned forward and tapped the cabdriver on the shoulder and told him to take them to the Brasserie Flo. He wanted a plate of oysters and a bottle of Sancerre. They jumped from the cab with four pieces of luggage and settled around a table. Flo was crowded and cheerful. The oysters arrived, along with the Sancerre. They ate a dozen oysters apiece and ordered a second bottle. They were trying to remember the precise moment when they fell in love; it was eleven years before, and they had both been married to other people. He insisted it had to be the same moment, and she said that was just like a man, an *American* man, searching for symmetry when there was no symmetry. She offered a preposterous version of events that had him roaring with laughter. She insisted that he had entrapped her, a kind of sting. They were leaning across the table, head to head, talking now in their private language, on familiar ground. They remained that way for some time in the amiable boozy atmosphere of Flo. They had finished the second bottle and knew now that it was time to go. But no one wanted to speak first, to break the spell and reintroduce the old world of promises and obligations. Knowing that, they looked up simultaneously and winked at each other. Time for the check. Time to go meet Harry.

They were very late, but in any event Harry was not at home. He had left them a note in his difficult spidery handwriting. Make free with the apartment. He had gone to Cyprus on assignment; it was either assignment or assignation, hard to tell which. There was altogether too much commotion and turbulence in Paris. Too much anxiety and the weather had been lousy, pissing down rain. However, he and Antoinette had reached an accommodation; in fact, she was with him in Cyprus, surprise surprise. It turned out that the quarrel had been the result of a simple misunderstanding, and he had taken her to Kyrenia to sort it out once and for all. She was a good egg, really, though a little off the wall. Wish me luck. There was a bottle of champagne in the fridge. How was your trip? Did you like the Jerries?

Marshall and Jan tumbled into bed and it was after nine when they rose and bathed. Marshall wandered into the kitchen and popped the bottle. It was warm in the apartment, and he opened one of the kitchen windows. He poured two glasses and walked into the living room, pausing at the bookcase to look for Antoinette in deshabille.

He heard Jan laughing in the tub.

She called to him, Remember the German on the mountain in the Kleinwalsertal?

He did, vaguely. They had taken a picnic into the mountains, leaving the hotel at noon, winding higher and higher along the macadam path. The view was gorgeous. There were many hikers in lederhosen, carrying backpacks and walking sticks, who looked at them with disapproval. They were dressed for a stroll on Boston Common. Marshall carried a plastic bag from the supermarket, with sausage and cheese and a bottle of wine. At mid-afternoon they left the path and began to strike for the summit, ascending through pastureland in lazy S-curves. They stopped to eat, wondering whether to resume the climb or start back. It was then that Jan saw the German and called to him.

She was still laughing, recalling the conversation, a clutter of German, French, and English. No, the German had said, they must not go higher. The north slope was already in shadows, and the snow six inches deep. He pointed at their shoes and laughed. They were not properly equipped for the journey. Heavy sweaters were required, darkness came quickly on the mountain, and with it the cold, and it was so very easy to lose your way. He produced a map that explained the difficulty. He said, Take the funicular, it's only five minutes. And you only have to hike one way and it's easier walking down than walking up. Or take the funicular both ways and save your energy. They had shared their wine with him. He was an engineer from Darmstadt, on a hiking holiday in the Kleinwalsertal. Leaving them, he wagged a finger and pointed at their feet. Next time, bring boots! He strode away very confidently, descending, and in a few minutes he was an inch high, merging with the other hikers on the lower slopes, heading for the village in the valley.

She laughed again. He could hear her splashing in the tub.

He had forgotten all about the hiker, a large good-looking German of the blond, Nordic type. He had given them sound advice. Marshall stood in front of the bookcase, two glasses of champagne in his hand. Jan called to him but he did not answer. He felt the beginnings of a headache and looked at his watch. In fourteen hours they would board their plane for Boston. Seven hours across the Atlantic, then customs at Logan, and another forty-five minutes by train to the anonymous suburb, a tedious day; he looked around the apartment, depressed by its sudden familiarity. It was only a bachelor's pad, with the bachelor's fussy confusion of transience and stability, but its atmosphere nagged at him. His eyes swept the bookcase—a pretty edition of Proust, Baedekers, histories of European wars, biographies of statesmen—but Antoinette's photograph was not to be seen. He searched and searched, then found it tucked between volumes four and five of Proust. He looked at her, a captivating off-focus European, a woman about to spill her wine. She had a carnival aura, a danger-ous woman worth worrying about. That seemed to be what careless Harry desired. It was what made him laugh. No doubt he was attracted to her ironic glare, and her bad crowd. Marshall stood motionless, staring at the photograph, stunned, knowing the most profound ambivalence.

Jan was in the doorway then, naked, dripping water.

He turned to face her, the headache beginning to tighten behind his eyes.

She said, Are you all right?

I'm all right, he said.

You look so sad.

No, he said, forcing a smile. I was just remembering us, a couple of middle-aged Bostonians, touring Europe. Thinking about Harry, and what made him laugh. Thinking about this apartment, thinking about us. Thinking about tomorrow.

Tomorrow, she said. Well then, where's the champagne?

He said, You're drinking too much, and extended to her the hand that held the two glasses. She took one, sipping it thoughtfully, then draining the glass—and with a triumphant look that went back to the first day they met, flung it with all her force into Harry's tiny fake fireplace. The glass exploded into bits, fragments everywhere, and he recoiled, surprised. *There*, she said, laughing. Isn't that what you're supposed to do at a celebration?

He said, What's the celebration?

Oh, Marsh. This is our last night! She laughed. And here I am, naked in Paris.

La gloire, he thought. He realized he was still holding Antoinette's photograph, and gently pushed it back between volumes four and five. He said, I found Antoinette.

I didn't know she was lost, Jan said, looking at him, grinning, giving a little toss of her head; droplets flew from her hair, catching the light. The glow from the single floor lamp accentuated the lines of her breasts and belly. She spread her arms wide and popped open the palms of her hands, an actress accepting the applause of a grateful audience.

But he was in another realm, forced there against his will; in the end, no one could know another, even if they loved each other and travelled well together. He thought of Harry and modern history, and remembered suddenly the trench of bayonets. He said, I hate the thought of going home. Maybe this is where we belong.

Not me, she said.

Yes, he said. That's right. Not you.

She said, There's always a limit to things, a time to say Enough. I'm ready to leave. We've had a fine time. We had a fine time this afternoon, and we're having a fine time now. Aren't we? But I want to go home. We're only visitors here.

He listened carefully, but did not commit himself.

It's been a strange time, she continued. At Verdun I didn't think it was going to be so great. We didn't seem to know who we were, and what we were seeing. It was all so alien, and grim. It didn't seem—safe. Freiburg so weird, and the mountain, the pictures that we bought, and the last night in Berlin . . . She turned, presenting her profile. His headache, forgotten these last few moments, returned. He stepped to her side and they stood together at Harry's picture window, looking out over the rooftops, sharing the last glass.

Really, she murmured. Do you want to stay?

Yes, he said. But his voice did not carry conviction and of course she perceived that, having lived with him so long, knowing him so well. Marsh always had trouble letting go. She put her bare arm around his waist. She said, I understand.

I know you do, he said.

Europe would always be there, she thought. But the idea did not console her, so she said nothing; in any case, it was true whether she said it or not.

NORTH LIGHT

by Mark Helprin

A RECOLLECTION
IN THE
PRESENT TENSE

We are being held back. We are poised at a curve in the road on the southern ridge of a small valley. The sun shines from behind, illuminating with flawless light the moves and countermoves of several score tanks below us. For a long time, we have been absorbed in the mystery of matching the puffs of white smoke from tank cannon with the sounds that follow. The columns themselves move silently: only the great roar rising from the battle proves it not to be a dream.

A man next to me is deeply absorbed in sniffing his wrist. "What are you doing?" I ask.

"My wife," he says. "I can still smell her perfume on my wrist, and I taste the taste of her mouth. It's sweet."

We were called up this morning. The war is two days old. Now it is afternoon, and we are being held back—even though our forces below are greatly outnumbered. We are being held back until nightfall, when we will have a better chance on the plain; for it is packed with tanks, and we have only two old half-tracks. They are loaded with guns—it is true—but they are lightly armored, they are slow, and they present high targets. We expect to move at dusk or just before. Then we will descend on the road into the valley and fight amid the shadows. No one wants this; we all are terrified.

The young ones are frightened because, for most of them, this is the first battle. But their fear is not as strong as the blood which is rising and fills their chests with anger and strength. They have little to lose, being, as they are, only eighteen. They look no more frightened than members of a sports team before an important match: it is that kind of fear, for they are responsible only to themselves.

Married men, on the other hand, are given away by their eyes and faces. They are saying to themselves, "I must not die; I *must not die*." They are remembering how they used to feel when they were younger; and they know that they have to fight. They may be killed, but if they don't fight they will surely be killed, because the slow self-made fear which demands constant hesitation is the most efficient of all killers. It is not the cautious who die, but the overcautious. The married men are trying to strike an exact balance between their responsibility as soldiers, their fervent desire to stay alive, and their only hope—which is to go into battle with the smooth, courageous, trancelike movements that will keep them out of trouble. Soldiers who do not know how (like dancers or mountain climbers) to let their bodies think for them are very liable to be killed. There is a flow to hard combat; it is not (as it has often been depicted) entirely chance or entirely skill. A thousand signals and signs speak to you, much as in music. And what a sad moment it is when you must, for one reason or another, ignore them. The married men fear this moment. We should have begun hours ago. Being held back is bad luck.

"What time is it?" asks one of the young soldiers. Someone answers him.

"Fourteen hundred." No one in the Israeli Army except high-ranking officers (colonels, generals—and we have here no colonels or generals) tells time in this fashion.

"What are you, a general?" asks the young soldier. Everyone laughs, as if this were funny, because we are scared. We should not be held back like this.

Another man, a man who is close to fifty and is worrying about his two sons who are in Sinai, keeps on looking at his watch. It is expensive and Japanese, with a black dial. He looks at it every minute to see what time it is, because he has actually forgotten. If he were asked what the time was, he would not be able to respond without checking the watch, even though he has done so fifty times in the last hour. He too is very afraid. The sun glints off the crystal and explodes in our eyes.

As younger men who badly wanted to fight, we thought we

knew what courage was. Now we know that courage is the forced step of going into battle when you want anything in the world but that, when there is every reason to stay out, when you have been through all the tests, and passed them, and think that it's all over. Then the war hits like an artillery shell and you are forced to be eighteen again, but you can't be eighteen again; not with the taste of your wife's mouth in your mouth, not with the smell of her perfume on your wrists. The world turns upside down in minutes.

How hard we struggle in trying to remember the easy courage we once had. But we can't. We must either be brave in a different way, or not at all. What is that way? How can we fight like seasoned soldiers when this morning we kissed our children? There is a way, hidden in the history of war. There must be, for we can see them fighting in the valley; and, high in the air, silver specks are dueling in a dream of blue silence.

Why are we merely watching? To be restrained this way is simply not fair. A quick entrance would get the fear over with, and that would help. But, then again, in the Six Day War, we waited for weeks while the Egyptian Army built up against us. And then, after that torture, we burst out and we leapt across the desert, sprinting, full of energy and fury that kept us like dancers— nimble and absorbed—and kept us alive. That is the secret: You have to be angry. When we arrived on the ridge this morning, we were anything but angry. Now we are beginning to get angry. It is our only salvation. We are angry because we are being held back.

We swear, and kick the sides of the half-tracks. We hate the voice on our radio which keeps telling us to hold to our position. We hate that man more than we hate the enemy, for now we want engagement with the enemy. We are beginning to crave battle, and we are getting angrier, and angrier, because we know that by five o'clock we will be worn out. They should let us go now.

A young soldier who has been following the battle, through binoculars, screams. "God!" he says. "Look! Look!"

The Syrians are moving up two columns of armor that will overwhelm our men on the plain below. The sergeant gets on the radio, but from it we hear a sudden waterfall of talk. Holding the microphone in his hand, he listens with us as we discover that they know. They are demanding more air support.

"What air support?" we ask. There is no air-to-ground fighting that we can see. As we watch the Syrians approach, our hearts are full of fear for those of us below. How did our soldiers know? There must be spotters or a patrol somewhere deep in, high on a hill, like us. What air support? There are planes all over the place, but not here.

Then we feel our lungs shaking like drums. The hair on our arms and on the back of our necks stands up and we shake as flights of fighters roar over the hill. They are no more than fifty feet above us. We can feel the heat from the tailpipes, and the orange flames are blinding. The noise is superb. They come three at a time; one wave, two, three, four, five, and six. These are our pilots. The mass of the machinery flying through the air is so great and graceful that we are stunned beyond the noise. We cheer in anger and in satisfaction. It seems the best thing in the world when, as they pass the ridge (How they hug the ground; what superb pilots!) they dip their wings for our sake. They are descending into a thicket of anti-aircraft missiles and radar-directed guns—and they dip their wings for us.

Now we are hot. The married men feel as if rivers are rushing through them, crossing and crashing, for they are angry and full of energy. The sergeant depresses the lever on the microphone. He identifies himself and says, "In the name of God, we want to go in *now*. Damn you if you don't let us go in."

There is hesitation and silence on the other end. "Who is this?" they ask.

"This is Shimon."

More silence, then, "Okay, Shimon. Move! Move!"

The engines start. Now we have our own thunder. It is not even three o'clock. It is the right time; they've caught us at the right time. The soldiers are not slow in mounting the half-tracks. The sound of our roaring engines has magnetized them and they *jump* in. The young drivers race the engines, as they always do.

For a magnificent half minute, we stare into the north light, smiling. The man who tasted the sweet taste of his wife kisses his wrist. The young soldiers are no longer afraid, and the married men are in a perfect sustained fury. Because they love their wives and children, they will not think of them until the battle is over. Now we are soldiers again. The engines are deafening. No longer are we held back. We are shaking; we are crying. Now we stare into the north light, and listen to the explosions below. Now we hear the levers of the gearshifts. Now our drivers exhale and begin to drive. Now we are moving.

SOLDIER'S JOY
by Tobias Wolff

On Friday Hooper was named driver of the guard for the third night that week. He had recently been broken in rank again, this time from corporal to Pfc., and the first sergeant had decided to keep Hooper's evenings busy so that he would not have leisure to brood. That was what the first sergeant told Hooper when Hooper came to the orderly room to complain.

"It's for your own good," the first sergeant said. "Not that I expect you to thank me." He moved the book he'd been reading to one side of his desk and leaned back. "Hooper, I have a theory about you," he said. "Want to hear it?"

"I'm all ears, Top," Hooper said.

The first sergeant put his boots up on the desk and stared out the window to his left. It was getting on toward five o'clock. Work details had begun to return from the rifle range and the post laundry and the brigade commander's house, where Hooper and several other men were excavating a swimming pool without aid of machinery. As the trucks let them out they gathered on the barracks steps and under the live oak beside the mess hall, their voices a steady murmur in the orderly room where Hooper stood waiting for the first sergeant to speak.

"You resent me," the first sergeant said. "You think you should be sitting here. You don't know that's what you think because you've totally sublimated your resentment, but that's what it is all right, and that's why you and me are developing a definite conflict profile. It's like you have to keep fucking up to prove to yourself that you don't really care. That's my theory. You follow me?"

26

"Top, I'm way ahead of you," Hooper said. "That's night school talking."

The first sergeant continued to look out the window. "I don't know," he said. "I don't know what you're doing in my army. You've put your twenty years in. You could retire to Mexico and buy a peso factory. Live like a dictator. So what are you doing in my army, Hooper?"

Hooper looked down at the desk. He cleared his throat but said nothing.

"Give it some thought," the first sergeant said. He stood and walked Hooper to the door. "I'm not hostile," he said. "I'm prepared to be supportive. Just think nice thoughts about Mexico, okay? Okay, Hooper?"

Hooper called Mickey and told her he wouldn't be coming by that night after all. She reminded him that this was the third time in one week, and said that she wasn't getting any younger.

"What am I supposed to do?" Hooper asked. "Go AWOL?"

"I cried three times today," Mickey said. "I just broke down and cried, and you know what? I don't even know why. I just feel bad all the time anymore."

"What did you do last night?" Hooper asked. When Mickey didn't answer, he said, "Did Briggs come over?"

"I've been inside all day," Mickey said. "Just sitting here. I'm going out of my tree." Then, in the same weary voice, she said, "Touch it, Hoop."

"I have to get going," Hooper said.

"Not yet. Wait. I'm going into the bedroom. I'm going to pick up the phone in there. Hang on, Hoop. Think of the bedroom. Think of me lying on the bed. Wait, baby."

There were men passing by the phone booth. Hooper watched them and tried not to think of Mickey's bedroom, but now he could think of nothing else. Mickey's husband was a supply sergeant with a taste for quality. The walls of the bedroom were knotty pine he'd derailed en route to some colonel's office. The brass lamps beside the bed were made from howitzer casings. The sheets were parachute silk. Sometimes, lying on those sheets, Hooper thought of the men who had drifted to earth below them. He was no great lover, as the women he went with usually got around to telling him, but in Mickey's bedroom Hooper had turned in his saddest performances and always when he was most aware that everything around him was stolen. He wasn't exactly sure why he kept going back. It was just something he did, again and again.

"Okay," Mickey said. "I'm here."

"There's a guy waiting to use the phone," Hooper told her.

"Hoop, I'm on the bed. I'm taking off my shoes."

Hooper could see her perfectly. He lit a cigarette and opened the door of the booth to let the smoke out.

"Hoop?" she said.

"I told you, there's a guy waiting."

"Turn around, then."

"You don't need me," Hooper said. "All you need is the telephone. Why don't you call Briggs? That's what you're going to do after I hang up."

"I probably will," she said. "Listen, Hoop, I'm not really on the bed. I was just pulling your chain. I thought it would make me feel better but it didn't."

"I knew it," Hooper said. "You're watching the tube, right?"

"Somebody just won a saw," Mickey said.

"A saw?"

"Yeah, they drove up to this man's house and dumped a truckload of logs in his yard and gave him a chainsaw. This was his fantasy. You should see how happy he is, Hoop. I'd give anything to be that happy."

"Maybe I can swing by later tonight," Hooper said. "Just for a minute."

"I don't know," Mickey said. "Better give me a ring first."

After Mickey hung up Hooper tried to call his wife, but there was no answer. He stood there and listened to the phone ringing. Finally he put the receiver down and stepped outside the booth, just as they began to sound retreat over the company loud-speaker. With the men around him Hooper came to attention and saluted. The record was scratchy, but, as always, the music caused Hooper's mind to go abruptly and perfectly still. The stillness spread down through his body. He held his salute until the last note died away, then broke off smartly and walked down the street toward the mess hall.

The officer of the day was Captain King from Headquarters Company. Captain King had also been officer of the day on Monday and Tuesday nights, and Hooper was glad to see him again because Captain King was too lazy to do his own job or to make sure the guards were doing theirs. He stayed in the guard-house and left everything up to Hooper.

Captain King had gray hair and a long grayish face. He was a West Point graduate with twenty-eight years of service behind him, just trying to make it through another two years so he could retire at three-quarters pay. All his classmates were generals or at least bird colonels, but he himself had been held back for good reasons, many of which he admitted to Hooper their first night together. It puzzled Hooper at first, this officer telling him about his failures to perform, his nervous breakdowns and Valium habit, but finally Hooper understood: Captain King regarded him, a Pfc. with twenty-one years' service, as a comrade in dereliction, a disaster like himself with no room left for judgment against anyone.

The evening was hot and muggy. Little black bats swooped overhead as Captain King made his way along the rank of men drawn up before the guardhouse steps. He objected to the alignment of someone's belt buckle. He asked questions about the chain of command but gave no sign whether the answers he received were right or wrong. He inspected a couple of rifles and pretended to find something amiss with each of them, though it was clear that he hardly knew one end from the other, and when he reached the end of the line he began to deliver a speech. He said that he had never seen such sorry troops in his life. He asked how they expected to stand up to a determined enemy. On and on he went. Captain King had delivered the same speech on Monday and Tuesday, and when Hooper recognized it he lit another cigarette and sat down on the running board of the truck he'd been leaning against.

The sky was gray. It had a damp, heavy look and it felt heavy too, hanging close overhead, nervous with rumblings and small flashes in the distance. Just sitting there made Hooper sweat. Beyond the guardhouse a stream of cars rushed along the road to town. From the officers' club farther up the road came the muffled beat of rock music, which was almost lost, like every other sound of the evening, in the purr of crickets that rose up everywhere and thickened the air like heat.

When Captain King had finished talking he turned the men over to Hooper for transportation to their posts. Two of them, both privates, were from Hooper's company and these he allowed to ride with him in the cab of the truck while everybody else slid around in back. One was a cook named Porchoff, known as Porkchop. The other was a radio operator named Trac who had managed to airlift himself out of Saigon during the fall of the city by hanging from the skids of a helicopter. That was the story

Hooper had heard, anyway, and he had no reason to doubt it; he'd seen the slopes pull that trick plenty of times, though few of them were as young as Trac must have been then—nine or ten at the most. When Hooper tried to picture his son Wesley at the same age doing that, hanging over a burning city by his fingertips, he had to smile.

But Trac didn't talk about it. There was nothing about him to suggest his past except perhaps the deep, sickle-shaped scar above his right eye. To Hooper there was something familiar about this scar. One night, watching Trac play the video game in the company rec room, he was overcome with the certainty that he had seen Trac before somewhere—astride a water buffalo in some reeking paddy or running alongside Hooper's APC with a bunch of other kids all begging money, holding up melons or a bag full of weed or a starving monkey on a stick.

Though Hooper had the windows open, the cab of the truck smelled strongly of after-shave. Hooper noticed that Trac was wearing orange Walkman earphones under his helmet liner. They were against regulations but Hooper said nothing. As long as Trac had his ears plugged he wouldn't be listening for trespassers and end up blowing his rifle off at some squirrel cracking open an acorn. Of all the guards only Porchoff and Trac would be carrying ammunition, because they had been assigned to the battalion communications center where there was a tie-in terminal to the division main-frame computer. The theory was that an intruder who knew his stuff could get his hands on highly classified material. That was how it had been explained to Hooper. Hooper thought it was a load of crap. The Russians knew everything anyway.

Hooper let out the first two men at the PX and the next two at the parking lot outside the main officers' club, where lately there'd been several cars vandalized. As they pulled away, Porchoff leaned over Trac and grabbed Hooper's sleeve. "You used to be a corporal," he said.

Hooper shook Porchoff's hand loose. He said, "I'm driving a truck, in case you didn't notice."

"How come you got busted?"

"None of your business."

"I'm just asking," Porchoff said. "So what happened, anyway?"

"Cool it, Porkchop," said Trac. "The man doesn't want to talk about it, okay?"

"Cool it yourself, fuckface," Porchoff said. He looked at Trac. "Was I addressing you?"

Trac said, "Man, you must've been eating some of your own food."

"I don't believe I was addressing you," Porchoff said. "In fact, I don't believe that you and me have been properly introduced. That's another thing I don't like about the Army, the way people you haven't been introduced to feel perfectly free to get right into your face and unload whatever shit they've got in their brains. It happens all the time. But I never heard anyone say 'Cool it' before. You're a real phrasemaker, fuckface."

"That's enough," Hooper said.

Porchoff leaned back and said, "That's enough," in a falsetto voice. A few moments later he started humming to himself.

Hooper dropped off the rest of the guards and turned up the hill toward the communications center. There were oleander bushes along the gravel drive, with white blossoms going gray in the dusky light. Gravel sprayed up under the tires and rattled against the floorboards of the truck. Porchoff stopped humming. "I've got a cramp," he said.

Hooper pulled up next to the gate and turned off the engine. He looked over at Porchoff. "Now what's your problem?" he said.

"I've got a cramp," Porchoff repeated.

"For Christ's sake," Hooper said. "Why didn't you say something before?"

"I did. I went on sick call, but the doctor couldn't find it. It keeps moving around. It's here now." Porchoff touched his neck. "I swear to God."

"Keep track of it," Hooper told him. "You can go on sick call again in the morning."

"You don't believe me," Porchoff said.

The three of them got out of the truck. Hooper counted out the ammunition to Porchoff and Trac and watched as they loaded their clips. "That ammo's strictly for show," he said. "Forget I even gave it to you. If you run into a problem, which you won't, use the phone in the guard shack. You can work out your own shifts." Hooper opened the gate and locked the two men inside. They stood watching him, faces in shadows, black rifle barrels poking over their shoulders. "Listen," Hooper said. "Nobody's going to break in here, understand?"

Trac nodded. Porchoff just looked at him.

"Okay," Hooper said. "I'll drop by later. Me and the captain." Hooper knew that Captain King wasn't about to go anywhere, but Trac and Porchoff didn't know that. Hooper behaved better when he thought he was being watched and he supposed that the same was true of other people.

Hooper climbed back inside the truck and started the engine. He gave the V sign to the men at the gate. Trac gave the sign back and turned away. Porchoff didn't move. He stayed where he was, fingers laced through the wire. He looked about ready to cry. "Damn," Hooper said, and hit the gas. Gravel clattered in the wheel wells. When Hooper reached the main road a light rain began to fall, but it stopped before he'd even turned the wipers on.

Hooper and Captain King sat on adjacent bunks in the guardhouse, which was empty except for them and a bat that was flitting back and forth among the dim rafters. As on Monday and Tuesday nights, Captain King had brought along an ice chest filled with little bottles of Perrier water. From time to time he tried pressing one on Hooper, but Hooper declined. His refusals made Captain King apologetic. "It's not a class thing," Captain King said, looking at the bottle in his hand. "I don't drink this stuff because I went to the Point or anything like that." He leaned down and put the bottle between his bare feet. "I'm allergic to alcohol," he said. "Otherwise I'd probably be an alcoholic. Why not? I'm everything else." He smiled at Hooper.

Hooper lay back and clasped his hands behind his head and stared up at the mattress above him. "I'm not much of a drinker myself," he said. He knew that Captain King wanted him to explain why he refused the Perrier water but there was really no reason in particular. Hooper just didn't like the idea.

"I drank eggnog one Christmas when I was a kid and it almost killed me," Captain King said. "My arms and legs swelled up to twice their normal size. The doctors couldn't get my glasses off because my skin was all puffed up around them. You know the way a tree will grow around a rock. It was like that. A few months later I tried beer at some kid's graduation party and the same thing happened. Pretty strange, eh?"

"Yes, sir," Hooper said.

"I used to think it was all for the best. I have an addictive personality, and you can bet your bottom dollar I would have been a problem drinker. No question about it. But now I wonder. If I'd had one big weakness like that, maybe I wouldn't have had all these little pissant weaknesses I ended up with. I know that sounds like bull-pucky, but look at Alexander the Great. Alexander the Great was a boozer. Did you know that?"

"No, sir," Hooper said.

"Well he was. Read your history. So was Churchill. Churchill drank a bottle of cognac a day. And of course Grant. You know what Lincoln said when someone complained about Grant's drinking?"

"Yes, sir. I've heard the story."

"He said, 'Find out what brand he uses so I can ship a case to the rest of my generals.' Is that the way you heard it?"

"Yes, sir."

Captain King nodded. "I'm all in," he said. He stretched out and assumed exactly the position Hooper was in. It made Hooper uncomfortable. He sat up and put his feet on the floor.

"Married?" Captain King asked.

"Yes, sir."

"Kids?"

"Yes, sir. One. Wesley."

"Oh my God, a boy," Captain King said. "They're nothing but trouble, take my word for it. They're programmed to hate you. It has to be like that, otherwise they'd spend their whole lives moping around the house, but just the same it's no fun when it starts. I have two and neither of them can stand me. Haven't been home in years. Breaks my heart. Of course, I was a worse father than most. How old is your boy?"

"Sixteen or seventeen," Hooper said. He put his hands on his knees and looked at the floor. "Seventeen. He lives with my wife's sister in San Diego."

Captain King turned his head and looked at Hooper. "Sounds like you're not much of a dad yourself."

Hooper began to lace his boots up.

"I'm not criticizing," Captain King said. "At least you were smart enough to get someone else to do the job." He yawned. "I'm whipped," he said. "You need me for anything? You want me to make the rounds with you?"

"I'll take care of things, sir," Hooper said.

"Fair enough." Captain King closed his eyes. "If you need me, just shout."

Hooper went outside and lit a cigarette. It was almost midnight, well past the time appointed for inspecting the guards. As he walked toward the truck mosquitoes droned around his head. A breeze was rustling the treetops, but on the ground the air was hot and still.

Hooper took his time making the rounds. He visited all the guards except Porchoff and Trac and found everything in order.

There were no problems. Finally he started down the road toward the communications center, but when he reached the turnoff he kept his eyes dead ahead and drove past. Warm, fragrant air rushed into his face from the open window. The road ahead was empty. Hooper leaned back and mashed the accelerator. The engine roared. He was moving now, really moving, past darkened barracks and bare flagpoles and bushes whose flowers blazed up in the glare of the headlights. Hooper grinned. He felt no pleasure, but he grinned and pushed the truck as hard as it would go.

Hooper slowed down when he left the post. He was AWOL now. Even if he couldn't find it in him to care much about that, he saw no point in calling attention to himself.

Drunk drivers were jerking their cars back and forth between lanes. Every half mile or so a police car with flashing lights had someone stopped by the roadside. Other police cars sat idling behind billboards. Hooper stayed in the right lane and drove slowly until he reached his turn, then he gunned the engine again and raced down the pitted street that led to Mickey's house. He passed a bunch of kids sitting on the hood of a car with cans of beer in their hands. The car door was open, and Hooper had to swerve to miss it. As he went by he heard a blast of music.

When he reached Mickey's block Hooper turned off the engine. The truck coasted silently down the street, and again Hooper became aware of the sound of crickets. He stopped on the shoulder across from Mickey's house and sat listening. The thick pulsing sound seemed to grow louder every moment. Hooper drifted into memory, his cigarette dangling unsmoked, burning its way toward his fingers. At the same instant that he felt the heat of the ember against his skin Hooper was startled by another pain, the pain of finding himself where he was. It left him breathless for a moment. Then he roused himself and got out of the truck.

The windows were dark. Mickey's Buick was parked in the driveway beside another car that Hooper didn't recognize. It didn't belong to her husband and it didn't belong to Briggs. Hooper glanced around at the other houses, then walked across the street and ducked under the hanging leaves of the willow tree in Mickey's front yard. He knelt there, holding his breath to hear better, but there was no sound but the sound of the crickets and the rushing of the big air-conditioner Mickey's husband had taken from a helicopter hangar. Hooper saw no purpose in staying under the tree, so he got up and walked over to the house. He looked around again, then went into a crouch and began to work his way along the wall. He rounded the corner of the house and was starting up the side toward Mickey's bedroom when a circle of light burst around his head and a woman's voice said, "Thou shalt not commit adultery."

Hooper closed his eyes. There was a long silence. Then the woman said, "Come here."

She was standing in the driveway of the house next door. When Hooper came up to her she stuck a pistol in his face and told him to raise his hands. "A soldier," she said, moving the beam of light up and down his uniform. "All right, put your hands down." She snapped the light off and stood watching Hooper in the flickering blue glow that came from the open door behind her. Hooper heard a dog bark twice and a man say, "Remember—nothing is too good for your dog. It's 'Ruff ruff' at the sign of the double R." The dog barked twice again.

"I want to know what you think you're doing," the woman said.

Hooper said, "I'm not exactly sure." He saw her more clearly now. She was thin and tall. She wore glasses with black "frames," and she had on a white dress of the kind girls called formals when Hooper was in high school—tight around the waist and flaring stiffly at the hip, breasts held in hard-looking cups. Shadows darkened the hollows of her cheeks. Under the flounces of the dress her feet were big and bare.

"I know what you're doing," she said. She pointed the pistol, an Army .45, at Mickey's house. "You're sniffing around that whore over there."

Someone came to the door behind the woman. A deep voice called out, "Is it him?"

"Stay inside, Dads," the woman answered. "It's nobody."

"It's him!" the man shouted. "Don't let him talk you out of it again! Do it while you've got the chance, sweetie pie."

"What do you want with that whore?" the woman asked Hooper. Before he could answer, she said, "I could shoot you and nobody would say boo. I'm within my rights."

Hooper nodded.

"I don't see the attraction," she said. "But then, I'm not a man." She made a laughing sound. "You know something? I almost did it. I almost shot you. I was that close, but then I saw the uniform." She shook her head. "Shame on you. Where is your pride?"

"Don't let him talk," said the man in the doorway. He came down the the steps, a tall white-haired man in striped pajamas.

"There you are, you sonofabitch," he said. "I'll dance on your grave."

"It isn't him, Dads," the woman said sadly. "It's someone else."

"So he says," the man snapped. He started down the driveway, hopping from foot to foot over the gravel. The woman handed him the flashlight and he turned it on in Hooper's face, then moved the beam slowly down to his boots. "Sweetie pie, it's a soldier," he said.

"I told you it wasn't him," the woman said.

"But this is a terrible mistake," the man said. "Sir, I'm at a loss for words."

"Forget it," Hooper told him. "No hard feelings."

"You are too kind," the man said. He reached out and shook Hooper's hand. "You're alive," he said. "That's what counts." He nodded toward the house. "Come have a drink."

"He has to go," the woman said. "He was looking for something and he found it."

"That's right," Hooper told him. "I was just on my way back to base."

The man gave a slight bow with his head. "To base with you, then. Good night, sir."

Hooper and the woman watched him make his way back to the house. When he was inside, the woman turned to Hooper and said, "If I told him what you were doing over there it would break his heart. But I won't tell him. There've been disappointments enough in his life already and God only knows what's next. He's got to have something left." She drew herself up and gave Hooper a hard look. "Why are you still here?" she asked angrily. "Go back to your post."

Captain King was still asleep when Hooper returned to the guardhouse. His thumb was in his mouth and he made little noises as he sucked it. Hooper lay in the next bunk with his eyes open. He was still awake at 4:00 in the morning when the telephone began to ring.

It was Trac calling from the communications center. He said that Porchoff was threatening to shoot himself, and threatening to shoot Trac if Trac tried to stop him. "This dude is mental," Trac said. "You get me out of here, and I mean now."

"We'll be right there," Hooper said. "Just give him lots of room. Don't try to grab his rifle or anything."

"Fat fucking chance," Trac said. "Man, you know what he

called me? He called me a gook. I hope he wastes himself. I don't need no assholes with loaded guns declaring war on me, man."

"Just hold tight," Hooper told him. He hung up and went to wake Captain King, because this was a mess and he wanted it to be Captain King's mess and Captain King's balls that got busted if anything went wrong. He walked over to Captain King and stood looking down at him. Captain King's thumb had slipped out of his mouth but he was still making sucking noises and pursing his lips. Hooper decided not to wake him after all. Captain King would probably refuse to come anyway, but if he did come he would screw things up for sure. Just the sight of him was enough to make somebody start shooting.

A light rain had begun to fall. The road was empty except for one jeep going the other way. Hooper waved at the two men in front as they went past, and they both waved back. Hooper felt a surge of friendliness toward them. He followed their lights in his mirror until they vanished behind him.

Hooper parked the truck halfway up the drive and walked the rest of the distance. The rain was falling harder now, tapping steadily on the shoulders of his poncho. Sweet, almost unbreathable smells rose from the earth. He walked slowly, gravel crunching under his boots. When he reached the gate a voice to his left said, "Shit, man, you took your time." Trac stepped out of the shadows and waited as Hooper tried to get the key into the lock. "Come on, man," Trac said. He knelt with his back to the fence and swung the barrel of his rifle from side to side.

"Got it," Hooper said. He took the lock off and Trac pushed open the gate. "The truck's down there," Hooper told him. "Just around the turn."

Trac stood close to Hooper, breathing quick, shallow breaths and shifting from foot to foot. His face was dark under the hood of his glistening poncho. "You want this?" he asked. He held out his rifle.

Hooper looked at it. He shook his head. "Where's Porchoff?"

"Around back," Trac said. "There's some picnic benches out there."

"All right," Hooper said. "I'll take care of it. Wait in the truck."

"Shit, man, I feel like shit," Trac said. "I'll back you up, man."

"It's okay," Hooper told him. "I can handle it."

"I never cut out on anybody before," Trac said. He shifted back and forth.

"You aren't cutting out," Hooper said. "Nothing's going to happen."

Trac started down the drive. When he disappeared around the turn Hooper kept watching to make sure he didn't double back. A stiff breeze began to blow, shaking the trees, sending raindrops rattling down through the leaves. Thunder rumbled far away.

Hooper turned and walked through the gate into the compound. The forms of the shrubs and pines were dark and indefinite in the slanting rain. Hooper followed the fence to the right, squinting into the shadows. When he saw Porchoff, hunched over the picnic table, he stopped and called out to him, "Hey, Porchoff. It's me—Hooper."

Porchoff raised his head.

"It's just me," Hooper said, following his own voice toward Porchoff, showing his empty hands. He saw the rifle lying on the table in front of Porchoff. "It's just me," he repeated, as monotonously as he could. He stopped beside another picnic table ten feet or so from the one where Porchoff sat, and lowered himself onto the bench. He looked over at Porchoff. Neither of them spoke for a while. Then Hooper said, "Okay, Porchoff, let's talk about it. Trac tells me you've got some kind of attitude problem."

Porchoff didn't answer. Raindrops streamed down his helmet onto his shoulders and dripped steadily past his face. His uniform was soggy and dark, plastered to his skin. He stared at Hooper and said nothing. Now and then his shoulders jerked.

"Are you gay?" Hooper asked.

Porchoff shook his head.

"Well then, what? You on acid or something? You can tell me, Porchoff. It doesn't matter."

"I don't do drugs," Porchoff said. It was the first time he'd spoken. His voice was calm.

"Good," Hooper said. "I mean, at least I know I'm talking to you and not to some fucking chemical. Now, listen up, Porchoff— I don't want you turning that rifle on me. Understand?"

Porchoff looked down at the rifle, then back at Hooper. He said, "You leave me alone and I'll leave you alone."

"I've already had someone throw down on me once tonight," Hooper said. "I'd just as soon leave it at that." He reached under his poncho and took out his cigarette case. He held it up for Porchoff to see.

"I don't use tobacco," Porchoff said.

"Well, I do," Hooper said. He shook out a cigarette and bent to light it. "Hey," he said. "All right. One match." He put the case back in his pocket and cupped the cigarette under the picnic table to keep it dry. The rain was falling lightly now in fine fitful gusts like spray. The clouds had gone the color of ash. Misty gray light was spreading through the sky. Hooper saw that Porchoff's shoulders twitched constantly now, and that his lips were blue and trembling. "Put your poncho on," Hooper told him.

Porchoff shook his head.

"You trying to catch pneumonia?" Hooper asked. He smiled at Porchoff. "Go ahead, boy. Put your poncho on."

Porchoff bent over and covered his face with his hands. Hooper realized that he was crying. He smoked his cigarette and waited for Porchoff to stop, but Porchoff kept crying and finally Hooper grew impatient. He said, "What's all this crap about you shooting yourself?"

Porchoff rubbed at his eyes with the heels of his hands. "Why shouldn't I?" he asked.

"Why shouldn't you? What do you mean, why shouldn't you?"

"Why shouldn't I shoot myself? Give me a reason."

"This is baloney," Hooper said. "You don't run around asking why shouldn't I shoot myself. That's decadent, Porchoff. Now, do me a favor and put your poncho on."

Porchoff sat shivering for a moment. Then he took his poncho off his belt, unrolled it, and began to pull it over his head. Hooper considered making a grab for the rifle but held back. There was no need, he was home free now. People who were going to blow themselves away didn't come in out of the rain.

"You know what they call me?" Porchoff said.

"Who's 'they,' Porchoff?"

"Everyone."

"No. What does everyone call you?"

"Porkchop. *Porkchop*."

"Come on," Hooper said. "What's the harm in that? Everyone gets called something."

"But that's my *name*," Porchoff said. "That's *me*. It's got so even when people use my real name I hear 'Porkchop.' All I can think of is this big piece of meat. And that's what they're seeing too. You can say they aren't, but I know they are."

Hooper recognized some truth in this, a lot of truth in fact, because when he himself said Porkchop that was what he saw: a porkchop.

"I hurt all the time," Porchoff said, "but no one believes me. Not even the doctors. You don't believe me, either."

"I believe you," Hooper said.

Porchoff blinked. "Sure," he said.

"I believe you," Hooper repeated. He kept his eyes on the rifle. Porchoff wasn't going to kill himself, but the rifle still made Hooper uncomfortable. He was about to ask Porchoff to give it to him but decided to wait a little while. The moment was wrong somehow. Hooper pushed back the hood of his poncho and took off his fatigue cap. He glanced up at the pale clouds.

"I don't have any buddies," Porchoff said.

"No wonder," Hooper said. "Calling people gooks, making threats. Let's face it, Porchoff, your personality needs some upgrading."

"But they won't give me a chance," Porchoff said. "All I ever do is cook food. I put it on their plates and they make some crack and walk on by. It's like I'm not even there. So what am I supposed to act like?"

Hooper was still gazing up at the clouds, feeling the soft rain on his face. Birds were starting to sing in the woods beyond the fence. He said, "I don't know, Porchoff. It's just part of this rut we're all in." Hooper lowered his head and looked over at Porchoff, who sat hunched inside his poncho, shaking as little tremors passed through him. "Any day now," Hooper said, "everything's going to change."

"My dad was in the National Guard back in Ohio," Porchoff said. "He's always talking about the great experiences he and his buddies used to have, camping out and so on. Nothing like that ever happens to me." Porchoff looked down at the table, then looked up and said, "How about you? What was your best time?"

"My best time," Hooper said. The question made him feel tired. He thought of telling Porchoff some sort of lie, but the effort of making things up was beyond him and the memory Porchoff wanted was close at hand. For Hooper it was closer than the memory of home. In truth it was a kind of home. It was where he went to be back with his friends again, and his old self. It was where Hooper drifted when he was too low to care how much lower he'd be when he drifted back, and lost it all again. He felt for his cigarettes. "Vietnam," he said.

Porchoff just looked at him.

"We didn't know it then," Hooper said. "We used to talk about how when we got back in the world we were going to do this and we were going to do that. Back in the world we were going to have it made. But ever since then it's been nothing but confusion." Hooper took the cigarette case from his pocket but didn't open it. He leaned forward on the table.

"Everything was clear," he said. "You learned what you had to know and you forgot the rest. All this chickenshit. This clutter. You didn't spend every living minute of the day thinking about your own sorry-ass little self. Am I getting laid enough. What's wrong with my kid. Should I insulate the fucking house. That's what does it to you, Porchoff. Thinking about yourself. That's what kills you in the end."

Porchoff had not moved. In the gray light Hooper could see Porchoff's fingers spread before him on the tabletop, white and still as if they had been drawn there in chalk. His face was the same color.

"You think you've got problems, Porchoff, but they wouldn't last five minutes in the field. There's nothing wrong with you that a little search-and-destroy wouldn't cure." Hooper paused, smiling to himself, already deep in the memory. He tried to bring it back for Porchoff, tried to put it into words so that Porchoff could see it, too, the beauty of that life, the faith so deep that in time you were not separate men anymore but part of each other.

But the words came hard. Hooper saw that Porchoff did not understand, and then he realized that what he was trying to describe was not only faith but love, and that it couldn't be done. Still smiling, he said, "You'll see, Porchoff. You'll get your chance."

Porchoff stared at Hooper. "You're crazy," he said.

"We're all going to get another chance," Hooper said. "I can feel it coming. Otherwise I'd take my walking papers and hat up. You'll see, Porchoff. All you need is a little contact. The rest of us, too. Get us out of this rut."

Porchoff shook his head and murmured, "You're really crazy."

"Let's call it a day," Hooper said. He stood and held out his hand. "Give me the rifle."

"No," Porchoff said. He pulled the rifle closer. "Not to you."

"There's no one here but me," Hooper said.

"Go get Captain King."

"Captain King is asleep."

"Then wake him up."

"No," Hooper said. "I'm not going to tell you again, Porchoff, give me the rifle." Hooper walked toward him but stopped when Porchoff picked up the weapon and pointed it at his chest. "Leave me alone," Porchoff said.

"Relax," Hooper told him. "I'm not going to hurt you." He held out his hand again.

Porchoff licked his lips. "No," he said. "Not you."

Behind Hooper a voice called out, "Hey! Porkchop! Drop it!"

Porchoff sat bolt upright. "Jesus," he said.

"It's Trac," Hooper said. "Put the rifle down, Porchoff—now!"

"Drop it!" Trac shouted.

"Oh Jesus," Porchoff said and stumbled to his feet with the rifle still in his hands. Then his head flapped and his helmet flew off and he toppled backward over the bench. Hooper's heart leapt as the shock of the blast hit him. Then the sound went through him and beyond him into the trees and the sky, echoing on in the distance like thunder. Afterwards there was silence. Hooper took a step forward, then sank to his knees and lowered his forehead to the wet grass. He spread his fingers through the grass beside his head. The rain fell around him with a soft whispering sound. A blue jay squawked. Another bird called out, and then the trees grew loud with song.

Hooper heard the swish of boots through the grass behind him. He pushed himself up and sat back on his heels and drew a deep breath.

"You okay?" Trac said.

Hooper nodded.

Trac walked on to where Porchoff lay. He said something in Vietnamese, then looked back at Hooper and shook his head.

Hooper tried to stand but went to his knees again.

"You need a hand?" Trac asked.

"I guess so," Hooper said.

Trac came over to Hooper. He slung his rifle and bent down and the two men gripped each other's wrists. Trac's skin was dry and smooth, his bones as small as a child's. This close, he looked more familiar than ever. "Go for it," Trac said. He tensed as Hooper pulled himself to his feet and for a moment afterwards they stood facing each other, swaying slightly, hands still locked on each other's wrists. "All right," Hooper said. Each of them slowly loosened his grip.

In a soft voice, almost a whisper, Trac said, "They gonna put me away?"

"No," Hooper said. He walked over to Porchoff and looked down at him. He immediately turned away and saw that Trac was still swaying, and that his eyes were glassy. "Better get off those legs," Hooper said. Trac looked at him dreamily, then unslung his rifle and leaned it against the picnic table farthest from

Porchoff. He sat down and took his helmet off and rested his head on his crossed forearms.

The clouds had darkened. The wind was picking up again, carrying with it the whine of distant engines. Hooper fumbled a cigarette out of his case and smoked it down, staring toward the woods, feeling the rain stream down his face and neck. When the cigarette went out Hooper dropped it, then picked it up again and field-stripped it, crumbling the tobacco around his feet so that no trace of it remained. He put his cap back on and raised the hood of his poncho. "How's it going?" he said to Trac.

Trac looked up. He began to rub his forehead, pushing his fingers in little circles above his eyes.

Hooper sat down across from him. "We don't have a whole lot of time," he said.

Trac nodded. He put his helmet on and looked over at Hooper, the scar on his brow livid where he had rubbed it.

"All right, son," Hooper said. "Let's get our story together."

SEEDS OF CONFLICT

by Kathryn Kramer

It was an earlier decade, in Arborville, where Cyrus was born. In other places the world was changing fast, but here it continued to be an era of rest and relaxation, a still-innocent time of picnics and funny new dance steps, of cars as round and homey-looking as that pie made out of the fruit of Eve's fall, which everyone in the country ate with such gusto. It was a peaceful time, of sparkling days lapsing unmourned into velveteen nights, a landscape of the mind without electric wires. This might be the most volatile century in the history of the world, but in Arborville people were content just to enjoy life, make some money and have children, give their children the childhoods they themselves had missed. And in Arborville, in the heart of the country, childhood lasted longer than anywhere else.

Childhood is belief, and Cyrus believed in the world of his big white house, which stood in the middle of a big flat lawn surrounded by rosebushes and lilacs and forsythias. A cement walk ran from the sidewalk to the front steps, then around the side of the house to the backyard, where a swing set stood beside a sandbox (though he and Betsy no longer played in it). Here Cyrus had always lived with his mother and his father, his sister, Betsy, and his grandfather, Charles, who used to be a general. But he had resigned his commission and moved to Arborville when he heard that Cyrus was born because he wanted to make sure his grandson was brought up right. Cyrus's mother, Rose, mostly stayed in the house. Sometimes she was busy and put on a big apron and hummed and straightened things, but other times she lay in her room with the shades down and no one was allowed to make any noise. Cyrus hated it then—it felt like a rainy day.

In the morning Cyrus's father, Harold, went to work; at breakfast he went around the table tightening his tie, kissing Betsy and Cyrus good-bye. Back at his place, he stopped to drink the rest of his coffee, bending over his placemat so he wouldn't spill on his shirt; then he kissed their mother. Cyrus and Betsy watched; they reminded him if he forgot. "You kids have all the luck," he said. The house was different once he left.

When he came home, the house changed back. The furniture seemed bigger, as though, if Cyrus wasn't careful, he might bump into it. Harold sat in the living room; Cyrus could go in but if he tried to tell his father something he had to talk quickly because his father was always listening for an end in the talk. If Cyrus didn't get there soon enough Harold would say, "Well, that's very interesting, Son," and pull the newspaper up in front of his face. When he came home, he liked his peace and quiet.

Cyrus's grandfather didn't go to work. His uniform hung in a closet upstairs. When Cyrus was bigger, he could try it on. His grandfather mainly told stories, and Cyrus loved to listen to them. His grandfather's voice was deep and soft like a lap, and when he began, "Once upon a time . . ." it made Cyrus feel as if he were about to eat something he had waited all day to eat. He felt cozy, yet also big, as if, should he go outside, he would find that his yard didn't stop at the sidewalk as it usually did, but instead rolled on, green and soft, covering the whole world.

Almost every day, between the time Cyrus came home from school and the time Harold came home from work, Cyrus and Charles would sit—in the kitchen if it was winter, on the front steps if it was summer—and Charles would tell Cyrus about the past. Charles had been a boy once too, but then he had grown up and gone to war and seen the world change. The world had been a happier place, where people did what they wanted without fretting about what other people might do to them if they turned their backs. But then all of this was ruined. People had to start worrying about things they'd never even thought about before and that made them cross.

"What's more, Corporal," Charles said to Cyrus, "people are getting crosser all the time, and why? Because they've come to realize that, no matter what they do or how hard they work, at any minute some imbecile can decide he's going to fight some other imbecile and pretty soon one of them will get mad enough and push a button and make the whole world pop like a balloon."

"What button, Granddad?"

"The one at the Imbecile Control Tower, Cyrus. It's a big black button and every time an imbecile walks by it big red letters flash and say, PUSH ME! PUSH ME!"

"They do?"

"Yes, and there's a kind of high screech at the same time, a very long shrill squeak that would make you or me shiver like fingernails down a blackboard do, but all the imbeciles love it. It makes them feel terrific. They dance around like a bunch of hooligans as if they're listening to the sweetest music."

Rose, sitting on the porch in a rocking chair, called out, "Mercy, Dad, what an optimist you are! To hear you talk, we might as well hide under the beds and wait for the sky to fall."

"If the sky falls you won't be any safer under your bed than out on the porch," Charles said. But he turned to smile at his daughter. He ought to keep his mouth shut. Why intone doom when she was happy? That happened too rarely these days.

Rose smiled back, and Charles saw her again as the child she had been before Sophie left them: like Cyrus, curious, alert, eager to right every wrong.

"Your mother's in a good mood today," Charles stage-whispered. "I like it when she's in a good mood, don't you?"

"Yes." But the subject made Cyrus uncomfortable and he said, "Tell me another story about the king, Granddad. Okay?"

"What king is that, Cyrus?" Rose asked sharply.

"The king," he said. He turned to look at her. "Once there was a king and he was a very contented man, he just sat around in his castle with his pipe and slippers and listened to the court jester's jokes, but all the imbeciles were always trying to get him to fight someone and finally this gave him such a big headache that he packed up his crown and snuck out of his castle in the middle of the night with the queen and the princes and princesses and came to America. Except he's hiding. It's up to us to find him and convince him to sit on the throne again."

"It is, is it?" Rose said. "I must say, Dad, you haven't wasted any time in indoctrinating the younger generation."

"Time is running out, Rosie." He winked at her, but she was no longer smiling.

"Let me ask you something, Cyrus," she said. "What makes you think there really is a king?"

"Mom . . ."

"Think about it. How do you know Granddad's not just making it up?"

"Are you making it up, Granddad?"

Charles laughed. "Ganging up on poor old Grandfather now, are you? For your information, Cyrus, the reason I know about the king is because I met him in the war."

Cyrus looked at his mother looking at his grandfather.

"Don't worry, I'm not going to reveal any state secrets." To Cyrus, Charles continued, "He was disguised as a common soldier. He thought that if everybody liked to fight wars so much, he ought to find out what they were all about. We got to be good friends, and he told me about his family, what life in hiding was like—he and his brothers and sisters, who lived with him, couldn't get to know anyone else for fear someone might discover they were of royal blood and turn them over to the imbeciles. It was awful always worrying about that. So he left his family and tried to be like everybody else."

"Dad . . ."

"It was the truth. And he tried. He didn't go back to his family and he met a very nice woman and they got married."

"What happened?"

Charles laid a hand on Cyrus's head. "I wish I could tell you, Corporal, that they lived happily ever after, but they didn't. You see, the king made a big mistake."

"What mistake?"

"He didn't tell his wife who he was. He wanted to forget about his past. Unfortunately, once you've got royal blood in your veins, you can't just pretend you don't. It's always there, boiling up and making you wish you were sitting on the throne, even if you really *hate* sitting on the throne. But I'll tell you something, Cyrus. People always know if you're keeping a secret. The king's wife kept asking him what the matter was but he wouldn't tell her. After a while she got fed up and ran away." Charles paused. "You see, Cyrus, secrets cause more trouble than they solve."

"Where did she go?"

"She went far away."

"Was the king sad?"

"He was very sad. In fact, I expect he never got over it."

"Where is he?"

"I'm afraid I don't know. I lost touch with him after the war."

"Then how do you know he got married?" Cyrus asked.

"You don't miss much, do you, Corporal?"

"No," Cyrus said, looking at his mother.

Charles looked over his shoulder to share his amusement at this reply with Rose, but she was not looking at either of them. She was sitting in the rocking chair, not rocking. Her face was lowered and she gripped each arm of the chair as if to keep herself from floating off. She was silent, but both Charles and Cyrus knew she was weeping.

Little by little, anxiety increased around the country, but the people of Arborville remained content. They thought all this talk of approaching war was so much hooey. They heard of people stocking food in their basements, building special shelters for protection during air raids, and they slapped their thighs and roared.

"They're out of their minds. Who would dream of attacking us?"

Arborville's nonchalance became so notorious that representatives from the government and the press arrived to determine why the Arborvilleans were so sure of themselves.

"Aren't you worried about another war?" they were asked. "Aren't you afraid of the effect it would have on your lives?"

"Hell, no, we're not worried about any war!"

"War! In Arborville?"

"We don't believe all that stuff on the news. We think the government's just trying to get everybody all stirred up for some reason."

"What reason?"

"How in tarnation should we know?"

Arborvilleans slouched in groups outside the hardware store around the questioner or peered at him down the Formica counter of the drugstore like planes waiting in line for an opportunity to take off. At first their self-assurance intimidated the pollster, but soon he became irritated and exclaimed, "But you're all asleep here! Can't you see what's happening in the world around you?"

"Now, now," the Arborvilleans soothed. "Don't get yourself worked up. It's just that we like things the way they are. We're not always looking for more in life than is there." They grinned at the interviewer. "You will report it as it really is here, won't you?"

But the interviewers suspected Arborville's complacence. They felt certain some arcane violence must lie dormant beneath the tidy lawns and trimmed bushes of the town, hidden antagonisms that, if left unexpressed, would have cruel repercussions in the later lives of the children who grew up there. They would move away and live in scantily furnished apartments in gridded cities, their cupboards empty except for a bottle of gin and maybe a jar of olives, and they would slam doors and sing whenever they came home in order to avoid noticing the silence. . . . They would go to any lengths not to be left alone with the terrors that, now that they were far from Arborville, could no longer be kept repressed. The interviewers strove to induce the Arborvilleans to confess to feelings of enmity, distrust, and fear. "Don't you realize that at any moment we could all be killed?" they pleaded. But the Arborvilleans merely felt sorry for the interviewer.

"Cripes, you really think about that?" asked an Arborville farmer in ruddy-faced perplexity. "You poor dog. Better come out here and stay with us for a while. We'll straighten you out."

Then they would invite the pollster in for some pie—"lemon meringue, our favorite," unless, that is, it was peach, or blueberry, or butterscotch cream—and the pollsters succeeded only in getting fat in Arborville—Arborville! where everyone got up early and ate a hearty breakfast, where a day contained a day's work, where after work people sat on their porches and rested their eyes on the wheat gilded by the setting sun, or in town on the huge elms, miraculously free from disease. Arborville—where bronzed men on tractors enjoyed the atavistic companionship of their forefathers as they guided the plow in the furrow. Arborville—where nobody suffered from insomnia, where the air smelled of freshly baked bread and newly mown grass. . . .

Arborvilleans thought the outsiders were just envious. Arborville, they believed, was a wonderful place to live, a town anyone would be proud of, and, in the evening, when they sat out on their porches and chatted as dusk fell unnoticed about them, they told themselves how lucky they were to live in Arborville, when the outside world was such a mess.

"Couldn't be a better place in the universe to bring up kids," parents congratulated one another. "Let the Martians look down and drool. It's safe; the schools are good; the air is fresh, the morals untarnished."

"We used to go away for vacations," the people of Arborville told the visitors, when asked if they didn't "come on, admit it, just get the littlest bit bored?"

Well, they used to think they were obliged to get away. They'd pack the kids into the station wagon, drive out to measure the Redwoods, holler down into the Grand Canyon. Even went one year to Bermuda! But then it struck them as silly. Why should they leave the place they loved best on earth whenever they got a moment's spare time? The rest of the country could travel full time if it wanted, but Arborvilleans no longer had any desire to go out and explore the world. Everyone else was welcome to come to them, if they wished, but they didn't like visiting other people. As far as they were concerned, Arborville was the center of the universe, and, one by one, the world's riches were sucked into Arborville's category of extraneous things. The pyramids of Egypt went tumbling, like dice, into the vortex of their self-satisfaction, the Taj Mahal, the jungles of Africa, the Eiffel Tower went end over end; the castles in Scotland, the white villas of Greece and Morocco—these in their turn were swallowed up, and then closer and closer to home: the Statue of Liberty, the Lincoln Memorial, the faces on Mt. Rushmore . . . until even the city fifty miles down the Interstate, where they had attended movies and fairs, was too much trouble to think about anymore. "Oh, it's just such a long way down, is the thing, and then you've got to come all the way back, and the kids are sleepy and cross. . . ." Hell, if they felt like going anywhere, why not go for a drive through Arborville itself, whose handsome founding houses still stood, capacious dwellings with enough clear space, front and back, to prevent any inimical party from reaching the porches unobserved, whose lilac and forsythia hedges kept the lines of demarcation cleanly drawn between neighbors? So they got into their station wagons, and, full of pride, ran the gantlets of huge elms that bent over the streets called Pleasant, Forest, Harvest, Oak, and so on out into the countryside, where lazy fields of corn and wheat stretched to the edge of the world.

"It doesn't make sense," the reporters said. "Someone will have to pay the piper." But, after all, they had their own careers to attend to. They had to go find out how the Vienna choirboys felt about their voices changing, get the scoop on the latest First Lady's plans for redecorating the White House. . . . They couldn't spend the rest of their lives in Arborville waiting for the towns-folk to confess they were just putting on a good show.

"So what's wrong with the Quinces?" Hugh Greenmantle, their next-door neighbor, asked his wife June impatiently. He was trying to read the sports section and he wished June would come to the point. "They've always seemed perfectly happy to me."

"I know, that's just it! How long can we keep pretending we don't hear the fighting going on next door?"

"Everyone has arguments from time to time, June."

"You know that mechanical bird Cyrus traded Huey for the aircraft carrier? The one that actually flew? Apparently Harold bought it for Cyrus on a business trip. Rose told me that when he found out Cyrus had gotten rid of it, he cried. He cried, Hugh!"

"June . . ."

"Well, Hugh, doesn't it make you think? If people like the Quinces, who we all thought had such a solid marriage, are having problems, how can we feel sure any of us are safe?"

Hugh frowned. "All I know is that if there are problems they must be Rose's fault. Hal Quince is an excellent fellow. I've known him since kindergarten. I'd trust him with my life!"

"What's going on with Hal lately?" Joe Williams remarked to his golfing partner, Tom Boxford. "He hasn't been himself in months."

"I know," replied Tom, choosing an iron for his drive. "He doesn't seem to want to discuss it though."

"Do you think something's wrong at home? Rose has always seemed kind of unstable to me. That way she looks at you like you might secretly be a maniac who carries a strangling stocking in your pocket. I remember once at a party she asked me if I had to drown or burn to death which I would choose."

Tom laughed. "Which did you?"

"I changed the subject, I think."

"Yes," said Susie Silton to Carrie Johnson over coffee, "I'm afraid there's definitely a snake in the garden. I finally got Rose alone after the bridge club and asked her if anything was wrong and she burst into tears. It seems the argument's over General Street. Harold thinks Cyrus and Betsy spend too much time with him; he complains General Street fills their heads with all kinds of unrealistic ideas. Rose thinks Harold's just jealous. But I don't know. I can see his point of view. It does seem odd, her dad living with them all these years."

"I agree," Carrie said. "It's not as if he's ill or can't afford to live anywhere else."

"Rose had a pretty rough childhood, I understand. She's never wanted to talk about it, but Harold told Bill once that her mother ran out on her dad when Rose was just a kid. Left her kind of fragile. Maybe her father feels she needs help with the children."

"She *is* pretty dreamy. Still, she's a grown woman. I'm sure she can manage on her own. I sometimes get the impression she thinks she's better than those of us who were born and raised here. Not that I like seeing her so unhappy."

"Yes, I know."

Carrie sighed. Susie refilled their coffee cups, and, thoughtfully, they sat sipping.

Meanwhile, in the Quince household (which the interviewers had not investigated), tensions increased. Harold, like the majority of fathers in Arborville who weren't farmers, worked at a job that made his existence away from the dining table, and apart from the weekends he spent working in the yard, impossible for his children to imagine. Yet he had never given this fact much thought until those jokers from out of town had started prying into everybody's private affairs. Their insinuating remarks had shaken Harold up more than he liked to admit. The things they said sounded so much like Charles. All this tomfoolery about the next war. Recently Harold had told Cyrus that he didn't want that ratty old cat of Cyrus's sleeping in his room anymore—the thing had fleas—and Cyrus had replied that Jonzo had to be there in case there was a night attack so Cyrus could carry him down to the basement.

"Blast it, Cyrus!" Harold had shouted. "How many times have I told you there's not going to be a war? There's not going to be any attack!"

Cyrus raised an eyebrow—he'd learned that trick from Charles—and said, "I don't know, Dad. Granddad says you can never be too careful."

"Careful of what, young man? Would you mind explaining yourself?"

"Of the enemy, Dad," Cyrus said patiently. He sounded as if he felt sorry for Harold for being so dimwitted. "You should never volunteer information," he recited. "You should suspect everyone. Spies are everywhere."

"Spies!" Harold exploded. "All I know is that your grandfather is the one who'd better start being careful. One of these days he may find himself sitting up for a pretty little court-martial!"

Harold had tried to discuss his concern with Rose, but she was impatient with the subject. "Oh, Harold," she said, "it's just a game." A game! Couldn't she even see what was happening in her own house?

"What do you want me to do? Forbid my father to talk to his own grandchildren?"

He reminded Rose that they had agreed Cyrus would do something with other kids after school—take swimming lessons or join the Little League—but she always had some explanation for his failure to be involved in such activities. Either he didn't get along with the coach or the class was full or ... He couldn't understand Rose's attitude. When pressed, she said, "There's a world outside Arborville, you know. And Dad encourages Cyrus's imagination." Imagination! Well, fine, but when a kid woke himself and the whole house up in the middle of the night screaming, "They're going to push the button! They're going to push the button!" it had gone too far.

For ages now, it seemed to Harold, he had been chanting: "*I'm* his father, Rose. *I'm* his father," though he hadn't said it to her. He kept seeing Cyrus sitting with Charles on the steps, the two of them staring at him when he came home from work, as if he were a stranger.

Harold had always been proud to go to work. He was employed by one of the country's most venerable industries—it had grown to its tremendous size during the last war, but, unlike most of its counterpart war-boom firms, had been able to maintain its profit margin ever since by altering its capabilities to keep pace with the times. Harold had relished being a part of this industrial empire, but now he suffered because his children showed no interest in what he did. They preferred to be with Charles, acting out his military games.

Harold had tried to reassure himself that this was all right, that his was a life they would respect when they had grown up and moved away from Arborville and gone on to bigger and better things—progress his own efforts would have made possible. Then, he had thought, they would speak reverently of how he had instilled the basic values; they would think with tears in their eyes of his decades of uncomplaining support of his family and feel terrible that they had taken him for granted. Someday, Harold had believed, Cyrus and Betsy would come home to Arborville with their hearts in their mouths, their eyes glistening as old Hal, giving old Rose his hand to steady her, walked down the porch steps to greet them.

"This is what life's all about," sighed the major's wife. (This was in the good old days.) The major and his wife sat before a fire, she sewing, he reading and smoking his pipe. Their two children, a boy and a girl, were asleep in the nursery; the servants, though about, were unobtrusive.

She gazed at him fondly. Smiling to herself, she took a deep breath and it seemed to her the house itself pulsed through her blood. She breathed in at the front door and out through the dormers. She stretched and a board creaked. She could feel the kitchen dark and quiet now; upstairs, her bedroom waiting; beyond, the dormant life of the attic. The clock in the lamplit room where she sat gazing at her husband might have been ticking in her heart.

The major took his pipe from his lips and looked up. "Darling . . ." he began, then sighed.

"What is it?"

"I have decided to volunteer for active duty."

He heard her sharp intake of breath and saw her sewing drop from her hands. "But you said . . ."

"Neither I nor anyone else expected it to go on for so long. It's not right for me to sit comfortably at home while so many are dying on the battlefield."

"But it will be right for you to mingle your blood with everyone else's?"

"My country needs my services. It is my duty to go."

She looked at him, betrayed. He went on, "Let me remind you of how many women have bravely given their husbands and sons to the cause."

"Given . . ." she scoffed.

Scorn was not the weapon he had expected. Still, he wanted to fight a fair fight.

"Would you wish me to be a coward? To skulk at home while my countrymen fall?"

"A coward or a corpse," she said bitterly. "It is not much of a choice, is it?"

"What you should do, you see, is take notes."

"Notes, Granddad?"

Charles, Cyrus, and Betsy sat in the backyard, at the picnic table, having a "summit conference." They were drinking lemonade and eating chocolate-covered graham crackers. Harold and Rose, who were temporarily on better terms since Rose had discovered that she was pregnant, had gone away for the weekend to visit Harold's mother, who was ill in a nursing home in nearby Riverton. The instant the car was out of sight, a holiday had been declared at the Quince residence. Cyrus and Betsy had rigged a tarpaulin in the backyard—"on maneuvers," Charles said—and were going to sleep under it all weekend. They had persuaded Charles to go to the store for hot dogs and marshmallows—"not exactly battle rations," he complained, "but it will have to do." Now the coals glowed in the grill, and the outlines of things were growing blurred.

"Notes about what, Granddad?"

"What kind of notes?"

"Did you read in the paper recently where some people said they met some visitors from other planets, who came down to get acquainted?"

"Martians!"

"You have too conventional a notion of outer space, Granddaughter. No—we spend so much time wondering what our next-door neighbors on Venus and Mars are up to that we forget there's a whole universe out there. We should be prepared for the visitors to be completely different from anything we've imagined, to have ways of doing things we've never dreamed of, ways of understanding things . . ."

"Like what?" Cyrus asked.

"I was afraid you'd want to know. Well, maybe they can fly. Maybe they never need to sleep. Maybe they can find where they're going without maps, like Jonzo. Maybe they have ways of living many lives at once—say, if you wanted to be here and visiting your Grandma Quince at the same time."

"Ugh," Cyrus said.

"Yuck," said Betsy.

"Now, now. It's not her fault she's a crotchety old hag."

Cyrus and Betsy giggled.

"See, if she lived in outer space," Charles went on, talking to himself, "maybe she wouldn't be so unhappy. Maybe in outer space people don't misunderstand each other, don't leave each other like they do down here. Maybe in outer space they don't feel they have to keep secrets."

"What secrets?"

"That's what you have to find out, Corporal. Maybe in outer space they don't have wars. Anyhow, you two should be good at taking notes. Being officers, you already have sharper powers of observation than most people."

"Mine are sharp, Granddad. Betsy's the one who sleeps at her post."

"I do not!" Betsy, indignant, stomped off.

"You see, Corporal," Charles went on, "the world, at least as we have known it, might end in your lifetime." Charles scrutinized Cyrus, but he didn't flinch. Or was he getting sleepy?

"It may not, of course, but, if it does, it would be sad if no one had taken notes on what it had been like here in case anyone visited afterward. That's why I'm doing my best to teach you—train you to keep your eyes peeled."

"Keep my eyes peeled!"

Charles laughed. "You're a good soldier, Cyrus. I'm sure you'll make an excellent ambassador to other planets if you ever get a chance."

"I'll zap them right away with my space weapons!"

"Oh, no you won't. That's pure imbecile talk, Cyrus, imagining everyone in outer space is out to get us. Think how it must hurt their feelings. They want to come down and have a nice chat and ask us how things have been going on earth lately but, if they attempt to, imbeciles run out with guns and start shooting."

"But they might shoot us first. They might be on the wrong side."

"True, they might." Charles laughed. "The point is, Cyrus, one hopes that visitors won't be bound by the same distrust and suspicion that shackle us poor benighted human beings. In the meantime, pay attention to what goes on around you. Then at some point you can compile the information you've acquired. Make a sort of guidebook, a handbook—something to fit in the hand . . ."

"What if they don't have hands?"

"Insubordination! Something they can carry around with them, like a book you take on field trips to identify plants, or that tourists carry to inform them about architectural monuments and historical sites. Doctors have handbooks that help them diagnose ailments. . . . You listening, Corporal?"

"Yes, Granddad."

"You have to look at the world from their point of view. They might never have seen a house, for instance, or a yard, or a cat. If nobody's around to explain these things to them, well, they may not understand what anything is *for*. But if somebody had left behind some notes, they'd feel a lot more comfortable, don't you think?"

"Yes," Cyrus said. He yawned.

Charles smiled.

The moon edged up behind the roof, round and molten—the identical moon that through the ages had been responsible for the melancholy of princesses, for the madness of sailors, for the quickening of everyone's blood.

"It would be nice if we could go out there too," Charles said softly. "I'm all for intergalactic travel, aren't you?"

An airplane crossed the moon, like a bug. This airplane could have come from anywhere. It could have been going anywhere too: tracing a line from Arborville to a little house in the suburbs of Winston City or to an eccentric mansion in the New Jersey countryside. Maybe those who dwelled there would also look up and wonder about the plane. Charles sighed. Cyrus shivered suddenly and woke up.

"What?" he exclaimed, hearing the plane overhead. "Wait . . . four, five . . . six! Six airplanes today so far, Granddad."

"Good boy, Cyrus," Charles said. "If you only knew how happy you make me."

After Lark was born, there was whispering. This was worse than when Harold and Rose had yelled at each other. Now they scarcely spoke at all except during the long hours in which they shut themselves up in their bedroom. Cyrus, crouched at the keyhole, trying to hear what was going on, learned that it had something to do with the baby and whose fault it was he was the way he was. Over and over Harold asked Rose what about her past she was hiding from him, and over and over she said, "Nothing. Why would I hide anything?" Why would she? Cyrus wondered.

Sometimes Harold grabbed Betsy and squeezed her until she cried for him to let her go. Both Harold and Rose bestowed on the older children sudden, violent affections that frightened them.

Even Charles seemed affected. He wouldn't plan maneuvers and Cyrus was forced to resort to his friends, whose idea of battle was to hide in the bushes and jump out when he wasn't expecting it. But he soon tired of their crude concepts and instead spent his time patrolling the town with Jonzo, looking for things to record.

Then, mysteriously, the atmosphere would clear; Rose would sing about the house, and Harold renew his shouting at Jonzo. Cyrus and Betsy would play happily with their brother—Edgar Francis, Harold and Rose had named him; Lark he was called, because Rose said he was as happy as one. He was a baby who loved to be spoken to, and Cyrus and Betsy, who both adored him, could tell him anything and he'd grin and chortle, as long as they kept talking.

However, during his third year, when Cyrus was twelve and Betsy ten, Lark fell victim to obscure terrors. Discovering himself alone in a room, he would scream for "Granny."

"Lord knows where he got that from," Harold said. "My mother's been dead a year and yours he's never seen. Cyrus, Betsy," he called, "come in here a minute. You kids been telling Edgar stories?"

"Stories?"

"What kind of stories?"

"*Any* stories. You been making things up around him?"

"No, Dad."

"No, Daddy."

"Well, I don't want you starting either, do you hear me?"

"Okay."

"We won't."

But Lark was too small to understand that Granny was half invention. The only way to quiet him was to go on as they had begun; they first told him stories about Granny to entertain him anyway, just as they had once been entertained by Charles (who, though he had gone so far as to give Cyrus and Betsy each a photograph of their missing grandmother, with her address written on the back, had exacted from them their promise to keep this secret). So Betsy and Cyrus told Lark how nice Granny was, how she always had cookies in her pocket. "Cookies," Lark repeated, happy again.

"And she never gets mad," Cryus went on, "although sometimes she gets a little sad."

"Don't tell him she gets sad, Cyrus."

"Well, she does."

"You don't know. You're just saying that because Granddad did."

"She doesn't have us," Cryus retorted.

They argued, and Lark began to cry.

"Don't worry, Lark," Cyrus comforted him. "When you visit her she'll cheer up immediately."

"*I'll* tell you about the house Granny lives in," Betsy said. "It's a very small house, because she lives all by herself, but it's very pretty and there are lacy curtains at all the windows."

"Granny has lots of cats and dogs, Lark, and she talks to all of them."

"She sleeps upstairs in a big four-poster bed with pillows twice as long as the ones we have."

"*What*?"

"Because that's the kind people have who think in bed, stupid. And there's a tall clock downstairs and sometimes Granny wakes up in the middle of the night and hears it strike but always goes right back to sleep."

"Except sometimes . . ."

"Stop interrupting. Then, Lark, when Granny wakes up in the morning, she always goes to the window and looks out over the town. . . ."

"Now who's saying what Granddad said?"

Betsy glared at Cyrus. "After she gets dressed she goes downstairs and has breakfast. And then you know what she does? She makes a cake."

"What cake?" Lark inquired.

"You're such an idiot, Betsy. Someday she'll make you one, Lark. We'll all go to visit her, with Granddad, and then we'll all live together for the rest of our lives."

It was a day so bright there seemed to be no shadows. Cyrus sat on the front steps of his house, a big white house on a street of big white houses, all freshly painted, with shutters that were never closed. Huey Greenmantle's father was waxing his car, rubbing it with a rag and then standing back and looking at his reflection in the newly polished surface. He saw Cyrus watching him and called, "What you up to, Cyrus?" but went back to rubbing his fender without waiting for an answer. Four doors down, across the street, Mr. Silton was clipping a hedge. Every few minutes he sang, "I wandered today to the hill, Maggie, to watch the scene below ..." and then hummed the rest of the verse. Max, the Fosters' collie, ambled across the Fosters' yard to the sidewalk, stopping every few feet to sniff at something. When he reached Cyrus's lawn, Jonzo, sitting on the steps beside Cyrus, arched his back. "Just relax, Jonzo," Cyrus said. "It's only Max."

Then slowly he got up, went down into the basement, and removed his sneakers from the dryer, where they lay like two dead birds, put them on, and set off, pursued by Jonzo, on his usual rounds. He strolled down to Main Street, still quiet for a Saturday, past the gas station: We Sell/Rain or Shine, into the hardware store, where he inspected the nail bins while he listened to the Saturday fathers greeting each other, "How goes the battle?" but his heart wasn't in it. So he left and walked back home again, rewinding the squares, each of which contained a smug-looking white house and a smug-looking green lawn, until he reached his own, which today looked no different from all the others. Charles was now sitting on the steps.

"Hey," he said, "aren't you going to salute?"

Cyrus flopped his arm to his forehead.

"At ease, soldier." Cyrus sat down a step below his grandfather. Jonzo turned in to the walk and meowed.

"Come on, Jonzo, knock it off!"

"How did inspection go? See anything out of the ordinary?"

"No."

"Hmm," Charles said. "Did you see anything?"

Cyrus shrugged.

At that moment, Harold came walking down the street, Lark on his shoulders, Lark's plump legs on either side of his neck, Lark's hands on his head: Lark was now three and a half years old. "Look out for the trees," Harold warned, whenever they passed under low-hanging branches, and Lark ducked. He was laughing, but with an undertone of fear, as if he thought his father had lowered the trees' branches on purpose.

"Stop, stop!" he panted, giggling harder as his father instead began to jog. "Daddy! Daddy!"

"Look out for the trees! Look out for the trees!" Harold shouted, and Lark shut his eyes as a fringe of maple feathered across his face, opened them just in time to close them again for the onslaught of fat, splayed oak leaves.

"Look out, buddy, look out for the trees!"

Slowing down, they turned in to the walk. Rose had been watching them anxiously from the porch.

"For goodness' sake, Harold!" she exclaimed, holding out her arms.

"For goodness' sake what, Rose?" He handed Lark up to her, over Cyrus's head.

"I . . ." she began, but then merely clutched Lark and hurried into the house.

With an effort Harold smiled at Cyrus and Charles. "Interrupting something? I wouldn't want to overhear anything top secret."

"Very funny," Cyrus said.

"Take it easy, Corporal," Charles said gently, but at this Harold lost control.

"Damn it all, Charles, I've asked you, over and over, to cut out the malarkey! What are you trying to do? Push me to the point where I have no choice but to ask you to leave the house?"

"Don't you dare ask him to leave the house! Don't you dare!"

"Hush, Cyrus," Charles said sharply. Cyrus, wounded, stared at him. Then Charles stood. He entered the house and climbed upstairs. Pausing at the door to Rose and Harold's bedroom, he saw Rose leaning out the window, trying to free a kite that had become entangled in the branches of a tree growing close to the house. "Rosie?" he said.

"I've meant to get this down for ever so long," she said brightly. "I keep forgetting to get around to it."

"Where's Lark?"

"In the kitchen with Betsy."

"Sweetheart . . ."

"I want to be alone, Dad."

He nodded, although she hadn't turned to look at him, and went from the room.

Cyrus had fled to the backyard and was scuffing the bare patch of ground under the swing set where he and Charles had often traced battle plans. Harold followed.

"Hey, champ," he pleaded.

Cyrus turned and swung. The punch landed on Harold's arm; Harold tried to grab Cyrus and hug him, but Cyrus wriggled loose and kept pummeling, though his swings were wild and landed without force.

"Hey, Cy," Harold said, ducking. "Hey, come on, now." He wanted to laugh but was afraid that if he did he would cry, so he stood still, accepting Cyrus's punches on his forearms, repeating, "Cy, come on now, come on."

Suddenly Rose screamed from the bedroom window. "Cyrus!" she cried, as if Harold were in grave danger. "Stop it! Stop it this instant!"

Startled, Cyrus looked up. While he was off-guard Harold made another grab for him, but he struggled free and then turned and ran out of the yard and down the street. Jonzo, who saw him take off, leapt yowling after.

"Stay home, Jonzo!" Cyrus yelled. "Why don't you just stay home?"

"Now look what you've done!" Rose cried.

Harold Quince lowered his head and accepted his wife's blame. But this did not change anything. Someone still had to make decisions, even if they were painful ones, like taking Lark away from home because under the circumstances it was the only thing that might save his life. And today was the day that, over two months ago, they had agreed Harold would take Lark to the Institute, which was located in New Jersey. Rose refused to look at the reality of the situation; he couldn't permit himself that luxury. Nevertheless, all during the plane trip east that afternoon, the only thing he could hear was her parting words to him, "You know what this will do to me, don't you, Harold?" "I'm not *doing* it to hurt you, Rose," he had reminded her, but he didn't even know if she heard him.

Harold recoiled as, at dusk, he and Lark drove down the wide, heavily traveled highway on the hour's drive from the airport to the Institute. On either side of the road lay an area resembling a battlefield after it was all over: mountains of debris in the midst of which elephantine pipes rose into the sky, belching pale yellow smoke. A foul smell hung over everything. Lark, huddled in the far corner of the front seat, stared out the window. When Harold asked him if he was hungry, he jumped. Instead of replying he asked again, "Where are we going, Daddy?" He sounded so normal and healthy. Yet hidden in his genes were the agents of his destruction, already, if the doctors were to be believed, at work.

"To a school, Lark," Harold said gently. "I've already explained to you."

"I don't want to go, Daddy," Lark quavered. "I want to go home."

He jumped again when Harold yelled, "Damn it, Lark, that's enough whining!" But though his eyes filled Lark didn't cry but pressed himself even farther into his corner and mumbled, "Granny, Granny loves Lark."

"Granny!" Harold thundered. Then his vision blurred, and he pulled off the road. He sat hunched over the wheel, racked by sobs, while long trucks roared by and sleek limousines whished past, underlining his presence in the middle of nowhere, a place he would always be, alone with his inarticulate love.

He sat up at last; Lark was watching him, terrified.

"Daddy loves you too, Lark, do you understand that?" Harold asked, trying to smile. Lark didn't answer, and Harold reached over and gathered him into his arms.

"Don't cry, Daddy," Lark pleaded. "Don't cry anymore."

"No, Daddy won't cry anymore, Lark. I promise."

"They said he'll be fine, Rose," Harold said in a tired voice. (Charles had retired early, and Betsy and Cyrus had been sent to bed but were listening from the landing.) "They said he'll adjust in no time, so that by the time it . . . by the time he requires more help he'll feel at home there. They said that the younger they see these children, the better chance there is of helping them. And, with all the research being done, they said it's entirely possible that he may be able to lead a relatively normal life someday."

"He already was leading a 'relatively normal life,' Harold!" Rose cried. "What do they think they can do for him that I can't?"

"Now, darling . . ." Harold began.

"Don't talk to me as if I were a child," she said.

Harold closed his eyes. When he opened them, Rose was still

there, a sentry guarding all sorrow, forbidding him to show any pain.

"I know you can care for him now," he went on, "but how would you cope later? The people at the Institute are trained to deal with children like Lark and we have to consider his welfare in the long run. We should also think of Betsy and Cyrus, whether it would be fair to them. . . ."

"Now, now, that's too much, Harold! If anything, Lark kept Cyrus and Betsy gentle and considerate."

"What I was going to say, Rose . . ."

"No, Harold, you're the only one who was uncomfortable having him around. He wasn't perfect enough for Arborville, was he? You were afraid the perfect Arborvilleans would shy away from us!"

Upstairs, Betsy began to cry, and Cyrus put his arms around her, whispering "Shh," but they had been heard, and Harold stormed up the stairs.

"You were eavesdropping!" he bellowed. "Get in your rooms!"

"You don't love Lark," Cyrus accused him. "If you loved him, you wouldn't have sent him away."

Harold stared. Then he slapped Cyrus twice, hard. "Don't you ever, ever say that again. Do you hear me? Do you?"

Cyrus shrugged.

"You had better not." He grabbed Cyrus and pulled him down the hallway and into his room. He shouted at Betsy, who had taken refuge in the doorway to hers, to shut her goddamn door that instant and quit staring at him as if he were a freakshow. Then he followed Rose, who had come upstairs, into their bedroom.

"What the hell were you doing?" she demanded.

He stared at her. Then he pleaded, "You're my *wife*. Why aren't you on my side?"

Cyrus, lying facedown on his bed, muffling his sobs in his pillow, vowed never to forgive his father.

COMMUNIST

by Richard Ford

My mother once had a boyfriend named Glen Baxter. This was in 1961. We—my mother and I—were living in the little house my father had left her up the Sun River, near Victory, Montana, west of Great Falls. My mother was thirty-one at the time. I was sixteen. Glen Baxter was somewhere in the middle, between us, though I cannot be exact about it.

We were living then off the proceeds of my father's life insurance policies, with my mother doing some part-time waitressing work up in Great Falls and going to the bars in the evenings, which I know is where she met Glen Baxter. Sometimes he would come back with her and stay in her room at night, or she would call up from town and explain that she was staying with him in his little place on Lewis Street by the GN yards. She gave me his number every time, but I never called it. I think she probably thought that what she was doing was terrible, but simply couldn't help herself. I thought it was all right, though. Regular life it seemed, and still does. She was young, and I knew that even then.

Glen Baxter was a Communist and liked hunting, which he talked about a lot. Pheasants. Ducks. Deer. He killed all of them, he said. He had been to Vietnam as far back as then, and when he was in our house he often talked about shooting the animals over there—monkeys and beautiful parrots—using military guns just for sport. We did not know what Vietnam was then, and Glen, when he talked about that, referred to it only as "the far east." I think now he must've been in the CIA and had been disillusioned by something he saw or found out about and been thrown out, but that kind of thing did not matter to us. He was a tall, dark-eyed man with thick black hair, and was usually in a good humor. He had gone halfway through college in Peoria, Illinois, he said, where he grew up. But when he was around our life he worked wheat farms as a ditcher, and stayed out of work winters and in the bars drinking with women like my mother, who had work and some money. It is not an uncommon life to lead in Montana.

What I want to explain happened in November. We had not been seeing Glen Baxter for some time. Two months had gone by. My mother knew other men, but she came home most days from work and stayed inside watching television in her bedroom and drinking beers. I asked about Glen once, and she said only that she didn't know where he was, and I assumed they had had a fight and that he was gone off on a flyer back to Illinois or Massachusetts, where he said he had relatives. I'll admit that I liked him. He had something on his mind always. He was a labor man as well as a Communist, and liked to say that the country was poisoned by the rich, and strong men would need to bring it to life again, and I liked that because my father had been a labor man, which was why we had a house to live in and money coming through. It was also true that I'd had a few boxing bouts by then—just with town boys and one with an Indian from Choteau— and there were some girlfriends I knew from that. I did not like my mother being around the house so much at night, and I wished Glen Baxter would come back, or that another man would come along and entertain her somewhere else.

At two o'clock on a Saturday, Glen drove up into our yard in a car. He had had a big brown Harley-Davidson that he rode most of the year, in his black-and-red irrigators and a baseball cap turned backwards. But this time he had a car, a blue Nash Ambassador. My mother and I went out on the porch when he stopped inside the olive trees my father had planted as a shelter belt, and my mother had a look on her face of not much pleasure. It was starting to be cold in earnest by then. Snow was down already onto the Fairfield Bench, though on this day a chinook was blowing, and it could as easily have been spring, though the sky above the Divide was turning over in silver and blue clouds of winter.

"We haven't seen you in a long time, I guess," my mother said coldly.

"My little retarded sister died," Glen said, standing at the door of his old car. He was wearing his orange VFW jacket and canvas shoes we called wino shoes, something I had never seen him wear before. He seemed to be in a good humor. "We buried her in Florida near the home."

"That's a good place," my mother said in a voice that meant she was a wronged party in something.

"I want to take this boy hunting today, Aileen," Glen said. "There're snow geese down now. But we have to go right away, or they'll be gone to Idaho by tomorrow."

"He doesn't care to go," my mother said.

"Yes, I do," I said, and looked at her.

My mother frowned at me. "Why do you?"

"Why does he need a reason?" Glen Baxter said and grinned.

"I want him to have one, that's why." She looked at me oddly. "I think Glen's drunk, Les."

"No, I'm not drinking," Glen said, which was hardly ever true. He looked at both of us, and my mother bit down on the side of her lower lip and stared at me in a way to make you think she thought something was being put over on her and she didn't like you for it. She was very pretty, though when she was mad her features were sharpened and less pretty by a long way. "All right then, I don't care," she said to no one in particular. "Hunt, kill, maim. Your father did that too." She turned to go back inside.

"Why don't you come with us, Aileen?" Glen was smiling still, pleased.

"To do what?" my mother said. She stopped and pulled a package of cigarettes out of her dress pocket and put one in her mouth.

"It's worth seeing."

"See dead animals?" my mother said.

"These geese are from Siberia, Aileen," Glen said. "They're not like a lot of geese. Maybe I'll buy us dinner later. What do you say?"

"Buy what with?" my mother said. To tell the truth, I didn't know why she was so mad at him. I would've thought she'd be glad to see him. But she just suddenly seemed to hate everything about him.

"I've got some money," Glen said. "Let me spend it on a pretty girl tonight."

"Find one of those and you're lucky," my mother said, turning away toward the front door.

"I already found one," Glen Baxter said. But the door slammed behind her, and he looked at me then with a look I think now was helplessness, though I could not see a way to change anything.

*   *   *

My mother sat in the back seat of Glen's Nash and looked out the window while we drove. My double gun was on the seat between us beside Glen's Belgian pump, which he kept loaded with five shells in case, he said, he saw something beside the road he wanted to shoot. I had hunted rabbits before, and had ground-sluiced pheasants and other birds, but I had never been on an actual hunt before, one where you drove out to some special place and did it formally. And I was excited. I had a feeling that something important was about to happen to me and that this would be a day I would always remember.

My mother did not say anything for a long time, and neither did I. We drove up through Great Falls and out the other side toward Fort Benton, which was on the benchland where wheat was grown.

"Geese mate for life," my mother said, just out of the blue, as we were driving. "I hope you know that. They're special birds."

"I know that," Glen said in the front seat. "I have every respect for them."

"So where were you for three months?" she said. "I'm only curious."

"I was in the Big Hole for a while," Glen said, "and after that I went over to Douglas, Wyoming."

"What were you planning to do there?" my mother asked.

"I wanted to find a job, but it didn't work out."

"I'm going to college," she said suddenly, and this was something I had never heard about before. I turned to look at her, but she was staring out her window and wouldn't see me.

"I knew French once," Glen said. "*Rose*'s pink. *Rouge*'s red." He glanced at me and smiled. "I think that's a wise idea, Aileen. When are you going to start?"

"I don't want Les to think he was raised by crazy people all his life," my mother said.

"Les ought to go himself," Glen said.

"After I go, he will."

"What do you say about that, Les?" Glen said, grinning.

"He says it's just fine," my mother said.

"It's just fine," I said.

Where Glen Baxter took us was out onto the high flat prairie that was disked for wheat and had high, high mountains out to the east, with lower heartbreak hills in between. It was, I remember, a day for blues in the sky, and down in the distance we could see the small town of Floweree, and the state highway running

past it toward Fort Benton and the high line. We drove out on
top of the prairie on a muddy dirt road fenced on both sides,
until we had gone about three miles, which is where Glen stopped.

"All right," he said, looking up in the rearview mirror at my
mother. "You wouldn't think there was anything here, would
you?"

"*We're* here," my mother said. "You brought us here."

"You'll be glad, though," Glen said, and seemed confident to
me. I had looked around myself but could not see anything. No
water or trees, nothing that seemed like a good place to hunt
anything. Just wasted land. "There's a big lake out there, Les,"
Glen said. "You can't see it now from here because it's low. But
the geese are there. You'll see."

"It's like the moon out here, I recognize that," my mother said,
"only it's worse." She was staring out at the flat, disked wheatland
as if she could actually see something in particular, and wanted to
know more about it. "How'd you find this place?"

"I came once on the wheat push," Glen said.

"And I'm sure the owner told you just to come back and hunt
any time you like and bring anybody you wanted. Come one, come
all. Is that it?"

"People shouldn't own land anyway," Glen said. "Anybody
should be able to use it."

"Les, Glen's going to poach here," my mother said. "I just
want you to know that, because that's a crime and the law will get
you for it. If you're a man now, you're going to have to face the
consequences."

"That's not true," Glen Baxter said, and looked gloomily out
over the steering wheel down the muddy road toward the mountains. Though for myself I believed it was true, and didn't care. I
didn't care about anything at that moment except seeing geese fly
over me and shooting them down.

"Well, I'm certainly not going out there," my mother said. "I
like towns better, and I already have enough trouble."

"That's okay," Glen said. "When the geese lift up you'll get to
see them. That's all I wanted. Les and me'll go shoot them, won't
we, Les?"

"Yes," I said, and I put my hand on my shotgun, which had
been my father's and was heavy as rocks.

"Then we should go on," Glen said, "or we'll waste our light."

We got out of the car with our guns. Glen took off his canvas
shoes and put on his pair of black irrigators out of the trunk.
Then we crossed the barbed-wire fence and walked out into the

high, tilled field toward nothing. I looked back at my mother when we were still not so far away, but I could only see the small, dark top of her head, low in the back seat of the Nash, staring out and thinking what I could not then begin to say.

On the walk toward the lake, Glen began talking to me. I had never been alone with him, and knew little about him except what my mother said—that he drank too much, or other times that he was the nicest man she had ever known in the world and that some day a woman would marry him, though she didn't think it would be her. Glen told me as we walked that he wished he had finished college, but that it was too late now, that his mind was too old. He said he had liked "the far east" very much, and that people there knew how to treat one another, and that he would go back some day but couldn't go now. He said also that he would like to live in Russia for a while and mentioned the names of people who had gone there, names I didn't know. He said it would be hard at first, because it was so different, but that pretty soon anyone would learn to like it and wouldn't want to live anywhere else, and that Russians treated Americans who came to live there like kings. There were Communists everywhere now, he said. You didn't know them, but they were there. Montana had a large number, and he was in touch with all of them. He said that Communists were always in danger and that he had to protect himself all the time. And when he said that, he pulled back his VFW jacket and showed me the butt of a pistol he had stuck under his shirt against his bare skin. "There are people who want to kill me right now," he said, "and I would kill a man myself if I thought I had to." And we kept walking. Though in a while he said, "I don't think I know much about you, Les. But I'd like to. What do you like to do?"

"I like to box," I said. "My father did it. It's a good thing to know."

"I suppose you have to protect yourself too," Glen said.

"I know how to," I said.

"Do you like to watch TV?" Glen said, and smiled.

"Not much."

"I love to," Glen said. "I could watch it instead of eating if I had one."

I looked out straight ahead over the green tops of sage that grew at the edge of the disked field, hoping to see the lake Glen said was there. There was an airishness and a sweet smell that I thought might be the place we were going, but I couldn't see it. "How will we hunt these geese?" I said.

"It won't be hard," Glen said. "Most hunting isn't even hunting. It's only shooting. And that's what this will be. In Illinois you would dig holes in the ground to hide in and set out your decoys. Then the geese come to you, over and over again. But we don't have time for that here." He glanced at me. "You have to be sure the first time here."

"How do you know they're here now?" I asked. And I looked toward the Highwood Mountains twenty miles away, half in snow and half dark blue at the bottom. I could see the little town of Floweree then, looking shabby and dimly lighted in the distance. A red bar sign shone. A car moved slowly away from the scattered buildings.

"They always come November first," Glen said.

"Are we going to poach them?"

"Does it make any difference to you?" Glen asked.

"No, it doesn't."

"Well then we aren't," he said.

We walked then for a while without talking. I looked back once to see the Nash far and small in the flat distance. I couldn't see my mother, and I thought that she must've turned on the radio and gone to sleep, which she always did, letting it play all night in her bedroom. Behind the car the sun was nearing the rounded mountains southwest of us, and I knew that when the sun was gone it would be cold. I wished my mother had decided to come along with us, and I thought for a moment of how little I really knew her at all.

Glen walked with me another quarter mile, crossed another barbed wire fence where sage was growing, then went a hundred yards through wheatgrass and spurge until the ground went up and formed a kind of long hillock bunker built by a farmer against the wind. And I realized the lake was just beyond us. I could hear the sound of a car horn blowing and a dog barking all the way down in the town, then the wind seemed to move and all I could hear then and after then were geese. So many geese, from the sound of them, though I still could not see even one. I stood and listened to the high-pitched shouting sound, a sound I had never heard so close, a sound with size to it—though it was not loud. A sound that meant great numbers and that made your chest rise and your shoulders tighten with expectancy. It was a sound to make you feel separate from it and everything else, as if you were of no importance in the grand scheme of things.

"Do you hear them singing?" Glen asked. He held his hand up to make me stand still. And we both listened. "How many do you think, Les, just hearing?"

"A hundred," I said. "More than a hundred."

"Five thousand," Glen said. "More than you can believe when you see them. Go see."

I put down my gun and on my hands and knees crawled up the earthwork through the wheatgrass and thistle, until I could see down to the lake and see the geese. And they were there, like a white bandage laid on the water, wide and long and continuous, a white expanse of snow geese, seventy yards from me, on the bank, but stretching far onto the lake, which was large itself— a half-mile across, with thick tules on the far side and wild plums farther and the blue mountain behind them.

"Do you see the big raft?" Glen said from below me, in a whisper.

"I see it," I said, still looking. It was such a thing to see, a view I had never seen and have not since.

"Are any on the land?" he said.

"Some are in the wheatgrass," I said, "but most are swimming."

"Good," Glen said. "They'll have to fly. But we can't wait for that now."

And I crawled backwards down the heel of land to where Glen was, and my gun. We were losing our light, and the air was purplish and cooling. I looked toward the car but couldn't see it, and I was no longer sure where it was below the lighted sky.

"Where do they fly to?" I said in a whisper, since I did not want anything to be ruined because of what I did or said. It was important to Glen to shoot the geese, and it was important to me.

"To the wheat," he said. "Or else they leave for good. I wish your mother had come, Les. Now she'll be sorry."

I could hear the geese quarreling and shouting on the lake surface. And I wondered if they knew we were here now. "She might be," I said with my heart pounding, but I didn't think she would be much.

It was a simple plan he had. I would stay behind the bunker, and he would crawl on his belly with his gun through the wheatgrass as near to the geese as he could. Then he would simply stand up and shoot all the ones he could close up, both in the air and on the ground. And when all the others flew up, with luck some would turn toward me as they came into the wind, and then I could shoot them and turn them back to him, and he would shoot them again. He could kill ten, he said, if he was lucky, and I might kill four. It didn't seem hard.

"Don't show them your face," Glen said. "Wait till you think you can touch them, then stand up and shoot. To hesitate is lost in this."

"All right," I said. "I'll try it."

"Shoot one in the head, and then shoot another one," Glen said. "It won't be hard." He patted me on the arm and smiled. Then he took off his VFW jacket and put it on the ground, climbed up the side of the bunker, cradling his shotgun in his arms, and slid on his belly into the dry stalks of yellow grass out of my sight.

Then for the first time in that entire day I was alone. And I didn't mind it. I sat squat down in the grass, loaded my double gun, and took my other two shells out of my pocket to hold. I pushed the safety off and on to see that it was right. The wind rose a little then, scuffed the grass, and made me shiver. It was not the warm chinook now, but a wind out of the north, the one geese flew away from if they could.

Then I thought about my mother, in the car alone, and how much longer I would stay with her, and what it might mean to her for me to leave. And I wondered when Glen Baxter would die and if someone would kill him, or whether my mother would marry him and how I would feel about it. And though I didn't know why, it occurred to me then that Glen Baxter and I would not be friends when all was said and done, since I didn't care if he ever married my mother or didn't.

Then I thought about boxing and what my father had taught me about it. To tighten your fists hard. To strike out straight from the shoulder and never punch backing up. How to cut a punch by snapping your fist inwards, how to carry your chin low, and to step toward a man when he is falling so you can hit him again. And most important, to keep your eyes open when you are hitting in the face and causing damage, because you need to see what you're doing to encourage yourself, and because it is when you close your eyes that you stop hitting and get hurt badly. "Fly all over your man, Les," my father said. "When you see your chance, fly on him and hit him till he falls." That, I thought, would always be my attitude in things.

And then I heard the geese again, their voices in unison, louder and shouting, as if the wind had changed and put all new sounds in the cold air. And then a *boom*. And I knew Glen was in among them and had stood up to shoot. The noise of geese rose and

grew worse, and my fingers burned where I held my gun too tight
to the metal, and I put it down and opened my fist to make the
burning stop so I could feel the trigger when the moment came.
Boom, Glen shot again, and I heard him shuck a shell, and all the
sounds out beyond the bunker seemed to be rising—the geese,
the shots, the air itself going up. *Boom*, Glen shot another time,
and I knew he was taking his careful time to make his shots good.
And I held my gun and started to crawl up the bunker so as not to
be surprised when the geese came over me and I could shoot.

From the top I saw Glen Baxter alone in the wheatgrass field,
shooting at a white goose with black tips of wings that was on the
ground not far from him, but trying to run and pull into the air.
He shot it once more, and it fell over dead with its wings
flapping.

Glen looked back at me and his face was distorted and strange.
The air around him was full of white rising geese and he seemed
to want them all. "Behind you, Les," he yelled at me, and
pointed. "They're all behind you now." I looked behind me, and
there were geese in the air as far as I could see, more than I knew
how many, moving so slowly, their wings wide out and working
calmly and filling the air with noise, though their voices were not
as loud or as shrill as I had thought they would be. And they were
so close! Forty feet, some of them. The air around me vibrated
and I could feel the wind from their wings and it seemed to me I
could kill as many as the times I could shoot—a hundred or a
thousand—and I raised my gun, put the muzzle on the head of a
white goose, and fired. It shuddered in the air, its wide feet sank
below its belly, its wings cradled out to hold back air, and it fell
straight down and landed with an awful sound, a noise a human
would make, a thick, soft, *hump* noise. I looked up again and shot
another goose, could hear the pellets hit its chest, but it didn't fall
or even break its pattern for flying. *Boom*, Glen shot again. And
then again. "Hey," I heard him shout. "Hey, hey." And there
were geese flying over me, flying in line after line. I broke my gun
and reloaded, and thought to myself as I did: I need confidence
here, I need to be sure with this. I pointed at another goose and
shot it in the head, and it fell the way the first one had, wings out,
its belly down, and with the same thick noise of hitting. Then I
sat down in the grass on the bunker and let geese fly over me.

By now the whole raft was in the air, all of it moving in a slow
swirl above me and the lake and everywhere, finding the wind
and heading out south in long wavering lines that caught the last
sun and turned to silver as they gained a distance. It was a thing

to see, I will tell you now. Five thousand white geese all in the air around you, making a noise like you have never heard before. And I thought to myself then: This is something I will never see again. I will never forget this. And I was right.

Glen Baxter shot twice more. One shot missed, but with the other he hit a goose flying away from him, and knocked it half falling and flying into the empty lake not far from shore, where it began to swim as though it was fine and make its noise.

Glen stood in the stubbly grass, looking out at the goose, his gun lowered. "I didn't need to shoot that, did I, Les?"

"I don't know," I said, sitting on the little knoll of land, looking at the goose swimming in the water.

"I don't know why I shoot 'em. They're so beautiful." He looked at me.

"I don't know either," I said.

"Maybe there's nothing else to do with them." Glen stared at the goose again and shook his head. "Maybe this is exactly what they're put on earth for."

I did not know what to say because I did not know what he could mean by that, though what I felt was embarrassment at the great numbers of geese there were, and a dulled feeling like a hunger because the shooting had stopped and it was over for me now.

Glen began to pick up his geese, and I walked down to my two, which had fallen close together and were dead. One had hit with such an impact that its stomach had split and some of its inward parts were knocked out. Though the other looked unhurt, its soft white belly turned up like a pillow, its head and jagged bill-teeth and its tiny black eyes looking as if they were alive.

"What's happened to the hunters out here?" I heard a voice speak. It was my mother, standing in her pink dress on the knoll above us, hugging her arms. She was smiling, though she was cold. And I realized that I had lost all thought of her in the shooting. "Who did all this shooting? Is this your work, Les?"

"No," I said.

"Les is a hunter, though, Aileen," Glen said. "He takes his time." He was holding two white geese by their necks, one in each hand, and he was smiling. He and my mother seemed pleased.

"I see you didn't miss too many," my mother said and smiled. I could tell she admired Glen for his geese, and that she had done some thinking in the car alone. "It *was* wonderful, Glen," she said. "I've never seen anything like that. They were like snow."

"It's worth seeing once, isn't it?" Glen said. "I should've killed more, but I got excited."

My mother looked at me then. "Where's yours, Les?"

"Here," I said, and pointed to my two geese on the ground beside me.

My mother nodded in a nice way, and I think she liked everything then and wanted the day to turn out right and for all of us to be happy. "Six, then. You've got six in all."

"One's still out there," I said, and motioned where the one goose was swimming in circles on the water.

"Okay," my mother said, and put her hand over her eyes to look. "Where is it?"

Glen Baxter looked at me then with a strange smile, a smile that said he wished I had never mentioned anything about the other goose. And I wished I hadn't either. I looked up in the sky and could see the lines of geese by the thousands shining silver in the light, and I wished we could just leave and go home.

"That one's my mistake there," Glen Baxter said, and grinned. "I shouldn't have shot that one, Aileen. I got too excited."

My mother looked out on the lake for a minute, then looked at Glen and back again. "Poor goose." She shook her head. "How will you get it, Glen?"

"I can't get that one now," Glen said.

My mother looked at him. "What do you mean?" she said.

"I'm going to leave that one," Glen said.

"Well, no. You can't leave one," my mother said. "You shot it. You have to get it. Isn't that a rule?"

"No," Glen said.

And my mother looked from Glen to me. "Wade out and get it, Glen," she said, in a sweet way, and my mother looked young then for some reason, like a young girl, in her flimsy short-sleeved waitress dress and her skinny, bare legs in the wheatgrass.

"No." Glen Baxter looked down at his gun and shook his head. And I didn't know why he wouldn't go, because it would've been easy. The lake was shallow. And you could tell that anyone could've walked out a long way before it got deep, and Glen had on his boots.

My mother looked at the white goose, which was not more than thirty yards from the shore, its head up, moving in slow circles, its wings settled and relaxed so you could see the black tips. "Wade out and get it, Glenny, won't you, please?" she said. "They're special things."

"You don't understand the world, Aileen," Glen said. "This can happen. It doesn't matter."

"But that's so cruel, Glen," she said, and a sweet smile came on her lips.

"Raise up your own arms, Leeny," Glen said. "I can't see any angel's wings, can you Les?" He looked at me, but I looked away.

"Then you go on and get it, Les," my mother said. "You weren't raised by crazy people." I started to go, but Glen Baxter suddenly grabbed me by my shoulder and pulled me back hard, so hard his fingers made bruises in my skin that I saw later.

"Nobody's going," he said. "This is over with now."

And my mother gave Glen a cold look then. "You don't have a heart, Glen," she said. "There's nothing to love in you. You're just a son of a bitch, that's all."

And Glen Baxter nodded at my mother as if he understood something that he had not understood before, but something that he was willing to know. "Fine," he said, "that's fine." And he took his big pistol out from against his belly, the big blue revolver I had only seen part of before and that he said protected him, and he pointed it out at the goose on the water, his arm straight away from him, and shot and missed. And then he shot and missed again. The goose made its noise once. And then he hit it dead, because there was no splash. And then he shot it three times more until the gun was empty and the goose's head was down and it was floating toward the middle of the lake where it was empty and dark blue. "Now who has a heart?" Glen said. But my mother was not there when he turned around. She had already started back to the car and was almost lost from sight in the darkness. And Glen smiled at me then and his face had a wild look on it. "Okay, Les?" he said.

"Okay," I said.

"There're limits to everything, right?"

"I guess so," I said.

"Your mother's a beautiful woman, but she's not the only beautiful woman in Montana." I did not say anything. And Glen Baxter suddenly said, "Here," and he held the pistol out at me. "Don't you want this? Don't you want to shoot me? Nobody thinks they'll die. But I'm ready for it right now." And I did not know what to do then. Though it is true that what I wanted to do was to hit him, hit him as hard in the face as I could, and see him on the ground bleeding and crying and pleading for me to stop. Only at that moment he looked scared to me, and I had never seen a grown man scared before—though I have seen one since—and I felt sorry for him, as though he was already a dead man. And I did not end up hitting him at all.

A light can go out in the heart. All of this went on years ago, but I still can feel now how sad and remote the world was to me. Glen Baxter, I think now, was not a bad man, only a man scared of something he'd never seen before—something soft in himself—his life going a way he didn't like. A woman with a son. Who could blame him there? I don't know what makes people do what they do or call themselves what they call themselves, only that you have to live someone's life to be the expert.

My mother had tried to see the good side of things, tried to be hopeful in the situation she was handed, tried to look out for us both, and it hadn't worked. It was a strange time in her life then and after that, a time when she had to adjust to being an adult just when she was on the thin edge of things. Too much awareness too early in life was her problem, I think.

And what I felt was only that I had somehow been pushed out into the world, into the real life then, the one I hadn't lived yet. In a year I was gone to hardrock mining and no-paycheck jobs and not to college. And I have thought more than once about my mother saying that I had not been raised by crazy people, and I don't know what that could mean or what difference it could make, unless it means that love is a reliable commodity, and even that is not always true, as I have found out.

Late on the night that all this took place I was in bed when I heard my mother say, "Come outside, Les. Come and hear this." And I went out onto the front porch barefoot and in my underwear, where it was warm like spring, and there was a spring mist in the air. I could see the lights of the Fairfield Coach in the distance on its way up to Great Falls.

And I could hear geese, white birds in the sky, flying. They made their high-pitched sound like angry yells, and though I couldn't see them high up, it seemed to me they were everywhere. And my mother looked up and said, "Hear them?" I could smell her hair wet from the shower. "They leave with the moon," she said. "It's still half wild out here."

And I said, "I hear them," and I felt a chill come over my bare chest, and the hair stood up on my arms the way it does before a storm. And for a while we listened.

"When I first married your father, you know, we lived on a street called Bluebird Canyon, in California. And I thought that was the prettiest street and the prettiest name. I suppose no one brings you up like your first love. You don't mind if I say that, do you?" She looked at me hopefully.

"No," I said.

"We have to keep civilization alive somehow." And she pulled her little housecoat together because there was a cold vein in the air, a part of the cold that would be on us the next day. "I don't feel part of things tonight, I guess."

"It's all right," I said.

"Do you know where I'd like to go?" she said.

"No," I said. And I suppose I knew she was angry then, angry with life, but did not want to show me that.

"To the Straits of Juan de Fuca. Wouldn't that be something? Would you like that?"

"I'd like it," I said. And my mother looked off for a minute, as if she could see the Straits of Juan de Fuca out against the line of mountains, see the lights of things alive and a whole new world.

"I know you liked him," she said after a moment. "You and I both suffer fools too well."

"I didn't like him too much," I said. "I didn't really care."

"He'll fall on his face. I'm sure of that," she said. And I didn't say anything because I didn't care about Glen Baxter anymore, and was happy not to talk about him. "Would you tell me something if I asked you? Would you tell me the truth?"

"Yes," I said.

And my mother did not look at me. "Just tell the truth," she said.

"All right," I said.

"Do you think I'm still very feminine? I'm thirty-two years old now. You don't know what that means. But do you think I am?"

And I stood at the edge of the porch, with the olive trees before me, looking straight up into the mist where I could not see geese but could still hear them flying, could almost feel the air move below their white wings. And I felt the way you feel when you are on a trestle all alone and the train is coming, and you know you have to decide. And I said, "Yes, I do." Because that was the truth. And I tried to think of something else then and did not hear what my mother said after that.

And how old was I then? Sixteen. Sixteen is young, but it can also be a grown man. I am forty-one years old now, and I think about that time without regret, though my mother and I never talked in that way again, and I have not heard her voice now in a long, long time.

THE DARK MEN
by Andre Dubus

Their dark civilian clothes defied him. They were from the Office of Naval Intelligence, they sat in his leather chairs in his cabin, they poured coffee from his silver pot, and although they called him Captain and Sir, they denied or outmaneuvered his shoulder boards by refusing to wear their own. He did not know whether they were officers or not, they could even be civilians, and they came aboard his ship and into his cabin, they told him names which he had already forgotten and, in quiet inflectionless voices, as if they were bringing no news at all, they told him that three months ago, during a confession in San Francisco, someone gave them Joe Saldi's name; and they told him what they had been doing for those three months, and what they had discovered. Then for a few moments they were talking but he wasn't listening and there were no images in his mind, not yet; he didn't see their faces either, though he was looking at them. If he was seeing anything at all, he was seeing the cold, sinking quickening of his heart. Then he entered their voices again, met their eyes, these men who looked for the dark sides of other men, and then he looked at his watch and said: "I've forgotten your names."

They told him. He offered them more coffee and they took it, and as they poured he watched their hands and faces: they appeared to be in their late thirties. Their faces were drained of color, they were men who worked away from the sun. Todd pinched his earlobe; Foster breathed through his mouth. At times it was audible. Foster now had a dispatch case on his lap; the raised top of it concealed his hands, then he lifted a large manila envelope and handed it to Captain Devereaux. The Captain laid it in front of him; then slowly, with a forefinger, pushed it aside, toward the photograph of his wife.

"I wonder how much you've missed," he said.

"We have enough," Foster said.

"That's not what I meant. I suppose he doesn't have much of a chance."

"I wouldn't think so," Foster said. "But we don't make recommendations. We only investigate."

"They always resign," Todd said.

Captain Devereaux looked at him. Then he picked up the envelope and dropped it across his desk, near Foster.

"I don't want to read it."

Foster and Todd looked at each other; Todd pinched his ear.

"Very well," Foster said. "Then I suppose we could see him now."

"I suppose you could." He dialed Joe's stateroom, waited seven rings, then hung up and told them Commander Saldi's plane was ashore and he might have gone flying. He went to the door and opened it and the Marine orderly saluted. The Captain told him to get Commander Saldi on the phone; he told him to try the pilots' wardroom and the commanders' wardroom and the officers' barber shop.

"I'll try the OOD too, sir."

"Do that last."

Then he sat at his desk and looked at them. Out of habit he was thinking of a way to make conversation but then he decided he would not. He looked away and tried not to hear Foster breathing.

"He should be flown home tomorrow," Foster said. "It's better for everyone that way."

"Before the word gets out," Todd said. "It always gets out."

"You shouldn't complain."

"What's that, Captain?"

"It's how you make your living, isn't it? On word that gets out?" Now he looked at them. "And where do you think he'll be flown to? I mean where do you think he will choose?"

"I don't know where he'll go, Captain," Foster said. "Our job is only to make sure he does."

"You contradict yourself. You said your job was only to investigate."

"Captain—"

"Yes, Mr. Foster?"

"Never mind, Captain."

"Have some coffee, Mr. Foster. Don't be disappointed because I'm not making your work easy. Why should it be?"

"We understand you're a friend of his," Todd said. He was trying to sound gentle. "We understand that."

"Do you, Mr. Todd?" The orderly knocked. "It's strange to talk to you gentlemen; you don't wear ribbons. I have no way of knowing where you've been."

"It doesn't matter where we've been," Foster said.

"Maybe that's my point."

He rose and went to the door. The orderly saluted.

"Sir, the OOD says Commander Saldi went ashore. He'll be back at eighteen hundred."

"When did the boat leave?" Foster said.

Captain Devereaux looked at him. He was twisted around in his chair.

"What boat is that, Mr. Foster?"

"The one Commander Saldi took."

Captain Devereaux looked at the orderly.

"Fifteen minutes ago, sir."

Foster took the envelope from the Captain's desk, put it in his dispatch case, and he and Todd stood up. Captain Devereaux held the door. When they were abreast of him they stopped.

"I don't know what you think you've gained," Foster said.

"Have a good day in Iwakuni," the Captain said.

"We'll be back tonight."

From his door he watched them cross the passageway and start down the ladder. Then he turned to the orderly.

"Have my boat alongside in thirty minutes. Wait: do you know Commander Saldi? What he looks like?"

"Yes sir."

"Then make it an hour for the boat. Then go eat your lunch. I want you to come with me."

The carrier was huge, it was anchored far out, and the ride in the launch took twenty minutes. It was a warm blue summer day and, to go ashore, he had changed from khakis to whites. He sat in the rear of the launch, his back against the gunwale, holding his cap so it wouldn't blow off; Corporal Swanson sat opposite him, wearing a white pistol belt and a .45 in a spit-shined holster, his cap chin-strapped to his head, dozing in the warm sun, his chin sinking slowly till it touched his necktie, then he snapped his head up and glanced at the Captain who pretended he hadn't seen, and in a few moments the sun did its work again and

Swanson—who looked hung over—fought it for a while and then lost until his chin again touched the knot of his tie, and it stayed there; soon his mouth was open. The Captain looked back at the carrier, diminished now but still huge against the sky and the sea beyond; then he turned away and looked up at the blue sky and at the green and rocky shore, his vision broken once by the hull of a British freighter, then shore line again, while in his mind he saw Joe in the orange flight suit, helmet under his arm, crossing the flight deck and turning his face into the wind; sometimes Joe looked up at the bridge and smiled and waved: thinning black hair, a suntanned face that never seemed weary, and the Captain, looking down through glass and lifting his arm in a wave, felt his own weariness, and he yearned for the wind out there, away from the bridge that could make him an admiral, and away from the cabin where he slept little and badly and smoked too much and drank too much coffee and took Maalox after his meals; and Joe would move on to his plane near the catapult and beyond him the Pacific glittered under the sun, and the endless blue sky waited to lift him up; but now images collided in the Captain's mind, images of night and shame, and he actually shook his head to cast them out and to cast out memory too, thinking he must move from one moment to the next and that no matter what he did the day held no hope, and that memory and imagination would only make it worse; he gazed ahead at the white buildings of the Marine air base and he looked at the boat's wake, and kept himself from thinking about what had happened in his heart this morning when, as soon as Foster spoke Joe's name, he had known what was coming next and though he had been Joe's friend for thirteen years this was the first time he knew that he knew it.

As the boat neared the wharf Corporal Swanson was rubbing his neck and blinking his eyes. When the engine slowed, the Captain leaned forward and told him what to do.

"After that," he said, "you can sack out till I get back."

It was early Thursday afternoon, so there weren't many people in the Officers' Club. A commander and his handsome wife were finishing lunch. The commander was a flight surgeon. Three Marine pilots were drinking at the bar. They were loud and happy and the Captain liked being near them. He chose a small polished table with two leather chairs, and he sat facing the door. A Japanese girl took his order. She was pretty and she wore a purple kimono of silk brocade, and as she walked back to the bar he felt an instant's yearning and then it was gone and he was both amused and wistful because either age or responsibility or both had this year kept him clean. He was finishing his second drink when Joe stepped in, wearing whites with short sleeves, four rows of ribbons under the gold wings on his breast, his white cap under his arm like a football; he stood looking about the room while his eyes adjusted and Captain Devereaux raised his hand and Joe saw him and waved and came forward. The Captain stood and took his hand and nodded toward the laughing pilots at the bar.

"It is peacetime and the pilots are happy pretending to make war. I'm about to start my third gimlet. Are you behind?"

"I am."

They sat, and the Captain signalled to the Japanese girl at the end of the bar, pointed at his glass and at Joe and then himself. Under the table Joe clicked his heels, and briskly raised his hand and held it salute-like at his brow: "Commander Saldi, sir. Captain Devereaux wishes the Commander to join him at the O Club sir. In the bar sir. He says if the Commander wishes to go back to the ship instead, sir, he is to send me to get the Captain and the Captain will take the Commander back to the ship in the Captain's boat. Sir." He snapped off the salute. "Jesus Christ, Ray, I'll drink with you. You don't have to send them out with .45's."

The girl lowered the drinks and Joe reached for his wallet but the Captain was quicker and paid.

"What about lunch," Joe said. "Have you had lunch?"

The girl was waiting.

"I'll buy you a lunch," the Captain said.

He watched the girl going back to the bar, then he looked at Joe, and Joe raised his glass and the Captain raised his and they touched them over the table.

"Old Captain Devereaux."

"Old is right. I don't sleep much, out there. My gut's going too."

"Gimlets'll back up on you."

"It's the lime, not the gin."

"Right."

"How do you know? Is yours on the blink too?"

"Not now. It has been."

"Not an ulcer."

"Oh hell no. *You* don't have one, do you?"

"Just acid. I ought to retain the booze and get rid of cigarettes and coffee."

The girl gave them the menus and then went away.

"You ought to have the lasagna, Joe."

"Where is it?"

"It's spelled sukiyaki."

"I don't like lasagna anyway."

"Really?"

"Too heavy."

"I'll have the sukiyaki."

"So will I."

"Should we have sake too?"

"How's your gut?"

"Fine. I'm going to lay off this lime juice."

"Then let's have hot sake."

When they laid down the menus the girl came and took their order and the Captain told her to bring his friend another drink but to leave him out.

"It's my stomach," he told her. "It needs gentleness."

"Oh? I could bring you some nice milk."

"No, not milk, thanks."

"What about Asahi?"

"Yes; fine. Bring me a big Ashia."

She brought Joe's gimlet and his beer, and after a glass of it he quietly belched and felt better but not good enough, so he told Joe he'd be right back and he went to the men's room and took from his pocket the aspirin tin containing six Maalox tablets and chewed two of them. He went back into the bar, approaching the table from Joe's rear and, looking at his shoulders and the back of his head, he felt a power he didn't want but had anyway, and he felt like a traitor for having it.

"You ought to get up more," Joe said.

"I know."

"Let's do it then."

"When?"

"After lunch. We can walk over to the field and go up for an hour."

"With gin and beer and sake."

"Oxygen'll fix you up."

"I can't though. I have things at the ship."

"Let them wait."

"They won't."

"Tomorrow then."

"Tomorrow?" He frowned, pretending he was trying to remember what tomorrow held for him, then he said: "All right. Tomorrow," and saying the word gave him a sense of plaintive hope that somehow and impossibly this moment with drinks and waiting for lunch would flow into a bright afternoon of tomorrow with Joe off his wing as they climbed from Iwakuni and out over the blue sea. And with that hope came longing: he wanted Foster and Todd to vanish, he wanted to go to sea next week and launch Joe into the wind, he wanted to not know what he knew and, with this longing, fear came shivering into his breast, and he did what he could not recall doing since he was a boy trying to talk to his father, a young boy, before he finally gave up and became silent: he promised himself that when a certain thing happened he would tell Joe: when his cigarette burned down; when he finished his beer; when the girl brought the sukiyaki; when Joe finished telling his story; and as each of these occurred, a third and powerful hand of his clutched his throat and squeezed.

The girl stood smiling and serving them until all the sukiyaki was on their plates and then she left, and he was chilled by her leaving because he had been flirting with her, praising the meal and her kimono and her face and small delicate hands, he had been cocking his head to her and glancing up at her, not up very high because he was a tall man and sat tall and she was barely over five feet and maybe not even that; now she was gone. He started to look at Joe, then poured sake into the china tumbler and carefully pinched rice with his chopsticks and dipped it into raw egg and, leaning forward, quickly raised it to his mouth, and heard over Joe's voice the drinking talk of the Marines at the bar, and he chewed his rice and hated his fear and silence and when he took another swallow of sake the acid rose to his throat and he held his breath for a moment till it went down, and then took another swallow and that one was all right. Joe was laughing: "—and he said I couldn't bail out, Commander. I'm afraid of sharks. You see, he really meant it but the bombardier and the crewman didn't believe him. They thought he believed he had a chance to make it, and he was just being cheerful to help them along. Truth was, he thought he'd go down, but he wasn't going into the water without that plane around him. So he kept telling them: look, you guys better jump, and they'd say what about you, and he'd say not me, I ain't getting down there with no sharks. So they stuck with him and he hit the ship first try, he said if he'd got waved off that time he'd have gone in and too low for anybody to bail out and he was cussing the other two for making him responsible for them going down too. But then he made it and I gave him a shot of rye in my room and he told me, You see, I don't even wade. Not in salt water. I haven't been in salt water for fourteen years. He was shot down, you see, in the Pacific, and

he swam to his raft and he was climbing aboard when a shark got
his co-pilot. He said the water turned red. He said I heard that
scream every night for ten years. He said I ain't been in the water
ever since and if any shark's going to get Chuck Thomson he's
going to be the most disguised shark you ever saw because he's
going to cross two hundred feet of sand walking on his tail and
wearing a double-breasted pinstripe suit and some of them re-
flecting sunglasses—" Then Joe was laughing again, and the Captain was too, his body jerked and made sounds and then he was
telling a story too, listening to it as it took shape, just as he had
watched and listened to his own laughter: another story of men
who had nearly gone into the sea and then had laughed, and after
that Joe told one and then he told another, and they kept going.
They did not tell stories of valor without humor, as though valor
were expected but humor was not, and the man who had both
was better. And they did not talk about the dead. Sometimes they
spoke a name but that was all. Three o'clock came and the girl
brought more tea and Captain Devereaux went to the men's room
and chewed two more tablets, standing alone at the mirror, but
Joe's ghost was with him, and he went back to the table and
looked at Joe and he could not feel the wine now, his heart was
quick, his fingers tight on the tumbler of tea, and he said: "There
are two men, Joe. On my ship. Or they were. They're coming
back tonight." And already Joe's eyes brightened, even before the
Captain said: "They're from ONI, Joe, and it's about you."

Joe turned in his chair and gazed off toward the bar and shut
his eyes and rubbed his forehead and murmured something he
couldn't hear and didn't want to, and then it was over, the long
bantering friendship between them, he felt it go out of him like
dry tears through his ribs and for an instant, watching Joe's
profiled face that could never look at him again, he raged at the
other face he had never seen, impassioned and vulnerable in the
night, then the rage was gone too and he sat watching Joe
rubbing his forehead, watched Joe profiled in that place of pain
and humiliation where he had fallen and where the Captain could
never go. Yet still he kept talking, threw words into the space,
bounced them off the silent jaw and shoulder: "Listen, I hate the
bastards. I don't want you to see them. They're going to tell you
general court or resign, but I'm going to tell them to get the hell
off my ship, and I'll handle it. No one will know anything. Not
for a while anyway. Not till you've written your letter and gone.
And still they won't know why. I don't care about what they told
me, I want you to know that. They brought paperwork and it was

sealed and it still is and it'll stay that way. I don't give a good Goddamn and I never *did*. You hear me, Joe?"

He waited. Joe nodded, looking at the bar.

"I hear you, Captain."

For perhaps a minute they sat that way. Then Captain Devereaux got up and touched Joe's shoulder and walked out.

Corporal Swanson was sleeping in the sun, his cap over his eyes, and he did not wake when the Captain and the coxswain and crew descended into the gently rocking boat, did not wake until Captain Devereaux softly spoke his name. Then he stood quickly and saluted and the Captain smiled and asked if he'd had a good nap. All the way back to the ship he talked to Swanson; or, rather, asked him questions and watched him closely and tried to listen. Swanson was not staying in the Marines; in another year he'd get out and go to college in South Dakota. He wasn't sure yet what he wanted to be. He had a girl in South Dakota and he meant to marry her. The Captain sat smiling and nodding and asking, and sometimes he leaned forward to listen over the sound of the engine, and it wasn't until the launch drew within a hundred yards of the ship that he knew Joe wasn't coming back, and then at once he knew he had already known that too, had known in the Club that Joe's isolation was determined and forever, and now he twisted around and looked back over his shoulder, into the sky above the air base, then looked forward again at the huge ship, at its high gray hull which now rose straight above him, casting a shadow across the launch.

At six-thirty Foster and Todd found him on the flight deck. He had been there for an hour, walking the thousand feet from fore to aft, looking into the sky and out at the sea. When they emerged from the island and moved toward him, walking abreast and leaning into the wind, he was standing at the end of the flight deck. He saw them coming and looked away. The sun was going down. Out there, toward the open sea, a swath of gold lay on the water. When they stopped behind him he did not turn around. He was thinking that, from a distance, a plane flying in the sunset looks like a moving star. Then shutting his eyes he saw the diving silver plane in the sunset, and then he was in it, his heart pounding with the dive, the engine roaring in his blood, and he saw the low red sun out the cockpit and, waiting, the hard and yielding sea.

"Commander Saldi is not here," he said.

"Not here?" It was Foster. "Where is he?"

"He's out there."

Foster stepped around and stood in front of him, and then Todd did, and they stood side by side, facing him, but he continued to stare at the sun on the water.

"Out there?" Foster said. "You let him fly? In a million dollar—"

Captain Devereaux looked at him, and he stopped.

"Iwakuni lost contact with him an hour ago," the Captain said.

"You told him," Foster said. "You told him and let him go up—"

This time the Captain did not bother to look at him; he stepped through the space between them and stood on the forward edge of the flight deck. He stood there, motionless and quiet, then he heard Foster and Todd going away, only a moment's footsteps on the deck before all sound of them was gone in the wind, and still he watched as the sun went down, and under the pale fading light of the sky the sea darkened until finally it was black.

LOST SONS

by James Salter

All afternoon the cars, many with out-of-state plates, had been coming along the road. The long row of lofty brick quarters appeared above. The gray walls began.

In the reception area a welcoming party was going on. There were faces that had hardly changed at all and others like Reemstma's whose name tag was read more than once. Someone with a camera and flash attachment was running around in a cadet bathrobe. Over in the barracks they were drinking. Doors were open. Voices spilled out.

"Hooknose will be here," Dunning promised loudly. There was a bottle on the desk near his feet. "He'll show, don't worry. I had a letter from him."

"A letter? He's never written a letter."

"His secretary wrote it," Dunning said. He looked like a judge, large and well fed. His glasses lent a dainty touch. "He's teaching her to write."

"Where's he living now?"

"Florida."

"Remember the time we were sneaking back to Buckner at two in the morning and all of a sudden a car came down the road?"

Dunning was trying to arrange a serious expression.

"We dove in the bushes. It turned out it was a taxi. It slammed on the brakes and backed up. The door opens and there's Klingbeil in the back seat, drunk as a lord. Get in, boys, he says."

Dunning roared. His blouse with its rows of colored ribbons was unbuttoned, gluteal power hinted by the width of his lap.

"Remember," he said, "when we threw Devereaux's Spanish

90

book with all his notes in it out the window? Into the snow. He never found it. He went bananas. You bastards, I'll kill you!"

"He'd have been a star man if he wasn't living with you."

"We tried to broaden him," Dunning explained.

They used to do the sinking of the *Bismarck* while he was studying. Klingbeil was the captain. They would jump up on the desks. *Der Schiff ist kaputt!* they shouted. They were firing the guns. The rudder was jammed, they were turning in circles. Devereaux sat head down with his hands pressed over his ears. Will you bastards shut up, he screamed.

Bush, Buford, Jap Andrus, Doane, and George Hilmo were sitting on the beds and windowsill. An uncertain face looked in the doorway.

"Who's that?"

It was Reemstma whom no one had seen for years. His hair had turned gray. He smiled awkwardly.

"What's going on?"

They looked at him.

"Come in and have a drink," someone finally said.

He found himself next to Hilmo, who reached across to shake hands with an iron grip. "How are you?" he said. The others went on talking. "You look great."

"You do too."

Hilmo seemed not to hear. "Where are you living?" he said.

"Rosemont. Rosemont, New Jersey. It's where my wife's family's from," Reemstma said. He spoke with a strange intensity. He had always been odd. Everyone wondered how he had ever made it through. He did all right in class but the image that lasted was of someone bewildered by close order drill, which he seemed to master only after two whole years and then with the stiffness of a cat trying to swim. He had full lips which were the source of an unflattering nickname. He was also known as To The Rear March because of the disasters he caused at the command.

He was handed a used paper cup. "Whose bottle is this?" he asked.

"I don't know," Hilmo said. "Here."

"Are a lot of people coming?"

"Boy, you're full of questions," Hilmo said.

Reemstma fell silent. For half an hour they told stories. He sat by the window, sometimes looking in his cup. Outside, the clock with its black numerals began to brighten. West Point lay majestic in the early evening, its dignified foliage was still. Below, the river was silent, mysterious islands floating in the dusk. Near the corner of the library a military policeman, his arm moving with precision, directed traffic past a sign for the reunion of 1960, a class on which Vietnam had fallen as stars fell on 1915 and 1931. In the distance was the faint sound of a train.

It was almost time for dinner. There were still occasional cries of greeting from below, people talking, voices. Feet were leisurely descending the stairs.

"Hey," someone said unexpectedly, "what the hell is that thing you're wearing?"

Reemstma looked down. It was a necktie of red, flowered cloth. His wife had made it. He changed it before going out.

"Hello, there."

Walking calmly alone was a white-haired figure with an armband that read, 1930.

"What class are you?"

"Nineteen-sixty," Reemstma said.

"I was just thinking as I walked along, I was wondering what finally happened to everybody. It's hard to believe but when I was here we had men who simply packed up after a few weeks and went home without a word to anyone. Ever hear of anything like that? Nineteen-sixty, you say?"

"Yes, sir."

"You ever hear of Frank Kissner? I was his chief of staff. He was a tough guy. Regimental commander in Italy. One day Mark Clark showed up and said, Frank, come here a minute, I want to talk to you. Haven't got time, I'm too busy, Frank said."

"Really?"

"Mark Clark said, Frank, I want to make you a B.G. I've got time, Frank said."

The mess hall, in which the alumni dinner was being held, loomed before them, its doors open. Its scale had always been heroic. It seemed to have doubled in size and was filled with the white of tablecloths as far as one could see. The bars were crowded, there were lines fifteen and twenty deep of men waiting patiently. Many of the women were in dinner dresses. Above it all was the echoing clamor of conversation.

There were those with the definite look of success, like Hilmo who wore a gray summer suit with a metallic sheen and to whom everyone liked to talk, although he was given to abrupt silences, and there were also the unfading heroes, those who had been cadet officers, come to life again. Early form had not always held. Among those now of high rank were men who in their schooldays had been relatively undistinguished. Reemstma, who had been out of touch, was somewhat surprised by this. For him the hierarchy had never been altered.

A terrifying face blotched with red suddenly appeared. It was Cranmer, who had lived down the hall.

"Hey, Eddie, how's it going?"

He was holding two drinks. He had just retired a year ago, Cranmer said. He was working for a law firm in Reading.

"Are you a lawyer?"

"I run the office," Cranmer said. "You married? Is your wife here?"

"No."

"Why not?"

"She couldn't come," Reemstma said.

His wife had met him when he was thirty. Why would she want to go? she had asked. In a way he was glad she hadn't. She knew no one and given the chance she would often turn the conversation to religion. There would be two weird people instead of one. Of course, he did not really think of himself as weird, it was only in their eyes. Perhaps not even. He was being greeted, talked to. The women, especially, unaware of established judgments, were friendly. He found himself talking to the lively wife of a classmate he vaguely remembered, R. C. Walker, a lean man with a somewhat sardonic smile.

"You're a what?" she said in astonishment. "A painter? You mean an artist?" She had thick, naturally curly blond hair and a pleasant softness to her cheeks. Her chin had a slight double fold. "I think that's fabulous!" She called to a friend, "Nita, you have to meet someone. It's Ed, isn't it?"

"Ed Reemstma."

"He's a painter," Kit Walker said exuberantly.

Reemstma was dazed by the attention. When they learned that he actually sold things they were even more interested.

"Do you make a living at it?"

"Well, I have a waiting list for paintings."

"You do!"

He began to describe the color and light—he painted landscapes—of the countryside near the Delaware, the shape of the earth, its furrows, hedges, how things changed slightly from year to year, little things, how hard it was to do the sky. He described the beautiful, glinting green of a hummingbird his wife had brought to him. She had found it in the garage; it was dead, of course.

"Dead?" Nita said.

"The eyes were closed. Except for that, you wouldn't have known."

He had an almost wistful smile. Nita nodded warily.

Later there was dancing. Reemstma would have liked to go on talking but people had drifted away. Tables broke up after dinner into groups of friends.

"Bye for now," Kit Walker had said.

He saw her talking to Hilmo, who gave him a brief wave. He wandered about for a while. They were playing "Army Blue." A wave of sadness went through him, memories of parades, the end of dances, Christmas leave. Four years of it, the classes ahead leaving in pride and excitement, unknown faces filling in behind. It was finished, but no one turns his back on it completely. The life he might have led came back to him, almost whole.

Outside the barracks, late at night, five or six figures were sitting on the steps, drinking and talking. Reemstma sat near them, not speaking, not wanting to break the spell. He was one of them, as he had been on frantic evenings when they cleaned rifles and polished their shoes to a mirror-like gleam. The haze of June lay over the great expanse that separated him from those endless tasks of years before. How deeply he had immersed himself in them. How ardently he had believed in the image of a soldier. He had known it as a faith. He had clung to it dumbly, as a cripple clings to God.

In the morning Hilmo trotted down the stairs, tennis shorts tight over his muscled legs, and disappeared through one of the salley-ports for an early match. His insouciance was unchanged. They said that before the Penn State game when he had been first-string the coach had pumped them up telling them they were not only going to beat Penn State, they were going to beat them by two touchdowns, then turning to Hilmo, "And who's going to be the greatest back in the East?"

"I don't know. Who?" Hilmo said.

Empty morning. As usual, except for sports there was little to do. Shortly after ten they formed up to march to a memorial ceremony at the corner of the Plain. Before a statue of Sylvanus Thayer they stood at attention, one tall maverick head in a cowboy hat, while the choir sang "The Corps." The thrilling voices, the solemn, staggered parts rose through the air. Behind Reemstma someone said quietly, "You know, the best friends I ever had or ever will have are the ones I had here."

Afterward they walked out to take their places on the parade ground. The superintendent, a trim lieutenant general, stood not far off with his staff and the oldest living graduate, who was in a wheelchair.

"Look at him," Dunning said. He was referring to the superintendent. "That's what's wrong with this place. That's what's wrong with the whole army."

Faint waves of band music beat toward them. It was warm. There were bees in the grass. The first miniature formations of cadets, bayonets glinting, began to move into view. Above, against the sky, a lone distinguished building, and that a replica, stood. The chapel. Many Sundays with their manly sermons on virtue and the glittering choir marching toward the door with graceful, halting tread, gold stripes shining on the sleeves of the leaders. Down below, partly hidden, the gymnasium, the ominous dark patina on everything within, the floor, the walls, the heavy boxing gloves. There were champions enshrined there who would never be unseated, maxims that would never be erased.

At the picnic it was announced that of the 550 original members, 529 were living and 176 present so far.

"Not counting Klingbeil!"

"Okay, one seventy-six plus a possible Klingbeil."

"An *im*possible Klingbeil," someone called out.

There was a cheer.

The tables were in a large, screened pavilion on the edge of the lake. Reemstma looked for Kit Walker. He'd caught sight of her earlier, in the food line, but now he could not find her. The class president was speaking.

"We got a card from Joe Waltsak. Joe retired this year. He wanted to come but his daughter's graduating from high school. I don't know if you know this story. Joe lives in Palo Alto and there was a bill before the California legislature to change the name of any street an All-American lived on and name it after him. Joe lives on Parkwood Drive. They were going to call it Waltsak Drive, but the bill didn't pass, so instead they're calling him Joe Parkwood."

The elections were next. The class treasurer and the vice-president were not running again. There would have to be nominations for these.

"Let's have somebody different for a change," someone commented in a low voice.

"Somebody we know," Dunning muttered.

"You want to run, Mike?"

"Yeah, sure, that would be great," Dunning said.

"How about Reemstma?" It was Cranmer, the blossoms of alcoholism ablaze in his face. The edges of his teeth were uneven as he smiled, as if eaten away.

"Good idea."

"Who, me?" Reemstma said. He was flustered. He looked around in surprise.

"How about it, Eddie?"

He could not tell if they were serious. It was all off-handed—the way Grant had been picked from obscurity one evening when he was sitting on a bench in St. Louis. He murmured something in protest. His face had become red.

Other names were being proposed. Reemstma felt his heart pounding. He had stopped saying, no, no, and sat there, mouth open a bit in bewilderment. He dared not look around him. He shook his head slightly, no. A hand went up.

"I move that the nominations be closed."

Reemstma felt foolish. They had tricked him again. He felt as if he had been betrayed. No one was paying any attention to him. They were counting raised hands.

"Come on, you can't vote," someone said to his wife.

"I can't?" she said.

Wandering around as the afternoon ended, Reemstma finally caught sight of Kit Walker. She acted a little strange. She didn't seem to recognize him at first. There was a grass stain on the back of her skirt.

"Oh, hello," she said.

"I was looking for you."

"Would you do me a favor?" she said. "Would you mind getting me a drink? My husband seems to be ignoring me."

Though Reemstma did not see it, someone else was ignoring her too. It was Hilmo, standing some way off. They had come back to the pavilion separately. The absence of the two of them during much of the afternoon had not been put together yet. Friends who would soon be parting were talking in small groups, their faces shadowy against the water that flashed in the light behind them. Reemstma returned with some wine in a plastic glass.

"Here you are. Is anything wrong?"

"Thank you. No, why? You know, you're very nice," she said. She had noticed something over his shoulder. "Oh, dear."

"What?"

"Nothing. It looks like we're going."

"Do you have to?" he managed to say.

"Rick's over by the door. You know him, he hates to be kept waiting."

"I was hoping we could talk."

He turned. Walker was standing outside in the sunlight. He was wearing an aloha shirt and tan slacks. He seemed somewhat aloof. Reemstma was envious of him.

"We have to drive back to Belvoir tonight," she said.

"I guess it's a long way."

"It was very nice meeting you," she said.

She left the drink untouched on the corner of the table. Reemstma watched her white skirt make its way across the floor. She was not like the others, he thought. He saw them walking to their car. Did she have children? he found himself wondering. Did she really find him interesting?

In the hour before twilight, at six in the evening, he heard the noise and looked out. Crossing the area toward them was the unconquerable schoolboy, long-legged as a crane, the ex-infantry officer now with a small, well-rounded paunch, waving an arm.

Dunning was bellowing from a window. "Hooknose!"

"Look who I've got!" Klingbeil called back.

It was Devereaux, the tormented scholar. Their arms were around each other's shoulders. They were crossing together, grinning, friends since cadet days, friends for life. They started up the stairs.

"Hooknose!" Dunning shouted.

Klingbeil threw open his arms in mocking joy.

He was the son of an army officer. As a boy he had sailed on the Matson Line and gone back and forth across the country. He was irredeemable, he had the common touch, his men adored him. Promoted slowly, he had gotten out and become a land developer. He drove a green Cadillac famous in Tampa. He was a king of poker games, drinking, late nights.

She had probably not meant it, Reemstma was thinking. His experience had taught him that. He was not susceptible to lies.

"Oh," wives would say, "of course. I think I've heard my husband talk about you."

"I don't know your husband," Reemstma would say.

A moment of alarm.

"Of course, you do. Aren't you in the same class?"

He could hear them downstairs.

"*Der Schiff ist kaputt!*" they were shouting. "*Der Schiff ist kaputt!*"

The Honored Dead

by Breece D'J Pancake

Watching little Lundy go back to sleep, I wish I hadn't told her about the Mound Builders to stop her crying, but I didn't know she would see their eyes watching her in the dark. She was crying about a cat run down by a car—her cat, run down a year ago, only today poor Lundy figured it out. Lundy is turned too much like her momma. Ellen never worries because it takes her too long to catch the point of a thing, and Ellen doesn't have any problem sleeping. I think my folks were a little too keen, but Lundy is her momma's girl, not jumpy like my folks.

My grandfather always laid keenness on his Shawnee blood, his half-breed mother, but then he was hep on blood. He even had an oath to stop bleeding, but I don't remember the words. He was a fair to sharp woodsman, and we all tried to slip up on him at one time or another. It was Ray at the sugar mill finally caught him, but he was an old man by then, and his mind wasn't exactly right. Ray just came creeping up behind and laid a hand on his shoulder, and the old bird didn't even turn around; he just wagged his head and said, "That's Ray's hand. He's the first fellow ever slipped up on me." Ray could've done without that, because the old man never played with a full deck again, and we couldn't keep clothes on him before he died.

I turn out the lamp, see no eyes in Lundy's room, then it comes to me why she was so scared. Yesterday I told her patches of stories about scalpings and murders, mixed up the Mound Builders with the Shawnee raids, and Lundy chained that with the burial mound in the back pasture. Tomorrow I'll set her straight. The only sure fire thing I know about Mound Builders is they must have believed in a God and hereafter or they never would have made such big graves.

I put on my jacket, go into the foggy night, walk toward town. Another hour till dawn, and both lanes of the Pike are empty, so I walk the yellow line running through the valley to Rock Camp. I keep thinking back to the summer me and my buddy Eddie tore that burial mound apart for arrowheads and copper beads gone green with rot. We were getting down to the good stuff, coming up with skulls galore, when of a sudden Granddad showed out of thin air and yelled, *"Wah-pah-nah-te-he."* He was waving his arms around, and I could see Eddie was about to shit the nest. I knew it was all part of the old man's Injun act, so I stayed put, but Eddie sat down like he was ready to surrender.

Granddad kept on: *"Wah-pah-nah-te-he.* You evil. Make bad medicine here. Now put the goddamned bones back or I'll take a switch to your young asses." He watched us bury the bones, then scratched a picture of a man in the dust, a bow drawn, aimed at a crude sun. "Now go home." He walked across the pasture.

Eddie said, "You Red Eagle. Me Black Hawk." I knew he had bought the game for keeps. By then I couldn't tell Eddie that if Granddad had a shot at the sixty-four-dollar question, he would have sold them on those Injun words: *Wah-pah-nah-te-he*—the fat of my ass.

So I walk and try to be like Ellen and count the pass-at-your-own-risk marks on the road. Eastbound tramples Westbound: 26–17. At home is my own darling Ellen, fast asleep, never knowing who won. Sometimes I wonder if Ellen saw Eddie on his last leave. There are lightning bugs in the fog, and I count them until I figure I'm counting the same ones over. For sure, Lundy would call them Mound Builder eyes, and see them as signals without a message, make up her own message, get scared.

I turn off the Pike onto the oxbow of Front Street, walk past some dark store windows, watch myself moving by their gloss, rippling through one pane and another. I sit on the Old Bank steps, wait for the sun to come over the hills; wait like I waited for the bus to the draft physical, only I'm not holding a bar of soap. I sat and held a bar of soap, wondering if I should shove it under my arm to hike my blood pressure into the 4-F range. My blood pressure was already high, but the bar of soap would give me an edge. I look around at Front Street and picture people and places I haven't thought of in years; I wonder if it was that way for Eddie.

I put out my hand like the bar of soap was in it and see its whiteness reflect blue from the streetlights long ago. And I remember Eddie's hand flattened on green felt, arched knuckles cradling the cue for a tough eight-ball shot, or I remember the way his hand curled around his pencil to hide answers on math tests. I remember his hand holding an arrowhead or unscrewing a lug nut, but I can't remember his face.

It was years ago, on Decoration Day, and my father and several other men wore their Ike jackets, and I was in the band. We marched through town to the cemetery in the rain; then I watched the men move sure and stiff with each command, and the timing between volleys was on the nose; the echoes rang four times above the clatter of their bolt weapons. The rain smelled from the tang of their fire, the wet wool of our uniforms. There was a pause and the band director coughed. I stepped up to play, a little off tempo, and another kid across the hills answered my taps. I finished first, snapped my bugle back. When the last tone seeped through to mist, it beat at me, and I could swear I heard the stumps of Eddie's arms beating the coffin lid for us to stop.

I look down at my hand holding the bugle, the bar of soap. I look at my hand, empty, older, tell myself there is no bar of soap in that hand. I count all five fingers with the other hand, tell myself they are going to stay there a hell of a long time. I get out a cigarette and smoke. Out on the Pike, the first car races by in the darkness, knowing no cops are out yet. I think of Eddie pouring on the gas, heading with me down the Pike toward Tin Bridge.

That day was bright, but the blink of all the dome lights showed up far ahead of us. We couldn't keep still for the excitement, couldn't wait to see what happened.

I said, "Did you hear it, man? I thought they'd dropped the Bomb."

"Hear? I felt it. The damn ground shook."

"They won't forget that much noise for a long time."

"For sure."

Cars were stopped dead-center of the road, and a crowd had built up. Eddie pulled off to the side behind a patrol car, then made his way through the crowd, holding his wallet high to show his volunteer fireman's badge. I kept back, but in the break the cops made, I saw the fire was already out, and all that was left of

Beck Fuller's Chevy was the grille, the rest of the metal peeled around it from behind. I knew it was Beck's from the '51 grille, and I knew what had happened. Beck fished with dynamite and primer cord, and he was a real sport to the end. Beck could never get into his head he had to keep the cord away from the TNT.

Then a trooper yelled: "All right, make way for the wrecker."

Eddie and the other firemen put pieces of Beck the Sport into bags, and I turned away to keep from barfing, but the smell of burning hair drifted out to me. I knew it was the stuffing in old car seats, and not Beck, but I leaned against the patrol car, tossed my cookies just the same. I wanted to stop being sick because it was silly to be sick about something like that. Under the noise of my coughings I could hear the fire chief cussing Eddie into just getting the big pieces, just letting the rest go.

Eddie didn't sit here with any bar of soap in his hand. He never had much gray matter, but he made up for it with style, so he would never sit here with any bar of soap in his hand. Eddie would never think about blowing toes away or cutting off his trigger finger. It just was not his way to think. Eddie was the kind who bought into a game early, and when the deal soured, he'd rather hold the hand a hundred years than fold. It was just his way of doing.

At Eight Ball, I chalked up while Eddie broke. The pool balls cracked, but nothing went in, and I moved around the table to pick the choice shot. "It's crazy to join," I said.

"What the hell—I know how to weld. They'll put me in welding school and I'll sit it out in Norfolk."

"With your luck the ship'll fall on you."

"Come on, Eagle, go in buddies with me."

"Me and Ellen's got plans. I'll take a chance with the lottery." I shot, and three went in.

"That's slop," Eddie said.

I ran the other four down, banked the eight ball to a side pocket, and stood back, made myself grin at him. The eight went where I called it, but I never believed I made the shot right, and I didn't look at Eddie, I just grinned.

I toss my cigarette into the gutter, and it glows back orange under the blue streetlight. I think how that glow would be just another eye for Lundy, and think that after a while she will see so many eyes in the night they won't matter anymore. The eyes will go away and never come back, and even if I tell her when she is grown, she won't remember. By then real eyes will scare her enough. She's Ellen's girl, and sometimes I want to ask Ellen if she saw Eddie on his last leave.

Time ago I stood with my father in the cool evening shadow of the barn to smoke; he stooped, picked up a handful of gravel, and flipped them away with his thumb. He studied on what I said about Canada, and each gravel falling was a little click in his thoughts; then he stood, dusted his palms. "I didn't mind it too much," he said. "Me and Howard kept pretty thick in foxhole religion—never thought of running off."

"But, Dad, when I seen Eddie in that plastic bag . . ."

He yelled: "Why the hell'd you look? If you can't take it, you oughtn't to look. You think I ain't seen that? That and worse, by god."

I rub my hand across my face, hang my arm tight against the back of my neck, think I ought to be home asleep with Ellen. I think, if I was asleep with Ellen, I wouldn't care who won. I wouldn't count or want to know what the signals mean, and I wouldn't be like some dog looking for something dead to drag in.

When Eddie was in boot camp, me and Ellen sat naked in the loft at midnight, scratching fleas and the itch of hay. She went snooping through a box of old books and papers, and pulled out a bundle of letters tied with sea-grass string. Her flashlight beamed over my eyes as she stepped back to me, and watching her walk in the color tracings the light left in my eyes, I knew she would be my wife. She tossed the package in my lap, and I saw the old V-mail envelopes of my father's war letters. Ellen lay flat on her back, rested her head on my thigh, and I took up the flashlight to read.

"*Dear folks. We are in*—the name's been cut out."

"Why?" She rolled to her stomach, looked up at me.

I shrugged. "I guess he didn't know he couldn't say that. *The way they do thes people is awful bad. I found a rusky prisoner starven in the street and took him to a german house for a feed.*" I felt Ellen's tongue on the inside of my thigh and shivered, tried to keep reading. "*They didn't do nothin for him till I leveled off with my gun and Howard he raised hell with me only I seen that rusky eat one damn fine meal.*" I turned off the flashlight, moved down beside Ellen. He had never told that story.

But it's not so simple now as then, not easy to be a part of Ellen without knowing or wanting to know the web our kisses make. It was easy to leave the house with a bar of soap in my pocket; only the hardest part was sitting here, looking at it, and remembering.

I went through the hall with the rest of the kids between classes, and there stood Eddie at the top of the stairs. He grinned at me, but it was not his face anymore. His face had changed; a face gone red because the other kids snickered at his uniform. He stood at parade rest, his seaman's cap hanging from his belt, his head tilting back to look down on me, then he dragged his hands around like Jackie Gleason taking an away-we-go pool shot. We moved on down the hall to ditch my books.

"You on leave?" I said.

"Heap bad medicine. Means I'm getting shipped."

"How long?" I fumbled with the combination of my locker.

"Ten days," he said, then squinted at the little upside-down flag on my open locker door. "You sucker."

I watched him until he went out of sight down the steps, then got my books, went on to class.

The butt of my palm is speckled with black spots deep under the skin: cinders from a relay-race fall. The skin has sealed them over, and it would cost plenty to get them out. Sometimes Ellen wants to play nurse with a needle, wants to pry them out, but I won't let her. Sometimes I want to ask Ellen if she saw Eddie on his last leave.

Coach said I couldn't run track because anyone not behind his country was not fit for a team, so I sat under the covered bridge waiting for the time I could go home. Every car passing over sprinkled a little dust between the boards, sifted it into my hair.

I watched the narrow river roll by, its waters slow but muddy like pictures I had seen of rivers on the TV news. In history class, Coach said the Confederate troops attacked this bridge, took it, but were held by a handful of Sherman's troops on Company Hill. Johnny Reb drank from this river. The handful had a spring on Company Hill. Johnny croaked with the typhoid and the Yankees moved south. So I stood and brushed the dust off me. My hair grew long after Eddie went over, and I washed it every night.

I put my fist under my arm like the bar of soap and watch the veins on the back of my hand rise with pressure. There are scars where I've barked the hide hooking the disk or the drag to my tractor; they are like my father's scars.

We walked the fields, checked the young cane for blight or bugs, and the late sun gave my father's slick hair a sparkle. He chewed the stem of his pipe, then stood with one leg across a knee and banged tobacco out against his shoe.

I worked up the guts: "You reckon I could go to college, Dad?"

"What's wrong with farming?"

"Well, sir, nothing, if that's all you ever want."

He crossed the cane rows to get me, and my left went up to guard like Eddie taught me, right kept low and to the body.

"Cute," he said. "Real cute. When's your number up?"

I dropped my guard. "When I graduate—it's the only chance I got to stay out."

He loaded his pipe, turned around in his tracks like he was looking for something, then stopped, facing the hills. "It's your damn name is what it is. Dad said when you was born, 'Call him William Haywood, and if he ever goes in a mine, I hope he chokes to death.'"

I thought that was a shitty thing for Granddad to do, but I watched Dad, hoped he'd let me go.

He started up: "Everybody's going to school to be something better. Well, when everybody's going this way, it's time to turn around and go that way, you know?" He motioned with his hands in two directions. "I don't care if they end up shitting gold nuggets, somebody's got to dig in the damn ground. Somebody's got to."

And I said, "Yessir."

The sky is dark blue and the fog is cold smoke staying low to the ground. In this first hint of light my hand seems blue, but not cold; such gets cold sooner or later, but for now my hand is warm.

Many's the time my grandfather told of the last strike before he quit the mines, moved to the valley for some peace. He would quit his Injun act when he told it, like it was real again, all before him, and pretty soon I started thinking it was *me* the Baldwin bulls were after. *I* ran through the woods till my lungs bled. *I* could hear the Baldwins and their dogs in the dark woods, and *I* could remember machine guns cutting down pickets, and all *I* could think was how the One Big Union was down the rathole.

Then I could taste it in my mouth, taste the blood coming up from my lungs, feel the bark of a tree root where I fell, where I slept. When I opened my eyes, I felt funny in the gut, felt watched. There were no twig snaps, just the feeling that something was too close. Knowing it was a man, one man, hunting me, I took up my revolver. I could hear him breathing, aimed into the sound, knowing the only sight would come with the flash. I knew all my life I had lived to kill this man, this goddamned Baldwin man, and I couldn't do it. I heard him move away down the ridge, hunting his lost game.

I fold my arms tight like I did the morning the bus pulled up. I was thinking of my grandfather, and there was a bar of soap under my arm. At the draft physical, my blood pressure was clear out of sight, and they kept me four days. The pressure never went down, and on the fourth day a letter came by forward. I read it on the bus home.

Eddie said he was with a bunch of Jarheads in the Crotch, and he repaired radio gear in the field. He said the USMC's hated him because he was regular Navy. He said the chow was rotten, the quarters lousy, and the left side of his chest was turning yellow from holding smokes inside his shirt at night. And he said he knew how the guy felt when David sent him into the battle to get dibs on the guy's wife. Eddie said he wanted dibs on Ellen, ha, ha. He said he would get married and give me his wife if I would get him out of there. He said the beer came in Schlitz cans, but he was sure it was something else. Eddie was sure the CO was a fag. He said he would like to get Ellen naked, but if he stayed with this outfit he would want to get me naked when he came back. He asked if I remembered him teaching me to burn off leeches with a cigarette. Eddie swore he learned that in a movie where the hero dies because he ran out of cigarettes. He said he had plenty of cigarettes. He said he could never go Oriental because they don't have any hair on their twats, and he bet me he knew what color Ellen's bush was. He said her hair might be brown, but her bush was red. He said to think about it and say Hi to Ellen for him until he came back. Sometimes I want to ask Ellen if she saw Eddie on his last leave.

When I came back, Ellen met me at the trailer door, hugged me, and started to cry. She showed pretty well with Lundy, and I told her Eddie's letter said to say Hi. She cried some more, and I knew Eddie was not coming back.

*   *   *

Daylight fires the ridges green, shifts the colors of the fog, touches the brick streets of Rock Camp with a reddish tone. The streetlights flicker out, and the traffic signal at the far end of Front Street's yoke snaps on; stopping nothing, warning nothing, rushing nothing on.

I stand and my joints crack from sitting too long, but the flesh of my face is warming in the early sun. I climb the steps of the Old Bank, draw a spook in the window soap. I tell myself that spook is Eddie's, and I wipe it off with my sleeve, then I see the bus coming down the Pike, tearing the morning, and I start down the street so he won't stop for me. I cannot go away, and I cannot make Eddie go away, so I go home. And walking down the street as the bus goes by, I bet myself a million that my Lundy is up and already watching cartoons, and I bet I know who won.

TAN

by John Sayles

Con Tinh Tan sits in the waiting room. She avoids looking directly at the other patients. The Americans. She can see them partially reflected in the mirror that is the back pane of the fish tank. She can look past the underwater flash of lionfish, saltwater angels, yellow tangs, rock beauties, sea robins, past a ceramic replica of the Golden Gate Bridge, to watch the Americans, sitting and waiting.

There is music playing around Tan, music so quiet and without edge that sometimes it is like she is humming it to herself, though none of the songs are familiar. A single receptionist shuffles file cards at a desk. The window behind her overlooks the Golden Gate Park. The receptionist has large, blue eyes, made rounder and bluer with liner and shadow, made larger still by the tinted aviator glasses she wears. Tan wonders if the receptionist could ever keep a secret, could ever hide a fear behind such open, blue eyes.

Tan can see a small boy reflected from the fish tank, half obscured by a drowsy grouper, a small boy with a harness strapped around his head, cinching into his mouth. When he turns to talk with his mother his lips stretch far back over his gums and he looks like a small muzzled animal. He seems not to notice or care.

In 1963 Tan was thirteen and in the mornings would bicycle with her two younger brothers along the walls of Hue to the nuns' school. Her little sister Xuan went to grammar school closer to home, inside of the Citadel, and her older brother Quat crossed the river to go to high school. The nuns taught Tan

107

poetry in Vietnamese, prayers in French, mathematics and history in English. She was a good student, which pleased Father very much. Your father expects you to do well in school, he would tell them at dinner. Only the educated person can save himself. Father never said what the person was saving himself from. Tan believed it was the lake of fire the nuns warned about, and she worked very hard.

Each night they faced the family altar to think about their ancestors, beginning with Mother. Then they'd say French prayers. All of Tan's ancestors, back as far as Father knew, had lived in Hue. But none lived and worked in the Citadel like Father did. Father had grown up with the Ngo family, had been a high-school friend of Ngo Dinh Diem. When Diem received the Mandate of Heaven he remembered his friend, and Father was given an important job in the city government. In Tan's house Diem was always spoken of in the same tones as the ancestors. They called him the Virgin Father and he was included in Tan's nightly prayers.

Tan liked mornings best, when she could take her time riding to school, surrounded by the high walls and the moats, the tiled roofs and gardens. She could look over the walls to see the mist rising off the Perfume River, could stop and rest by the Emperor's Gate and watch the city waking up. Hue was a walled garden.

The ride home was too hurried to enjoy. Tan was the eldest daughter, responsible for dinner and cleaning. It never bothered her. If she waited around school too long the boys' section would let out and they would tease her. Monkey. Tan had an extra pair of canine teeth that pushed her upper lip out and made her nose look fatter. Face like a monkey! the boys would cry and bicycle circles around her. Monkeymonkeymonkey.

But sometimes Tan would sit with the picture of Mother they kept on the altar and see the same teeth, the same lips and nose. It was her connection with Mother. It was her face.

Quat mostly stayed out with his friends from the high school. He came home just before dinner, tried not to get in an argument with Father, and then went out again. Father was a quiet and gentle man but Quat always managed to make him angry. Quat did well in school but didn't like the priests. Quat would speak against the priests or the government at dinner and Father would remind him where he was. They would begin to shout and Xuan would cry and then they would stop speaking to each other. Your father has work to do, Father would say to them, and move to his desk facing the far wall. Your brother is going out, Quat would say to them, and he would leave, grabbing a few last bites of food.

When they were younger Quat would sit with Tan in the walled garden behind the house and tell her stories. He told of the wars with the Chinese, and the one Tan liked best was about the Trung sisters who rose up to fight the invaders on elephant-back. She felt very safe and very peaceful, sitting inside the garden behind their house in the Citadel of the walled city of Hue. The stories Quat told were often bloody and terrible, but the Chinese had been defeated long ago.

Father arranged to have Tan's teeth taken care of. Their own dentist had said there was nothing to be done, but Father went to the Americans.

The Americans were there to fight the country people. The Virgin Father had allowed them to come. They lived in a place beyond the walls and across the river and weren't allowed to come into Hue. Tan had seen people who weren't Vietnamese, like the French priests, but she hadn't ever seen an American. She had heard stories, though, and was scared of them.

Father worked with the Americans sometimes. Sometimes he did favors for them and they returned the favors. He said they were very strange people, always laughing, like children. Father did some favors and arranged for an American dentist to work on Tan's extra teeth.

Father went with her the first time. The American was a young man who laughed and made faces for her, like a child. He was so big she didn't know how his fingers would ever fit in her mouth. He gave her shots till she could no longer feel any of her face but her eyes. She was too scared to make a sound or move. She felt that if she closed her eyes she might disappear. Though she studied English in school the American mostly used a kind of sign language with her. He slipped tongue sticks under his lip for fangs and made a deep monkey growl. Ugly. Then he yanked them out with a pair of pliers and smiled, showing all his white teeth. *Dep.* Pretty. That was what he was going to do to Tan.

Tan lay back and watched the huge fingers work over her and tried to keep her eyes open.

When she came home that first time her lip and gums were so swollen that she looked more like a monkey than ever and Father let her stay home from school for two days. Quat had an argument with Father about the Americans. But on the third day most of the swelling had gone down and Father was very pleased. He told Tan that she would go back to school, and that she would go back to the American for follow-up treatments.

She got used to eating and talking again and the boys no longer called her monkey. The nuns said it was wonderful. Tan was not so sure. Looking in a mirror, all she recognized were her eyes. The American had taken her face.

It was after the last visit to the American that Tan saw the bonze. He was trying to sit on the sidewalk just outside of the gate to the American compound. American soldiers were forcing him to move away and a crowd had gathered around. There were three or four other bonzes in the crowd, sunlight flashing off their shaven heads. Tan rode closer on her bicycle. The monks scared her, scared her even more than her Catholic nuns did. Father said that the Buddhists would never get ahead, would never move into the twentieth century, and that the monks were traitors to their people. The bonze who was trying to sit was very young, no older than Quat. Tan could see that he had let the nails on his little fingers grow long. The American soldiers pushed gently with the sides of their rifles and the bonze and the other Vietnamese moved across the bridge.

Tan followed, pedaling slowly. The crowd grew as the bonze walked through the edge of the city, they whispered and kept their eyes on him. He walked solemnly, looking straight ahead.

The bonze tried to sit in front of a huge pagoda. The people inside came out to watch but government soldiers roared up in a truck and began to push them away. The soldiers jabbed and threatened with the barrels of their rifles, and soon the bonze had to get up and move again.

He was crying a little. The crowd began to drop away. He no longer looked straight ahead, he wandered in a wide arc looking about for a place to sit. The section of town was familiar, he was leading Tan home.

He finally settled by the Emperor's Gate. He sat and began to pray and the crowd ringed around him. Three of the other monks sat to pray a few feet away from him, while another placed a metal gallon can at his feet like an offering. The bonze finished praying and dumped the contents of the can over himself. The crowd stepped back a few paces, and Tan held her breath against the fumes. The young man burst into flame.

Tan watched. No one in the crowd spoke. The bonze was the black center of a sheet of flame, he began to rock forward, began to fall, then straightened and held himself upright, still praying. The only sound was the burning. Tan watched and wondered if it was a sin to watch. She smelled him, meat burning now and not gasoline. He fell over stiffly on his side, a crisp sound like a log shifting in a cooking fire, and as if a spell had been broken sirens came to life and the crowd moved away. Tan pedaled home as fast as she could. She didn't tell what she had seen. She fixed dinner but couldn't eat, saying that her teeth hurt from the American.

Shortly after that the Virgin Father and his brother Nhu were murdered in Saigon. People shouted in the streets, honking horns and raising banners and the nuns kept Tan's class inside all day and told them stories of King Herod. Father was put in jail. He was a loyal friend of the Ngo family. Some government soldiers came during dinner and drove him away for questioning. Quat tried to stop them but Father told him to sit and finish his meal. He would be back after the questioning. He told them all to pray for him. The soldiers took Father away. Quat sat at Father's desk, facing the wall, and cried.

One of the office doors opens and a doctor walks into the waiting room. He nods to the boy in the face harness. The boy closes his mouth tightly and shakes his head. His mother whispers to him. He won't go. The doctor leans down next to him, talking in calm, fatherly tones. The boy's face turns red, he presses his knees together and clamps his fingers to the edge of his chair. The mother whispers through her teeth, the doctor takes hold of the boy's arm and squeezes. The boy goes with the doctor, looking to his mother like he'll never see her again.

The sergeant major darts after the Moorish idol, seeming to nip at its tail. They shoot through the tank in jumps and spurts till finally the bigger idol turns and chases the sergeant major all the way back under the shelter of the Golden Gate.

When Tan was sixteen she lived in the Phu Cam section of the right bank with Dr. Co, one of Mother's brothers. He didn't allow Tan and Quat and the others to call him Uncle. Always Dr. Co. He was older than Father. Father died in the jail from tuberculosis. A man came from the government and said that was what happened. Father was buried in the Catholic cemetery.

Most of the Catholics in Hue lived in Phu Cam. Dr. Co was political chief of their ward. He had eight children of his own and now five of his sister's to care for. The house was very crowded. Sometimes Tan rode her bicycle back into the center of town, to their old house in the Citadel. She would watch it from across the street until she saw someone moving around in it. Everything had to be sold or left behind, there wasn't even room for the family altar. Dr. Co kept Father's desk.

It wasn't good living with Dr. Co and his wife. Their children teased the younger brothers and Xuan all the time. Tan was the oldest girl and had to work hard in the house. Quat and Dr. Co hardly spoke to each other. Quat was going to Hue University with the money Father had put aside for him, money that Dr. Co thought should be used to run the combined family. Quat drove a taxi and brought some money home but it didn't seem to please Dr. Co. He said the university teachers were Communists. And that the Communists were responsible for Father's death. Quat spent much of his time with his friend Buu, who was working in the Struggle Movement. Dr. Co said the Struggle Movement was backed by the Communists, and that Quat or Buu or anyone else who got involved with the crazy Buddhists and their burnings and demonstrations would end in serious trouble. Quat never argued, he just walked away.

Tan went to the Dong Kanh girls' high school. She would ride along the river on Le Loi Street on school mornings, enjoying her freedom from the Co house. She did well in her studies and was considered one of the prettiest girls. The boys from Quoc Hoc would say things sometimes when she rode past but not in a mean way.

Dr. Co had late-night meetings at the house. All the children would be crowded into one room and Madame Co would go to sleep, but Tan had to serve the men. There were politicians from the ward and men who must have been doctors or worked at a hospital. They spent the night buying and selling medicines. Tan was tired at school the next day and she hated the way the men looked at her and made jokes when she brought them their food and drinks.

Tan tried to be obedient and agreeable in the Co house and tried to make sure everyone got enough to eat. Quat had his dinner out and the younger brothers could fight for themselves, but Xuan was small and thin and Tan had to save something out of her own bowl to give to her when the rest were sleeping. They would sit up and Tan would try to tell the stories Quat had told her, but the only one she could remember completely was about the Trung sisters. Xuan loved that one and always asked for it. Tan left off the last part, the part where the Chinese came back and the sisters had to drown themselves.

One day in the spring Tan and her classmates were let out of school early. People were milling in the streets, radios blasted news at every corner. Everyone had a different rumor about what was happening. Tan tried to bicycle home, but the way was too full of people. They were crowded around an old man carrying a radio and Quat's voice was coming from it.

Tan was excited and scared. Quat said that the Struggle Movement was coming to fruit all over the country and that here in Hue the Buddhists and their friends had control of the city. Control that they meant to keep until their demands for reform were met. After each demand that Quat read, the people in the street cheered.

It was a strange kind of control. There weren't soldiers in the streets with guns like there had been after the Virgin Father was killed. The soldiers were all staying in their barracks in the Citadel. The city-government people were staying inside too, and there was no one guarding them. There were Buddhist flags flying everywhere. The Buddhists had the radio stations and the people in the streets. Tan had never seen so many people outside at once in her life.

The people in the streets were saying that they couldn't be beaten, the soldiers in the barracks were on their side and the Americans wouldn't dare interfere. The generals in Saigon would have to have elections, for none of them had the Mandate of Heaven.

In Phu Cam people were in the streets too, but they were much quieter. Trucks drove through with loudspeakers saying not to worry, they wouldn't be hurt. No one seemed to believe them.

There was a meeting at the Co house late that night. The doctor and his politician friends from the ward were there. Quat was there, and Buu, and several other people from the Struggle Movement, including two bonzes. They talked about peace, talked about how to avoid having people get hurt. Tan listened from the next room. Buu explained how the Buddhists had control of the city, how the First Division was staying neutral and the Americans were all hiding in their compound. He explained that it was important for the city officials to cooperate if they were going to avoid violence. That much of the violence might be directed at the city officials themselves. Dr. Co and his friends pledged to do anything they could to help in the difficult times ahead.

People waited to see what would happen. There were demonstrations but no government soldiers to break them up. Tan went to school, people went to their jobs, but there was a feeling of waiting, that no normal routine could be taken up till the demands were resolved one way or the other.

Quat started coming home for dinner. He talked openly about politics, about what he thought should be done to choose new leaders. Dr. Co hardly spoke. Quat talked constantly and in ways that were not right in front of one's uncle. It frightened Tan. Often at night now she could hear through the wall that Dr. Co was hitting his wife. Tan felt like she did after Confession, waiting to her the Penance the Father would give her.

The rumors came first. Ky. Ky was coming to attack them. He was coming, closer, closer. It was hard to get reliable reports. They lived in a walled city and were afraid to travel far. They waited. They wondered if the Americans would let Ky come. One night when Quat was out Dr. Co said that Ky was a good man. He might not have the Mandate of Heaven but he knew how to get things done.

Buu brought the news that General Ky was in Da Nang, fighting the people there. So close. Ky's men were fighting the soldiers who had been stationed there, were shooting civilians in the streets and in the pagodas. The Americans had helped them transport the troops and weapons. Hue would be next.

Dr. Co didn't say anything. He went to bed. Madame Co looked relieved and said maybe the best thing would be to surrender. Quat and Buu talked late into the night. The only way to save it, to keep the Struggle Movement alive, was if Hue could present a united front against Ky. The Buddhists and the Catholics and the soldiers in the Citadel and the city-government people—all standing together.

School ended for Tan. Ky was coming, he had cut off food and supplies. Dr. Co brought home some bags of rice and boxes of medicine one night and hid them in the attic. They were for the siege, he said. When things got really tight he would ration them out to the people in his ward. He didn't tell Quat about them. Every day people said that Ky would come tomorrow. They waited. Rumors went around about the killing in Da Nang. But Da Nang was different, people said. Da Nang was crowded with refugees and Communists and Americans. The Americans walked around in the city like they owned it and dumped mountains of garbage alongside the roads. It was the kind of place you could expect a lot of killing. Ky would never dare to do the same thing in the Imperial City, would never march shooting into Hue.

A nun burned herself. Somebody burned the American library, and the American consulate. The leader of the Buddhists, Thich

Tri Quang, told people to pray and be very holy. Buddhists planned to put their family altars out on the streets to stop Ky's tanks when he came. Everyone listened to the radio station. Quat spent most of his time there, and Tan heard his voice often.

One day Quat gave her a message to bring to Dr. Co. The doctor was gone when she reached home. She tried the house of one of his political friends. The friend's wife said he had left with Dr. Co, in a hurry. Tan tried the ward hall. No one was inside but an old man who said Dr. Co had been there with the other politicians but had left.

Tan rode into the center of Hue, to the city offices. There was no one but janitors in the City Clerk's office and the District Court was empty. Tan went to the soldiers' barracks.

The soldiers were gone. The people in the streets in the Citadel said the soldiers had gotten into trucks and jeeps and had driven northward out of town. Ky was to the south, in Da Nang.

Tan started back to the station. Thich Tri Quang was on the speakers telling people to stay off the streets. Ky was on his way and there was no one left to stop him. They had been betrayed. Tri Quang told people not to resist, he didn't want Buddhists killed like in Da Nang.

Before Tan reached the station the talking had stopped and there was music playing. When she arrived there were government soldiers standing guard at the entrance with their rifles pointing out.

Dr. Co came home three nights later in a very good mood. He said the traitors would be taught a lesson. He said that he was glad that order had come back to Hue. He didn't mention what he was going to do with the supplies in the attic. Quat didn't come home. Dr. Co said he must have run off to join the Communists. He was lazy, he wanted other people to do all the work, then come along and take it over. Dr. Co had a lot to drink and said more about Quat. Quat was twenty years old, he said, and yet without a wife or a job. He would never amount to anything, never be able to take care of a wife and twelve children, four of them orphans, like Dr. Co did. When Dr. Co and Madame Co went to bed there was noise, but not because he was beating her.

A week later a boy gave Tan a note from Buu. He had hidden in a Catholic church when the soldiers came and now he was going into the country. He had seen Quat captured by the Ky soldiers and taken away for questioning. When Tan went to the soldiers they said she should try the city police. The city police had a record proving the existence of a Con Tinh Quat, but had no idea of his whereabouts. He was wanted for questioning.

Quat didn't come back. Sometimes late at night Tan and the younger brothers and Xuan would sit facing one another in a small circle and pray for him and cry. But quietly, so as not to wake Dr. Co.

Tan sees a little girl watching her in the fish-tank mirror. The girl is maybe five years old, sitting with her mother. One side of her face is puckered with burnt skin, a nostril and the corner of her lip eaten away. Her blond hair is tied up in pale blue ribbons. She smiles at Tan through the fish and plastic eelgrass and Tan smiles back. The little girl takes her fingers and folds her lids down to make thin eye slits like Tan's. The mother looks up from her magazine and gives the girl a quick slap on the wrist.

Tan was eighteen. It was very early morning, only a few hours into the Year of the Monkey, when she was wakened by the popping. Close, a sporadic hollow popping and flashes like heat lightning in the sky. Dr. Co had just come back from a Tet party at the ward hall, he was still in his rumpled street clothes when he wandered out from his bedroom. It was monsoon season and had been drizzling on and off all night. Dr. Co held newspapers over his head and went out. He came back without the papers, hair plastered to his head, looking very pale. The Communists were attacking all over, he said—trying to take over the city. It would be best to stay in and wait for the Americans to come out of their compound and chase the Communists away.

They sat in the dark, no one sleeping, no one speaking, and listened to the popping. The sounds grew very close, the house shuddered a few times, and then they moved away. That was the Americans, said Dr. Co from the corner he was huddled in. When the ground shakes like that it is the Americans chasing Communists with their big guns.

At dawn Dr. Co and Tan went out to look. It was very quiet, raining lightly. Soldiers walked in the street carrying rifles— Vietnamese soldiers. They weren't the ones from the Citadel though. These men wore khaki uniforms and green-and-red armbands, and called to each other in the rapid dialect of northerners. Dr. Co hurried Tan back inside.

Dr. Co sent Madame Co and the young children to shelter at the Phu Cam Cathedral, a little ways across the railroad tracks. The soldiers wouldn't bother a woman and children. Tan had to stay and help him gather their valuables. When it was dark they would try to reach the Cathedral.

Now and then Dr. Co had Tan peek into the street. There were people with rifles in everyday clothes, and the people with their hair in buns, the country people in black pajamas. The popping and explosions came from up by the American compound now, and from the walled city across the river. The Communists were in control of Phu Cam.

Dr. Co cursed the Saigon generals and the Americans. This was what came of declaring a truce with the Communists. Dr. Co gathered his papers and money and some of the medicines he had stored in the attic. Ever since the Struggle Movement failed, Dr. Co had been bringing home supplies and storing them in the attic. Things he said the Americans had given him. He put the medicines and a few cartons of cigarettes in his suitcases, but he left the American ham and beef upstairs.

In the early evening someone pounded on the door. Dr. Co told Tan to say he had gone to the hospital to treat casualties, and ran up into the attic. The pounding continued, someone yelled that they should come outside, that no one would be harmed. Dr. Co was called by name. Tan sat on the floor, too scared to answer the pounding. It stopped. After several quiet hours Dr. Co came down.

They tried to sneak out late at night. At the railroad tracks someone called for them to stop and searchlights came on. Dr. Co ran into the darkness and Tan tried to follow. The suitcase she'd been given was heavy and when she heard men close behind her she had to drop it and scurry away. Tan spent an hour squatting in the shelter of a small pagoda and then found her way home. Dr. Co slapped her for leaving the suitcase behind. How would the family eat, he asked, now that she had thrown all their money away? Tan saw no sign of the suitcase Dr. Co had been carrying.

They lay on mats in the children's room, several feet of darkness between them. They didn't speak for over an hour. Neither slept. Then there was pounding on a door down the street. Voices shouting. Screaming and a shot, very loud, very close, and a woman wailing on the street. Pounding on a door, closer. Dr. Co came over and lay by Tan, putting his arms around her. She couldn't tell which one of them was shaking so hard. Pounding right next door, more shots, more crying. Tan held her breath. She felt Dr. Co's heart beating against her back. The pounding came again, on the other side of the house. They had been passed over. The pounding moved on down the street.

Tan felt Dr. Co's breath hot on the back of her neck. He pushed his face through her hair and kissed her there. She was the one shaking now, she was sure of that. He rolled her onto her belly and pulled her clothes up. The northerners were near, she couldn't cry out. She couldn't think who she would cry to.

Tan felt crushed under his weight, the matting dug into her breasts. She tried to think of prayers. She was glad she didn't have to see his face. Tan bit her lip against the pain and he pushed into her from behind. That evening, frightened by the pounding, she had forgotten and not called him Dr. Co, had not even called him Uncle. Father, she had said, what will we do?

Dr. Co lay still on top of her when he had finished. He lay so still and so long that Tan thought he must have fallen asleep. But then he rolled off her and she groped her way to where she could wash herself. Tan sat shivering under her father's desk until dawn.

It rained heavily all morning and the fighting sounds were muffled. Dr. Co didn't meet her eyes or speak. When Tan looked out she saw a few of the country people riding by on bicycles. They didn't seem to notice how wet they were getting.

The pounding came in the afternoon. Dr. Co was called by name. He went up in the attic to hide. The people outside said they would start shooting if no one came out. Tan opened the door.

There were country people and a few people dressed in city clothes. They all wore red armbands. One was a girl who went to the Dong Kanh high school with Tan, a very pretty, popular girl. She wore a pair of pistols in her belt. Another of the people was Buu.

He looked much older. He held a clipboard in a hand with only one finger and a thumb on it. He pretended he didn't know Tan.

Buu asked where Dr. Co was. Tan said he had gone to the hospital. Buu said they knew that wasn't true. The people stood in the house, dripping, and told her not to be afraid, they were here to protect the Vietnamese from the Americans and the Saigon generals. Tan was too frightened to speak. Father, her uncle, the nuns in school—all had told of the terrible things that the Communists did to people.

Buu sat on the ladder leading to the attic and asked if they were hoarding meat in the house. Tan shook her head. Buu said he had learned about decay since he had been away from the city. If you lived too close to it you never noticed the smell, but any outsider could tell right off that things were rotten. Buu led the people up into the attic and they found Dr. Co hiding behind containers of American beef.

Dr. Co cried and pleaded. They bound his hands behind his back with wire, told him not to worry. They were only taking him for questioning. Buu told Tan to stay in the house until told what to do by the People's Army. The country people carried the meat out into the rain. Dr. Co didn't say good-bye.

Tan dressed in black and waited for night. There was no trouble at the railroad tracks and she reached the Phu Cam Cathedral. Women inside were wailing, beating their faces with their hands. There were no men. No men and almost no boys.

The Communists had come that morning, sobbed Madame Co, and had taken all the men and boys away. Just to a political meeting, they said, and then they would be brought back. They had taken Madame Co's four sons and Tan's two brothers. No one had returned. Xuan had volunteered to go for help to the government soldiers. She knew her way in the Citadel.

Tan told Madame Co her husband had gone to work at the hospital.

She started after Xuan in the morning. Rain beat down and there was fighting everywhere. She ran north toward the river, ducking between buildings when the fighting came close. She saw northern soldiers. She saw Americans. Loudspeakers said the People's Army was winning. A sound truck blared that the government soldiers were in control.

Tan was knocked to the pavement by an explosion. Her head hurt. She went on. Somebody shot at her. She felt the bullet pass, dove to the ground and cut her hands open. She stumbled onto a man lying dead in a puddle on the street. Tan crawled off him and ran for the river. The fight roared around her, trucks burning, houses burning, flames sizzling up to meet the rain. Tan saw blood running through the gutters with the rain. A flying piece of brick hit her, her side burning, and an old man fell in front of her, bleeding, tangled with his bicycle. It was the lake of fire the nuns had told of, it was the Day of Atonement. Her head hurt. Tan ran upright down the middle of the street, knowing only that she had to reach the river.

The bridge was gone. There was no way back to the Imperial City. Her head hurt. She had to get across. She held her head in her hands, tried to remember. She was the sister of—there was someone floating by in the water, face down. She was the daughter of—the water was gray, its surface alive with rain. Glowing embers blew from the fires in the walled city and died as they landed on the water. She held her head and sat on the bank of the Perfume River, trying to remember who she was.

The air conditioner blows on Tan, her nipples stand up and hurt a little. She folds her arms across her breasts. They are so big, so hard, since the Chinese doctor did them. She is a tiny, thin woman with huge breasts. She wonders if they'll ever be small again, be soft. If she gives him her eyes maybe he'll let her have her body back.

There are pictures on the wall. Chins pushed back or strengthened, noses straightened and reduced, harelips mended. Oriental eyes made round. Before and After, say the pictures.

When Tan went back to the Co house it was full of government soldiers hiding from their commanding officer. They sat halfnaked on the floor with their clothes hanging to dry, eating what was left of the food, cooking on a fire made from Father's desk. They called for Tan to come in and sleep with them. She ran. The Americans and Communists fought in the Bien Hoa suburb to the north. The Americans built a pontoon bridge and Tan crossed with thousands of other homeless people. The people said the Americans would feed them.

Tan wandered in the walled city, looking for Xuan, looking for food. Thousands wandered with her. The walls had crumbled under the bombing, half the houses were knocked down. People looted what they could before the soldiers came back. The soldiers had guns and took the best of everything.

The sun came out for one day and the bodies in the streets began to stink. Families, dressed in white for mourning, made circular graves for their dead in the red earth of the parks and schoolyards. The bodies were wrapped in black cloth, then in white, and buried in the mud. The Americans wrapped their dead in green plastic bags and left them on the curb for trucks to pick up.

Tan found Madame Co at a refugee center the government soldiers had set up. There was no food. Dr. Co had been found with his hands still bound behind his back, buried alive. There was no word of Madame Co's sons or Tan's brothers. No word of Xuan.

Tan wandered in the monsoon. Sometimes Americans would give her food. She was afraid to approach them alone, but joined groups of begging children. Tan found the men gave more if she talked like the little children. Hey, you, GI, she would call, you numba one. You give gell to eat, yes?

The Americans would smile if they weren't too tired and hand out a little food. People cooked what they could beg or steal right on the street, in water pots made from artillery shells.

The first time Tan saw Supply Sergeant Plunkett he was wrapped around a case of Army K-rations. He grinned at her as he hurried across the rubble, rattling his cans of beans and processed ham. Care for a bite? Tan was too hungry to be scared. His legs were so long that she had to run to keep up with him.

You, me, pom-pom, he said to her in the abandoned house they sheltered in. Boom-boom. Fuckee-fuckee?

He seemed very pleased when she didn't understand what he meant.

You vir-gen gell?

She told him she was.

Vary good. Me show you boom-boom. Then you eat. Beaucoup food.

He did what Dr. Co had done to her, but he looked her in the eyes afterward and smiled.

You no vir-gen now. You Plunkett gell.

Tan smiled back at him like she had learned from the young children, smiled and said you numba-one GI. Numba-one boom-boom. Me eat now?

The Communists disappeared and bulldozers came to bury the walls and buildings that had been blown down. Tan went with Plunkett to Da Nang. He would give her money. If the Communists had taken her brothers and Xuan she would become wealthy enough to buy them back.

Plunkett set her up in a house on the edge of the sand flats in Da Nang, close to the refugee camps. There were four other girls who had American soldiers. Plunkett paid her rent and gave her money for food and clothes. She sewed most of it into a chair. It was nice having the other girls to talk to, there was a mama-san to keep the house and always enough food. Plunkett visited at least twice a week.

There was garbage everywhere in Da Nang, small mountains of it that little boys fought and played on. People in the camps sat all day waiting for food, crowded together like insects. There were girls on the streets, country girls who had sold eggs and produce in the market before the fighting. Buy me, buy me, they said. Me numba-one gell, suckee-suckee, six-hundred pi.

Plunkett would come to drink and for boom-boom. He liked

how thin her body was, how her breasts barely stuck out. My little girl, he called her. He asked if she had a little sister he could meet. Tan said she had no sisters. He showed pictures of his little daughters back in America. Plunkett didn't like the name Tan, he called her Betsy. It was the same name as one of his daughters.

He smiled and laughed constantly, like a child. He said he didn't like her eyes. They looked like she was hiding something from him. You trick me, he would say. Alla time same-same. You Betsy unscrutable gell. He gave her money to have the round-eye operation like Madame Ky, like the other girls in the house. She sewed it in the chair.

Tan had been in Da Nang three months when the word came about the men and boys taken from the Phu Cam Cathedral. Their bones were found buried together in the jungle a few miles from Hue. Most shot, some buried alive. Over four hundred men and boys. Plunkett gave Tan money to send to care for her brothers' bones.

Her belly grew. The other girls noticed first, then Plunkett. He was very angry and took her to his friend Dr. Yin.

Dr. Yin was Chinese and smelled of ammonia. Tan was terrified. Plunkett reassured her that Dr. Yin was an American, a soldier, and his friend. But Chinese was Chinese. Tan screamed and had to be given a shot when the young doctor approached her.

She was thin again then, but Plunkett didn't seem to like her so much. He brought her a Catholic-schoolgirl's uniform, like she had worn when she was little, and had her put it on for the boom-boom. Sometimes he made her bend over so he could hit her with his belt. He didn't smile or laugh so much anymore.

Plunkett left things at the apartment, medicines, food, sometimes guns. He ordered Tan not to touch them. She listened for hours to the American radio he had given her. She would lie in the dark at night twisting the dial back and forth, listening to all the different languages, all the voices blending into one another. She felt like she was floating, hearing everyone's private thoughts. When she woke the batteries would be dead and she'd be without a radio till Plunkett came. He always had batteries with him.

Tan was twenty, had been in Da Nang two years, when she saw her sister on the street. Two Americans were walking with their Vietnamese girls. One of them was Xuan. She looked like all the other street girls, looked like she could take care of herself. Her American called her Sue-Anne. Tan followed, listening to her sister laugh at what the Americans were saying, and then let them walk out of sight. A moment later she thought better of it and tried to catch up, but Xuan had turned some corner and was gone.

Plunkett said he would send Tan to America. She would help him be a rich man. He explained that in America opium was used just like money, better than money. But government police would steal it from you, just like in Vietnam. It was hard to bring opium to America, but Tan could help him.

He took her back to his friend Dr. Yin. They explained how much just a little opium was worth if it was pure. She watched the doctor put it into the implants. They would be like a cyst, he said, like a thorn that the skin grows over. Harmless.

Tan lay on the slab and remembered all the stories Quat had told her. Dr. Yin put her under. She dreamed of riding a bicycle in a quiet, walled city.

When she woke her breasts felt mammoth, they jutted out stiffly from her body. The skin was stretched taut, the nipples pointing up and out. There was a scar in the crease beneath each breast, creases she had never had before. The breasts didn't feel a part of her. They belonged to Plunkett. He loved to grab them in bed. The future is in my hands, he would say, and smile like he used to.

He arranged for her to go to the American city of San Francisco. He would come later. Tan was afraid to tell him about the money she had hoarded, afraid he wouldn't understand. It was in piasters, and wouldn't be any good in America. It wasn't opium. The day before the plane took her, Tan ripped the money out of the chair and gave it to the other girls in the house.

It would be good in San Francisco, she thought. No one was fighting and there was always enough food.

A nurse, a young American girl, calls Tan into the office. She is seated in a leather reclining chair. Doctor is in the back washing his hands, says the nurse, I'm his assistant. The nurse asks Tan if she is sure she wants to go through with the eye operation, says she is a very pretty woman already. Tan says she wants to go ahead. The nurse leaves.

There are more pictures on the walls inside the office. Before and After pictures, profiles of breasts enlarged or made smaller. A picture of the doctor in Army fatigues sitting on a pile of sandbags. Tan closes her eyes, tries to steady her heartbeat.

*   *   *

Tan lived in a bad-smelling Mission Street hotel run by an old Thai man. The rent seemed high, but that was something the nuns hadn't taught about in English. Tan avoided talking to anyone, she took all her money with her if she went out and never walked more than a few blocks from the hotel. She waited for Plunkett.

A young brown-skinned woman with a little baby lived in the next room. Sometimes at night she would play her radio, slow, sad songs in Spanish to keep her baby from crying. Tan would lie in bed, listening through the wall, and think how nice it would be if she could be friends with the woman.

Tan waited. Her American money began to run out. She ate rice at a Vietnamese restaurant on Powell Street. On the sign out front was a map of Vietnam with the northern half painted red and the southern half painted green and all the major cities labeled. Young American men would come by with their girls and point to spots on the map, but very few came inside. Mr. Thuong, who ran the restaurant, would talk with Tan while she ate. He had come to America during the fighting between the French and the Communists. He seemed very kind, but Tan was careful not to tell much about herself. Her bill never came to what it said on the menu.

Tan waited in her room on Mission Street. She was afraid. Afraid of the Americans, afraid of being alone, afraid of being caught with the opium. They had searched her when she got to the Hawaii airport, a woman had put her hands up in Tan's private parts.

Plunkett wrote her a letter saying when he was coming. He wrote in the child-language he had used to talk with her. It was very hard to read. Tan went to the docks to meet him.

Passengers came off the big boat, but Plunkett was not among them. Tan asked a man from the boat, who took her to a policeman. The policeman said that Plunkett had been taken for questioning. He asked Tan's name and address and she gave him false ones. Plunkett never showed up at the hotel. Questioning meant the same thing in America that it did in Vietnam.

Mr. Thuong gave Tan a job at the restaurant when her money was gone. She made salads in the kitchen and tried to avoid the busboys and dishwashers, who were all Chinese. Mr. Thuong couldn't pay her much, she didn't have a Green Card, but if she ate at the restaurant she had enough to pay her rent.

One of the waitresses, a Korean girl named Kim, was friendly to her. Kim had another job, being a girl in a Chinese bar on Pacific

Street. The Chinese men would come in a little drunk and Kim would sit by them and talk and they would buy her drinks. It made more money for the bar. The Chinese tried to do more and you could make extra. Kim let them touch her breasts. Kim said she was willing to sell her breasts but nothing beyond that. The girls in the bar were all Koreans and had American boyfriends or husbands. They had come over from their country with soldier husbands. Kim said it would pay much more than making salads, said the Chinese men would like Tan. She was small and delicate but had big breasts for them to touch.

Kim told her to have the round-eye operation. If she ever wanted to get an American boyfriend, to be able to become a citizen and get papers so she could have a nice job, she would have to have her eyes changed. That was how they wanted it. Tan said she was interested, but kept putting it off.

One morning Mr. Thuong came out from listening to the news and began to paint the bottom half of the Vietnam map red. There were tears in his eyes as he painted. At least, he said, it is all the same color now. It was that morning Tan decided for the operation.

Kim showed her the ad for the plastic surgeon in the yellow pages, a big ad with a picture of the doctor. Tan recognized his face.

Tan lies in the reclining chair wondering what he'll do. If he'll remember her. If he'll steal it from her or give her to the police. But one way or the other, she'll be free of it. The last of Vietnam locked inside her, next to her heart, will be gone.

The doctor comes in rubbing his hands on a towel. Tan catches her breath, tries to look calm. She wonders what she'll do when her eyes are round and unguarded.

Hello Tan, says Dr. Yin. I've been expecting you.

NOVEMBER AND DECEMBER: BILLY, 1969

by Jayne Anne Phillips

NOVEMBER

Riding the bus in from South Campus, Billy looked at the University's new indoor athletic stadium. Its overhanging roof dominated an expanse of green field like the giant fluted cap of a cement mushroom. Long sidewalks led over the hill to the med school, to married students' housing, to the four towers of the dorm complex where he'd lived for two months. He balanced his biology text and spiral notebook on his knees. Touching the face of the notebook, he thought about his parents' handwriting on birthday cards he'd opened that morning. Words in his mother's cursive hand contained modest loops, the writing was large, and the sentences ran on to comprise one form, one image. It was a funny card, a dog on the front with big eyes and a gap-toothed grin; couldn't picture it exactly but the thought bubble referred to some pun on doggone it etc. your birthday. Inside, a check for twenty dollars and her message, which he remembered exactly: *I wish I could do more, honey, but things are a little tight this month. When you come home next, I'll make you a special birthday dinner. Things all right? Need anything? Love, Mom.* Mitch had sent him fifty dollars. Since the divorce he'd tried to give Billy too much money; Billy would have to persuade his father to take half the fifty back. The card was a money envelope from Central National Bank in Bellington. A paper flap lifted to reveal an oval cutout and the face of Andrew Jackson; near it Mitch had printed *Happy Birthday* and underlined the words. At the bottom, under the money, *Love, Mitch.* And he underlined his name. Lately he signed himself "Mitch" in letters, one every couple of weeks, Bess's address printed in the top left corner of the envelopes as return. Each letter was neatly typed and nearly telegraphic in nature. *Fall has arrived here, nights are cold and fog of a morning. Better to winterize your car before snow, here is a check. Upshur Drill bought the County Bldg. & are adding on, tore hell out of East Main.* He typed one-fingered on the big manual Billy had moved from the basement on Labor Day weekend; the typewriter sat on top of his metal desk just as before. His bedroom at Bess's easily held all his possessions: his clothes, the Formica-topped desk in the corner, a swivel desk chair, a file cabinet. His construction manuals, loose-leaf in vinyl-covered notebooks, displayed between steel bookends. Small graduation photos of Billy and Danner in a plastic frame Mitch must have bought at the five and ten on Main Street. A metal nameplate that read MITCH HAMPSON in white letters on fake wood. This was his father's room and it had existed all along, unacknowledged by anyone, in the basement—in the same cement-block room as the ironing board and the single bed where Jean used to sleep.

Despite the awkward pain of his father's anger, Billy was glad Jean and Mitch finally lived apart. Purposefully, Billy stayed out of the cross fire. Bess was his father's ally, silently, constantly, in companionship, in their familial bickering over when to bring in more coal, over how warm to keep the fire that had burned in the grate of the sitting room since October. Mitch sat in front of the color television in a big-seated upholstered rocker, stoking the fire with a poker. He sat forward, elbows on his knees, feet flat on the floor, his hands touching contemplatively. Or he leaned back, the chair in motion, one arm extended on the broad oak armrest, the other crooked as he stroked the back of his neck. Bess sat in the corner in a small white rocker with her handwork, out of viewing range of the picture constantly beamed by the TV. *I don't watch anyway,* she confided to anyone, telling a joke on herself, *I only listen to the stories*—the stories being several afternoon soap operas. She sat in near darkness doing cross-stitch, a kind of touch braille, Billy thought, since she couldn't possibly see the patterns. Her glasses were thick and their lenses made her eyes seem too large for her thin face. If Billy stood close enough he saw pale blue whorls in her brown irises, a milky flaring of age near the tight dots of her pupils. She stood up from her chair carefully, touching the top of the warm television for support.

They didn't talk about the divorce in front of Billy. *Lord save us,* Bess would comment good-humoredly while Mitch complained about potholes on Main Street or prices at the grocery store. When Billy went by the house on weekends home, they had Saturday lunch in the kitchen: chicken baked in the oven until it was hard and salty, mashed potatoes, soup beans. Flour gravy Bess made at the stove, Mitch pouring the milk into the pan as she stirred. Afterward she insisted on cleaning up alone. *You go on and visit with your father.* Back to the sitting room, Billy rolling his sleeves up in the warmth. Mitch taking his usual seat, then talk, generalities with specific meanings. Long pauses, expected, not uncomfortable. Crackling of the coal fire. Billy never mentioned his mother; Mitch never asked. Jean did discuss the divorce; Billy knew it was final in February.

They all wanted to put Billy somewhere safe while things settled and time passed, but he couldn't cooperate any longer. He'd thought carefully and wondered for weeks; this was the day to go ahead. Withdrawal from the University wasn't difficult. He'd fill out the form and decide what to do next. At home they'd think it was the divorce, or Vietnam and the times, or Kato—or maybe they thought she was out of the picture. *Gone but not forgotten.* Whose phrase was that really, who first said it? The bus pulled at a crawl across crowded Stadium Bridge, a one-way wooden lane, and the Student Union was in sight.

Yesterday he'd taken most of the money out of his checking account at a downtown bank—$400. Tuition at the state school was inexpensive, less than two hundred, but Jean must have paid nearly a thousand for room and board at the dorm. He'd get a job here or in Bellington and pay the rest before he went south, or into the army. The army. Supposedly the first few minutes of the lottery drawing in December were going to be broadcast on television. Just like TV, catch it on film up to about number 30.

Well, numbers were pure if television wasn't. Now it was a matter of numbers, published in a newspaper list. No more dodg'em plans or 1S deferments: fuck up, drop your grades, and you're gone. He'd know once and for all in December; he wouldn't have to argue it out in his head. It was a joke, really. His birthday—today—written on a white plastic ball and bounced around in a machine. Exactly whose hand would touch the machine? Sometimes Billy dreamed about the lottery, a close-up interior view: hundreds of days of white balls tumbling in a black sphere, silent and very slow, moving as though in accordance with physical laws. A galaxy of identical white planets. No sun. Cold, charged planets, simple, symmetrical, named with months and numbers. *Nov. 1, no. 305 of 365.* Universe stops. Hand reaches in. Suddenly everything in color, and the black sphere turns midnight blue. Crazy dream. The black and white beginning, when the balls moved around and through each other slowly, must be a Bio I flash: all those films of microorganisms, bacteria, swimming shapes.

Billy wasn't worried about the lottery, he wasn't hassled. The lottery was an ingenious system, better than the draft. Having your birthday picked early in the countdown was a completely coincidental happening, like being struck by lightning. Your birthday had been all those cakes and tricycles and new shirts: now pay up. The government could claim near innocence. Of course, they'd set up the system. Supposedly they'd set up the war, too, but Billy wasn't sure. He didn't know histories or politics—he didn't want to know. Knowing wouldn't change what was going to happen. It had no more to do with him than this bus ride, but maybe it would hurt him a lot worse. And it was two years.

His roommate joked over beer and pretzels. *December 1 you're going to see me drop acid and park in front of the tube in Towers Lounge, watch it all on the big screen.* Then, more seriously: *Look, Vietnam is practically over. Suppose we do get drafted, might not even go to Nam. Might go to Hawaii. Be fun. Surfboards.* That was DeCosto, the loony Italian from Scranton, Pa.

Some of Billy's friends had talked to draft counselors. Various tables were set up every weekend outside the Student Union: sorority and fraternity rush sign-ups (GO GREEK), Environment Club ski trip sign-ups (PRAY FOR SNOW), Mobilize Against Strip Mining sign-ups, Draft Counseling (PLAN NOW). DeCosto said he planned every Friday so he could get dates with older women on Saturday nights: most of the draft counselors were women grad students. They wore baggy clothes; they looked pale and studious, in wire-frame glasses, or they were clean and energetic, like campers. Occasionally the counselors were men, a hippie law student or a vet. The Vets were usually skinny, long-haired, never glossy. One guy sat there in a wheelchair at the side of the table. Always—in the milling of students, honking of traffic, barking of mutt dogs wearing bandannas—short, intense conversations took place at the draft-counseling tables. Billy never went near them. He would take his cue from the numbers. He thought he would. Numbers were his plan while the pattern held.

The bus pulled up to the Student Union steps. Billy knew that General Studies students had to withdraw from the Dean of Students' offices upstairs in the Union. As he left the bus and walked into the building, he wished himself a happy birthday. This might not be his best birthday—not like his sixteenth, the day he took his driver's test in a blue secondhand Falcon he already owned. Or his eighteenth, when Kato made him a chocolate cake full of melted M&Ms and gave him a watch she must have saved all year to buy. He checked the watch on the way upstairs: one o'clock. But this birthday would be okay; he was doing exactly what he wanted to do. He opened the door marked DEAN OF STUDENTS.

The woman behind the counter looked up expectantly. She was alone in the room. Behind her a carpeted hallway led out of sight. "Can I help you?"

"I want to withdraw from school," Billy said.

"You want to withdraw now, in November? There's no refund on tuition this late."

"I know. Which form do I use?"

She put both hands flat on the counter. "Wait a minute. Mind if I ask—it's my job to ask—why you're withdrawing? Are your grades bad?"

"They're not good, but they're not bad." He didn't think his grades were any of her business. "I'm withdrawing for personal reasons."

She folded her hands and smiled. "Perhaps I can help you."

"No, I don't think so. I'd just like the form, please." He put his books on the counter near her hands and stood waiting, watching her. He wouldn't let himself look away.

"Would you like to come into the office? If you're so sure about doing this, would it hurt to talk it over?"

"I don't want to talk it over, thanks. If you'll just give me the form, I'll fill it out right here."

She gave him the form, one white sheet in triplicate. He filled in the blanks, signed it, and handed the form back to her.

She looked at his name. "You'll receive official notification in the mail, Mr. Hampson."

He nodded. At least she hadn't called him Billy. "I wanted to ask—will I have to move out of the dorm right away?"

"Well, you're paid up. If you don't turn in your key, I suppose you're free to stay until the end of the term." She paused. "Look, I hope you'll re-enroll at some point. Please phone here at the Dean of Students' office if we can assist you in any way."

He thanked her and walked back downstairs, then out the double doors of the Student Union to the street. He waited for some precise feeling to wash over him, but nothing came. Almost out of habit, he crossed the street and entered Sumner Hall for bio class. He was a little late.

The room was a sort of tiered concrete arena with semicircular rows of desks bolted in place on descending levels all the way to the bottom. There, a graduate proctor sat silently behind a long table, reading a book. Far above him, suspended in both forward corners of the ceiling, were the two thirty-inch televisions that taught the course. MITOSIS, said the screens in black and white. Notebooks shuffled open, lights dimmed slightly. The screens were brighter now, more exclusively boring. Billy resolved to pay close attention, not to "mitosis" but to the room, the people, what they did. He'd watch the screens as well. Maybe bio was interesting and he hadn't noticed because he hated the whole setup—or didn't hate it, thought it was silly. He always sat in the back row; now and then he smoked a joint, which didn't prevent him from taking notes. Actually, he took more explicit notes when he was a little stoned.

He fixed his gaze on the screen. Here came the definition, printed out a few words at a time. *Usual method of cell division. Resolving of the chromatin. Of the nucleus. Into a threadlike form.* It was a weird language really; they should have someone reciting in a sci-fi thriller voice. Instead, a taped professorial drone pronounced the words as they appeared, or lagged a little behind the pictures; the bio department filmed the lessons themselves and narrated the course. Every freshman at the University had to take Bio I and II, and the big room seated five hundred. But it was never full. Billy envisioned the wonderful confusion if all freshmen, each carefully assigned a numbered section of Bio I, showed up for the same class. Billy listened to the scratching of pens and pencils, the ripping open of cellophane bags of junk food. A few students were sleeping. Innumerable others sat doing nothing, watching. He watched. The illustration, cells dividing under the scrutiny of a microscope, proceeded jerkily, in silence. Maybe if they synced in music, rock music, even classical music. Maybe if the films were in color. What color were cells? Billy thought the endless tones of gray were sad as hell.

His thoughts drifted. Last night Danner had come out to Towers to bring him a birthday cake. She brought a boyfriend with her, Jim his name was, a nice enough guy, and two pints of ice cream. The cake was chocolate with white icing, and Danner put twenty candles on it, one to grow on. They'd set the cake up on the only table in his dorm room, all of them laughing, and when she leaned over, lighting matches, the ends of her long hair caught fire. Billy put it out fast with his hands, but a few strands near her face were scorched. She made a joke about Buddhist protests; no harm was done and they ate cake until most of it was gone. This morning, pulling on his jeans, he'd thought he smelled the acrid odor of burnt hair, and he remembered the scared look on her face as she pulled back from the candles. Billy shifted in his seat. There was no smell at all in the bio classroom of Sumner Hall.

The bell rang. All around him books slammed shut, bodies shuffled. Everyone got up at once and moved, a bored herd on its way to cafeteria lines. He sat and let them pass, watching the tiers of seats reassert their emptiness. All summer, he'd waited to come to college. After he was in college, it seemed he was waiting for something else. What was he waiting for now?

He figured he would drive to Bellington. It wasn't fair if he didn't tell Jean right away.

The summer before he started college, Billy worked as a life-guard at the State Park, a wilderness of rhododendron and pine crossed with trails. The trails were steep and rocky above the winding river, dotted with bridges, picnic tables, stone-hewn barbecue pits, fireplaces built in the Depression by CCC men. The river wound or rushed according to season; every spring someone drowned in the rapids, the river twisting violently around boulders and big rocks that created deep pools in the current. Teenagers from nearby towns went camping or tubing; they hiked the trails back along the river, toting beer and food far from the park entrance. They waded out to favorite rocks, awkwardly carrying ice chests, blankets, radios. Couples staked space on a flat rock and swam off the side in summer when the river was calm; they grew drunk slowly and necked in the sun.

Families stayed farther up where there were guards, where the river was cordoned off near the refreshment stand and restrooms. Billy sat there in his tall white chair, a silver whistle on a chain around his neck, and watched dragonflies skim across the water. Weekends the park was crowded, the stretch of paved riverbank spread with towels and bathers. Transistor radios blared pop legends. Young mothers, high-school girls a few years before, lay insensate, their faces blank. They listened to Top 40 and oiled their thighs. Sometimes they started conversations. *Hey there, aren't you Billy Hampson? What class was it you were in—two years ago, right?* Or *I knew your sister, she was just three years behind me. Where was it she went off to?* Billy watched toddlers in the wading pool, a shallows roped off with plastic cord and multicolored floats. Even on weekends, the young mothers were alone. They were girls whose husbands worked Saturdays or watched TV ballgames; they bought new bathing suits every summer at K-Mart and read romance paperbacks. Already they seemed transformed into an isolated species; groups of boys who came to the park in such numbers never glanced at them. *You're a Hampson. Aren't you Billy Hampson? I thought you were.* They pulled piles of plastic toys from beach bags, watched their charges wade into the water, then lay down and abandoned consciousness for a semiwakeful trance. The older women, whose children were eight and ten and twelve, came in couples and played cards. They refereed their kids' quarrels, drank iced tea from a thermos, smoked endless cigarettes; they were stolid, asexual, and self-contained. They didn't notice Billy unless he reprimanded their children, blowing the whistle and signaling them back to the bank for dunking or straying too far. Then the women stood up in their solid-color, one-piece suits, shouting threats and directions, snapping down the legs of the suits to cover a half-moon of sagging derrière.

Weekdays were long, lazy, the park nearly empty and the swimming area frequented only by a country family or two. The men were present then: they were truckers between hauls, or miners or plant workers on night shift, or they were out of work. Never less than five or six kids, and the parents middle-aged on wool blankets. The kids wore shorts and T-shirts; the babies went naked. They brought big rubber innertubes and tires instead of toys. No radios, no plastic bottles of oil. There was little talk and easy silence; the kids could all swim and were usually obedient, and the older ones took care of the younger. Billy sat all day in the swoony heat. By four in the afternoon everyone was gone from the swimming area; he put away life jackets and guard poles, checked the bathrooms, picked up litter. He would lock up at five. Just before, he knelt by the river with a set of corked vials to take a water sample. The river was getting dirtier; mine drainage striped the rocks orange just a few miles up. In a year, two years, swimming would be officially disallowed. Billy held the vials to the sun, watched the water cloud, then wrote dates and acidity registration in the record book. The days smelled of pollen. Close insects sounded, faint stirrings, dollop of a fish breaking. Billy would dump the vials, rinse them, put them back in the case and shut the lid. He stood looking at the water and then went in, swimming underwater. He cleared the river to the opposite bank in five powerful strokes and long glides, surfaced, and moved back across with a regular butterfly stroke, hearing only the quick, flat impact of his limbs cutting water.

Often on the way home he stopped at a small beer joint called Bartley's. It was a peaceful red-neck bar not big enough for fights or dancing. The interior was just nine bar stools, the bar itself, and five square tables arranged across the slanted wood floor in front. A closet to the right of the bar held a stained toilet. The insulbrick-sided building had been some worker's shanty house back in the days when there were lumber mills. Narrow second-ary roads near the park were dotted with such houses, some of them fallen away to frames and inverted roofs, the struts pointing into air. Trees grew up through the floors where there was sun enough.

At Bartley's the sun was muted by brown paper blinds; the blinds were old and faded and strained the light to a dull gold. Unhurried conversations continued at the tables. The patrons were mostly men in their fifties or sixties who lived nearby in Hampton or Volga, rural settlements begun as mill towns along the river. Billy's grandfather had built Hampton, had owned a mill. But the man, his mother's father, had died when Jean was a girl; Hampton had died before he did. Even then, it must have been steamy in summer. Country near the State Park was brushy and still forested, valleys overhung by hills. The old air condi-tioner at Bartley's wheezed over the entrance, and a small rotating fan, its face no bigger than a pie plate, stood on the bar. Billy drank one or two cold beers in tall Stroh's glasses, and wondered about Kato with little urgency. He thought in terms of 'getting rid of her,' getting her out of his mind. But four years back, things referred to her. Summers, winters, high school, movie houses. His car reminded him of her. His friends reminded him. Girls he went out with now reminded him; even the best ones seemed coy and mannered. They were willing to different degrees but wanted something in exchange for their loyalty, their favors—some assur-ance. They all had plans, secretarial school or college, and they believed in their plans as though the future were cast in iron. His sister, Danner, was a little like that too, but Danner was smart enough it seemed reasonable she'd have plans. And she could veer off course suddenly. Most girls around Bellington didn't. And to Billy, who'd been sleeping with Kato for nearly two years, the proceeding and backing off in parked cars, the lines drawn, the expectations, seemed a waste of time. He wouldn't make any promises.

Kato hadn't needed promises. He guessed they might have slept together even sooner if he'd tried. Somehow his getting a car had started them off. He wasn't the first; Kato told him candidly she'd been with another boy before, twice. She attached no judgments and neither did Billy. He took her to school every morning and took her home in the afternoon, except during football season, when he was team manager and stayed late. Afternoons, she worked with her father in the billiard room, doing food orders for customers while Shinner poured drafts and saw to the tables. Billy played pool or shot the bull with Shinner until he had to go home to supper. Later, he phoned. Saturday nights they went to the movies at the Colonial, then walked across the street and upstairs to Kato's room. They were always alone then and they didn't have to hurry. Sometimes Billy fell asleep afterward, as though her bedroom were his own, then got up and left after midnight.

He supposed they'd acted grown-up long before they really were. But in some ways Kato was never a kid. Her mother had died a long time before, and she and her brothers had raised themselves. Shinner didn't impose many rules, and he drank. Billy had cleaned him up a few times to save Kato's doing it. Shinner wasn't a mean drunk but he was fairly dependable; twice a month he'd drink himself into a stupor. One of the brothers or even Kato ran the billiard room then, though it meant she served beer. She hadn't turned drinking age until recently, but the cops knew the story and looked the other way.

Billy had gotten used to it all gradually, so nothing had seemed odd. Only now he wondered, because he wondered about everything. Shinner had bought the building outright with an inheritance years before, and the family lived upstairs. He had no overhead and a pretty good business; there weren't money problems but the rooms upstairs looked impoverished. A rug, one long couch, a cheap maple coffee table, and a color TV console in the living room. Arrangement of blue plastic flowers on the console. The kitchen with its Formica table and chairs, its prefab cabinets and old sink. A dishwasher, outcast and new, off by itself on one wall. A low ceiling full of pipes. Kato's bedroom: white child's bureau, big stuffed animals, presents from Billy, on the floor a double bed on a frame. Dime store full-length mirror he'd helped her mount on the back of the door, the closed door. They kept a box of rubbers under the bed, though Shinner would never have bothered looking.

He liked Billy well enough. Sundays, Billy ate dinner with them in the kitchen, Rice-a-Roni and pork chops Kato cooked in a big frying pan. The two brothers, three and four years older than Kato, ate when they passed through the kitchen. The boys more or less roomed above the billiard hall and kept no particular hours. The older one was 4F—*basketball, hell,* Shinner said, *he messed up that elbow leaning on too many pool tables*—and worked in the mines near town. The other played football at Lynchburg State. Week nights, whoever was around ate downstairs at the counter: hot dogs, fries, hamburgers made at the grill, and beer. Sundays, anytime, Billy loved being with Kato above the billiard hall. He liked all the nearly empty rooms. He loved how she looked, like she didn't need anything else around her.

Last spring, senior year, when it was certain he'd go away to college, things had gotten bad between them. She flirted with other guys and went out with some. He wasn't about to ask her why or yell at her; he just got his class ring back and stayed away. Now she was going out with some city cop who hung around the billiard room; cops ate lunch there. Billy saw her now and then, not much; she didn't hang around with the high-school crowd anymore. The cop was seven or eight years older—apparently they went to Winfield to supper clubs, and skeet shooting. Maybe it wasn't so strange; cops around town had always gone easy on Shinner, and the whole family had reason to be nice to them. But what did she think was happening to her?

Danner had asked Billy, around graduation, if he'd thought of marrying Kato. He hadn't. He didn't want to be married. He couldn't see Kato married either, to anybody. But nothing was right anymore.

His parents were glad when it ended, especially Jean. She'd talked to him about it in July or so. She was sorry, she told him, but after all, he and Kato were so young. And Kato might be a nice person—her father and Jean had gone to high school together and, no matter what anyone said, there wasn't a better person in this town than Shinner Black—but Kato had never had a mother to teach her certain things. Would she ever have made the kind of home Billy had grown up in, the kind he might someday want?

Billy didn't know what he wanted. Jean had gone on speaking softly, with such worry in her voice that Billy didn't say anything back, only nodded. But all he could think of while she talked was the sound of her footsteps, every early morning all summer, up the stairs from the basement. Ever since they'd moved from the house on Brush Fork, almost two years ago, she'd slept down there in a single bed. Billy hadn't paid much attention before, but that summer he began to notice everything. He got up early, drove the fifteen miles to his job, opened the swimming area by nine; but before he could drive to the park, where it was quiet and lush, he had to listen to his mother's footsteps. He lay in bed, waking up, and listened. Her steps were heavy with a resignation he couldn't fathom. Later he sat by the river and heard the rush of water. He stared at the moving surface, and finally all other sounds left his mind.

After he went away to school, he missed the river badly.

He was in Bellington by four in the afternoon. November light went fast and it was already dusk. On impulse, he drove through an alley off Main Street and pulled up behind the billiard room. The barbecue grill he'd bought the previous spring was still on the fire escape landing; it would rust in the winter if she didn't take it inside soon. Didn't seem right to use the fire escape steps, so he went around front. He didn't want to walk through the billiard room and see people and talk, so he went in the other door, up the dark, narrow stairs that led to the upstairs apartment. His walking was loud in the enclosed hallway. Before he got to the top to ring the bell, she opened the door and looked down. He stopped, waiting.

Dressed in a T-shirt and jeans, barefoot, she hugged her arms in the chilly hallway. "Billy."

He thought he must seem like a fool. He said nothing and leaned against the wall. She looked like she'd been sleeping, her hair tousled. It occurred to him she might be with someone. "Anyone here?"

"No. I was taking a nap." She walked down two steps. "Billy, is anything wrong?"

He shook his head. "Just wanted to talk to you. Haven't seen you in a while. How you doing?"

"Okay. . . ."

"Can I come in, or do you want me to go?"

"You want to come in?" She shrugged, flustered. "Sure. Come in."

He followed her inside. She shut the door behind them and he looked around. After the carpeted dorm with its modernistic furniture, the square room looked even more spare. She sat down on the couch a little nervously; he sat beside her but not too near. "So," he asked, "how have you been?"

"Pretty good. I've been working downstairs, but last week I got a job at the newspaper."

"Yeah? Reporting?" *Keep talking,* he thought, *it'll get better.*

"Just typing, but maybe later they'll let me do more. I mean, at least write up birth announcements and things."

"Kato, that's good."

She nodded and took a cigarette from a pack on the table. She tamped it down and lit it, then picked up an ash tray and put it on the cushion between them. She tucked her legs under her and turned toward him. "So. You met any nice people up there?"

At first he thought she was mocking him, then understood again that she was nervous. He didn't want her to be, but it encouraged him. She was asking him about girls. "Well, yeah, I mean it's real easy. But no one special."

Her face betrayed no relief. "How is school?"

"I quit school this morning." It was the first time he'd said it. He leaned a little forward and put his hands on his knees, then clasped them. He realized he was sitting as his father did, and he sat back. "Maybe I shouldn't have come by, but I wanted to talk to someone before I told my parents. I guess I wanted to talk to you."

She didn't answer right away but looked across the room at the window. Then she tapped the ash of the cigarette and looked at him. "Why did you quit?"

"I didn't want to be there. I was just waiting until December really, to find out what my number was. Like, if I did what I was supposed to do and sat through all the classes, my number would be high, and then I could quit." He shook his head. "Stupid. The number is going to be the same, whatever. If it's low, there's no deferment anyway. School isn't going to help. And later, I don't want these grades on my record. I haven't really tried. I couldn't get myself to care."

"You thought about what you're going to do?"

"Maybe stay up there, get a job. I've got the dorm room anyway until the term ends. Or I could come back here. I might go south after Christmas. I could always get a job tending bar in a resort town."

"What would you do if you stayed in Bellington?"

He felt flushed, listening to her simple questions. He heard her talk with an almost physical ache of pleasure. "Would you like it if I stayed around?" He asked uncertainly; he was sure she'd tell him the truth.

She raised her brows in puzzlement and spoke slowly. "I don't know. It would be kind of complicated for me."

"You mean because of this guy you're going out with."

She held the cigarette high in her hand and the smoke, a thin, constant smoke, disappeared into the room. "You know, it wasn't like things were great for me over the summer, when you never even came around. I used to just talk to him once in a while, when he came in for lunch. He was new around here and kind of quiet, old-fashioned. Finally he asked my father if he could take me out sometime."

Billy imagined Shinner's befuddlement and smiled. "What did Shinner say?"

"He said, 'It's no business of mine. Ask her.'" Kato laughed.

Billy nodded. He said, after a pause, "I kept wondering if it wasn't strange, going out with a cop. Does he get upset about some of your habits?"

She put the cigarette out. "I don't do dope in front of him. I don't smoke much dope at all anymore. Turning into a drinker, I guess."

"What?"

"Not like that, Billy. I'm not that dumb."

Maybe Shinner was worse. "I never thought you were dumb at all," Billy said softly.

Far off, they heard a siren. Fire truck barreling up Quality Hill and on out. The corners of her mouth tightened. "Sorry. It's just that Dad is driving me crazy lately. Soon as I save up some money at the paper, I might get my own place."

"He drinking more?"

She opened one hand in a dismissive gesture. "Anyway. You ought to stay around if you want to. Don't let it depend on me, but I mean, maybe the Park Service would hire you back."

Billy let himself imagine it. "I liked the Park Service, even if the pay was bad. I guess they need people in winter. Be nice there in the snow."

She nodded. "They patrol the park in jeeps. You have to have four-wheel drive on those roads."

"Yeah." He touched her shoulder, then moved his hand away. "You could ride around with me and help put out hay for the deer. Or maybe not. Your friend would get mad."

"He doesn't tell me what to do," she said flatly.

"That would be a mistake," Billy agreed.

She smiled a little and leaned forward to touch the edge of the ash tray.

"Does he try to tell you what to do?" Billy watched her hand, her long fingers.

"Not exactly. He just . . . expects me to be more, like, ladylike, than I am. He seems surprised sometimes. I don't know, he's nothing like me. He says most girls he knows only sleep with the one they're going to marry. I told him I was kind of married to you, if he wants to think of it that way."

"Is that how you thought of it?"

She looked up guiltily, as though she'd admitted too much. "No. Not until lately anyway."

It was dark outside. The room had gotten dark, and it was cold. The small neon light that advertised Black's Billiards blinked on and off downstairs, throwing up a muted rosiness that came and went beyond the living room windows. They could hear, through the floor, the soft clicks of pool cues, the thumps of balls dropping into pockets. The sounds were so known and so familiar, so comforting. Billy felt an edge release inside him. "Quiet down there," he said. "No jukebox?"

"Broken," Kato said. "Dad hasn't got it fixed yet."

"Well, I better go." He started to stand but she stood first.

She walked over and said, from above him, very near, "I don't mean we should change things, but I wish you wouldn't leave yet."

He stood to meet her halfway but they were on the couch again and he couldn't hold her close enough, hard enough, his face pressed tight against her, sounds of surprise and relief in his throat. She felt more real than anything had felt in all these months.

Though it was only ten, his mother's house was in darkness. He stood on the stoop and considered sleeping in his car but, no, he'd driven here to tell her. He rang the bell. Inside, the hallway light went on. As the doorknob turned and the door swung open, he realized she might have wakened out of sleep to loud and unexpected sounds. "Mom," he called, "it's just me, Billy."

"Billy?" She was at the door, her face in shadow. "What's wrong?"

"Nothing's wrong. Everything is fine."

"What do you mean? Don't you have classes tomorrow?" She opened the door wide and stepped back to let him enter.

"No, not tomorrow. I'm sorry I woke you up." He took his

jacket off and hung it over the newel post, and hugged her. "You're turning in early these days."

"I wasn't really sleeping." She looked at him confusedly. "Did you eat dinner? Are you hungry?"

"No, I'm not hungry."

She drew her robe closer around her, the long red woolen robe he remembered from last year and other years. She'd worn it every night, sitting in a straight-backed chair in the small den, reading or knitting while the television droned low in a corner. Last winter, Billy had come in late to find his father asleep in the downstairs bedroom, and Jean in the den with both doors of the little room shut, *to keep the heat in.* Sometimes he sat down with her to watch the last of the eleven o'clock news or a few minutes of a late movie. She was quiet and relaxed; Billy felt as though they were alone in the house. Later he walked upstairs soundlessly on the carpeted steps; Danner was at college and the whole upstairs was his domain.

"I don't even have a bed made for you," Jean said. "I'll have to get some sheets out of the closet." She turned.

"Mom," he said, and waited until she faced him. "I withdrew from school today."

"You what?" She sat down on the piano bench in the living room.

"Here's the refunded tuition, and I'll pay you back for the dorm costs." He took two hundred-dollar bills from his pocket and, standing beside her, put the money on top of the piano.

She made no move and only stared at him, bewildered.

He sat down on the couch opposite her. "I knew during the summer that I'd made plans for school because there was really no other choice, with the draft. I was accepted and I thought I should go, give it a chance. The longer I went to classes, the surer I was . . . that I don't know what I want to do."

"Billy, no nineteen-year-old kid has to decide in the first semester of college what he wants to do. You're there to take your time and find out what you want to do."

"I found out I don't want to be in school."

"When you find yourself in basic training you may wish you were in school."

He smiled at her. "That doesn't work anymore, Mom. No more school deferments after December. Wouldn't matter if I was number one on the honor roll. Quitting school doesn't affect my draft status one way or the other." He paused, watching her.

He didn't want to sound fresh. "Listen, it's a waste of money for me to go to college right now."

The tick of the kitchen clock was loud in the house. She looked at him angrily. "Since it's my money, why don't you let me decide when it's wasted. And I know they didn't give you any refund this late."

He didn't answer.

She sighed. "Isn't it a waste to quit now, when the semester is nearly over?"

His eyes were tired and he fought the impulse to touch them. He felt as though he'd been en route to this house for weeks. "When I really decide, for myself, that I want to go to school, I want to start clean. These grades, these courses some adviser signed me up for at registration, mean nothing to me."

His mother looked at him levelly. "Were you failing, Billy? Why didn't you tell me if you were having trouble? You always said you were doing fine."

"I was. My grades weren't good but I wasn't failing." Now he did rub his eyes, and he touched his forehead. He could smell Kato on his hand, the perfumed, musky smell of her neck and throat. He didn't want to think about her now; he wanted to talk to Jean and make her understand. "Mom, if it turns out my number is high, I want to work for a year. I'll get a job, either here or maybe farther south, and save some money. If my number is low and I go into the army, I don't want to have spent these weeks going to classes. Either way, I did the right thing."

Jean's hands were open in her lap. She looked down at her palms and said slowly, "Is this my fault? Have I made things so confusing?"

"No, Mom. Maybe I went along with going to school because I didn't want to cause trouble when everyone was upset anyway. But keeping on with that mistake isn't going to help—"

"With my mistakes?" she asked gently.

"I don't think you made a mistake. You did what you had to do. I just wish you'd understand—I did, too. I'm in a bind like yours in a way." He looked up at her, as though for help with words. "I guess that doesn't make any sense."

"No, it does." She looked at the floor and bent over to pick up a bit of fuzz from the carpet. Absently she held a blur of gold threads, her fingers touching lightly. "Lord," she said, "I hope you haven't given yourself a terrible birthday present."

"I don't think I have."

She nodded. Across the gulf of the floor between them, her

gaze was direct and quietly frightened. She looked more vulnerable than he'd ever seen her. Billy suddenly wondered if he'd ever sit across some room listening to his own kid and get scared.

"It's going to be all right," he told his mother now. "Things will turn out."

DECEMBER

Billy picked his sister up at the courthouse the night of December 2. Near evening the day-long drizzle had turned to constant rain. There was no bus station anymore in Bellington, and Trailways let people off on Main Street at the courthouse steps. Billy drove up and saw Danner standing under the portico of the domed building, alone, hems of her jeans wet to the ankles, collar of her denim jacket turned up. *After all the money she spent on clothes in high school,* Jean had said as Billy left the house, *Danner dresses like a bum.* Danner had no raincoat, no umbrella, but she had a larger suitcase than was necessary for a visit of a few days. Billy got out of the car to help her, but before he could cross the street she was halfway to him, the rain drenching her. They threw the suitcase in the back seat and pulled both doors shut; then he handed her a towel.

"You look drowned," he told her as she dried her face. "I can't believe you rode the bus to Bellington in a storm like this. They must have stopped at every little Podunk on Route 20. No wonder it took three hours."

Danner laughed. "At least it wasn't snow. The bus would have ended up in a drift in Peel Tree."

"You want to go down by Shinner's and have a beer with Kato before we go home?"

She looked up as Billy started the car, a little surprised. "Sure, I guess. You seeing Kato again since you came home?"

"Some." There were no cars on Main Street. Billy ran a red light and turned the corner down past the movie house. "Why didn't you wait until the weekend to come home?"

She threw the towel in the back seat. "I saw the lottery list this morning and I got the first bus that came through Bellington. I want to talk to you, Billy. Before we go inside."

Billy parked opposite the billiard room, then pointed across the street. "Take a look at Shinner's new sign." The long horizontal sign snapped lazily off and on behind the downward slant of the rain. BILLIARDS, it said in alternate hot pink and blue, waves of the colors rippling, muted in rain.

"Big," Danner said. "Not exactly classy, but very noticeable. Billy, can you turn the heat on?"

Billy did. "All right, I want a beer. What do you want to tell me?"

"Just hear me out, okay?" She looked down at her bare hands, her long hair dripping onto her jacket. With the heat on, Billy could smell the dampness on her, almost smell rain. She looked back up at him. "Billy, you've got to make some plans. You don't have to let them send you over there."

"You mean Fort Knox? Basic training?"

"You know what I mean, Billy. Don't make fun of me. This is not funny."

"I'm not laughing, Danner." The motor of the Camaro idled and the windshield wipers thwacked, regular as metronomes.

"I've brought some money with me, a thousand dollars. And an address in Canada. Saturday you're supposed to drive me back to the University. We'll say you're staying overnight with some school friends, and when we get to Montreal, we'll phone and say where we are. I'll stay a couple of days and take a bus back."

"Where did you get a thousand dollars?"

"Emergency Student Loans."

"You got the money that fast, in one day?"

"No. I applied last week, just in case." She gazed out the windshield, then turned to him. "Oh God, please listen to me. One way or the other, they're going to fuck you up. Look, if you're standing on a railroad track and a locomotive is coming closer, very fast, don't you step off the track? Don't you get the hell out of the way?"

"Not until the last minute." He looked away from her and switched off the wipers. Rain immediately runneled on the windshield, distorting the street to colors on a black shine.

"You can't wait, Billy. If you leave after you're inducted, you're AWOL, you're a criminal. If you leave now, you're a resister. A lot of people think resisters will be pardoned, maybe in just a few years."

"You mean the draft counselors at the University think so."

She didn't miss a beat. "Draft counselors everywhere think so. But I didn't get the address from them. A girl in my dorm has a sister in Montreal."

He smiled at her. Lighten it up. "A pretty sister?"

But she looked at him, frustrated, fearful, her face open and naked, and bit her lips. "Please," she said, "please think about this."

"What the fuck, Danner," he said quietly, "don't you know I've thought about it? I thought before I quit school and I've thought all month, selling trousers up there at Rossing's. Hardly anyone comes into Rossing's. I had time to think about it a lot."

Danner looked past his face at the billiards sign, but he knew she wasn't seeing it. She was planning her next remark, some way to convince him.

"Listen," he said, "if it was possible to avoid the army, I would. But my number is nineteen. I'm not going to Canada for ten years, I'm not going to Canada at all. I decided I'd go with the numbers."

"Don't be an idiot," she said angrily. "They're not your numbers."

"I don't feel that way," he said, raising his voice. "Things are in the cards. I could buy it right here in Bellington, crack up my car on the Winfield road, like that college kid did last weekend."

"That's stupid reasoning," she yelled back. "You don't put yourself where bad things happen."

"Bad things can happen anywhere!" He caught himself then and sat back. "You don't reason through these things. The best way to be lucky is to take what comes and not be a coward." He looked silently into the rain. "I'm going to go. It's in the cards."

"What cards?" She was almost whispering.

"Everyone's cards." He looked over at her. "It'll be different for you after I go."

"Jesus, I'm not worried about me."

Billy touched her hands and they were cold. He held both her hands hard between his. "The fuckers won't do me in. I'll stay off the ground if they send me, get into an air crew. I'll keep my ass in the air."

"Great. Then you'll have farther to fall." Danner had slumped down in the seat beside him, and she moved her legs toward the heating vent.

"Please," he said, encircling her forearm with his hand, "take the money back to Student Loans, and don't give me any more suggestions. Not about Canada and not about Nam. And don't mope around all through Christmas. Weren't you going to go to Florida for New Year's with your pals? I want you to go ahead and go."

She looked away from him, her eyes wet.

"Don't be a pain," he said gently. "You're not the one with the number. It's not your show."

"All right, all right. Let's go have a beer." She caught his arm

as he turned off the ignition. "But if you change your mind, you'll
tell me."

"I will." He opened the door of the car and the rain asserted
its steady patter. "When we get inside, be sure to tell Shinner you
like the sign."

The first heavy snow blanketed Bellington on Christmas Eve.
Billy sat in the living room. He listened to his mother and Danner
in the kitchen and gazed at the tree, a six-foot pine decked out in
lights and ornaments and gold trim. The thing had been hell to
get through the kitchen door and into the holder, since Danner
wasn't strong enough to help much. Jean had swathed the metal
holder with a wide length of hemmed red corduroy. Billy and
Danner had marked the change silently; always before there had
been a simple white bedsheet under the tree, to look like snow.
But the dining room table was familiar, set with the white damask
cloth, the silver service, the Havilland china. Billy knew the name
because Jean had always referred to the white, gold-scalloped
plates as *my mother's Havilland,* washed before and after use each
Christmas and Easter. The kitchen radio played carols and the
house was filled with smells of roast turkey and yams. The day
felt long and slow and full; since he'd left school, each day had
seemed completely separate from any other.

Jean was doing pretty well. She'd wept easily the first couple of
weeks after the lottery, but then she determined they'd have a
normal Christmas. Well, not exactly normal. Dinner on Christmas
Eve, since he and Danner would eat the big noon meal tomorrow
with all the relatives at Bess's, with Mitch.

"Billy, you want another egg nog?" Danner leaned out of the
kitchen doorway. "Or straight bourbon?"

Jean's voice, from the vicinity of the stove: "Don't you dare
give him straight bourbon."

"No thanks," Billy told them. "Since you two are drinking so
hard, I believe I'll stay sober."

Danner looked nice in black velvet. Jean's reproof: *I haven't
seen you in a dress since Billy's high-school graduation.* Now his
sister smiled and disappeared again. Billy knew she'd made careful preparations for tomorrow; a special joint rolled in red and
green papers to smoke in the car on the way to Bess's house. But
he wasn't sure he'd partake. Though he didn't leave for basic
until January 5, the relatives would all feel they had to mention
his going into the army. Only Mitch would not refer to it. *Damn*

it, was all he'd said to Billy, his face grave, the morning the lottery list was published.

Radio music in the kitchen increased slightly in volume; Danner came into the living room and sat with Billy on the couch. "How do you think Mom is doing?" she asked in a low voice.

"Good."

Danner nodded. "I think I may go to Florida, but I'll leave on the 26 and be back on the 2. Then stay a few days after you have to go. She shouldn't be alone then." She took a drink of her bourbon and Coke. "You and Kato exchanging presents?"

"Tomorrow night. I got her a gold necklace, a chain. Something she can keep. Real pretty."

"Want me to wrap it for you?"

"They wrapped it at the store. Otherwise, I would have already asked you."

Danner looked at the tree. "What ever happened to that cop of hers?"

"I guess he's biding his time. Kato must have told him I'm on my way to foreign parts, though so far it's only Kentucky." He touched Danner's arm. "You look cold, you've got goose bumps."

"It's colder out here than in the kitchen." She looked down at her drink.

"Kato told me he was in Nam in '65. He's only been a cop for a year."

"Gee, Kato's turning into a real heartbreaker. First you, now him."

"That's not how it is, Danner. We don't advertise things. I don't stay over there. Now we're like all the other couples in Bellington, we make it in my car."

She smiled. "Cars aren't bad."

"Takes flexibility."

A pause.

Danner frowned. "Do you think she's sleeping with both of you?"

Billy shook his head and gave his sister a sideways glance. "I don't worry about those details. I don't ask her if she sleeps with him. That's her business, and his.

"I bet she isn't," Danner said slowly, and folded her arms, "not now."

"I think you're right," Billy said.

"Right about what?" Their mother stood by the dinner table, holding the big platter of roast turkey.

"Mom," Danner reprimanded, "you should have let me bring that in for you."

"Who do you think carried it home from the store? It's not much heavier now." She smiled, pretty in her white wool dress. Billy had given her a corsage, a white gardenia, and she'd kept it in the refrigerator until five minutes ago. The white flower was just opening, ribboned with red satin and a sprig of holly. Billy knew she'd keep the ribbons in a drawer for years.

They put the rest of the food on the table together: potatoes, peas, yams, gravy, bread dressing with walnuts, relishes, all in china serving dishes. Finally they sat down.

"Enough for a party of eight," Danner said. "Mom, maybe we didn't need quite such a big turkey."

"We count for eight," Jean responded, "and this is a celebration. Besides, these leftovers will last until the army comes for us."

Billy caught Danner's warning glance. "Right," he said, "and then you can always ship crates of turkey sandwiches to Fort Knox."

Jean handed Billy the carving knife and fork. She'd put the platter of meat near his plate. "Really, there are things to celebrate. We're together, you don't have to leave until after the holidays, and your sister—did you know she'll make the dean's list this semester?"

"Mom," Danner said, "it's not for sure."

"A toast." Billy raised his glass, then asked in a stage whisper, "Who is the dean, anyway?"

"Bob Hope," Danner answered.

"Danner," Jean said seriously, "you should go ahead and go to Florida, since your friends are going and you have a ride. You've worked hard, and you've been such a help to me, too—." She stopped talking, her voice quavering.

"Come home with a tan like Bob Hope's," Billy injected quickly. "I'll supervise here in Bellington."

Danner unfolded her napkin. "You mean you'll supervise Black's Billiards."

"Exactly. But first I'll eat my dinner." He picked up the carving knife and made ready.

"Wait." Jean held up one hand. "Let's say the blessing."

"Good idea." Danner fixed Billy with an encouraging look. "Billy, the floor is yours."

"Do I know a blessing?" Billy put the knife down. "I'll make one up."

Their mother shook her head. "You act as though you were raised as heathens."

"We'll hold hands for luck." Danner crossed her wrists as though taken captive.

But they did hold hands, Jean at one side of the square table, Billy and Danner at either end. Danner couldn't quite reach Billy; she moved her chair closer and arched one arm over the steaming food. Their fingertips met in a pyramid.

"Secret signal," Billy said, and stood to grasp her hand. Pewter bells on the front door moved in the wind; he remembered the snow outside, drifting along the street. When they were children, in the country on Brush Fork, the snow drifted magically high. They'd worn bulky mittens impossible to lose, mittens strung on yarn around their necks and through the sleeves of their snowsuits.

"Start talking," Danner said, "it'll come to you." She and Jean bowed their heads and waited, smiling.

Billy spoke, words from one of the old prayers, but behind his closed eyes played a memory of startling clarity: watching the snow plow with Danner, both of them small, standing in snow to their knees. The big yellow machine rumbling by, slow, all-powerful. Engine roar, shrill jangling of chains. The powdery snow thrown up in fanned continuous spray as the heavy machine pressed on.

December 31. Snow on his boots, stamping his feet on the back porch of the white house beside the hospital. Chains of the dismantled swing moved in the wind, and the lattice of the porch roof was built up with thick snow so wet that the square spaces of the lattice work were solidly snowed in. Snow made the gray light whiter; he stamped his feet and heard them inside—his father and Aunt Bess moving from their chairs to the kitchen door: Mitch coughing, his tread heavy; and Aunt Bess moving stiffly, laced into her corsets. The coal bucket was full beside the door and laced with snow, the black lumps jagged and big, showing snow like a powder. Billy took off his gloves and brushed the snow away; the coal was so cold it left no smear on his fingers. By now they were at the door and the sound of the knob turning was loud. Aunt Bess was there, behind the screen, his father hovering beyond her like a wall. Her face wore that pleased, surprised question, the thick eyeglasses exaggerating her inquiring gaze.

"Well hello, Mister," she said. "You're up early."

Mitch motioned for Billy to come inside. "Get on in here, let's not let Bess get cold." He shut the door behind them all and clapped a hand on Billy's shoulder. "Got some spuds cooking. You want some eggs?"

"No thanks." Billy put his snowy gloves in his pocket and unzipped his jacket.

"Big mistake," Mitch said, "I make good eggs." He nodded at Bess. "Even Bess eats them, and she's hard to please."

"Your father is a wonderful cook," Bess told Billy. "Now, there's no question about it, we all know I can't cook." She went to the stove to pour hot water into two cups of instant coffee.

Mitch gave Billy an amused look, then sat down again.

Billy stood awkwardly in the small room as Bess brought the coffee to the table. Billy took a breath. He would just have to go ahead and tell them. "Mitch, Danner called last night from Florida. She got into some trouble. She got arrested for possession."

"Possession of what? What are you talking about?"

"Possession of marijuana. Danner got busted."

His father looked at him, incredulous. Behind him Aunt Bess touched the back of his chair.

"You mean drugs," Mitch said. "Is Danner in jail?"

"Yes. Mom went down to the bank this morning to borrow the money for bail. She had to borrow two thousand dollars."

"Jesus Christ." His father bowed his head and leaned his elbows on the table. He turned his head to one side and touched his forehead, then covered his eyes with his hand. For a strange moment Billy thought he was praying.

Aunt Bess still stood, gripping the back of Mitch's chair as though holding it in place. "But Danner is all right, she's not hurt."

"No, no, she's okay. She should be out of the jail by tonight." Billy stepped closer to the table but kept his hands in his pockets. His father sat silently, with no movement in his body. He moved his hand now to support his forehead and tears fell on the checked tablecloth. Billy felt very warm, as though he were going to be dizzy. Snow was falling past the kitchen windows in big wet flakes; the yard and bushes on the other side of the glass were a smooth, unbroken white. The kitchen was lit with snowlight, indirect and off-white. The warmth of the room was inconsistent with the light and the consciousness of snow; Bess was baking bread, that was it—Billy hadn't smelled it till now.

He looked at his great-aunt and she faced him from behind his father, unblinkingly. She seemed to be looking straight through Billy, through the walls of the house as well, sadly and evenly. She was very thin and held her rounded shoulders high, of some long habit; her stance lent the front of her body a concave aspect from chest to knees. Now she moved to give Mitch her white handkerchief, taking the small square from the pocket of her sweater, unfolding it, placing it near him. Her gesture was deliberate and unobtrusive. She sat down, very straight, on the tall stool beside the hoosier.

Mitch refolded the handkerchief, his eyes wet. "I hope your mother is satisfied now," he said.

"It's not her fault," Billy said.

Mitch continued as though Billy hadn't spoken. "This would never have happened."

They were all quiet. Snow was falling and a car moved through the alley, its motor muffled and sputtering. There was the sound of chains on ice as tires spun for traction. New snow would be flying up all around the wheels.

"You never know what can happen," Bess said.

Her words were so heavy in the room that Billy found himself saying more than he'd intended. "Dad, they only had a couple of grams between the four of them."

"Grams? What the hell do you mean? What do you know about grams?"

"I mean they only had a small amount."

His father made no response.

"I think she has to stay in the state about a week," Billy said, "until the arraignment. The father of one of the boys flew down last night. I guess he's arranging things. They already have a lawyer, and rooms in a motel."

"What motel?"

"A place called the Sea View. In Naples." Billy dropped his voice, uncertain how much Danner would want Mitch to know. "They were camping out on a beach in Naples."

Mitch stood, scowling. "You get me the phone number of that motel. I want to talk to Danner."

Billy nodded. "Mom has it. I'd better get back, she's pretty upset."

His father didn't answer. Billy gestured at Bess apologetically. "I'll call or come down as soon as I hear anything."

"Yes," Bess said, "of course you will."

He turned and let himself quietly out of the house, pulling the door tight behind him and closing the screen door so it latched. The look of the old woman's face stayed with him as he walked through deep snow to his car. He tried to imagine Danner in jail and couldn't. Bail would be arranged by afternoon. They wouldn't send four kids up for three grams of marijuana, especially when the nearly empty box of dope was found at the campsite and none of them admitted to possession anyway. Even though it was a felony charge, getting them off would probably be a technicality. . And the lawyer's making some money. But his parents wouldn't see it that way. They thought Billy was going into the army and Danner was going wrong, all in the same week.

When he touched her there, through her clothes, he felt a small hardness throbbing like a pulse point. Her whole body, spread-eagle on the seat of the car, turned on that hardness. Kato draped one leg over the back of the seat and the other over the column of the steering wheel so that Billy was just at the vee of her crotch, leaning back against the door on his side and watching her. She threw her arms out as though floating on water and kept her eyes closed, and Billy watched her with no self-consciousness. She worked up to her own feeling a little shyly, in private; when she couldn't keep her eyes closed any longer that was a signal. If he kept touching her then, it was an unspoken promise he wouldn't stop, and when she came her whole body rippled lengthwise with a delicate vibration that reminded Billy of horses shivering their flanks. Often he didn't let her go that far; he liked to feel the trembling tight around him, from inside her. Her muscles seemed to imitate a spastic lapping of water. It was so gentle and felt so foreign, so mysterious, something fluttering against the inner walls of a cage. To Billy it didn't seem part of either one of them; if he was lost in his own sensation, he missed hers altogether and couldn't tell if she'd felt it. So he tried to wait and while they were touching each other, taking turns and trading off, he was priming himself to wait; they were intent and usually stopped talking except for involuntary sounds. This was a drug between them; there was the weightless high of dope but they were excruciatingly alert and wound tight. They could go on for hours.

Finally they took their clothes off and the heated interior of the car was like a capsule with steamed windows, drifting in space. They lay down in this isolated nowhere and cried out with relief at his first thrust inside her. They made love every way possible in the cramped room of the front seat, one of them changing position when they felt him almost coming. At last they let go and rode their own movement, not thinking, racing: he opened his eyes for an instant and a small shape in the steamy window had teared clear. The snowy hill below the plant lot was a luminous slant in the winter dark. Far below, cars moved on the Winfield

road. Billy saw the lit points of headlights in the midnight blue of
the cold air, but knowledge of what he was looking at was
nowhere inside him.

First he was conscious again of sounds; he heard the hum of
the car heater, he heard Kato breathing. "You there?" he whispered.

"I'm here."

He sat up, pulling out of her as she touched him. She'd used
their clothes as a pillow; now she gave him his pants and shirt and
pulled her coat on over her nakedness. "I'd feel better if we
parked behind the drive-in," she said. "It's spooky here, all these
old trucks."

Billy zipped his Levi's. "You scared?" He circled her throat
with his hands, pulled her closer and kissed her forehead. "I used
to come here when I was a kid, same trucks. Doesn't seem spooky
to me. Besides, there are always two or three cars parked behind
the drive-in—the police swing by. And who knows which police."

"He wouldn't," Kato said. "I'd never speak to him again." She
pulled her jeans on under the coat.

"What have you told him, anyway, all this time?"

"I haven't told him anything lately. About a month ago, I just
said I couldn't see him for a while." She reached into her purse
for a cigarette.

"Kato, suppose I wasn't getting drafted?"

"We were seeing each other again before you knew you were
getting drafted."

"But not as much." He raised his brows, smiling. "Maybe you
have a thing for uniforms."

She lit the cigarette. Now he saw her clearly in the glow of the
match; her eyes glistened with moisture. What was she feeling?
Her eyes always looked wet after they made love, but the wetness
seemed an automatic response, like the tears of someone choking
or sneezing.

Kato held the cigarette and looked at Billy, her hand shaking a
little. "Maybe I do, Billy," she said, and her voice broke.

He touched the steering wheel. It was cold and suddenly he
was cold; he felt the cold dark seeping into the car. He leaned
forward, switched the heat on higher. The blower hummed.

"I'll write to you, Billy." She pursed her lips when she exhaled
smoke.

"Maybe you will at first," he said carefully. "But it's okay.
You've already written to me."

She flung her blond hair back from her face and moved over

near him. "Anytime you come home, call me. You'll be back on a leave before they send you anywhere, won't you? No matter what people tell you, get in touch with me."

They both sat looking at the patch of night framed in the windshield of the Camaro. It was snowing again. Kato rested one hand on Billy's thigh. There was no sense being jealous, or mad at her. She would always be herself, pretty and tarnished, but honest like a guy was honest. She didn't try to work things around.

"I don't know what will happen," she said. Her hand on his leg moved now, stroking him. "You can always reach me through my father."

Billy gazed into the snow, imagining himself a grunt with a shaved head, buying Shinner Black cups of coffee at the Tap Room or the Rainbow. *Where's Kato, Shinner? Give me a phone number.* Shinner would smell of Rebel Yell and he'd answer with a bleary, good-natured silence. Billy shook his head.

Kato glanced at him. "I know, but eventually he'd tell you."

"I suppose so."

"You heard anything else about Danner?"

"She's staying in a motel. Her arraignment isn't until the day after I leave. I bet she's having a great New Year's Eve."

"I guess." Kato leaned forward and put her cigarette out. "Do you want to go by that party?"

"No, this is my party. 1969 can end right here."

Kato laughed. "I think it already did."

Billy pulled her close and put his face against her hair, smelling a sweetish odor of cream rinse and tobacco smoke. Her hair wasn't usually so light in winter; she must be bleaching it again. She had a kind of sexiness that wouldn't diminish as she grew older. Middle-aged, she would look knowing and tired, he thought, her blondness brassier.

She rubbed her eyes with her hands, like a kid, then looped both arms in his and settled against him. "I wish we could just go to sleep," she said.

The snow blew now in minute flakes that swirled like sand. There must be a long narrow beach behind the Sea View Motel in Naples, Florida; Billy couldn't quite see it but he imagined the sound of surf. Here the wind was a constant murmur with snow inside it. His mother would be lying awake in the dark, listening.

GOOD MORNING TO YOU, LIEUTENANT

by Larry Heinemann

We can stand at the crest of the town's one good hill, James, and pause to get quiet and comfortable and still, and listen to the night sounds. At this late hour of the night the tranquil murmuring hum of the river, cascading over the rock-and-cement spillway under the bridge, yonder, is almost the only sound to be heard. That constant rush of water is the hush that has lulled many a strapping newborn infant to sleep in its time. That hush is the last sobering sound heard suddenly, abruptly, in many a death-bed room, as clean and even and smooth as the curl in the neck of a glass cider jug.

But that is not the only night sound to be heard in town, James. We can sit on the thick slate curb, under the parkway walnut trees, and hear the squeak of wicker chairs; the tumble of ice melting to slivers in glasses of Coke and tea and whiskey; the whisper of bedroom conversation that is all hisses, and the snapping and popping of buttons; women flapping and fluttering their light, summery dress fronts like bellows; the shrill squeal of children racing through swirling clouds of fireflies with quart canning jars, a game better than tag; someone spitting on dry pavement; the snick snick snick of the tails of a loose pack of town dogs on the schoolyard blacktop. Then the sound that all but stops the others, even the dogs—the tap, step-tap of that gimpy kid wounded in the war, that guy Paco, who washes dishes by hand at the Texas Lunch, that greasy spoon across the way from the Greyhound depot.

All those night sounds bristle, brushing back and forth under the trees, and everyone who's sitting back, listening, hears. And

155

we hear, don't we, James—the river pouring over the spillway, the ring of jar lids, the giggles, the clear click of the cast-brass tip of Paco's cane.

And that girl, with the rooms across the hall from the head of the stairs at the transient hotel where Paco lives, listens too. (The girl, James—her name Cathy—small-breasted and bony-armed, built small like a smooth-faced, tallish boy, and whenever Paco sees her she is wearing a man's dress shirt with the cuffs rolled a time or two to the middle of her forearms, the shirttails loose at her thighs, a collar as stiff as a military uniform tunic.) Nearly every night the girl will sit on the broad, dusty sill of the alley window over the head of her bed with her small, clean feet drawn up under her, and lean her cheek against the filthy screen. She listens to the river the way a meditative person will gaze into a bonfire, but she doesn't pay it so much as a never-you-mind; doesn't give it so much as a shake of her hair. No, no. She perks her ears with deliberate and uncanny intentness, listening ever so keenly for the sharp click of Paco's black hickory cane on the asphalt, and the sure and steady slight off-rhythm of his walk— tap, step-tap. Her moist sparkling eyes will dart this way and that around the room, and she'll glance out the window, rubbing the cool, smooth, nut-brown skin of her knee (her whole body as brown as toast, James) with the breezy heat of the tin-and-tar back-porch roof rising in her face, and she'll try to count the courses of smoothed herringbone brick in the alley below. She will absentmindedly stare at her own fingers as she strums a limp gold anklet with manicured fingernails. In her mind she will see Paco's hands, bleached-white and water-wrinkled, the sweat-soaked shirt clinging to the hard flat of his stomach; will see that glazed-over, glossy look in his eyes, which in most people is simply work weariness.

Every night when she hears the snap of his cane on the asphalt change to the mellow, hollow thump of the stoop, she will uncurl herself and crawl crablike across her bed. She will primp on the move and brush herself down, using her fingers for a whisk, smoothing down that lime- or peach- or cocoa-colored dress shirt (opened a couple of buttons at the neck), and strike a pose leaning against the warm wood of her door. Sometimes she will hold the door open just so far with her head leaned into the hall as though she's dripping wet and doesn't want to drip on the hallway rug, but the front of that shirt will be nearly all unbut-toned, and there's enough light shining down her front to be teasing, enticing. And sometimes she will put just her head in the light, with her body to one side, and she'll have a glittering gleam in her eye as though she doesn't have a stitch on. And you've got to know, James, that some nights she doesn't, but those nights are for *her* benefit, not Paco's, because being buck naked when she smiles that smirk down at Paco makes her feel so goosey and juicy and naughty, and sometimes she can't help but giggle. She will wait for Paco to come in the front, and stop at the bottom of the stairway and stand stoop-shouldered, leaning so heavily on that goddamned cane some nights it will bow. She will wait for him to raise his eyes and look up through the railing rungs, and see her in the dim amber light of the hallway (the light shining on the smooth, browned skin of her legs and face, looking like dry oval slivers of yellowed, antique ivory). She will stir slightly, waiting for that look in his eyes that is unmistakable in a man who has not been to bed with a woman for a long time. And Paco will nod, almost imperceptibly, and *then* will begin the race, the struggle to get to the top of the stairs before she slips back into her room and closes the door. It is the one solid rule of her game, James. If he can get so much as the tip of his cane in the door before she shuts it, he may come in. ("You can fuck me, Sugar.")

And Paco has struggled up those stairs many a night, ass-whipped tired, his legs tingling and throbbing, wobbly even, his feet sore and sweat-soaked, and that goddamned lye-soap rash on his arms as red as rope burns. Washing dishes by hand ain't no pleasure and it ain't no joke, James.

But tonight, getting in Cathy's doorway doesn't happen. No, no. Tonight he comes up the street and into the hotel, hits the stairs, and just keeps coming. Tonight Paco has been sitting on the damp hard clay of the river bank down by the spillway, listening to the skinny-dippers horsing around in the sand-bottomed shallows downriver from the railroad trestle, drinking beers with Jesse (that lanky, rangy cat with the brown ponytail) half the night, waiting for the air to cool, and there's no telling what time it is.

He limps up the hallway to the left with his skeleton key in one hand and his black hickory cane in the other, works the door open, steps in, and closes it behind him with a slow and heavy click (as firm and final a sound as we are likely to hear in that hotel, James). The hall light vanishes from the room except for a flat, slender sliver of light under the door not any bigger than a piece of oak lath. Paco squeezes his head against the warm and sticky door, squeezing his eyes shut from the pure relief of being home, taking a bit of a breather. Paco's got a still and stuffy, smothering little room, with a crumbling 8 × 10 linoleum sheet, a ragged mahogany dresser with the veneer shredding to splinters, and a coffee-colored bedstead with a brown bedspread. There is a scum of dust in all the corners, and fuzzy, flowered wallpaper you would swear was flocked if you brushed against it in the dark. He rattles around in his darkened room, peeling off his T-shirt, unbuckling his belt and unzipping his fly, scooting his pants down, skivvies and all. Then he flops back on his creaking bed, the way drunks do. His head and arms loll this way and that, and his legs hang over the edge of the bed with the balls of his feet brushing the floor. He sets his hands wide on the raspy, grayish sheets, stares hard at the curling chips of paint above his head, then takes a good long breath, and with a sudden, sharp exhalation, lifts his legs onto the bed. And it's god-awful painful, James. Sometimes the pain shoots straight up his legs and thighs (he can hear the pins grinding against the bone) to his back and arms and fingers, up to his eyes (oh, the grimacing squint wrinkles he will have). The very tips of his fingers tingle as though someone has pricked them.

He takes a long moment to settle in—to get his sore, throbbing legs and the small of his back just so among the lumps. The air is hot and heavy around him, and the sheets are as itchy and scratchy as snapping-dry flannel. (Everything has been warm and sticky and uncomfortable all day, every day, and all the night through, for weeks now. Bread won't rise right. Beer foam looks pale and greasy and slippery. Your clothes bunch thickly at the crotch and cling to your back and down under your arms, for instance, and folks are awkward and ill-tempered most of the time.)

We can take a pause now, and lean down over Paco's thighs and knees and calves, James, even in this little light of his room (there *is* a slice of moon, the 40-watt back-porch light, and the glow of the yellow hall light reflected into the room under the door; this faint, burdensomely warm and oppressive light that gives his room a welcome and intimate air nonetheless, as still and smothering a place as we are likely to come across these warm and stuffy nights, unrelieved by comfort), if we lean down, we could see the many razor-sharp, razor-thin surgical scars, the bone-fragment scars (going every which way) the size of pine-stump splinters, the puckered burn scars (from cooked-off ammunition), looking as though he'd been sprayed with a shovelful of glowing cinders, the deadened, discolored ring of skin at the meatiest part of his thigh where the Bravo Company medic wound the twisted tourniquet, using Paco's own bandanna, though the time for a tourniquet had long since passed. The sallow, thin-faced medic slapped the crook of Paco's elbow to get a vein, and Paco and half the company could hear him grumble, "Come on, you dumbshit grunt motherfucker, give me a goddamned vein," and Paco's arm stung like a son of a bitch, and the medic's dog tags jangled in Paco's face (the same as his old man would rattle the buckle end of his belt in Paco's face before he commenced a licking). And if we looked at Paco's arm we could see the scar of the gouge at the inside of his forearm the size of a pencil stub where the catheter ripped loose when those geek-fucking, shit-for-brains Bravo Company litterbearers dropped Paco down a rain-slick footpath, litter and all. ("You goddamned bullshit fucking Bravo Company Jesus Christ I hope you motherfuckers all die shit!")

We could lean down and take a good hard look, and see all that, James, even in this little light. We could back away, now that we know what we're looking at, and those scars will seem to wriggle and curl, snapping languidly this way and that the same as grubs and night crawlers when you prick them with the barb of a bait hook. It is only an illusion, James, a sly trick of the eye. But that is the way many a frightful thing in this world comes alive—in the dimmest, whitest moonlight, the lowest lamplight.

He lies on his bed, trying to nod off, trying to get as comfortable as the muggy air and sweat-filthy sheets and teasing, tickling ache will allow, but out his window, just the other side of her window, kitty-corner to his, he hears the girl, Cathy, and she's honey-fucking the everlasting daylights out of some guy (Marty-boy, she calls him). There's no mistaking that sloppy glucking sound, the bed squeaking effortlessly and meekly. (Fucking the girl is something Paco has dreamed over and over, James, sprawled spraddle-legged spread-eagle on his creaking, coffee-colored bed-stead bed with the filthy brown bedspread, with this flaccid cock flopped to one side of his aching thighs—oh, how his legs would ache on those nights—his pubic hair fluffy and prickly, almost crackling in the heat, like dry grass.)

Paco doesn't have to strain any to hear, because his bed is shoved alongside the wall under the window. He can slide his hand and arm out the window—over the dust and blistered nicotine streaks and coffee-cup rings—lean out a little, and fin-gertip touch the top of her hair. Cathy sighs slowly and calmly and soothingly—involuntary and contented, Paco thinks to himself—brimful of peace and pleasure.

Now, Cathy had heard Paco fiddle with his key in the lock, heard him fumbling around in his dingy little room, smelled the very beer on his breath. (She thinks his room is depressing—faded wallpaper, no telling *what* the motif was, and that tacky, shabby linoleum. And he's a dingy, dreary, smelly, shabby, *shabby* little man.) And now, with each slippery thrust, she stretches her thin little neck and exhales audibly toward the window. She pulls on Marty-boy's pale, shuddering hips, clawlike, with sedately manicured nails, and sways from side to side as though she were cooing and cuddling an infant (with her thin, pinkish lip between her teeth and a slap-happy grin on her face, as though to say, I get a nice little kick from teasing that gimp, but fucking is nice, and I love it too).

Paco sweats up a storm trying to wish himself sober, trying to wish himself up and out of his bed and straight to the foot of her bed. He wishes Marty-boy (some skinny primary-education major from a teachers' college just outside of town) to hell and gone. He lies on his back, smelling the starched linen and eau de cologne, the pungent tin-and-tar porch roof and the rank sweetness of their sweat. He stares up at the darkened ceiling and the curled chips of paint that hang down as thick as a shedding winter shag. Then suddenly, abruptly, he remembers Pfc. Randy Gallagher's Bangkok R and R tattoo of a red and black dragon that covered the inside of his forearm from his wrist to his elbow (that tattoo a goddamned work of art, everyone said, a regular fucking masterpiece).

Paco sees that tattoo, then suddenly, abruptly, remembers the rape of the VC girl, and the dreams he has had of the rape. He winces and squirms, and his whole body jerks, but he cannot choose but to remember. Gallagher's got this girl by the hair. She isn't just any girl, you understand—not some dirt farmer's wife or one of those god-awful ugly camp-following whores; she isn't some poor son of a bitch's tag-along sister pestering people with her whining, and she isn't some rear-rank slick-sleeve private (who doesn't know dismounted, close-order drill from shit and Shinola) who pushes a pencil or wraps field bandages and smiles big and pretty when the Swedish photographers shoot through on the grand tour. No, James, she is as hard a hardcore VC as they come (by the look of the miles on her face). She had ambushed the First Platoon's night Listening Post just shy of first light, shot two of them dead, and the company was hunkered down, wet and sullen, waiting for a medivac helicopter—dust-off we called it—and a couple of body bags. And Gallagher was nibbling from a bar of Hershey's Tropical Chocolate (the color of dogshit) and sipping heavily chlorinated canteen water, watching her squatting on her haunches, wolfing down a C-ration can of ham and eggs some fucking new guy had given her—she wolfed it down with the plastic spoon and her thumb—and finally Gallagher had had enough. He muttered something about only one way to cool out gooks, and the next thing you know, James, he had her by the hair and was hauling her this way and that (the spit bubbles at the corners of his mouth slurring his words) through the company to his brick-and-stucco hooch off to one side of the clearing that's roofless and fucked-up with mortar hits up one side and down the other.

Paco sees wiseacre ("Fuck-you-up-boy") Gallagher haul that girl through the night laager by the hair of her head; sees this dude and that dude peel off from their night positions and follow across the hard, bare clay, smacking their lips to a fare-thee-well—there's a bunch of dudes in that company want a piece of *that* gook. Gallagher waltzes her into the room at the side, perhaps a bedroom. The whole time the girl looks at that red and black tattoo out of the corners of her eyes like a fretted, hysterical dog. She can only see the slick-sweated tail curled and twisted and twined this way and that around itself, and the stumpy, lizardlike legs (the long, reddish tongue curls around the snout and head and long curving neck and forelegs, but she cannot see that much because of the way Gallagher has her by the hair).

(Take your hand, James, and reach around to the top of your head, grab as much hair as you can in one hand and yank, then press that arm tight against the side of your head and look over at your arm out of the corners of your eyes. That's as much of Gallagher's arm as the woman sees.)

The hooch is claustrophobic with thick walls and small rooms, and smells like an old wet dog. Gallagher and the others smell sourly of issue mosquito repellent and camouflage stick and marijuana, sopping-wet clothes and jungle rot. The woman smells of jungle funk and cordite—gunpowder, James—and piss.

(If the zip had been a man we would not have bothered with the motherfucker, you understand that, don't you, James? Gallagher, or whoever, would have grabbed that son of a bitch by his whole head of hair—that zip staring at the twined and twisted and curlicued red and black tail of that Bangkok R and R tattoo, knowing it would be the last thing he's likely to get a good clean look at in *this* life. Gallagher would have dragged him over to that hooch, jerking him clean off his feet every other step, snatching his head this way and that for good measure—long, filthy black hairs coming loose in his sweaty hand—Gallagher grumbling through his teeth about the one and only fucking way to put the chill on gooks. We would take him straight around to the side, hold him straight-backed against the beat-to-hell brick-and-stucco wall—his toes wiggling, just touching the ground, James—and that zip's eyes *that* big and his poor little asshole squeezed tighter than a four-inch wad of double sawbucks. We would pound on that poor cocksucker till his face was ragged, till our arms were tired. "Anybody else want a poke at 'im? Goin' once. Twice. *Three* fuckin' times." Then someone would hold him while Jonesy pulls out his pearl-handled straight razor just as slow and catlike and quiet as a barber commencing to trim around your ears, James. Jonesy would flick that sucker open with a flashy snap, showing that puffy-eyed, bloody-faced zip four inches of the goddamnedest Swedish steel he's likely to come across, and then just as slow and calm and cool as you would halve a melon, James, Jonesy would slit that zip's throat from nine to three. He wouldn't be cutting him the way he snipped ears; wouldn't cut him the way he whittled booby-trap tripwire stakes for Paco; no, he'd cut him with a slow sweep of the hand and arm the same as reapers sweep those long-handled scythes; that barebacked, bare-armed motion with the sweat popping on their arms and the yellow wheat laid back in thick armfuls. Beautiful and horrible.

The razor cut would bleed horrible abundance, the zip's life gushing from his neck with him watching it, not hardly believing—his face wax-white—bleeding in terrific spurts. It would be as though he'd been garroted, good and proper hard, only the razor cut would hiss and bubble and gurgle the way a garroting simply cannot.

You've got to understand, James, that if the zip had been a man we would have punched on him, then killed him right then and there, and left him for dead.)

So Gallagher is hauling the woman off by the hair and she's looking just as hard as hard can be at that red and black dragon tattoo. And she's naked from the waist up, but nothing much to look at so no one is much looking at her, and she's flailing her arms trying to gouge Gallagher's eyes out, and swinging her legs, trying to kick him in the balls, but Gallagher's doing a pretty good job of blocking her punches and holding her back (was a wrestler, Gallagher was). She's screaming in Viet and no one can understand, but can figure out pretty well, "*Pig*. You *pig*. GI beaucoup number-ten goddamn shit-eating fucking pig. I *spit* on you." Gallagher's dodging and bobbing and weaving, and chuckling, saying, "Sure, Sweet Pea, sure." Gallagher pulls her—arms flailing, legs kicking, screaming that hysterical bullshit at the top of her lungs. And everybody in the whole ballpark knows they aren't going in there to argue who could throw the blandest brush-back pitch—Lyle Walsh or Dub Paterson. Even Lieut. John Ridley Stennett (Dartmouth, 1967) knows for a refreshing fucking change. Good morning to you, Lieutenant!

We take her right into the side room, and there isn't much of a roof, but there are chunks of tile and snips of shrapnel and the ass end of some bullshit furniture littered around. You walk on the stone parquet floor of that mortared hooch, James, and the crumbs of red roofing tile and whatnot crunch underfoot, like picture-window glass will grind and snap and squeak underfoot. That hooch is a ruin, James, a regular stone riot of ruin. Gallagher and the girl and Jonesy and Paco and the others stand in the brightening overcast (more like bright, hazy glare) that makes you squint involuntarily, as though you're reading fine print.

Jonesy takes a long stretch of black commo wire and whips a handful of it into the open air. It loops high over the ridge pole and comes down, smacking Paco in the leg. Gallagher and Paco hold the girl down firmly while Jonesy ties her wrists together behind her back, then hauls on that wire the same as if he were hoisting the morning colors, just as crisp and snappy as The Book says. Well, James, she's got to bend over some or dislocate both arms, so she bends over this raw plank table about the size of a kitchen table. The girl is scared shitless, James, and shuddering, glossy and greasy with sweat, and chilly, and she's half tempted to ask them as one human being to another not to rape her, not to kill her, but she doesn't speak English.

There's considerable jostling and arm-punching and jawing back and forth, everyone forming a rough line, so just for that moment Paco gets to stand there and take a good long look. A peasant girl, not more than fourteen, say, or sixteen. And by the look of her back she has worked, *hard*, every day of her life. She's not beefy, though. None of the Viets are big. Isn't their nature most likely, but then sharecropping doesn't tend to turn out strapping, hale and hardy offspring. Ask anyone who knows shit from shit and Shinola about farming and he will tell you that sharecropping is a long, hard way to get down to business and get some. The dumbest dumbshit on the face of this earth, who knows just enough to follow a horse around with a coal shovel, knows that sharecropping sucks; knows you can't spend your time leaning on your hoe handle or the porch pillar and make a living sharing your crop with *yourself,* much less the Man. Who knows, maybe Viets enjoy being thin and frail, gaunt and rickety, rheumy and toothless. May be. They get along well enough on forty-and-found—what they can grow and what they can find— and it's a long, hard row to hoe, James. Viet sharecroppers eat rice and greens and fish heads, and such as that—whatever they can catch; whatever they can lay their bare hands on.

Jonesy steps up behind the woman, takes out his pearl-handled straight razor with a magician's flourish—acting real gaudy and showy the way he could—and slits her flimsy black pants from the cuffs to the waistband just the same as you'd zip a parka right to your chin. Then he hauls off and hoists her up another notch or two for good measure until her shoulders turn white (clear on the other side of the laager Lieutenant Stennett hears the commo wire squeak). Gallagher steps up behind her, between her feet, unbuttons his fly, and eases his cock out. He leans on her hard, James, rubbing himself up a hard-on, and slips it to her. Then he commences to fuck her, *hard,* with his big meaty hand pressed into the middle of her back.

Gallagher and Jonesy start to grin and want to laugh, and a couple of dudes *do* laugh, because no one in the company has had any pussy for a month of Sundays (except for Lieutenant Stennett, but he hasn't been in this man's army a month of Sundays).

And when Gallagher finishes, Jonesy fucks her, and when Jonesy is done half the fucking company is standing in line and commences to fuck her ragged. The girl bites the inside of her cheek to bite back the rancor. The line of dudes crowds the low and narrow doorway, drinking warm and bitterly sour canteen water and warm beers (they've been saving), smoking cigars and jays, watching one another while they grind the girl into the rubble. Her eyes get bigger than a deer's, and the chunks and slivers of tile and such get ground into her scalp and face, her breasts and stomach, and Jesus-fucking-Christ she's got her nostrils flared and her teeth clenched and her eyes are squinted and tearing from the sheer humiliating grinding pain of it. (Paco can remember feeling her whole body pucker down; can feel her bowels, right here and now, squeezing as tight as if you were wringing out a rag; can see that huge red mark in the middle of her back; can hear her involuntarily snorting and spitting; can see the broad smudge of blood on the table as clear as day; can hear all those dudes walking on all that rubble.) There's dudes still ambling over to the end of the line, coming in the doorway to watch, to call out coaching, taking their turn, hanging around the side of the building, after—some getting back in line again and again.

And clean across the clearing—way the hell on the other side of the laager; way the fuck out in left field on the other side of the moon—Lieutenant Stennett squats on his steel pot with his knees up and his back to the doings in that hooch, making himself a canteen cup of coffee. The dudes at the quiet end of the line hear the feathery hiss of the thumb-sized chunk of C-4 plastic explosive, and the clank of the green bamboo twig he stirs it with, but don't you know, James, they don't pay it so much as a never-you-mind. The lieutenant hears the grinding, raucous laughter behind him; hears that raw-wood table squeak and creak, creeping across the floor, shoved at and shoved at the way you might pound at the edge of a kitchen table with the heels of your hand. If he had a mind to he could glance back over his shoulder and see that line formed and that bit of commo wire looped over the ridge pole. He knows what's what in that hooch all right, all right—he may be a fool, James, but he ain't a *stone* fool. He works his shoulders, trying to work that damp, rawboned and rainy sweaty feeling of sleep out of his shoulders. He keeps his back bent and his head slumped, tending his hissing little C-4 fire, stirring the caked and lumpy thousand-year-old C-ration instant coffee furiously with a knotted bamboo stick until you would think he was going to wear a hole in it, if you didn't know any better. Well, good morning to you, Lieutenant! Is the coffee fried?

And when everyone has had as many turns as he wants (Paco fascinated by the huge red welt in the middle of her back), as many turns as he can stand, Gallagher takes the girl out behind that bullshit brick-and-stucco hooch, yanking her this way and that by her whole head of hair (that afternoon we notice long black hairs on the back of his arm). He's holding her the way you'd grab some shrimpy little fucker by the throat—mother-fuck-you-up street-mean and businesslike—and he slams her against the wall and hoists her up until her gnarled toes barely touch the ground. But the woman doesn't much fucking care, James. She's bloody up one side and down the other, as though someone had taken a handful of splinters and whatnot and smeared and ground them into her scalp and face and chest, and such as that. There's spit and snot and blood and drool all over her, and she's pissed herself. Her eyes have that dead stare to them, and she doesn't seem to know what's happening anymore. Gallagher slips his .357 Magnum out of its holster and touches her deftly just under the breastbone and says, "Who's it? Who's it?" just like tag, in a clear resonant voice, and jerks her once and her eyes snap. "She is, Jack."

Then he lays the muzzle to her forehead, between her eyebrows. He holds her up by the hair and works his fingers on the pistol grip, not to fuck with her more, but simply to get the best grip (a .357 isn't a metal-shop, hand-crank zip gun, James). The girl's glaring eyes watch the red and black tattoo of the dragon, and she's near enough to his hand to purse her lips and kiss the knuckles. And then in the middle of all this—dudes grabassing and fooling around—he squeezes off the round. Boom.

The pistol bucks, and Gallagher's whole body shimmers. Some of the fucking new guys flinch, and Lieutenant Stennett positively jerks his arms and splashes himself with scalding water. Smoke rises from the pistol and his hand in a cloud; in wisps. If you had been listening close, you would have heard the ring of metal on metal, the same way you can hear a 105 howitzer ring with a *tang* sound; that sound the same as if you whacked a thirty-foot I-beam with a ten-pound ball peen—a sound you feel in every bone in your body from the marrow out.

With her head so close against the hooch we hear the simultaneous shot and clack and clatter of bone chips against the brick and stucco. The slug and the hard, splintered chips of brick ricochet and strike her in the meatiest part of her back, between the shoulder blades. She is dead in that instant (and we mean *stone* dead, James), and just that quick there is blood all over everything and everyone, and splinters of bone and brick stuck in our clothes and the bare skin of our arms and chest and faces. The girl's body lies in its own abundant blood; her hands and fingers flutter the same as a dog's when it dreams.

Paco remembers the spray of blood and brick and bone chips on Gallagher and Jonesy, and everyone, as thick as freckles, and it sparkles. He remembers that quick tingling itch of the spray like a mist of rain through a porch screen. He remembers the brown blood stains down the front of his trousers for days afterward. He remembers Gallagher turning to us, him still holding the scalp and we making a path when he walked away, and hearing him say loud as if we were in an auditorium (the timbre and resonance of his voice reverberating superbly), "That's how you cool out gooks."

Most of us shake out of our reverie and walk away, too, but some of us stay, staring down at the bloody thighs, the filthy bottoms of her feet, the slumped head, and her flat, mannish face—that is both counting coup, in a way, and dumb, dull, and curious fascination. The whole expression of her face is drawn to the dry, drooping lips. We look at her and at ourselves, drawing breath again and again, knowing that this is a moment of evil, that we will never live the same. (It has even begun to dawn on Lieutenant Stennett, the English major from Dartmouth, who's been sitting, pucker-assed, on the other side of the laager with his back as round and smooth as a black beach pebble, minding his p's and q's like there was no tomorrow, still stirring his coffee.)

Soon enough we hear the thack thack thack, thomp thomp thomp, whap whap whap of the Huey dust-off chopper. It circles once around the laager, then comes upwind and lands. One by one we back away from the girl and the hooch, and go help load the body bags. By that time the girl—whatever her name was—is still. When the dust-off is loaded, it rises and is gone. Lieutenant Stennett gets the word to hit the road. We saddle our rucksacks and turn away from that hooch and leave that place, and never go back. Perhaps the girl's body was found later, and buried, but we would never know.

Paco sprawls spread-eagle in his bed in his one-room room, itchy hot and stinking drunk, thinking about Gallagher's tattoo and the girl, and the rape, and that look the dust-off medics gave us.

Cathy and Marty-boy are still fucking up a storm an arm's reach away, Cathy sighing contentedly. Paco's cock is iron hard and his groin aches. His knees and scars, and such, ache and throb. He knows he's not going to get any sleep this night (it isn't the first and it won't be the last, but not because of the heat).

And he's lying on his bed listening to Cathy finish ("Oh, Marty-boy, that was just super!"), and he cannot help his hard-on. The air is oppressively hot, squeeze you down hot and muggy and stifling. There is nothing to do for it but lie still; it is too much for anything else. Marty-boy hustles into his pants. The loose change jangles in his pockets, his keys rattle. He buckles his belt and ties his sneakers, all the while looking at Cathy lazily rolling and curling this way and that on her bed, cuddling herself. Paco hears Marty-boy pull her door open, step gingerly down the stairway, lay the screen door delicately back in its jamb, and leave.

He listens to Cathy loll on her bed, murmuring. Paco lies on *his* bed with his eyes closed but perfectly awake, daydreaming, brushing the fuzzy wallpaper with the back of his hand, waiting for first light, the coolest part of the day.

TANKS
by John Mort

The objective was a numbered patch of green, a rectangular slice of jungle twenty kilometers long and twelve wide, nestled against Cambodia. There was no village, no farmland, nothing; when the tanks had changed direction several times, Porter could not even have told which way was Tay Ninh. He scooted carefully, on the moving tank, to sit on his pack. It was cooler.

They'd make a fine target for mortars, he thought, as the two files of tanks merged, and rolled down an isthmus of grass connecting two fields. The jungle met above them, and a troupe of monkeys fled across the meshed sky, back into bamboo. But there were no mortars. Porter shifted hands on his grab bar, wiped off the sweat, studied the new woodlines.

Attaching infantry to armored had been Jolly Green's—the Colonel's—idea: more firepower, more kills. He flew over every day, like a businessman checking on his investment. He seldom landed, instead calling down the coordinates of where the enemy was likely to be; sometimes he flew ahead of them, a guidon, a god on a horse. Toward lunch he'd drop low, swoop back over them, and bank off into the sun.

So far they'd done little but burn gasoline. The infantry, needing camouflage to be whole, rode high for all to see, clutching at gear, hanging on. The rain scratched their eyes and the steel plate bruised their bones until, like so many RV's in a caravan, the tanks would park in a field. As long as they avoided contact, Porter was content, but he understood how Okie or Lieutenant Wolfe could feel superfluous. Rifles and tripflares and even mines were ridiculous things, alongside the defenses a tank could muster. The enemy would have needed to be both crazy and high to come charging across an open field, into howitzers and .50 caliber machine guns.

Now they halted on the long side of the rectangle and Cherokee platoon dismounted. They dropped into the tall grass as though into a pool, bobbed up, tried to group amid all the noise. There was a splash, a curse, someone laughing. Then they were zigzagging toward the woods, a zombie-like procession of floating heads. They gathered at the jungle's edge, which was tall old trees here, unscathed by artillery and with no brush beneath, a park.

The theory was that the North Vietnamese, assuming there were any, would run from the advance of the tanks and the remaining infantry, into Cherokee's ambush. Cherokee's was the safer assignment, since they wouldn't need to expose themselves, could burrow down, stick their rifles in front of their faces. Nonetheless it seemed to Porter like the main body was deserting them. When Cherokee had threaded into the trees, and the tanks were rolling again, Porter watched the squad radioman, Preacher. Preacher had the handset cupped to his ear. His face would change should Cherokee run into an ambush before it could construct one.

In another twenty minutes the tanks had reached their entry point on the short side of the triangle. They lined up parallel, fifteen meters apart, fifty meters from the jungle wall. Down the line Porter could see Captain Diemer and then Lieutenant Wolfe waving, and then the remaining infantry dropped into the grass, trying to land solidly.

Snowball waded the grass between first squad's point and gun teams, yelling at the new men, "Behind the tanks!" He grinned at Porter, his old friend, as if to demonstrate that such mundane advice was not meant for him. Porter threw him a mock salute, already too weary to attempt a shout above the engines. Snowball turned sharply, his face fluid, as though the salute had truly been mocking. He had been made platoon sergeant that morning. Maybe part of it too was that Snowball was black. He moved toward Wolfe's tank, huge, aloof, but not, Porter thought, truly ferocious.

Porter stumbled behind the Sheridan and knelt, not wanting to present a target before he had to, even if it were merely flashes of his head and shoulders. The ground was moist but the long shoots of grass were dry and brittle; he couldn't breathe, so he stood up again. The engines had throttled low, awaiting word from Cherokee. Porter pointed to the radio, but Preacher shook his head. Porter removed his helmet, dropped his pack, and searched for more Pall Malls.

Smoking absently, he watched the gunner atop the demolition track, twenty meters away. The man stood and ripped off his helmet. That would break his radio contact with the other vehicles, a minor taboo. But now he was simply a man, with shaggy hair and a ragged T-shirt, rather than a connection in a weapon in a long circuit of weapons, jerking and firing when whispers were in his ears. He stretched and scratched his chest, as though to say, "*There*. We got here, at least." He lit a cigarette, passed it down to the hand of the driver, reaching up from inside. The gunner took it back, said something, waited, nodded, smiled. Then he fell forward, looking puzzled. He struck his knee on a bolt head, and his face, with a quick pain, grew blank.

He was dead. So many engines were running that no one had heard the shot. Nonetheless every gunner tensed, hugged his weapon; surely ears were buzzing. When down the line the commander nodded, all the .50 calibers opened up, slicing down the bamboo that began the jungle here. It dropped delicately, sifting to the ground along with tall weeds and grass, as though with so many rounds it was momentarily suspended. The firing was vengeful, sustained and disciplined. It was pride, and nothing could withstand it.

When it had ceased Porter could see Captain Diemer talking on the battalion radio, and soon artillery was whistling in from the firebase. Fire flared in the grass where the rounds exploded, and smoke hung in layers beneath the jungle canopy. Deeper within, trees cracked and toppled.

Medics had picked up the dead man and were carrying him through the grass to a place further behind. The grass whipped round them: if fire caught it, everything would jump up in a quick terror. A detail sliced grass with machetes, to establish an Aid Station, and the medical track withdrew. Porter turned his eyes.

Word came that Cherokee had established its ambush. Two Sheridans, neither of them Porter's, rumbled forward for the point, and the other tanks moved laboriously into files behind them. Snowball spread his men out between the files. Porter concentrated on his footing.

There was a deeper rumble, like an unexpected chord in a piece of music. Porter saw lightning. He looked up and the rain was falling gently, the sun reflected in it still; he realized he hadn't lifted his head to the sky in several hours. The rain could become a problem, but for now it cooled him, offered a brief serenity. The tanks themselves steamed and seemed to run more quietly, as though they were drinking rain.

The tanks leaned up against, and then uprooted, trees six inches thick. The bamboo splintered and fell like wheat before combines, making a mat of arched branches, and shortly this was wet: Porter fell, ripped his pants at the knee.

Smoking another Pall Mall, he stared ahead into a jungle that had grown darker and more deceptive with the rain. He could see Captain Diemer, atop the command tank, speaking into a handset carried, now, by someone Porter didn't know. The black man Johnson, the Captain's radioman before this one, had long since left for a supply job in Tay Ninh: a bed to sleep in, good food, whores. Most important, he was certain to make it home. Porter had lobbied hard for Johnson's job, but Wolfe had blocked it. Wolfe had the deluded notion that Porter was a born point man, that pointing was his destiny. Porter understood that he'd never have a rear job. He barely knew Captain Diemer. He was where he'd started: nothing much learned, near to death as ever. Now it didn't matter. Black or white, soon they'd all be equal.

There was sporadic small arms fire a long way ahead. Porter glanced toward Preacher, who was near Snowball because of the radio; they stood in a mist of exhaust. Preacher nodded. "They're running into Cherokee."

"Maybe we won't have to go all the way in," a new man said.

"No way," Okie said, moving up.

Snowball danced about, trying to keep the squad apart should mortars begin; he walked back to confer with Wolfe, who was managing second squad. Dover and Billy Boy stood a distance from everyone else. Dover talked earnestly; Billy Boy giggled.

Heavy fire opened up on the right. From behind a shield, his body half out of the tube that plunged into the machine itself, the gunner atop the right point tank returned the fire, until his barrel steamed. Grenades went out; smoke drifted back and clung like fog. The gunner resumed his firing. Wolfe ordered the platoon out to the flank, and Porter crouched, trying to see something to aim at.

Now the gunner in the tube fired with one hand, his free arm twisting in the air, like a rodeo rider's. His tank wheeled beneath him to advance; there was a deep muffled explosion, and a clot of smoke, as the tank hit a mine. Part of a tread flew back and landed behind first squad. One side of the tank lifted off the ground, and when it fell the gunner was bucked into the air. He came down dead, slumped in his seat. A rocket sailed in and exploded below his neck; the head and chest disappeared.

Firing from the nearby tanks stopped abruptly, with men shouting, the smoke everywhere. Diemer stood, far up in the right column, and screamed that a jet was coming in. Porter crawled backward, gingerly on the bamboo, marveling that anyone would stand up in the middle of a firefight. He reached for another Pall Mall, but the pack was wet: no time to dig within his gear.

"Man hurt!" Billy Boy was shouting. "Man hurt!"

There were two neat small holes at Dover's wrist. Beside him, Billy Boy poked into the bamboo with his rifle barrel, and looked grim. Snowball and Wolfe came quickly.

"Let's see," said Wolfe. He glanced around him, at the rest of the squad. "Don't bunch up!"

"Fuck," said Okie. "He ain't hurt. It's just—"

Billy Boy brushed past, knelt, propped Dover up. "You gonna be all right, Dove?"

"Oh wow . . ." Dover said, faintly. "It *hurts.*"

"Jesus Fucking Christ," Okie said. "He done that himself."

"Well, I saw it," Billy Boy said, pointing down at the bamboo. "I *saw* it."

"Snake," murmured Porter, only now understanding.

"Maybe it wasn't poisonous," Wolfe said hopefully. He shook his head and looked anxiously toward Diemer, then Snowball. He opened his mouth to speak, but had to pause as the jet made its first attack, dropping two five-hundred pounders with a clunk and fiery crashing. Debris settled with the rain. "What do you think, Snow?" Wolfe asked, his voice, the entire matter, at odds with a burst of AK-47 fire that began before the jet was quite up the sky again.

"Wasn't no snake at all," Okie insisted.

"You don't know. You can't be sure, babes," said Snowball. He knelt. "You shamming it, Dove?"

"Lord . . ." Dover moaned. "Please, please . . ."

Okie turned angrily away. Wolfe stepped past Dover, moving toward Captain Diemer, who had motioned from atop the command tank. "I—don't—know," Wolfe said, his voice cut up again by small arms, like a bad radio transmission. "We have to let him go. Dover, if you . . . Yes. We'll let him go. Get two of the new men, Snow; they can carry him back to the field." Wolfe frowned. There was a momentary lull in the firing, and he sounded decisive. "Move it! Break it up here. Spread out!"

"You'll be okay, Dove," said Billy Boy.

". . . Shit," said Dover, shivering as though in withdrawal.

The jet pounced again, strafing; the empty shell casings pattered through the leaves overhead, like little bombs. Porter stood beside Okie. They watched until the jet veered up again. Two men—straining to conceal their delight—were carrying Dover away.

"I'd a fixed his black ass," Okie said. "I'd put him on the point, see how he liked that. You hear Snow? You don't catch the point team pulling that shit."

Porter shrugged. "Beats me, man. Some guys are smarter than we are."

Okie bent and held his hand near the bamboo. "Snake," he said. "Nice snake. *Here*, snake."

Porter glimpsed the belly of Jolly Green's bird, a dull green above the treetops, its landing lights flashing. More AK fire, and the bird lifted sharply from sight, high into the rain.

A burst of machine gun fire ripped across the demolition track. Soon the crew was leaping off, and smoke poured from within. Coils of white detonator cord leaped up, extended, snapped in the air like electric arcs. A man still on top was blown to the ground, and hunched along painfully, his shirt quickly soaking in blood. The track plowed off into the bamboo, stalled, died, sprouted flame.

Ahead, the disabled point tank looked like some blinded green beast as the driver tried to maneuver out of the way of the columns behind him, only to hit another mine. Steam hissed, and a fountain of coolant shot up, spraying the stump of the dead gunner. The driver climbed out and ran to another tank.

The platoon had moved up, and Porter could hear Diemer and the tank commander talking above. "He *what*?" said the commander.

"He says link up. Link up. My Cherokee platoon's running out of ammo."

"Fucking Pie-in-the-Sky. Goddam, man, I can't *move*. They got mines, Mister! Nobody said they'd have mines. I got nine men dead and two tracks down. Link up? That sorry sack of shit."

Diemer dipped his forehead into the palm of his hand, pinched his temples with a thumb and forefinger. The muscles in his arms flexed. "They're gonna get chewed up," he said, accusingly. "They're gonna get chewed up."

"Can't move! Except back. Out of here."

Lieutenant Wolfe looked meaningfully at Porter, and Porter stepped back, understanding that all of this was not for his ears. But he heard Wolfe say, "I'll go in, sir. We'll get through."

He was volunteering!

Diemer shook his head, not in refusal, seemingly, but with an inability to consider. The battalion radio crackled with Jolly Green's voice and Diemer reached for the handset.

Porter eased over to Preacher. "Turn around," he said when Preacher hesitated, he grabbed his shoulders and spun him around. He switched the radio to the battalion frequency and held the handset so they both could hear.

". . . Gooks not more than one-zero-zero meters east your point vehicle. Plain as day up here. Running into your ambush element. But link up! Link up! I say again: you *must* link up. Cherokee has a body count of two-six, were you aware?"

". . . Negative," said Diemer.

"Roger. You're kicking ass, pardner! Now get your patrol out there; we got 'em nailed. We'll run some interference up here, so sit tight zero-four, then move when the shit lifts. How copy?"

"Solid copy."

"Jolly Green, out."

"What is it, Porter?" Preacher asked.

Porter switched back to the company frequency. "It's *us*, Preacher. It's us."

A Cobra gunship dove, firing rockets that trailed plumes of purple smoke. Two jets came screeching. Then it was almost quiet: the engines idling low, no small arms, rain soft as thought.

Snowball approached, looking guilty. He put something of their old intimacy into his voice, but Porter refused to respond. Snowball's eyes rose mournfully, and when they met Porter's, leaped with surprise. Snowball stared off between the columns of tanks. "You gots to point, Porter."

"Right," Porter said, and picked up his rifle.

Preacher stepped near. "I wish you were a Christian, Porter."

Porter looked at him, opened his mouth to reply, but he couldn't.

It rained steadily. There was wind up high. The afternoon was nearly done: only a little firing came from Cherokee's direction now, none from behind him.

Once, when he dislodged its roost, a brightly-colored bird flew up at his face. He brushed the water from his eyes with a wet sleeve. He crouched, trying to see what lay ahead, fighting off something close to nausea. He hadn't realized how near to dark it was.

It might be that they were waiting until three or four had passed—they'd aim at Preacher because of his antenna, at Snowball because he was black. They hated black skin.

One thing: they would not have had the time to set booby traps.

Perhaps they were all gone, either dead or howling down a trail, cradling their wounds.

Porter moved forward another twenty meters. Further on he could see a slight path through the foliage. In five more steps he discovered a sandal imprint, melting in the rain. Enough of guesswork: they were here still, one at least, hardly a minute ahead. With a flooded eye he traced a line forward, trying to establish that shadows weren't bodies. Perhaps the man was wounded, running from them like a gutshot deer ... there was a burst of fire somewhere ahead, confirming the soldier's presence, possibly, or his death. Porter didn't want to go any further. He had spotted three small stumps, sawed off evenly.

He motioned, and Okie slid noiselessly to his side. "Through there," Porter murmured, pointing toward the stumps. "That'll be the bunker complex. You see that footprint?"

"Yeah." Okie nodded. "Be an observation bunker maybe fifty, sixty feet. He might be in there." He pivoted on his toes and motioned to Snowball. He gestured left and right: a new man and Billy Boy took positions looking out.

Snowball brought the machine gun down from his shoulder. "Know where they be?"

"Know where they *might* be," Okie whispered, motioning.

Porter could barely see. He was cold, slowly growing numb. He heard shouts a good distance behind, a deep groaning as the tanks turned around. There was no more firing, and the smoke had washed away. It was time to go: drink coffee, smoke cigarettes, read his mail.

"Bring in some artillery?" Snowball asked.

"Don't much want to," Porter said. "Can't see. We don't know for sure where Cherokee is: might hit 'em. '

"No, no," said Preacher, pointing at his handset. "I talked to 'em: they got out the back way. Tanks went after 'em."

"Well," said Snowball. "Where Jolly Green?"

"He headed for Tay Ninh. Said he wasn't gonna fly around in the rain if we were done killing bad guys."

"Back at the mess hall," Porter said. "Eating his curds and whey."

"Well, shit," said Okie. "Let's head on back. Get something to eat. Snow?"

"Good deal, Lucille," Porter said. "How about it, Preacher-Man?"

"Okay by me."

Snowball shook his head. "We can't, babes. Lieutenant Wolfe say we turn around, we turn around. You go on, Porter."

Porter couldn't believe it. "Go *on*, Porter?"

"You go on, now."

"Jesus H. Christ! I only got sixty-three days left. I don't have to listen to this shit. You goddamn . . . *coon!*"

"Porter!" said Snowball. "You—"

"You blackassed motherfucking lifer. What the hell you—"

"Shut up, Porter," Okie said. "You cain't talk like that. Hush!"

"You lay off me, motherfucker!"

"Porter," said Preacher, tapping Porter's shoulder. "Porter. No. No."

Porter turned his face to the rain. He heard them rustling confusedly behind, and at length Okie squatted nearby, started to speak, didn't. Porter found a dry Pall Mall, but the rain hit it, and he threw it angrily away. Okie passed him a lit Winston; Porter cupped it carefully, took several long drags, passed it back. Then Wolfe was bending over his shoulder. "What's the problem, Porter?"

"We're walking into bunkers."

"Cherokee killed a lot of gooks. What did you expect?"

"I saw a sandal imprint. It's *got* to be fresh, in all this rain. I'm not going anywhere."

"I been thinking, sir," Okie cut in. "Cherokee done got out, don't seem to be no reason to be *on* this patrol. Reckon we'll go on back?"

Wolfe bent his head, as though amused, and lit a cigarette beneath the bevel of his helmet. When he looked up it was through a wreath of smoke. "We have our orders. I'd like to go a little further."

"You could call up Captain Diemer, sir," Okie said. "I mean, here it is raining and going on dark. Anybody up there, Porter's right, they got us by the balls. We'll come back in the morning, sir. Be the whole company, daylight, tanks behind us."

Wolfe nodded as though to agree, but turned to Snowball. "How about it, Sergeant?"

The raindrops on Snowball's face caught the waning light, and seemed silvery. He stared steadily at Porter. At last he said, "Maybe one or two gooks."

Wolfe smiled and grasped Porter's shoulder. He tilted his head to one side, like an understanding father. "What say, point man? Let's go a little further, what say?"

"It's suicide."

The Lieutenant shook his head, still seemingly amused; Porter could have struck him. "I don't think so, Porter. I think Cherokee drove them all off; we'll just run a little inventory while their shit is weak. Get any documents they left before they can come back tonight. All right?"

"Nosir. I'm not going any direction but backwards. I can't see. Maybe *you'd* like to point into those bunkers . . . *sir*."

Porter cocked his head; the Lieutenant lowered his, slowly released a breath. Cigarette smoke hung on his face, like a beard. His eyes were only dark places. "You know that's not my function, Porter."

"What *is* your function? To get me killed? I'm sick of this teamwork crap, if I got to be the fucking football."

It was quiet. The insistent rain, the quickening darkness, merely shrouded them. Everyone stared at Porter; Preacher's face was incredulous, terrified.

The Lieutenant was rising. He cast his cigarette away. "All right, Porter. I'll point."

Surely no lieutenant in any army on earth was foolhardy enough to point. It was not what Porter had wanted. He had no interest in defiance. He had wanted someone to say, "You're right. Of course you're right." Now he felt robbed even of his minor status as a point man and would have shared in this lunacy. He fought an urge to run up from behind, take charge.

Wolfe was careful. He held his rifle as though it might shatter in his hands, and took steps only after he'd eyed every leaf. Several times, ignoring Porter, he motioned to Okie, for advice.

At last he reached the observation bunker. An arm lay atop it, at first looking like a fallen branch. Wolfe kicked it away, dropped to the mud, and snaked over the bunker's roof—as he'd seen in the movies, perhaps, learned in training. He held up a grenade and looked back at Porter, or so it seemed: faces no longer had expressions. Wolfe dropped the grenade through a firing portal, and somehow the muffled explosion took Porter far back, to that time he'd thrown a cherry bomb in the cistern. Even now he seemed eight years old, with his mother scolding him.

Wolfe stood and stared ahead, studying the dark buildings of the bunker complex. When he motioned, the men moved silently around him, fanning in a semicircle. Porter could make out bags of rice beneath a shed, cutting tools, broken weapons, an open-air kitchen where the coals, still warm, spluttered in the rain. Snowball brushed past to set up the machine gun, and Porter moved near him, feeling lonely. He struggled, in the darkness, for a way to apologize.

"Spread out along the edge," whispered the Lieutenant roughly, the beginning of a cold bubbling in his throat. "Okie, Billy Boy, when they get in position, check for documents and weapons. Preacher, let me have that radio."

Porter remained behind it all, near Snowball. He began to speak, but couldn't. Billy Boy, unbelievably, paused to compliment Wolfe on his job of pointing; the Lieutenant waved him away. Holding Preacher's handset, with Preacher shivering at his side, Wolfe spoke to Porter across the dark space: "I'll bust you."

"I know it, sir."

Wolfe shook his head. "I don't understand. I thought you were born to point. No nerves. Loose. I thought you loved it."

Porter was sorry now. "Nosir, I— How could anybody . . . like to—"

Wolfe cut him off with a wave of his hand. He brought the handset to his face, and his lips parted, probably to call Diemer. Three rounds popped out of the rain. Wolfe slumped and died.

Six more rounds: one of the new men fell, and Preacher died with a gurgle. Porter took a step forward.

"Down! Down! Down!" screamed Okie.

Snowball jumped behind the gun. Porter lay beside him, feeding ammo. Snowball fired fifty rounds, spraying wildly. What was the target? Bags of rice split open and peppered them. The belt grew short.

"Ammo! Ammo!" Porter yelled back, and two boxes came thudding at his feet. He reached around for them, and they were slick with mud, like flour paste, or grease, or blood. He turned to snap on a fresh belt, but Snowball lay still.

"Snow," Porter said. "Snow."

Porter rolled him over; he was bleeding at the neck. A hip was gone. Though his eyes were open, they were dark and Porter couldn't read them. "Snow? Snow?" Porter whispered.

"The tree!" Okie was yelling. He was pinned down. "The fucking tree!"

Porter couldn't move. He knew which tree Okie meant; he realized that a man was firing at him. Of course the man *would* fire at the gun. It made sense.

Billy Boy leaped in beside him, clawing at bodies, pushing Snowball aside. He tilted the gun up toward the tree. On and on now Billy Boy fired.

"Feed it!" Okie was screaming. "Porter, Porter, feed it!" So he did, clipping on another belt. Something fell from the tree.

"Hold it! Hold *on*," Okie said, standing.

Billy Boy kept firing.

"Stop it," Porter said. "Stop."

Billy Boy kept firing. Porter yanked at the belt, tore it apart. The gun jammed. "Billy Boy," Porter said.

Billy Boy was shaking all over.

All around the perimeter the armored and infantry had parted, as though there were shame in each other's company. The armored fired up their tapes of Hendrix and The Doors and disappeared inside the tanks. The infantry withdrew to the very center, and made a circle of its own.

A brand-new lieutenant, who'd flown out on the mail bird, came slogging through the mud to ask for the tank commander, but no one seemed to know where he was. The Lieutenant tried to talk to Captain Diemer, but Diemer wouldn't answer. Finally the Lieutenant withdrew. He hung at the fringes of various groups, then moved on again, unnoticed.

Captain Diemer was on the radio for a long time. His voice was shaky and self-conscious, as though he were auditioning for something. Occasionally he seemed angry. He was trying to call in the names of the dead, but Battalion was too far away, the rain interfered, and he couldn't seem to get through. "Say again," a voice at Battalion replied clearly. "Read you weak and distorted." Diemer repeated the men's names. "Say again," said Battalion, more faintly, down a river of static. "Say again."

Joint after joint went around, but it didn't make Porter sleepy, didn't make him float away. He walked around the perimeter, rubbing his neck. He ran into Okie, but they didn't speak.

The armored cook had made a great pot of bean soup, and put out a slab of Wisconsin cheese. Porter cut a piece of cheese, grabbed some bread, and stuffed it all inside his shirt. He continued walking the perimeter, sipping soup, smoking Pall Malls, staring into men's faces.

"They run right at me," Billy Boy was saying. "Wouldn't stop. I said, I told Shari, I said I wasn't ever gonna shoot nobody, I said that." He began to giggle. Slowly everyone grew silent, watching him. Porter stopped, waited, stood just into the darkness beyond the circle of light thrown by a diesel candle. Billy Boy spun around, holding an imaginary machine gun: John Wayne. "Eh-eh-eh-eheheh!" he said. "*Got* 'em."

"Hush, now," said Okie.

"Eh-eh-eh-eheheh! This foot comes back at me?" Billy Boy kept giggling. Slowly Porter eased in from the dark, though he wanted to run away. "It was still in the boot, like. Laced up? Clean, how it come off. Isn't that weird? They just kept coming. Eh-eh-eh—"

Okie grabbed him. Billy Boy tried to fight, and swung his arms wildly. One of the new men, still a stranger to Porter, stepped up to Billy Boy and slapped his face repeatedly, hard. Billy Boy slipped from Okie's arms down into the grass. "Mmmmmmmh-mmmmm," he said.

"Christ," Okie said, to the new man. "What you do that for? This ain't the fucking movies, troop."

The rain had slowed to a drizzle, but the moon hadn't come out. Porter wrapped his poncho liner tightly around him, like a bandage. He lay down and pulled the poncho over his head, and that was when he remembered his bread and cheese. He munched on it deep down under, where no one could see him. When he opened his eyes the sun was shining, and the cheese lay by his hand.

THE GHOST SOLDIERS
by Tim O'Brien

I was shot twice. The first time, out by Tri Binh, it knocked me against the pagoda wall, and I bounced and spun around and ended up on Teddy Thatcher's lap. Lucky thing, because Teddy was the medic. He tied on a compress and told me to get some sleep, then he ran off toward the fighting. For a long time I lay there all alone, listening to the battle, thinking, *I've been shot, I've been shot.* Winged, grazed, creased: all those Gene Autry movies I'd seen as a kid. In fact, I even laughed. Except then I started to think I might bleed to death. It was the fear, mostly, but I felt wobbly, and then I had a sinking sensation, ears all plugged up, as if I'd gone deep under water. Thank God for Teddy Thatcher. Every so often, maybe four times altogether, he trotted back to check me out. Which took guts. It was a wild fight, lots of noise, guys running and laying down fire, regrouping, running again, real chaos, but Teddy took the risks. "Easy does it," he said. "Just a side wound—no problem unless you're pregnant. You pregnant, buddy?" He ripped off the compress, applied a fresh one, and told me to clamp it in place with my fingers. "Press hard," he said. "Don't worry about the baby." Then he took off. It was almost dark before the fighting petered out and the chopper came to take me and two dead guys away. "Adios, amigo," Teddy said in his fake Mexican accent. I was barely up to it, but I said, "Oh, Cisco," and Teddy wrapped his arms around me and kissed my neck and said, "Oh, Pancho!" because we were buddies and that was how we did things.

On the ride in to Chu Lai, I kept waiting for the pain to

come but actually I couldn't feel much. A throb, that's all. Even in the hospital it wasn't bad.

When I got back to Delta Company twenty-six days later, in mid-March, Teddy Thatcher was dead, and a new medic named Jorgenson had replaced him. Jorgenson was no Teddy. Incompetent and scared. So when I got shot the second time, in the butt, along the Song Tra Bong, it took the son of a bitch almost ten minutes to work up the courage to crawl over to me. By then I was gone with the pain. Later I found out I'd almost died of shock. Jorgenson didn't know about shock, or if he knew, the fear made him forget. To make it worse, the guy bungled the patch job, and a couple of weeks later my ass started to rot away. You could actually peel off chunks of butt with your fingernail.

It was borderline gangrene. I spent a month flat on my belly—couldn't play cards, couldn't sleep. I kept seeing Jorgenson's scared-green face. Those buggy eyes and the way his lips twitched and that silly excuse for a moustache. After the rot cleared up, once I could think straight, I devoted a lot of time to figuring ways to get back at him.

Getting shot should be an experience you can take some pride from. I'm not talking macho crap; I'm not saying you should strut around with your Purple Hearts on display. All I mean is that you should be able to *talk* about it: the stiff thump of the bullet and the way it knocks the air out of you and makes you cough, how the sound comes about ten decades later, the dizzy feeling, the smell of yourself, the stuff you think about and say and do right afterward, the way your eyes focus on a tiny pebble or a blade of grass and how you think, man, that's the last thing I'll ever see, *that* pebble, *that* blade of grass, which makes you want to cry. Pride isn't the right word; I don't know the right word. All I know is, you shouldn't feel embarrassed. Humiliation shouldn't be part of it.

Diaper rash, the nurses called it. Male nurses, too. That was the worst part. It made me hate Jorgenson the way some guys hated Charlie—the kind of hate you make atrocities out of.

I guess the higher-ups decided I'd been shot enough. In early May, when I was released from the Ninety-first Evac Hospital, they transferred me over to headquarters company—S-4, the battalion supply section. Compared with the boonies, of course, it was cushy duty. Regular hours, movies, floor shows, the blurry slow motion of the rear. Fairly safe, too. The battalion firebase was built into a big hill just off Highway One, surrounded on all sides by flat paddy land, and between us and the paddies there were plenty of bunkers and sandbags and rolls of razor-tipped barbed wire. Sure, you could still die there—once a month or so we'd get hit with some mortar fire—but you could die in the bleachers at Fenway Park, bases loaded, Yaz coming to the plate.

I wasn't complaining. Naturally there were times when I half-way wanted to head back to the field; I missed adventure, even the danger. A hard thing to explain to somebody who hasn't felt it. Danger, it makes things vivid. When you're afraid, really afraid, you see things you never saw before, you pay attention. On the other hand, I wasn't crazy. I'd already taken two bullets; the odds were deadly. So I just settled in, took it easy, counted myself lucky. I figured my war was over. If it hadn't been for the constant ache in my butt, I guess things would've worked out fine.

But Jesus, it *hurt*.

Pain, you know?

At night, for example, I had to sleep on my belly. That doesn't sound so terrible until you consider that I'd been a back-sleeper all my life. It got to where I was almost an insomniac. I'd lie there all fidgety and tight, then after a while I'd get angry. I'd squirm around on my cot, cussing, half-nuts with hurt, then I'd start remembering stuff. Jorgenson, I'd think. Shock—how could the bastard forget to treat for shock? I'd remember how long it took him to get to me, how his fingers were all jerky and nervous, the way his lips kept twitching under that ridiculous mustache.

The nights were miserable.

Sometimes I'd roam around the base. I'd head down to the wire and stare out at the darkness, out where the war was, and I'd count ways to make Jorgenson suffer.

One thing for sure. You forget how much you use your butt until you can't use it anymore.

In July, Delta Company came in for stand-down. I was there on the helipad to meet the choppers. Curtis and Lemon and Azar slapped hands with me then I piled their gear in my jeep and drove them down to the Delta hootches. We partied until chow time. Afterward, we kept on partying. It was one of the rituals. Even if you weren't in the mood, you did it on principle.

By midnight it was story time.

"Morty Becker wasted his luck," said Lemon.

I smiled and waited. There was a tempo to how stories got told. Lemon peeled open a finger blister and sucked on it.

"Go on," Azar said. "Tell it."

"Becker used up his luck. Pissed it away."

"Oh *nothin,*'" Azar said.

Lemon nodded, started to speak, then stopped and got up and moved to the cooler and shoved his hands deep into the ice. He was naked except for his socks and his dog tags. In a way, I envied him—all of them. Those deep bush tans, the jungle sores and blisters, the stories, the in-it-togetherness. I felt close to them, yes, but I also felt separate.

Bending forward, Lemon scooped ice up against his chest, pressing it there for a moment, eyes closed; then he fished out a beer and snapped it open.

"It was out by My Khe," he said. "Remember My Khe? Bad-ass country, right? A blister of a day, hot-hot, and we're just sort of groovin' it, lyin' around, nobody bustin' ass or anything. I mean, listen, it's *hot*. We're poppin' salt tabs just to stay conscious. Finally somebody says, 'Hey, where's Becker?' The captain does a head count, and guess what? No Becker."

"Gone," Azar said. "Vanished." "*Poof,* no fuckin' Becker."

"We send out two patrols—no dice. Not a trace." Lemon poured beer on his open blister, slowly licked the foam off. "By then it's getting dark. Captain's about ready to have a fit—you know how he gets, right?—and then, guess what? Take a guess."

"Becker shows," I said.

"You got it, man. Becker shows. We've almost chalked him up as MIA, and then, bingo, he shows."

"Soaking wet," Azar said.

"Hey—"

"Okay, it's your story, but *tell* it."

Lemon frowned. "Soaking wet," he said.

"Ha!"

"Turns out he went for a swim. You believe that? All by himself, the moron just takes off, hikes a couple klicks, finds himself a river, strips, hops in, no security, no *nothin'*. Dig it? He goes swimming."

Azar giggled. "A hot day."

"Not that hot," said Curtis Young. "Not that fuckin' hot."

"Hot, though."

"Get the picture?" Lemon said. "I mean, this is fuckin My Khe we're talking about. Doomsville, and the guy goes for a *swim*."

"Yeah," I said. "Crazy."

I looked across the hootch. Thirty or forty guys were there, some drinking, some passed out, but I couldn't find Morty Becker among them.

Lemon grinned. He reached out and put his hand on my knee and squeezed.

"That's the kicker, man. No more Becker."

"No?"

"The kicker's this," Lemon said, "Morty Becker's luck gets all used up. See? On a lousy swim."

"And that's the truth. That's the truth," said Azar.

Lemon's hand still rested on my knee, very gently.

"What happened?"

"Ah, shit."

"Go on, tell."

"Fatality," Lemon said. "Couple days later, maybe a week, Becker gets real dizzy. Pukes a lot, temperature zooms way up. Out of sight, you know? Jorgenson says he must've swallowed bad water on that swim. Swallowed a virus or something."

"Jorgenson," I said. "Where is my good buddy Jorgenson?"

"Hey, look—"

"Just tell me where to find him."

Lemon made a quick clicking sound with his tongue. "You want to *hear* this? Yes or no?"

"Sure, but where's—"

"Listen up. Becker gets sick, right? Sick, sick, sick. Never seen nobody so bad off, *never*. Arms jerkin' all over hell, can't walk, can't talk, can't fart, can't nothin'. Like he's paralyzed. Can't move. Polio, maybe."

Curtis Young shook his head. "Not polio. You got it wrong."

"Maybe polio."

"No way," Curtis said. "Not polio."

"*Maybe*," Lemon siad. "I'm just saying what Jorgenson says.

Maybe fuckin' polio. Or that elephant disease. Elephantiasshole or whatever."

"But not polio."

Azar smiled and snapped his fingers. "Either way," he said, "it goes to show. Don't throw away luck on little stuff. Save it up."

"That's the lesson, all right."

"Becker was due."

"There it is. Overdue. Don't fritter away your luck."

"Fuckin' polio."

Lemon closed his eyes.

We sat quietly. No need to talk, because we were thinking about the same things: about Mort Becker, the way luck worked and didn't work, how it was impossible to gauge the odds. Maybe the disease was lucky. Who knows? Maybe it saved Morty from getting shot.

"Where's Jorgenson?" I said.

Another thing: Three times a day, no matter what, I had to stop whatever I was doing, go find a private place, drop my pants, bend over, and apply this antibacterial ointment to my ass. No choice—I had to do it. And the worst part was how the ointment left yellow stains on the seat of my trousers, big greasy splotches. Herbie's hemorrhoids, that was one of the jokes. There were plenty of other jokes, too—plenty.

During the first full day of Delta's stand-down, I didn't run into Jorgenson once. Not at chow, not at the flicks, not during our long booze sessions in the hootch.

I didn't hunt him down, though. I just waited.

"Forget it," Lemon said. "Granted, the man messed up bad, real bad, but you got to take into account how green he was. Brand new, remember?"

"I forget. Remind me."

"You survived."

I showed Lemon the yellow stain on my britches. "I'm in terrific shape. Really funny, right?"

"Not exactly," Lemon said.

But he was laughing. He started snapping a towel at my backside. I laughed—I couldn't help it—but I didn't see the big joke.

Later, after some dope, Lemon said: "The thing is, Jorgenson's doing all right. Better and better. People change, they adapt. I mean, okay, he's not a Teddy Thatcher, but the dude hangs in there, he knows his shit. Kept Becker alive."

"My sore ass."

Lemon nodded. He shrugged, leaned back, popped the hot roach into his mouth, chewed for a long time. "You've lost touch, man. Jorgenson . . . he's *with* us now."

"I'm not."

"No," he said. "I guess you're not."

"Good old loyalty."

Lemon shook his head. "We're friends, Herbie. You and me. But look, you're not *out* there anymore, and Jorgenson is. If you'd just seen him the past couple of weeks—the way he handled Becker, then when Pinko hit the mine—I mean, the kid did some good work. Ask anybody. So . . . I don't know. If it was me, Herbie, I'd say screw it. Leave it alone."

"I won't hurt him."

"Right."

"I won't. Show him some ghosts, that's all."

In the morning I spotted Jorgenson. I was up on the helipad, loading the resupply choppers, and then, when the last bird took off, while I was putting on my shirt, I looked up, and there he was. In a way, it was a shock. His size, I mean. Even smaller than I remembered—a little squirrel of a guy, five and a half feet tall, skinny and mousy and sad.

He was leaning against my jeep, waiting for me.

"Herb," he said, "can we talk?"

At first I just looked at his boots.

Those boots: I remembered them from when I got shot. Out along the Song Tra Bong, a bullet in my ass, all that pain, and the funny thing was that what I remembered, now, were those new boots—no scuffs; smooth, unblemished leather. One of those last details, Jorgenson's boots.

"Herb?"

I looked at his eyes—a long, straight-on stare—and he blinked and made a stabbing motion at his nose and backed off a step. Oddly, I felt some pity for him. The tiniest arms and wrists I'd ever seen—a sparrow's nervous system. He made me think of those sorry kids back in junior high who used to spend their time collecting stamps and butterflies, always off by themselves, no friends, no hope.

He took another half-step backward and said, very softly, "Look, I just wanted . . . I'm sorry, Herb."

I didn't move or look away or anything.

"Herb?"

"Talk, talk, talk."

"What can I say? It was—"

"Excuses?"

Jorgenson's tongue flicked out, then slipped away. He shook his head. "No, it was a bungle, and I don't ... I was *scared*. All the noise and everything, the shooting, I'd never seen that before. I couldn't make myself move. After you got hit, I kept telling myself to move, move, but I couldn't *do* it. Like I was full of Novocaine or something. You ever feel like that? Like you can't even move?"

"Anyway," I said.

"And then I heard how you ... the shock, the gangrene. Man, I felt like ... couldn't sleep, couldn't eat. Nightmares, you know? Kept seeing you lying out there, heard you screaming, and ... it was like my legs were filled up with cement. I *couldn't*."

His lip trembled, and he made a weird moaning sound—not quite a moan, feathery and high—and for a second I was afraid he might start crying. That would've ended it. I was a sucker for tears. I would've patted his shoulder, told him to forget it. Thank God he tried to shake my hand. It gave me an excuse to spit.

"Kiss it," I said.

"Herb, I can't go back and do it over."

"Lick it, kiss it."

But Jorgenson just smiled. Very tentatively, like an invalid, he kept pushing his hand out at me. He looked so mournful and puppy-doggish, so damned hurt, that I made myself spit again. I didn't feel like spitting—my heart wasn't in it—but somehow I managed, and Jorgenson glanced away for a second, still smiling a weary little smile, resigned-looking, as if to show how generous he was, how big-hearted and noble.

It almost made me feel guilty.

I got into the jeep, hit the ignition, left him standing there.

Guilty, for Chrissake. Why should it end up with *me* feeling the guilt? I hated him for making me stop hating him.

Thing is, it had been a vow. *I'll get him, I'll get him*—it was down inside me like a stone. Except now I couldn't generate the passion. Couldn't feel the anger. I still had to get back at him, but now it was a need, not a want. An obligation. To rev up some intensity, I started drinking a little—more than a little, a lot. I remembered the river, getting shot, the pain, how I kept calling out for a medic, waiting and waiting and waiting, passing out once, waking up, screaming, how the scream seemed to make new pain, the awful stink of myself, the sweating and shit and fear, Jorgenson's clumsy fingers when he finally got around to working on me. I remembered it all, every detail. *Shock,* I thought. *I'm dying of shock.* I tried to tell him that, but my tongue didn't connect with my brain. All I could do was go, "Ough! Ough!" I wanted to say, "You *jerk!* I'm *dying!* Treat for shock, treat for shock!" I remembered all that, and the hospital, and those giggling nurses. I even remembered the rage. Except I couldn't feel it anymore. Just a word—*rage*—spelled out in my head. No *feeling.* In the end, all I had were the facts. Number one: the guy had almost killed me. Number two: there had to be consequences. Only thing was, I wished I could've gotten some pleasure out of them.

I asked Lemon to give me a hand.

"No pain," I said. "Basic psy-ops, that's all. We'll just scare him. Mess with his head a little."

"Negative," Lemon said.

"Just spook the fucker."

"Sick, man."

Stiffly, like a stranger, Lemon looked at me for a long time. Then he moved across the hootch and lay down with a comic book and pretended to read. His lips were moving, but that didn't fool me a bit.

I had to get Azar in on it.

Azar didn't have Lemon's intelligence, but he had a better sense of justice.

"Tonight?" he said.

"Just don't get carried away."

"Me?"

Azar grinned and snapped his fingers. It was a tic. Snap, snap—whenever things got tight, whenever there was a prospect of action.

"Understand?"

"Roger-dodger," Azar said. "Only a game, right?"

We called the enemy "ghosts." "Bad night," we'd murmur. "Ghosts are out." To get spooked, in the lingo, meant not only to get scared but to get killed. "Don't get spooked," we'd say. "Stay cool, stay alive." The countryside was spooky; snipers, tunnels, ancestor worship, ancient papa-sans, incense. The land was haunted. We were fighting forces that didn't obey the laws of twentieth-century science. Deep in the night, on guard, it seemed that all of Nam was shimmering and swaying—odd shapes swirling in the dark; phantoms; apparitions; spirits in the abandoned pagodas; boogeymen in sandals. When a guy named Olson was killed, in February, everybody started saying, "The Holy Ghost took him." And when Ron Ingo hit the booby trap, in April, somebody said he'd been made into a deviled egg—no arms, no legs, just a poor deviled egg.

It was ghost country, and Charlie was the main ghost. The way he came out at night. How you never really saw him, just thought you did. Almost magical—appearing, disappearing. He could levitate. He could pass through barbed wire. He was invisible, blending with the land, changing shape. He could fly. He could melt away like ice. He could creep up on you without sound or footsteps. He was scary.

In the daylight, maybe, you didn't believe in all this stuff. You laughed, you made jokes. But at night you turned into a believer: no skeptics in foxholes.

Azar was wound up tight. All afternoon, while we made preparations, he kept chanting, "Halloween, Halloween." That, plus the finger snapping, almost made me cancel the whole operation. I went hot and cold. Lemon wouldn't speak to me, which tended to cool it off, but then I'd start remembering things. The result was a kind of tepid numbness. No ice, no heat. I went through the motions like a sleepwalker—rigidly, by the numbers, no real emotion, no heart. I rigged up my special effects, checked out the battle terrain, measured distances, gathered the ordnance and gear we'd need. I was professional enough about it, I didn't miss a thing, but somehow it felt as if I were gearing up to fight somebody else's war. I didn't have that patriotic zeal.

Who knows? If there'd been a dignified way out. I might've taken it.

During evening chow, in fact, I kept staring across the mess hall at Jorgenson, and when he finally looked up at me, a puzzled frown on his face, I came very close to smiling. Very, very close. Maybe I was fishing for something. A nod, one last apology—

anything. But Jorgenson only gazed back at me. In a strange way, too. As if he didn't *need* to apologize again. Just a straight, unafraid gaze. No humility at all.

To top it off, my ex-buddy Lemon was sitting with him, and they were having this chummy-chummy conversation, all smiles and sweetness.

That's probably what cinched it.

I went back to my hootch, showered, shaved, threw my helmet against the wall, lay down awhile, fidgeted, got up, prowled around, applied some fresh ointment, then headed off to find Azar.

Just before dusk, Delta Company stood for roll call. Afterward the men separated into two groups. Some went off to drink or sleep or catch a movie; the others trooped down to the base perimeter, where, for the next eleven hours, they would pull night guard duty. It was SOP—one night on, one night off.

This was Jorgenson's night on.

I knew that in advance, of course. And I knew his bunker assignment: number six, a pile of sandbags at the southwest corner of the perimeter. That morning I'd scouted every inch of his position; I knew the blind spots, the ripples of land, the places where he'd take cover in case of trouble. I was ready. To guard against freak screwups, though, Azar and I tailed him down to the wire. We watched him lay out his bedroll, connect the Claymores to their firing devices, test the radio, light up a cigarette, yawn, then sit back with his rifle cradled to his chest like a teddy bear.

"A pigeon," Azar whispered. "Roast pigeon on a spit. I smell it cookin'."

"Remember, though. This isn't for real."

Azar shrugged. He touched me on the shoulder, not roughly but not gently either. "What's real?" he said. "Eight months in Fantasyland, it tends to blur the line. Honest to God, I sometimes can't remember what real *is*."

Psychology—that was one thing I knew. I never went to college, and I wasn't exactly a whiz in high school either, but all my life I've paid attention to how things operate inside the skull. Example: You don't try to scare people in broad daylight. You wait. Why? Because the darkness squeezes you inside yourself, you get cut off from the outside world, the imagination takes over. That's basic psychology. I'd pulled enough night guard to know how the fear factor gets multiplied as you sit there hour after hour, nobody to talk to, nothing to do but stare blank-eyed into the Big Black Hole. The hours pile up. You drift; your brain starts to roam. You think about dark closets, madmen, murderers hiding under the bed, all those childhood fears. Fairy tales with gremlins and trolls and one-eyed giants. You try to block it out but you can't. You see ghosts. You blink and laugh and shake your head. Bullshit, you say. But then you remember the guys who died: Teddy, Olson, Ingo, maybe Becker, a dozen others whose faces you can't see anymore. Pretty soon you begin to think about the stories you've heard about Charlie's magic. The time some guys cornered two VC in a dead-end tunnel, no way out, but how, when the tunnel was fragged and searched, nothing was found but dead rats. A hundred stories. A whole bookful: ghosts swinging from the trees, ghosts wiping out a whole Marine platoon in twenty seconds flat, ghosts rising from the dead, ghosts behind you and in front of you and inside you. Your ears get ticklish. Tiny sounds get heightened and distorted, crickets become monsters, the hum of the night takes on a weird electronic tingle. You try not to breathe. You coil and tighten up and listen. Your knuckles ache, and your pulse ticks like an alarm clock. What's *that*? You jerk up. Nothing, you say, nothing. You check to be sure your weapon is loaded. Put it on full automatic. Count your grenades, make sure the pins are bent for quick throwing. Crouch lower. Listen, listen. And then, after enough time passes, things start to get bad.

"Come on, man," Azar said. "Let's *do* it." But I told him to be patient. "Waiting, that's half the trick," I said. So we went to the movies, *Barbarella* again, the sixth straight night. But it kept Azar happy—he was crazy about Jane Fonda. "Sweet Janie," he kept saying, over and over. "Sweet Janie boosts a man's morale." Then, with his hand, he showed me which part of his morale got boosted. An old joke. Everything was old. The movie, the heat, the booze, the war. I fell asleep during the second reel—a hot, angry sleep—and forty minutes later I woke up to a sore ass and a foul temper.

It wasn't yet midnight.

We hiked over to the EM club and worked our way through a six-pack. Lemon was there, at another table, but he pretended not to see me.

Around closing time, I made a fist and showed it to Azar. He smiled like a little boy. "Goody," he said. We picked up the gear, smeared charcoal on our faces, then moved down to the wire.

Azar lifted his thumb. The he grinned and peeled away from me and began circling behind Bunker Six. For a second I couldn't move. Not fear, exactly; I don't know what it was. My boots felt heavy.

In a way, it was purely mechanical. I didn't think. I just shouldered the gear and crossed quietly over to a heap of boulders that overlooked Jorgenson's bunker.

I was directly behind him. Thirty-two meters away, exactly. My measurements were precise.

Even in the heavy darkness, no moon yet, I could make out Jorgenson's silhouette: a helmet, his shoulders, the rifle barrel. His back was to me. That was the heart of the psychology. He'd be looking out at the wire, the paddies, where the danger was; he'd figure his back was safe.

Quiet, quiet.

I knelt down, took out the flares, lined them up in front of me, unscrewed the caps, then checked my wristwatch. Still five minutes to go. Edging over to my left, I groped for the ropes, found them wedged in the crotch of two boulders. I separated them and tested the tension and checked the time again. One minute.

My head was light. Fluttery and taut at the same time. It was the feeling I remembered from the boonies, on ambush or marching at night through ghost country. Peril and doubt and awe, all those things and a million more. You wonder if you're dreaming. It's like you're in a movie. There's a camera on you, so you begin acting, following the script: "Oh, Cisco!" You think of all the flicks you've seen, Audie Murphy and Gary Cooper and Van Johnson and Roy Rogers, all of them, and certain lines of dialogue come back to you—"I been plugged!"—and then, when you get shot, you can't help falling back on them. "Jesus, Jesus," you say, half to yourself, half to the camera. "I been fuckin' *plugged*!" You expect it of yourself. On ambush, poised in the dark, you fight to control yourself. Not too much fidgeting; it wouldn't look good. You try to grin. Eyes open, be alert—old lines, old movies. It all swirls together, clichés mixing with your own emotions, and in the end you can't distinguish. . . .

I fingered one of the ropes, took a breath, then gave it a sharp jerk.

Instantly there was a clatter outside the wire.

I expected the noise, I was even tensed for it, but still my heart took a funny little hop. I winced and ducked down.

"Now," I murmured. "Now it starts." Eight ropes altogether. I had four, Azar had four. Each rope was hooked up to a home-made noisemaker out in front of Jorgenson's bunker—eight tin cans filled with rifle cartridges. Simple devices, but they worked.

I waited a moment, and then, very gently, I gave all four of my ropes a little tug. Delicate—nothing loud. If you weren't listening, listening hard, you might've missed it. But Jorgenson was listening. Immediately, at the first low rattle, his silhouette seemed to freeze. Then he ducked down and blended in with the dark.

There—another rattle. Azar this time.

We kept at it for ten minutes. Noise, silence, noise, silence. Stagger the rhythm. Start slowly, gradually build the tension.

Crouched in my pile of boulders, squinting down at Jorgenson's position, I felt a swell of immense power. It was the feeling Charlie must have. Like a puppeteer. Yank on the ropes, watch the silly wooden puppet jump and twitch. It made me want to giggle. One by one, in sequence, I pulled on each of the ropes, and the sound came bouncing back at me with an eerie, in-definite formlessness: a rattlesnake, maybe, or the creak of a closet door or footsteps in the attic—whatever you made of it.

"There now," I whispered, or thought. "There, there."

Jorgenson wasn't moving. Not yet. He'd be coiled up in his circle of sandbags, listening.

Again I tugged on my ropes.

I smiled. Eyes closed, I could almost *see* what was happening down there.

Bang. Jorgenson would jerk up. Rub his eyes, and bend forward. Muscles hard, brains like Jell-O. I could *see* it. Right now, at this instant, he'd glance up at the sky, hoping for a moon, a few stars. But no moon, no stars. He'd start talking to himself: "Relax, relax." He'd try to bring the night into focus, but the effort would only cause distortions: objects would seem to pick them-selves up and twist and wiggle; trees would creep forward; the earth itself would begin to sway. Funhouse country. Trick mirrors and trapdoors and pop-up monsters. I could *see* it. It was as if I were down there *with* him, *beside* him. "Easy," he was muttering, "easy, easy, easy," but it didn't get easier.

*　　*　　*

"Creepy," Azar cackled. "Wet pants, goose bumps. Ghost town!" He held a beer out to me, but I shook my head.

We sat in the dim quiet of my hootch, boots off, smoking, listening to Mary Hopkin.

"So what next?"

"Wait," I said. "More of the same."

"Well, sure, but—"

"Shut up and *listen*."

That high elegant voice. That melody. Someday, when the war was over, I'd go to London and ask Mary Hopkin to marry me. Nostalgic and crazy, but so what? That's what Nam does to you. Turns you sentimental, makes you want to marry girls like Mary Hopkin. You learn, finally, that you'll die. That's what war does to you.

Azar switched off the tape.

"Shit, man," he said. "Don't you got some *music*?"

And now, finally, the moon was out. We slipped back to our positions and went to work again with the ropes. Louder, now, more insistently. The moon added resonance. Starlight shimmied in the barbed wire-reflections, layerings of shadow. Slowly, we dragged the tin cans closer to Jorgenson's bunker, and this, plus the moon, gave a sense of creeping peril, the slow tightening of a noose.

At 0300 hours, the very deepest part of the night, Azar set off the first trip flare.

There was a light popping sound out in front of Bunker Six. Then a sizzle. And then the night seemed to snap itself in half. The flare burned ten paces from the bunker.

I fired three more and it was instant daylight.

Then Jorgenson moved. There was a short, squeaky cry—not even a cry, really, just a sound of terror—and then a blurred motion as he jumped up and ran a few paces and rolled and lay still. His silhouette was framed like a cardboard cutout against the burning flares.

In the dark outside my hootch, even though I bent toward him, nose to nose, all I could see were Azar's white eyes.

"Enough," I told him.

"Oh, sure."

"Seriously."

"Serious?" he said. "That's too serious for me I'm a fun lover."

When Azar smiled I saw the quick glitter of teeth, but then the smile went away, and I knew it was hopeless. I tried, though. I told him the score was even—no need to rub it in.

Azar just peered at me, almost dumbly.

"Poor Herbie," he said.

Nothing dramatic. The rest was inflection and those white eyes.

An hour before dawn he moved up for the last phase. Azar was in command now. I tagged after him, thinking maybe I could keep a lid on.

"Don't take this personal," Azar whispered. "You know? It's just that I like to finish things."

I didn't look at him; I looked at my fingernails, at the moon. When we got down near the wire, Azar gently put his hand on my shoulder, guiding me over toward the boulder pile. He knelt down and inspected the ropes and flares, nodded, peered out at Jorgenson's bunker, nodded again, removed his helmet and sat on it.

He was smiling again.

"Herbie?" he whispered.

I ignored him. My lips had a waxy, cold feel, like polished rock. I kept running my tongue over them. I told myself to stop it, and I did, but then a second later I was doing it again.

"You know something?" Azar said, almost to himself. "Sometimes I feel like a little kid again. Playing war, you know? I get into it. I mean, wow, I *love* this shit."

"Look, why don't we—"

"Shhhh."

Smiling, Azar put a finger to his lips, partly as a warning, partly as a nifty gesture.

We waited another twenty minutes. It was cold now, and damp. I had a weird feeling of brittleness, as if somebody could reach out and crush me like a Christmas tree ornament. It was the same feeling out along the Song Tra Bong, when I got shot: I tried to grin wryly, like Bogie or Gable, and I thought about all the zingers Teddy Thatcher and I would use— except now Teddy was dead. Except when I called out for a medic, loud, nobody came. I started whimpering. The blood was warm, like dishwater, and I could feel my pants filling up with it.

God, I thought, all this blood; I'll be *hollow*. Then the brittle feeling came over me. I passed out, woke up, screamed, tried to crawl but couldn't. I felt alone. All around me there was rifle fire, voices yelling, and yet for a moment I thought I'd gone deaf: the sounds were in my head, they weren't real. I smelled myself. The bullet had smashed through the colon, and the stink of my own shit made me afraid. I was crying. Leaking to death, I thought— blood and crap leaking out—and I couldn't quit crying. When Jorgenson got to me, all I could do was go "Ough! Ough!" I tightened up and pressed and grunted, trying to stop the leak, but that only made it worse, and Jorgenson punched me and told me to cut it out, ease off. *Shock,* I thought. I tried to tell him that: "Shock, man! Treat for shock!" I was lucid, things were clear, but my tongue wouldn't make the right words. And I was squirming. Jorgenson had to put his knee on my chest, turn me over, and when he did that, when he ripped my pants open, I shouted something and tried to wiggle away. I was hollowed out and cold. It was the *smell* that scared me. He was pressing down on my back—sitting on me, maybe, holding me down—and I kept trying to buck him off, rocking and moaning, even when he stuck me with morphine, even when he used his shirt to wipe my ass, and tried to plug up the hole. Shock, I kept thinking. And then, like magic, things suddenly clicked into slow motion. The morphine, maybe: I focused on those brand-new black boots of his, then on a pebble, then on a single wisp of dried grass—the last things I'd ever see. I couldn't look away, I didn't dare, and I couldn't stop crying.

Even now, in the dark, I felt the sting in my eyes.

Azar said, "Herbie."

"Sure, man, I'm solid."

Down below, the bunker was silent. Nothing moved. The place looked almost abandoned, but I knew Jorgenson was there, wide awake, and I knew he was waiting.

Azar went to work on the ropes.

It began like a breeze: a soft, lush, sighing sound. I was hugging myself. You can *die* of fright; it's possible, it can happen. I'd heard stories about it, about guys so afraid of dying that they died. You freeze up, your muscles snap, the heart starts fluttering, the brain floats away. It can *happen*.

"Enough," I whispered. "Stop it."

Azar looked at me and winked. Then he yanked sharply on all four ropes, and the sound made me squeal and jerk up.

"Call it quits, right now. Please, man."

Azar wasn't listening. His white eyes glowed as he shot off the first flare. "Please," I said, but then I watched the flare arc up over Jorgenson's bunker, very slowly, pinwheeling, exploding almost without noise, just a sudden red flash.

There was a short whimper in the dark. At first I thought it was Jorgenson, or maybe a bird, but then I knew it was my own voice. I bit down and folded my hands and squeezed.

Twice more, rapidly, Azar fired off red flares, and then he turned and looked at me and lifted his eyebrows.

"Herbie," he said softly, "you're a sad case."

"Look, can't we—"

"Sad."

I was frightened—of him, of us—and though I wanted to do something, wanted to stop him, I crouched back and watched him pick up the tear-gas grenade, pull the pin, stand up, smile, pause, and throw. Then the gas puffed up in a smoky cloud that partly obscured the bunker. Even from thirty meters away, upwind, I could smell it: not really *smell* it, though. I could *feel* it, like breathing razor blades.

"Jesus," I said, but Azar lobbed over another one, waited for the hiss, then scrambled over to the rope we hadn't used yet.

It was my idea. That morning I'd rigged it up: a sandbag painted white, a pulley system, a rope.

Show him a ghost.

Azar pulled, and out in front of Bunker Six, the white sandbag lifted itself up and hovered in the misty swirl of gas.

Jorgenson began firing. Just one round at first—a single red tracer that thumped into the sandbag and burned.

"Ooooooh!" Azar murmured. "Star light, star bright. . . ."

Quickly, talking to himself, Azar hurled the last gas grenade, shot up another flare, then snatched the rope and made the white sandbag dance.

Jorgenson did not go nuts. Quietly, almost with dignity, he stood up and took aim and fired at the sandbag. I could see his profile against the red flares. His face seemed oddly relaxed. No twitching, no screams. He gazed out at the sandbag for several seconds, as if deciding something, and then he shook his head and smiled. Very slowly, he began marching out toward the wire. He did not crouch or run or crawl. He walked. When

he reached the sandbag he stopped and turned, then he shouted
my name, then he placed his rifle muzzle directly against the
bag.

"Herbie!" he hollered, and he fired.

Azar dropped the rope.

"Show's over," he said. He looked down at me with pity. "Sad,
sad, sad."

I was weeping.

"Disgusting," Azar said. "Herbie, you're the saddest fuckin'
case I ever seen."

Azar smiled. He looked out at Jorgenson, then at me. Those
eyes—falcon eyes, ghost eyes. He moved toward me as if to help
me up, but then, almost as an afterthought, he kicked me hard
in the knee.

"Sad," he murmured, then he turned and headed off to bed.

"No big deal," I told Jorgenson. "Leave it alone."

But he hooked my arm over his shoulder and helped me down
to the bunker. My knee was hurting bad, but I didn't say anything.

It was almost full dawn now, a hazy silver dawn. For a while
we didn't speak.

"So," he finally said.

"Right."

We shook hands. Neither of us put much emotion in it and
we didn't look at each other's eyes.

Jorgenson pointed out at the shot-up sandbag.

"That was a nice touch," he said. "No kidding, it had me . . . a
nice touch. You've got a real sense of drama, Herbie. Someday
maybe you should go into the movies or something."

I nodded and said, "Sure I've thought about that."

"Another Hitchcock. *The Birds.* You ever see it?"

"Scary shit, eh." I said.

We sat for a while longer, then I started to get up, except my
knee wasn't working right. Jorgenson had to give me a hand.

"Even?" he asked.

"Pretty much."

We almost shook hands again but we didn't. Jorgenson picked
up his helmet, brushed it off, touched his funny little moustache,
and looked out at the sandbag. His face was filthy.

Up at the medic's hootch, he cleaned and bandaged my knee,
then we went to chow. We didn't have much to say. Afterward,
in an awkward moment, I said, "Let's kill Azar."

Jorgenson smiled. "Scare him to death, right?"

"Right," I said.

"What a movie!"

I shrugged. "Sure. Or just kill him."

BIG BERTHA STORIES

by Bobbie Ann Mason

BIG BERTHA STORIES
by Bobbie Ann Mason

Donald is home again, laughing and singing. He comes home
from Central City, Kentucky, near the strip mines, only when he
feels like it, like an absentee landlord checking on his property.
He is always in such a good humor when he returns that Jeannette forgives him. She cooks for him—ugly, pasty things she gets
with food stamps. Sometimes he brings steaks and ice cream,
occasionally money. Rodney, their child, hides in the closet when
he arrives, and Donald goes around the house talking loudly
about the little boy named Rodney who used to live there—the
one who fell into a septic tank, or the one stolen by Gypsies. The
stories change. Rodney usually stays in the closet until he has to
pee, and then he hugs his father's knees, forgiving him, just as
Jeannette does. The way Donald saunters through the door, swinging a six-pack of beer, with a big grin on his face, takes her breath
away. He leans against the door facing, looking sexy in his
baseball cap and his shaggy red beard and his sunglasses. He
wears sunglasses to be like the Blues Brothers, but he in no way
resembles either of the Blues Brothers. I should have my head
examined, Jeannette thinks.

The last time Donald was home, they went to the shopping
center to buy Rodney some shoes advertised on sale. They stayed
at the shopping center half the afternoon, just looking around.
Donald and Rodney played video games. Jeannette felt they were
a normal family. Then, in the parking lot, they stopped to watch a
man on a platform demonstrating snakes. Children were petting a
12-foot python coiled around the man's shoulders. Jeannette felt
faint.

"Snakes won't hurt you unless you hurt them," said Donald as Rodney stroked the snake.

"It feels like chocolate," he said.

The snake man took a tarantula from a plastic box and held it lovingly in his palm. He said, "If you drop a tarantula, it will shatter like a Christmas ornament."

"I hate this," said Jeannette.

"Let's get out of here," said Donald.

Jeanette felt her family disintegrating like a spider shattering as Donald hurried them away from the shopping center. Rodney squalled and Donald dragged him along. Jeanette wanted to stop for ice cream. She wanted them all to sit quietly together in a booth, but Donald rushed them to the car, and he drove them home in silence, his face growing grim.

"Did you have bad dreams about the snakes?" Jeannette asked Rodney the next morning at breakfast. They were eating pancakes made with generic pancake mix. Rodney slapped his fork in the pond of syrup on his pancakes. "The black racer is the farmer's friend," he said soberly, repeating a fact learned from the snake man.

"Big Bertha kept black racers," said Donald. "She trained them for the 500." Donald doesn't tell Rodney ordinary children's stories. He tells him a series of strange stories he makes up about Big Bertha. Big Bertha is what he calls the huge strip-mining machine in Muhlenberg County, but he has Rodney believing that Big Bertha is a female version of Paul Bunyan.

"Snakes don't run in the 500," said Rodney.

"This wasn't the Indy 500, or the Daytona 500, none of your well-known 500s," said Donald. "This was the Possum Trot 500, and it was a long time ago. Big Bertha started the original 500, with snakes. Black racers and blue racers mainly. Also some red-and-white-striped racers, but those are rare."

"We always ran for the hoe if we saw a black racer," Jeannette said, remembering her childhood in the country.

In a way, Donald's absences are a fine arrangement, even considerate. He is sparing them his darkest moods, when he can't cope with his memories of Vietnam. Vietnam had never seemed such a meaningful fact until a couple of years ago, when he grew depressed and moody, and then he started going away to Central City. He frightened Jeannette, and she always said the wrong thing in her efforts to soothe him. If the welfare people find out he is spending occasional weekends at home, and even bringing some money, they will cut off her assistance. She applied for welfare because she can't depend on him to send money, but she knows he blames her for losing faith in him. He isn't really working regularly at the strip mines. He is mostly just hanging around there, watching the land being scraped away, trees coming down, bushes flung in the air. Sometimes he operates a steam shovel, and when he comes home his clothes are filled with the clay and it is caked on his shoes. The clay is the color of butterscotch pudding.

At first, he tried to explain to Jeannette. He said, "If we could have had tanks over there as big as Big Bertha, we wouldn't have lost the war. Strip mining is just like what we were doing over there. We were stripping off the top. The topsoil is like the culture and the people, the best part of the land and the country. America was just stripping off the top, the best. We ruined it. Here, at least, the coal companies have to plant vetch and loblolly pines and all kinds of trees and bushes. If we'd done that in Vietnam, maybe we'd have left that country in better shape."

"Wasn't Vietnam a long time ago?" Jeannette asked.

She didn't want to hear about Vietnam. She thought it was unhealthy to dwell on it so much. He should live in the present. Her mother is afraid Donald will do something violent, because she once read in the newspaper that a veteran in Louisville held his little girl hostage in their apartment until he had a shootout with the police and was killed. But Jeannette can't imagine Donald doing anything so extreme. When she first met him, several years ago, at her parents' pit-barbecue luncheonette, where she was working then, he had a good job at a lumberyard and he dressed nicely. He took her out to eat at a fancy restaurant. They got plastered and ended up in a motel in Tupelo, Mississippi, on Elvis Presley Boulevard. Back then, he talked nostalgically about his year in Vietnam, about how beautiful it was, how different the people were. He could never seem to explain what he meant. "They're just different," he said.

They went riding around in a yellow 1957 Chevy convertible. He drives too fast now, but he didn't then, maybe because he was so protective of the car. It was a classic. He sold it three years ago and made a good profit. About the time he sold the Chevy, his moods began changing, his even-tempered nature shifting, like driving on a smooth interstate and then switching to a secondary road. He had headaches and bad dreams. But his nightmares seemed trivial. He dreamed of riding a train through the Rocky Mountains, of hijacking a plane to Cuba, of stringing up barbed wire around the house. He dreamed he lost a doll. He got drunk and rammed the car, the Chevy's successor, into a Civil War statue in front of the courthouse. When he got depressed over the meaninglessness of his job, Jeannette felt guilty about spending money on something nice for the house, and she tried to make him feel his job had meaning by reminding him that, after all, they had a child to think of. "I don't like his name," Donald said once. "What a stupid name. Rodney. I never did like it."

Rodney has dreams about Big Bertha, echoes of his father's nightmare, like TV cartoon versions of Donald's memories of the war. But Rodney loves the stories, even though they are confusing, with lots of loose ends. The latest in the Big Bertha series is "Big Bertha and the Neutron Bomb." Last week it was "Big Bertha and the MX Missile." In the new story, Big Bertha takes a trip to California to go surfing with Big Mo, her male counterpart. On the beach, corn dogs and snow cones are free and the surfboards turn into dolphins. Everyone is having fun until the neutron bomb comes. Rodney loves the part where everyone keels over dead. Donald acts it out, collapsing on the rug. All the dolphins and the surfers keel over, everyone except Big Bertha. Big Bertha is so big she is immune to the neutron bomb.

"Those stories aren't true," Jeannette tells Rodney.

Rodney staggers and falls down on the rug, his arms and legs akimbo. He gets the giggles and can't stop. When his spasms finally subside, he says, "I told Scottie Bidwell about Big Bertha and he didn't believe me."

Donald picks Rodney up under the armpits and sets him upright. "You tell Scottie Bidwell if he saw Big Bertha he would pee in his pants on the spot, he would be so impressed."

"Are you scared of Big Bertha?"

"No, I'm not. Big Bertha is just like a wonderful woman, a big fat woman who can sing the blues. Have you ever heard Big Mama Thornton?"

"No."

"Well, Big Bertha's like her, only she's the size of a tall building. She's slow as a turtle and when she crosses the road, they have to reroute traffic. She's big enough to straddle a four-lane highway. She's so tall she can see all the way to Tennessee, and when she belches, there's a tornado. She's really something. She can even fly."

"She's too big to fly," Rodney says doubtfully. He makes a face like a wadded-up washrag and Donald wrestles him to the floor again.

Donald has been drinking all evening, but he isn't drunk. The ice cubes melt and he pours the drink out and refills it. He keeps on talking. Jeannette cannot remember him talking so much about the war. He is telling her about an ammunitions dump. Jeannette had the vague idea that an ammo dump is a mound of shotgun shells, heaps of cartridge casings and bomb shells, or whatever is left over, a vast waste pile from the war, but Donald says that is wrong. He has spent an hour describing it in detail, so that she will understand.

He refills the glass with ice, some 7-Up, and a shot of Jim Beam. He slams doors and drawers, looking for a compass. Jeannette can't keep track of the conversation. It doesn't matter that her hair is uncombed and her lipstick eaten away. He isn't seeing her.

"I want to draw the compound for you," he says, sitting down at the table with a sheet of Rodney's tablet paper.

Donald draws the map in red-and-blue ballpoint, with asterisks and technical labels that mean nothing to her. He draws some circles with the compass and measures some angles. He makes a red dot on an oblique line, a path that leads to the ammo dump.

"That's where I was. Right there," he says. "There was a water buffalo that tripped a land mine and its horn just flew off and stuck in the wall of the barracks like a machete thrown back-handed." He puts a dot where the land mine was, and he doodles awhile with the red ballpoint pen, scribbling something on the edge of the map that looks like feathers. "The dump was here and I was there and over there was where we piled the sandbags. And here were the tanks." He draws tanks, a row of squares with handles—guns sticking out.

"Why are you going to so much trouble to tell me about a buffalo horn that got stuck in a wall?" she wants to know.

But Donald just looks at her as though she has asked something obvious.

"Maybe I *could* understand if you'd let me," she says cautiously.

"You could never understand." He draws another tank.

In bed, it is the same as it has been since he started going away to Central City—the way he claims his side of the bed, turning away from her. Tonight, she reaches for him and he lets her be close to him. She cries for a while and he lies there, waiting for her to finish, as though she were merely putting on make-up.

"Do you want me to tell you a Big Bertha story?" he asks playfully.

"You act like you're in love with Big Bertha."

He laughs, breathing on her. But he won't come closer.

"You don't care what I look like anymore," she says. "What am I supposed to think?"

"There's nobody else. There's not anybody but you."

Loving a giant machine is incomprehensible to Jeannette. There must be another woman, someone that large in his mind. Jeannette has seen the strip-mining machine. The top of the crane is visible beyond a rise along the Western Kentucky Parkway. The strip mining is kept just out of sight of travelers because it would give them a poor image of Kentucky.

For three weeks, Jeannette has been seeing a psychologist at the free mental health clinic. He's a small man from out of state. His name is Dr. Robinson, but she calls him The Rapist, because the word *therapist* can be divided into two words, *the rapist*. He doesn't think her joke is clever, and he acts as though he has heard it a thousand times before. He has a habit of saying, "Go with that feeling," the same way Bob Newhart did on his old TV show. It's probably the first lesson in the textbook, Jeannette thinks.

She told him about Donald's last days on his job at the lumberyard—how he let the stack of lumber fall deliberately and didn't know why, and about how he went away soon after that, and how the Big Bertha stories started. Dr. Robinson seems to be waiting for her to make something out of it all, but it's maddening that he won't tell her what to do. After three visits, Jeannette has grown angry with him, and now she's holding back things. She won't tell him whether Donald slept with her or not when he came home last. Let him guess, she thinks.

"Talk about yourself," he says.

"What about me?"

"You speak so vaguely about Donald that I get the feeling that you see him as somebody larger than life. I can't quite picture him. That makes me wonder what that says about you." He touches the end of his tie to his nose and sniffs it.

When Jeannette suggests that she bring Donald in, the therapist looks bored and says nothing.

"He had another nightmare when he was home last," Jeannette

says. "He dreamed he was crawling through tall grass and people were after him."

"How do *you* feel about that?" The Rapist asks eagerly.

"I didn't have the nightmare," she says coldly. "Donald did. I came to you to get advice about Donald, and you're acting like I'm the one who's crazy. I'm not crazy. But I'm lonely."

Jeannette's mother, behind the counter of the luncheonette, looks lovingly at Rodney pushing buttons on the jukebox in the corner. "It's a shame about that youngun," she says tearfully. "That boy needs a daddy."

"What are you trying to tell me? That I should file for divorce and get Rodney a new daddy?"

Her mother looks hurt. "No, honey," she says. "You need to get Donald to seek the Lord. And you need to pray more. You haven't been going to church lately."

"Have some barbecue," Jeannette's father booms, as he comes in from the back kitchen. "And I want you to take a pound home with you. You've got a growing boy to feed."

"I want to take Rodney to church," Mama says. "I want to show him off, and it might do some good."

"People will think he's an orphan," Dad says.

"I don't care," Mama says. "I just love him to pieces and I want to take him to church. Do you care if I take him to church, Jeannette?"

"No. I don't care if you take him to church." She takes the pound of barbecue from her father. Grease splotches the brown wrapping paper. Dad has given them so much barbecue that Rodney is burned out on it and won't eat it anymore.

Jeannette wonders if she would file for divorce if she could get a job. It is a thought—for the child's sake, she thinks. But there aren't many jobs around. With the cost of a babysitter, it doesn't pay her to work. When Donald first went away, her mother kept Rodney and she had a good job, waitressing at a steak house, but the steak house burned down one night—a grease fire in the kitchen. After that, she couldn't find a steady job, and she was reluctant to ask her mother to keep Rodney again because of her bad hip. At the steak house, men gave her tips and left their telephone numbers on the bill when they paid. They tucked dollar bills and notes in the pockets of her apron. One note said, "I want to hold your muffins." They were real-estate developers and businessmen on important missions for the Tennessee Valley

Authority. They were boisterous and they drank too much. They said they'd take her for a cruise on the Delta Queen, but she didn't believe them. She knew how expensive that was. They talked about their speedboats and invited her for rides on Lake Barkley, or for spins in their private planes. They always used the word *spin*. The idea made her dizzy. Once, Jeannette let an electronics salesman take her for a ride in his Cadillac, and they breezed down The Trace, the wilderness road that winds down the Land Between the Lakes. His car had automatic windows and a stereo system and lighted computer-screen numbers on the dash that told him how many miles to the gallon he was getting and other statistics. He said the numbers distracted him and he had almost had several wrecks. At the restaurant, he had been flamboyant, admired by his companions. Alone with Jeannette in the Cadillac, on The Trace, he was shy and awkward, and really not very interesting. The most interesting thing about him, Jeannette thought, was all the lighted numbers on his dashboard. The Cadillac had everything but video games. But she'd rather be riding around with Donald, no matter where they ended up.

While the social worker is there, filling out her report, Jeannette listens for Donald's car. When the social worker drove up, the flutter and wheeze of her car sounded like Donald's old Chevy, and for a moment Jeannette's mind lapsed back in time. Now she listens, hoping he won't drive up. The social worker is younger than Jeannette and has been to college. Her name is Miss Bailey, and she's excessively cheerful, as though in her line of work she has seen hardships that make Jeannette's troubles seem like a trip to Hawaii.

"Is your little boy still having those bad dreams?" Miss Bailey asks, looking up from her clipboard.

Jeannette nods and looks at Rodney, who has his finger in his mouth and won't speak.

"Has the cat got your tongue?" Miss Bailey asks.

"Show her your pictures, Rodney." Jeannette explains, "He won't talk about the dreams, but he draws pictures of them."

Rodney brings his tablet of pictures and flips through them silently. Miss Bailey says, "Hmm." They are stark line drawings, remarkably steady lines for his age. "What is this one?" she asks. "Let me guess. Two scoops of ice cream?"

The picture is two huge circles, filling the page, with three tiny stick people in the corner.

"These are Big Bertha's titties," says Rodney.

Miss Bailey chuckles and winks at Jeannette. "What do you like to read, hon?" she asks Rodney.

"Nothing."

"He can read," says Jeannette. "He's smart."

"Do you like to read?" Miss Bailey asks Jeannette. She glances at the pile of paperbacks on the coffee table. She is probably going to ask where Jeannette got the money for them.

"I don't read," says Jeannette. "If I read, I just go crazy."

When she told The Rapist she couldn't concentrate on anything serious, he said she read romance novels in order to escape from reality. "Reality, hell!" she had said. "Reality's my whole problem."

"It's too bad Rodney's not here," Donald is saying. Rodney is in the closet again. "Santa Claus has to take back all these toys. Rodney would love this bicycle! And this Pac-Man game. Santa has to take back so many things he'll have to have a pickup truck!"

"You didn't bring him anything. You never bring him anything," says Jeannette.

He has brought doughnuts and dirty laundry. The clothes he is wearing are caked with clay. His beard is lighter from working out in the sun, and he looks his usual joyful self, the way he always is before his moods take over, like migraine headaches, which some people describe as storms.

Donald coaxes Rodney out of the closet with the doughnuts.

"Were you a good boy this week?"

"I don't know."

"I hear you went to the shopping center and showed out." It is not true that Rodney made a big scene. Jeannette has already explained that Rodney was upset because she wouldn't buy him an Atari. But she didn't blame him for crying. She was tired of being unable to buy him anything.

Rodney eats two doughnuts and Donald tells him a long, confusing story about Big Bertha and a rock-and-roll band. Rodney interrupts him with dozens of questions. In the story, the rock-and-roll band gives a concert in a place that turns out to be a toxic-waste dump and the contamination is spread all over the country. Big Bertha's solution to this problem is not at all clear. Jeannette stays in the kitchen, trying to think of something original to do with instant potatoes and leftover barbecue.

"We can't go on like this," she says that evening in bed. "We're just hurting each other. Something has to change."

He grins like a kid. "Coming home from Muhlenberg County is like R and R—rest and recreation. I explain that in case you think R and R means rock-and-roll. Or maybe rumps and rears. Or rust and rot." He laughs and draws a circle in the air with his cigarette.

"I'm not that dumb."

"When I leave, I go back to the mines." He sighs, as though the mines were some eternal burden.

Her mind skips ahead to the future: Donald locked away somewhere, coloring in a coloring book and making clay pots, her and Rodney in some other town, with another man—someone dull and not at all sexy. Summoning up her courage, she says, "I haven't been through what you've been through and maybe I don't have a right to say this, but sometimes I think you act superior because you went to Vietnam, like nobody can ever know what you know. Well, maybe not. But you've still got your legs, even if you don't know what to do with what's between them anymore." Bursting into tears of apology, she can't help adding, "You can't go on telling Rodney those awful stories. He has nightmares when you're gone."

Donald rises from bed and grabs Rodney's picture from the dresser, holding it as he might have held a hand grenade. "Kids betray you," he says, turning the picture in his hand.

"If you cared about him, you'd stay here." As he sets the picture down, she asks, "What can I do? How can I understand what's going on in your mind? Why do you go there? Strip mining's bad for the ecology and you don't have any business strip mining."

"My job is serious, Jeannette. I run that steam shovel and put the topsoil back on. I'm reclaiming the land." He keeps talking, in a gentler voice, about strip mining, the same old things she has heard before, comparing Big Bertha to a supertank. If only they had had Big Bertha in Vietnam. He says, "When they strip off the top, I keep looking for those tunnels where the Viet Cong hid. They had so many tunnels it was unbelievable. Imagine Mammoth Cave going all the way across Kentucky."

"Mammoth Cave's one of the natural wonders of the world," says Jeannette brightly. She is saying the wrong thing again.

At the kitchen table at 2:00 A.M., he's telling about C-5As. A C-5A is so big it can carry troops and tanks and helicopters, but it's not big enough to hold Big Bertha. Nothing could hold Big Bertha. He rambles on, and when Jeannette shows him Rodney's drawing of the circles, Donald smiles. Dreamily, he begins talking about women's breasts and thighs—the large, round thighs and big round breasts of American women, contrasted with the frail, delicate beauty of the Orientals. It is like comparing oven broilers and banties, he says. Jeannette relaxes. A confession about another lover from long ago is not so hard to take. He seems stuck on the breasts and thighs of American women—insisting that she understand how small and delicate the Orientals are, but then he abruptly returns to tanks and helicopters.

"A Bell Huey Cobra—my God, what a beautiful machine. So efficient!" Donald takes the food processor blade from the drawer where Jeannette keeps it. He says, "A rotor blade from a chopper could just slice anything to bits."

"Don't do that," Jeannette says.

He is trying to spin the blade on the counter, like a top. "Here's what would happen when a chopper blade hits a power line—not many of those over there!—or a tree. Not many trees, either, come to think of it, after all the Agent Orange." He drops the blade and it glances off the open drawer and falls to the floor, spiking the vinyl.

At first, Jeannette thinks the screams are hers, but they are his. She watches him cry. She has never seen anyone cry so hard, like an intense summer thundershower. All she knows to do is shove Kleenex at him. Finally, he is able to say, "You thought I was going to hurt you. That's why I'm crying."

"Go ahead and cry," Jeannette says, holding him close.

"Don't go away."

"I'm right here. I'm not going anywhere."

In the night, she still listens, knowing his monologue is being burned like a tattoo into her brain. She will never forget it. His voice grows soft and he plays with a ballpoint pen, jabbing holes in a paper towel. Bullet holes, she thinks. His beard is like a bird's nest, woven with dark corn silks.

"This is just a story," he says. "Don't mean nothing. Just relax." She is sitting on the hard edge of the kitchen chair, her toes cold on the floor, waiting. His tears have dried up and left a slight catch in his voice.

"We were in a big camp near a village. It was pretty routine and kind of soft there for a while. Now and then we'd go into Da Nang and whoop it up. We had been in the jungle for several months, so the two months at this village was sort of a rest—an R and R almost. Don't shiver. This is just a little story. Don't mean nothing! This is nothing, compared to what I could tell you. Just listen. We lost our fear. At night there would be some incoming and we'd see these tracers in the sky, like shooting stars up close, but it was all pretty minor and we didn't take it seriously, after what we'd been through. In the village I knew this Vietnamese family—a woman and her two daughters. They sold Cokes and beer to GIs. The oldest daughter was named Phan. She could speak a little English. She was really smart. I used to go see them in their hooch in the afternoons—in the siesta time of day. It was so hot there. Phan was beautiful, like the country. The village was ratty, but the country was pretty. And she was beautiful, just like she had grown up out of the jungle, like one of those flowers that bloomed high up in the trees and freaked us out sometimes, thinking it was a sniper. She was so gentle, with these eyes shaped like peach pits, and she was no bigger than a child of maybe thirteen or fourteen. I felt funny about her size at first, but later it didn't matter. It was just some wonderful feature about her, like a woman's hair, or her breasts."

He stops and listens, the way they used to listen for crying sounds when Rodney was a baby. He says, "She'd take those big banana leaves and fan me while I lay there in the heat."

"I didn't know they had bananas over there."

"There's a lot you don't know! Listen! Phan was twenty-three, and her brothers were off fighting. I never even asked which side they were fighting on." He laughs. "She got a kick out of the word *fan*. I told her that *fan* was the same word as her name. She thought I meant her name was banana. In Vietnamese the same word can have a dozen different meanings, depending on your tone of voice. I bet you didn't know that, did you?"

"No. What happened to her?"

"I don't know."

"Is that the end of the story?"

"I don't know." Donald pauses, then goes on talking about the village, the girl, the banana leaves, talking in a monotone that is making Jeannette's flesh crawl. He could be the news radio from the next room.

"You must have really liked that place. Do you wish you could go back there to find out what happened to her?"

"It's not there anymore," he says. "It blew up."

Donald abruptly goes to the bathroom. She hears the water running, the pipes in the basement shaking.

"It was so pretty," he says when he returns. He rubs his elbow absentmindedly. "That jungle was the most beautiful place in the

world. You'd have thought you were in paradise. But we blew it
sky-high."

In her arms, he is shaking, like the pipes in the basement,
which are still vibrating. Then the pipes let go, after a long
shudder, but he continues to tremble.

They are driving to the Veterans Hospital. It was Donald's
idea. She didn't have to persuade him. When she made up the
bed that morning—with a finality that shocked her, as though she
knew they wouldn't be in it again together—he told her it would
be like R and R. Rest was what he needed. Neither of them had
slept at all during the night. Jeannette felt she had to stay awake,
to listen for more.

"Talk about strip mining," she says now. "That's what they'll
do to your head. They'll dig out all those ugly memories, I hope.
We don't need them around here." She pats his knee.

It is a cloudless day, not the setting for this sober journey. She
drives and Donald goes along obediently, with the resignation of
an old man being taken to a rest home. They are driving through
southern Illinois, known as Little Egypt, for some obscure reason
Jeannette has never understood. Donald still talks, but very quietly, without urgency. When he points out the scenery, Jeannette
thinks of the early days of their marriage, when they would take a
drive like this and laugh hysterically. Now Jeannette points out
funny things they see. The Little Egypt Hot Dog World, Pharaoh
Cleaners, Pyramid Body Shop. She is scarcely aware that she is
driving, and when she sees a sign, Little Egypt Starlite Club, she
is confused for a moment, wondering where she has been
transported.

As they part, he asks, "What will you tell Rodney if I don't
come back? What if they keep me here indefinitely?"

"You're coming back. I'm telling him you're coming back
soon."

"Tell him I went off with Big Bertha. Tell him she's taking me
on a sea cruise, to the South Seas."

"No. You can tell him that yourself."

He starts singing a jumpy tune. He grins at her and pokes her
in the ribs.

"You're coming back," she says.

Donald writes from the VA Hospital, saying that he is making
progress. They are running tests, and he meets in a therapy group
in which all the veterans trade memories. Jeannette is no longer

on welfare because she now has a job waitressing at Fred's Family Restaurant. She waits on families, waits for Donald to come home so they can come here and eat together like a family. The fathers look at her with downcast eyes, and the children throw food. While Donald is gone, she rearranges the furniture. She reads some books from the library. She does a lot of thinking. It occurs to her that even though she loved him, she has thought of Donald primarily as a husband, a provider, someone whose name she shared, the father of her child, someone like the fathers who come to the Wednesday night all-you-can-eat fish fry. She hasn't thought of him as himself. She wasn't brought up that way, to examine someone's soul. When it comes to something deep inside, nobody will take it out and examine it, the way they will look at clothing in a store for flaws in the manufacturing. She tries to explain all this to The Rapist, and he says she's looking better, got sparkle in her eyes. "Big deal," says Jeannette. "Is that all you can say?"

She takes Rodney to the shopping center, their favorite thing to do together, even though Rodney always begs to buy something. They go to Penney's perfume counter. There, she usually hits a sample bottle of cologne—Chantilly or Charlie or something strong. Today she hits two or three and comes out of Penney's smelling like a flower garden.

"You stink!" Rodney cries, wrinkling his nose like a rabbit.

"Big Bertha smells like this, only a thousand times worse, she's so big," says Jeannette impulsively. "Didn't Daddy tell you that?"

"Daddy's a messenger from the devil."

This is an idea he must have gotten from church. Her parents have been taking him every Sunday. When Jeannette tries to reassure him about his father, Rodney is skeptical. "He gets that funny look on his face like he can see through me," the child says.

"Something's missing," Jeannette says, with a rush of optimism, a feeling of recognition. "Something happened to him once and took out the part that shows how much he cares about us."

"The way we had the cat fixed?"

"I guess. Something like that." The appropriateness of his remark stuns her, as though, in a way, her child has understood Donald all along. Rodney's pictures have been more peaceful lately, pictures of skinny trees and airplanes flying low. This morning he drew pictures of tall grass, with creatures hiding in it. The grass is tilted at an angle, as though a light breeze is blowing through it.

With her paycheck, Jeannette buys Rodney a present, a minia-

ture trampoline they have seen advertised on television. It is
called Mr. Bouncer. Rodney is thrilled about the trampoline, and
he jumps on it until his face is red. Jeannette discovers that she
enjoys it too. She puts it out on the grass, and they take turns
jumping. She has an image of herself on the trampoline, her sailor
collar flapping at the moment when Donald returns and sees her
flying. One day a neighbor driving by slows down and calls out to
Jeannette as she is bouncing on the trampoline, "You'll tear your
insides loose!" Jeannette starts thinking about that, and the idea
is so horrifying she stops jumping so much. That night, she has a
nightmare about the trampoline. In her dream, she is jumping on
soft moss, and then it turns into a springy pile of dead bodies.

OPERATE AND MAINTAIN

by Robert Stone

At 0401 Pablo Tabor signed himself off the circuit and put out the last cigarette of his watch. On his way through Search and Rescue to the Coke machine, he saw the sky through the Operations Room window, it was alight and clear, pale yellow.

"Ah me," he said softly.

Breedlove, the Operations yeoman, was watching him.

"Ol' Pablo must have smoked about a thousand cigarettes tonight," Breedlove told his yeoman striker. "I been watchin' him and he's smokin' the shit out over there."

"Leave me alone, Breedlove," Tabor said. "I already told you."

"Air," Breedlove said, winking at the striker. "Ay-er—that's what you need, Tabor."

"Give him air," the striker said busily.

Pablo was listening to his change rattle in the machine, to the bottle zip down its tin track. He picked it up, icy in his hot hand, and opened it.

"You know, you're just a couple of fucking noises in my head."

The striker smiled.

"That's all you are."

"We're all a deck of cards," Breedlove said.

"Hey, good night, Tabor," he called down the corridor when Tabor walked out. "Sleep well, hear?" He leaned over the Operations desk to see that Tabor was out of hearing and addressed himself to the striker.

"Don't think he ain't scoffin' those pills again. Tell by the little tiny eyes." He narrowed his own eyes to a squint. "Speed-freak

217

sparky. When he moves—it's jit jit jit." He moved the flat of his hand in little jits.

"Jitters," the striker said.

"Don't think they won't nail him," Breedlove said complacently.

"With this old man? Shit sure they'll nail him."

Some morning, Tabor thought, walking into the locker room, I'll kill that skinny prick. Except he wants me to so much, I won't.

He changed out of the dungaree uniform in which he had stood his watch and into civilian clothes. That morning he had brought a silky Western shirt, twill pants, a leather-like jacket and seven-stitch fancy boots. In the pocket of the jacket was a large aspirin bottle of Dexedrine and when he had changed he set the aspirin bottle beside his Coke and sat down on the wooden bench with his head in his hands.

Lord, he said to himself, the shit I sit still for. Make you weep, Jesus. He stood up suddenly and hit the tin grill of his locker with his left elbow and followed through with the palm of his right hand.

Just anybody calls me anything and I sit still for it. I don't know the fucking difference. He sat down again, unscrewed the cap on the aspirin bottle and tucked two Dex tabs in the pocket of his shirt. He swallowed two more with his Coke.

Now Breedlove, he thought, I'll tell him again and that'll be it. Breedlove's old lady worked in the supermarket, a good-looking head.

Gimme a break, God, Tabor prayed going out. Gimme a rush and ease my mind. A little good feeling.

On his way to sign out with JOD, he remembered the Coke bottle in his hand, so he went back around to Search and Rescue to stack it in the rack that held empties. When he left the bottle off, he saw Breedlove watching him.

He walked over and leaned on the Operations counter until Breedlove came over.

"I want to tell you something, Breedlove," he said, leaning close to the counter and speaking so softly that Breedlove had to incline his own head to hear him. "I want to tell you get off my case, man. Now if you don't do it I'm gonna transport your ass over to Gulfstream Plaza and I'm gonna beat the living shit out of you in front of that big old supermarket window. So your old lady can watch from the cash register."

Breedlove walked away pale, shaking his head.

Tabor checked out and went down the magnolia-lined walk that led to the gate and the parking lot. The lemon light was spreading across the sky, coloring the flat waters of the Gulf and the white hull of the fishery protection cutter that was tied up at the end of the pier. Eastward, night lights burned on the steel coils of the Escondido refinery and in the highway distance beyond it westbound headlights glowed snake eyes against the dawn.

"Gimme a rush, Jesus," Tabor said. He walked to his Chevy with the keys in his hand. He put the key in the door lock, smiled and licked his lips. One of these times, he thought, I'll have a car where you don't turn the key upside down. "Contact," he said. He was getting off a little and he turned to look at the sky over his shoulder.

"Gimme a rush, Jesus." He put the car in gear and rolled to the edge of the highway. "If you want me for a sunbeam."

A truck full of melons went by the gate and he smiled after it.

Gimme a rush if you truly want me for your personal sunbeam.

Once out of the gate, he ran in front of the drug, passing the melon truck with a grin.

Good morning, boys. What nice watermelons, yes indeed.

He cooled it at the town line, drove past the line of shrimp boats at the commercial pier, the fish market, the ceviche restaurant. First light hit the wide oily sidewalks of the main drag; a few Mexican women in tailored jeans walked toward the cannery.

He parked his Chevy just down the block from the Sullivan Hotel. The Sullivan was a three-story building with rounded corners of frosted glass and a sign beside the door that said "Locker Club, Servicemen Welcome." Tabor went in and across the small dusty lobby to the lounge out back. In the lounge there was a bar on rollers and a few plastic tables and chairs but the jukebox was the treasure of the Sullivan; it dated from World War II like the "Locker Club" sign by the street door. Linda Ronstadt's "Heart Like a Wheel" was spinning on it.

At one of the tables Mert McPhail, the station's chief radioman, was sitting with two girls in pants suits. The girls were drinking Jax; McPhail had a bottle of bourbon and a cardboard cup of ice beside his glass. They all looked up when Tabor walked in.

The older of the two girls with McPhail was named Nancy.

"Haayy, Pablo," she called as he walked toward them, "how're you keepin', keed?"

"Hey," Pablo said.

"You want a drink, honey? Want a whiskey? A cocktail?"

"Just a beer be nice. Why don't everybody have a beer?"

"Gracias, amigo," Nancy said, and went to the cooler. Tabor pulled up a chair and sat down beside McPhail.

"What say, McPhail?"

McPhail had been in the hotel most of the night. He was tired and drunk, a huge balding man with a brown, lined face—sloped-shouldered, six-six or -seven. He glanced at Tabor with distaste. The girl with him watched them both with a spacy smile.

"Real good," Tabor said. "Hey, you know," he told them after a minute, "it's such a nice morning I might just go after some birds. I got my Remington in the car. I might just go up back of the airport and get me a turk."

The girl at the table looked down at Tabor's feet.

"Gonna stomp through that old swamp with them pretty stitch boots on? Just get 'em all muddied up."

"I don't mind," Tabor said.

Nancy brought the beers to the table and set them out.

"Don't know about turkeys," she said. "But I bet you could get you a alligator back there."

"If I meet one I'll rassle with him. Hey, you think I could rassle a alligator, McPhail?"

McPhail had been studying the bare wall beside him.

"How the hell would I know?" he said.

"You could bring me back a pocketbook," Nancy said quickly. "But that's against the law now, ain't it? Alligator pocketbooks, they're against the law now."

"Ain't no more against the law than what's doin' in here," the younger girl said.

After a moment, McPhail stood up heavily and walked into the john. Tabor picked up his beer and drank half of it at a draw.

"Dry," he said.

The girls laughed as though he had told a joke.

"Hey, Pablo," Nancy said, "you goin' hunting right away or you gonna hang around awhile?"

"I don't know," Tabor said. He picked up his beer and walked into the men's room after McPhail.

In the men's room, he found McPhail flat-footed before the urinal, pissing contentedly. Holding the bottle in his hand, Tabor took up a position directly behind him and leaned against the wall.

"So I'm on report, huh, Chief?"

McPhail had turned his head as far to the side as he could, trying to see Tabor behind him.

"I did put you on report," he said as though he had just remembered it. "Chit's still on my desk. Straighten it out Monday."

He left off pissing and hastened to zipper his fly.

"Sure," Tabor said. "I'd really like to straighten it out, know what I mean, Chief?"

McPhail left quickly. When Tabor went back out, he found the chief radioman sitting on a barstool near the movable bar combing his thin black hair. Tabor watched him with what appeared to be good humor.

"What are you combing that with, McPhail? You combing it with piss? You didn't wash your hands in there."

The younger girl stood up at her place and walked straight out of the lounge into the lobby. McPhail struggled off his stool. His legs were trembling.

"I had just enough of you, you crazy son of a bitch," McPhail said, advancing on Tabor. "You damn psycho."

Tabor stood his ground, his hands by his sides.

"Don't let nothing hold you back but fear, McPhail."

Nancy moved between them, looking as though she were ready to duck.

"C'mon, now," she said. "C'mon, you all."

"What the hell's the matter with you, Tabor?" McPhail demanded. "You lost your goddamn marbles or something?"

"Maybe a lot the matter from your point of view, Chief," Tabor said. "But I don't appreciate your point of view. You don't even wash your hands when you go to the toilet."

McPhail stared at him, blank-eyed, silent, a head taller than Tabor.

"You're just nuts," the chief said finally. He took a step toward the door and lumbered on out, like an oversized old man. "You better see a doctor," he said.

Nancy fixed Pablo Tabor with a wise little mother look.

"Everybody's gonna be pissed at you, Pablo. Not just the Coast Guard but everybody."

"Well, that'll be too bad," Pablo said, and drank the rest of his beer. "I don't give a shit. I'm getting out here. Got to."

"You gonna request a transfer?"

"I'm gonna transfer myself," Tabor said. "This damn station is draggin' me down."

"Where would you go if you had a choice?"

"I'd wait for a message. When I got that message—goodbye. Could be any time. Maybe today."

"Well," Nancy said, "I hope you work it out okay." She lowered her voice a little and glanced toward the door that led to the lobby. "Hey, Pablo—you wouldn't have any extra speed around, would you?"

"Nope," Pablo said, and went out.

He drove to the inshore end of Main Street and turned west, through a neighborhood of old frame houses with peeling shutters and unfenced gardens gagged with kudzu. After a few blocks the houses and the paving ended and the road ran a course of sandy islands in the mud and saw grass that stretched to a distant line of pines. At the end of the roadway was a small square bungalow with some wooden dog pens beside it. Tabor parked in the muddy yard by the pens; as soon as he was out of his car, the dogs set up a barking.

"Hello, dogs," he said. His own two shorthairs were in the nearest pen, beside themselves at the sight of him, pressing their noses against the chicken wire, rearing and scratching against the boards of the pen gate.

"Wait a minute, wait a minute," Tabor said.

He took his twelve-gauge Remington from its cardboard box in the trunk, assembled it and stuffed his pockets with shells. The disc of the sun was over the horizon; he put his sunglasses on.

Freed, the shorthairs made a lightning circuit of the yard and hurried back to Tabor, bounding at his shoulders, climbing his legs until he put a knee up to force them down.

"Get down, fuckers," he told them. "What you think you're doin'? What you think you're doin', huh?"

An old black man came out of the bungalow holding a coffee pot in his hand.

"Gonna take 'em out?" he asked, glancing at Tabor's Saturday-night clothes.

"Sure am," Tabor said. He gave the old man three dollars, the dogs' boarding fee. Tabor lived in a trailer court where they didn't allow dogs.

"They been good dogs," the old man said. "Good dogs."

He followed the old man into the kitchen and accepted a half cup of coffee.

"See any birds?" Tabor asked.

"Le'see—I seen one, two up the other side of the airfield. That dry ground. Brush up there. Didn't have my gun at the time."

"Too bad," Tabor said.

The old man watched him take two pills from the aspirin bottle and swallow them with his coffee.

"I might have a shot at one of them airplanes back there," Tabor said. "Piss me off with the noise they make. Scaring the cows. And the dogs."

"Don't do that now."

Tabor set the cup down and picked up his gun.

"I been wasting my time around this place," Tabor told the old man. "Wasting the best years of my life, no shit."

"You got that feelin', huh?" He sat waiting for Tabor to take his dogs and go. "I s'pec' that's 'cause you a young man. Be restless. Nervous in the service, heh-heh."

"Nervous in the service," Tabor repeated in a lifeless voice. "Well, I'll see you."

"Sure enough," said the old man. "You might could get one outen that dry brush."

He set off along a raised trail through the swamp, the dogs running ahead, the sun behind him.

Nervous in the service. Okay, Tabor thought, he didn't mean nothing by it. Just an old nigger, shooting the shit.

The dogs closed over a rabbit scent, their snouts poking into the saw grass, haunches low and quivering, stub tails wagging out of control. Tabor kicked at the male.

"Get along, Trouble. Goddamn, it's a fucking rabbit."

The dogs, who dreaded his anger, took off through the grass, circled back to the trail and ran ahead looking busy. They had been good dogs to start with but they were too rarely hunted, gone to seed.

"Fucking morning," Tabor said.

From the airport off to his right, a Cherokee rose on a roar of engines and shot over his head toward the Gulf. Bound for the islands or Tampico, maybe Villahermosa, maybe Yucatán. There were clearings back in the swamp where the dope pilots landed their grass or Mexican brown—thousands of bills for a few hours' hauling. The dogs barked after the plane; Tabor watched the sunlight on its bright yellow wings as it gained altitude and settled in southwesterly.

"Very far from God this morning," he said. The second rush of speed began to jangle him. "Very far from you this morning, God."

The morning sun was raising the sweat beneath his shirt but his limbs felt cold and unconnected.

If I were God, Pablo Tabor thought, I wouldn't have mornings like this. The sun up on a swamp, two worthless dogs, a sparky with his blood full of speed and gasoline. No such morning could have a God over it.

If I were God, he thought, if I made mornings I wouldn't have no Pablo Tabor and his dogs in 'em.

"You do this, God?" he asked. "You operate and maintain mornings like this?"

He came to a fork in the raised trail and the dogs ran off to the right, toward the deeper swamp where the game was. Tabor turned left toward the shore. After a few minutes, the puzzled dogs fell in behind him; then, scenting the carrion of the beach, they whipped forward, running together.

The sun was partly in his eyes, his rush came up speckled, buzzing in his brain, old rages rose in his throat. Tasting the anger, he clenched his teeth.

Where the fuck to begin? he thought. But these people—there was hardly any getting at them.

"Usin' me," he sang out, "usin' me usin' me. Turning me and turning me and turning me around."

His mind's eye started flashing him shit—death's-heads, swastikas, the ace of spades. Dumbness. Dime-store badness. His anger rolled along, cooling and sharpening on the Dex. Before long he was standing on the beach, the sunlit Gulf spread out before him, coarse sand clinging to his wet cowboy boots. The dogs nosed along the waterline.

He walked down the beach, away from the sun, then stood with his eyes closed, his shotgun resting on his neck and shoulders, his forearms curled over it. His heart was throbbing in his side, in his temple, under his jaw. He eased the gun down and propped the stock against his thigh; from the jacket pocket he fished out two of the red and gold cartridges, forced them into the magazine of his shotgun, pumped them into place. Then a third—inserted it and pumped it forward.

The dogs had found the shell of a horseshoe crab and were worrying it, trying to lift it from the sand with their soft retriever's teeth. Tabor watched them.

If I moved, he thought, it would be like this.

The anger fell away from him as he raised the gun. He felt as though he were a metal image of himself, cool, without much reality.

Like this.

The charge drove the male dog's head down into wet sand, sent the rest of its body swinging on the pivot of its nearly severed neck to splash in the ebbing of a faint Gulf wave. Blood on the shimmering regular surface of the washed sand.

Tabor pumped the spent shell out. The female stood quivering at the shot, confused at what she saw, almost, it seemed, about to run. His second charge sent her into the air and she fell, still quivering, across a bough of flotsam mangrove.

He pumped the second shell out and licked his dry lips.

You happy now, you fool, you just murdered your dogs?

"I feel fine," Tabor said, "just fine." But it was not true. "They're fucking with my head this morning," he said.

He was walking away from the dogs, making himself not look back, when he caught sudden sight of two heads above the line of saw grass at the edge of the beach.

Stopping, he saw a boy and a girl in the grass not forty feet away from him. They stood in a peculiar crouch as though they had just stood up or were about to duck. He walked over to them.

The boy was blond, with a red bandana tied around his head; the girl almost as tall with shorter, darker hair. Tabor saw that she was crying.

"Had to be done," he told them. "They was sick, know what I mean? They had heartworm, had it real bad."

The young people seemed to relax a little. The girl wiped her sunburned cheek.

"Jeez," the boy said. "They were pretty dogs."

Tabor looked away from him.

"What the hell you know about it?"

He saw the girl's sad blue eyes on his shotgun.

"Don't you be crying over my dogs," he told her. "I'll cry over my own dogs."

They fell silent. The boy swallowed and twisted his mouth slightly.

"You want to chant with me?" Tabor asked them.

"I don't believe we know any chants," the boy said, with something like a smile. The girl clung to his arm.

"You think I'm gonna hurt you, don't you?"

"I hope not," the boy said softly. "We didn't mean any harm. We were just sad about the dogs."

You little bastard, Tabor thought, you got it all figured out. Humor the crazy man with the iron. Be gentle. Save your own and your girl friend's ass. Smart boy, Tabor thought. Smart boy.

"You're good kids," Tabor said. "I can see you are. You go to college, don't you?"

The boy nodded warily.

"Well I ain't gonna hurt you," Tabor told him. He turned from their frightened faces toward the sun. "Go ahead and have a nice day."

He walked off toward the water and they called "You too" in unison after him. As he passed between the corpses of his dogs, he turned back toward them and saw that they had not moved.

Cold to the marrow of his bones, he drove through town again and onto the Interstate, traveling west. The trailer court where he lived was beside an old canal, padded with water hyacinth. Across the highway was a brown slope where a billboard advertised a beach hotel and three derricks stood, their pistons rising and falling in perpetual motion.

Tabor's trailer was in the last row, the one furthest from the road and the most expensive.

He parked beside it, in a little driveway of crushed shell with a sick banana tree at the end of it. He had taken his sunglasses off getting out of the car, and the sun on the streamliner siding of his trailer dazzled his eyes. As he put the glasses back on, he looked toward the sorry little playground that stood fenced between two rows of trailers and saw his son. The boy was lying belly down on one of the rusty miniature slides, his arms dangling to the ground. With one hand he was sifting the surface of shredded shell and dried mud under the slide.

Tabor went to the playground gate.

"Billy."

The little boy started and turned over quickly, guiltily.

"How the hell come you ain't in school? Whatchyou doin' around here?"

Billy walked toward him ready to flinch.

"She didn't get you up, did she?" Tabor shouted. Billy shook his head. Tabor stood tapping his foot, looking at the ground.

"Dumb bitch," he whispered.

Hearing him, the boy wiped his nose, uneasily.

That could just do it, Tabor thought.

"Look here," he told the little boy, "I'm gonna drive you in after a while. Meantime you stay right out here and don't come in, hear?"

He went back to the trailer and let himself in. The living room had a sweet stale smell, spilled beer, undone laundry.

And it was just the sort of place you had to keep clean, he

thought. Like a ship. You had to keep it clean, or pretty soon it was like you were living in the back seat of your car.

Clothes were piled beside an empty laundry bag at one end of the pocket sofa—her blouses, work uniforms, Billy's dungarees. Spread out across the rest of the sofa were the sections of the past Sunday's paper. On the arm was a stack of Jehovah's Witness pamphlets she had let some missionaries give her.

She was asleep in their bedroom, the end compartment.

Tabor went quietly into the kitchen and opened the waist-high refrigerator. There were three shelves in it—the bottom shelf held nothing except cans of Jax beer. On the two top shelves were row upon row of hamburger patties each on its separate waxed-paper square. She brought them home frozen in cardboard boxes from the place she worked.

As he looked at the rows of hamburger, a curious impulse came into his mind. He straightened up and took a breath—he had the sensation of time running out, of seconds being counted off toward an ending. Finally, he took a can of Jax out, opened it and sat down on the living-room sofa facing the plastic door.

If he allowed himself one more, he thought, he might coax another rush. On the one hand go easy because things are getting fast and bad; on the other hand fuck it. He took a Dex out of the bottle, bit off half and swallowed it with the beer. After a few moments he swallowed the other half.

In the kitchen again, he threw the empty beer can away and stood looking out of the little window above the sink. Miles of bright green grass stretching to the cloudless blue, the horizon broken here and there by bulbous raised gas tanks on steel spider legs, like flying saucer creatures. You could picture them starting to scurry around the swamp and they'd be fast all right, they'd cover ground.

He opened the refrigerator and took one of the hamburger patties out.

"Now that's comical," he said, holding it over the sink. His chest felt hollow.

His hand closed on the hamburger, wadding it together with the waxed paper. A fat, dirty, greasy fucking thing. He couldn't stop squeezing on it. The ice in it melted with the heat of his hand and the liquid ran down the inside of his forearm. He took a couple of deep breaths; his heartbeat was taking off, just taking off on him. He dropped the meat in the sink.

When he had washed his hands, he went into the compartment at the opposite end of the trailer from their bedroom, the place where he kept his own things. Everything there was in good order.

There was a locked drawer under the coat closet where Tabor kept his electronics manuals and his military .45 automatic. He took the pistol out, inserted a clip and went back into the kitchen.

With the gun in his right hand, he gathered up as many of the hamburgers as he could manage with his left and went to the bedroom.

"Meat trip," he said.

She had the blue curtains drawn against the morning light. The covers were pulled up over her ears; in the space between her pillow and the wall were a rolled magazine and a spilled ashtray that had fouled the sheet with butts. Tabor moved around her bed, delicately setting hamburger patties at neat intervals along the edge.

"Kathy," he called softly.

She stirred.

"I killed the dogs," he said.

"You did what?" she said, and as she came awake she saw the little circle of meat in front of her.

She started to turn over; Tabor let her see the barrel of the gun and forced her back down on the pillow with its weight.

"Pab," she said, in a small broken voice. He held the gun against the ridge of bone beside her eye and let her listen to the tiny click the safety made when he released it.

She had begun to tremble and to cry. Her nose was scarcely two inches from the waxed-paper edge of the hamburger in front of her.

"You want to go out on a meat trip, Kathy? Just you and all those ratburgers all over hell?"

"Oh, God," she whispered. "Oh, Pab."

He was thinking that when he had pressed the safety the thing was as good as done. If I moved, he thought, it would be like the dogs.

"Shall I count off for you? You want to read one of them Jehovah books before you go out?" He reached behind him and pulled a little chair nearer the bed and sat down on it. "No use in getting out of bed, baby. 'Cause it's good-night time."

He watched her mouth convulse as she tried to breathe, to speak. Like the dogs, he thought.

A fecal smell rose from the covers; he lifted them and saw the bottom sheet soiled with bile. He covered her again.

"You fuckin' little pig," he said wearily.

The voice broke from her trembling body.

"Baby," she said. "Oh, baby, please."

He stood up and put the gun down on the chair. From his wallet he took two singles and dropped them on her covers.

"That there's for all the good times," he told her, and picked up the gun and put it in his pocket.

She was still screaming and sobbing when he went out with his bag. It was like a bad dream outside—the traffic on the highway just shooting on by, the derricks across the highway up and down up and down. Craziness. He was weak in the knees; he put the bag in the back seat and walked to the playground to call his son.

"Hey, you gonna drive me now, Daddy?"

"Looks like I ain't today. I gotta go somewhere, so you can just hang out and play."

"Neat," the boy said. "You ain't goin' to sea, are ya, Daddy?"

"Yeah, I am," Tabor said. "The South Sea."

He leaned on the wire fence and took a deep breath.

"You be good to your mother, hear? She needs you to be real good to her."

"Yes, sir," the boy said.

WHERE PELHAM FELL
by Bob Shacochis

Less than a year after Colonel Taylor Coates had been told not to drive he was behind the wheel again, smoking Chesterfields, another habit he had been warned not to pursue, clear-headed and precise in his own opinion, holding the patriotic speed limit north on Route 29 away from Culpeper in a flow of armies and horses and artillery across the battlefields of Virginia. On one flank the landscape pitched toward a fence of Blue mountains, on the other it receded through the bogs and level fields of Tidewater and as far as Colonel Coates was concerned, there was no better frame for a gentleman's life. There never had been, there never would be, which wasn't just a guess because the Corps of Engineers had made him world-sore, a forty-year migrant before they discharged him in the direction of the Piedmont.

The Confederate John Mosby came onto the road at the Remington turnoff and galloped alongside the car for a mile or two, spurring his Appaloosa stallion. The Colonel deaccelerated so he wouldn't lose him. Mosby pointed to a field map clutched in the same hand that held the reins. His boots were smeared with red clay, the tails of his longcoat flapped, and he held his head erect, his beard divided by the wind. Colonel Coates rolled down the car window and shouted over into the passing lane. *You!* Mosby arched an eyebrow and leaned to hear the Colonel's voice in the thunder of a diesel truck prepared to overtake them. The breeze flipped the Colonel's walking hat into the passenger seat, exposing the white brambles of his hair, blew cigarette ash into his eyes. *Your grandson honored me with a button off that coat you're wearing.* The Gray Ghost, as Mosby was known to those who loved or feared him, saluted and rode off onto the shoulder of the pike. The truck rumbled past between them followed by a long stream of gun caissons pulled by teams of quarter horses showering froth into the air.

Well, now, in the presence of consecrated ground, even the imaginations of simple men are stirred to hazy visions, and Colonel Coates wasn't simple, only old, recuperating from the shingles and a number of years of puzzling spiritual fatigue, being given too many years on earth. He had snuck out onto the road to buy dogfood but had never reached the store and was returning home with two dirty burlap sacks full of what had been described to him as noisy bones. Bones they were, laced with rotted scraps of wool and leather, too sacred for canine bellies and tasteless anyway. But no noise to them that the Colonel could detect other than the dull rattle and chalky shift they made when he and the old black fellow carried them out of the shed and hoisted them into the rear of the station wagon. The black man had what he and the Colonel agreed was accurately called nigger notion: the bones talked too much, the men whose flesh once hung on these disjointed skeletons were still in them, like the tone in a tuning fork, refusing the peace of afterlife in favor of their military quarrels. That's a voodoo I never had use for, the Colonel said. Men our age find queer ways to pass the time. I ain't yo age as yet, the fellow answered back, and I never said I had trouble fillin' a day like some folks I know.

Colonel Coates wasn't a man to heed mere telling, nor to concede to age what age had not yet earned or taken. All right, he said to the black man, whose name was President Trass. With all respect for your habits, I am obliged to recover the remains of these brave boys.

You take dem bones you might be gettin' some nigger notions yo'self, President Trass said. Prob'ly do you some good.

I've been waiting half my life for a younger fellow to set me straight, the Colonel said—and I don't reckon you're him.

Well, Colonel, President said with a tight smile, winking at the sacks of bones in the car. You finally get in with the right crowd to tell you a thing or two.

Dippy was born in 1899, which put her a year and a century ahead of Colonel Taylor Coates and allowed her certain privileges as his wife of sixty-four years. She could shut him up by reminding him of the fact because the Colonel was vulnerable to the past, and jealous of anyone who had a greater access to it than

him. That was the advantage her one hundred years gave her. As
for her extra year, a young woman with that sort of lead on a
young man cannot be reckoned with quite so easily. In the eyes of
her affection, men are found in one direction, boys in the opposite. When they met at a chorale program on a blizzardy evening
the winter of 1919 in Leadville, Colorado, Dippy was anything
but coy with the young junior surveyor sent fresh from the
University of Virginia. She suspected correctly that he was a mere
teenager despite his shiny moustaches, the tips of which could
still be seen when his back was turned. They were introduced by
her cousin, a supplier of dynamite, when the artists had ended their
hymns and the audience squeezed around the coal stove at the
back of the town hall, sipping hot chocolates and coffees brewed
by the Christian Women's League. He had a shy face and over-
practiced manners. From his eastern suit came the faint tangy
fragrance of the saddle. Dippy, who was self-assured, a pretty
dark-haired Tennessee belle with unformed ambitions, offered
him none of the deference a youth needed when he set out to make
an impression on women. Even at first sight, Taylor knew Dippy
was his elder, at least his equal, unquestionably a lady.

What a curious name you have, he said to her, tucking the
fingers of his right hand into his dove-gray waistcoat. I believe it
makes me want to smile. Taylor tried to smile but he couldn't,
nervous as he was. His mouth formed what Dippy felt was a
sincere grimace. Surely it's a sobriquet, he said.

Ah *what*? she asked, bemused, thickening her voice. Taylor
thought she was mocking his Rappahannock drawl. The girls in
Charlottesville never seemed so threatening as this petticoated
creature in the snowy mountains. He flushed and mumbled, Not
your full name, is it? I mean to say, Christian.

She spoke with a parlor-room formality when she answered,
more nasal and northern, and she said to him straight-faced, No,
Mister Coates, you are correct. My real name, received under the
waters of baptism, is Diphtheria. I was named for the disease that
makes men weak, and causes them difficulty in breathing.

Of course the women nearby squealed and the men slapped
their legs. Somebody called out, That boy seems to have a touch
of it himself, Dippy. In the short gloom of Taylor's humiliation he
discovered he was fascinated by her. She had only intended to
bait this newcomer, not sink a hook into a fish that was barely
keeper size. It was as though she had worked a spell on him and
he adored her immediately, Dippy Barrington, and badgered her

into a proper courtship, wise and restrained, that ended two years later in marriage.

Well, you've made a damn fool out of me, he said that night after the laughter had died down. At least you could tell me your true name so I'll know to steer away from other women who carry it. She took him aside and told him that before she was born her father was refused a job on a newspaper in Nashville because he had no diploma to certify his ability. Come back when you got one, the editor ordered. Dippy arrived seven months later, Barrington's first child, and he felt such an occasion was diploma enough for anybody, verifying that belief by naming her so. He went back to the newspaper and found the same editor. I got that diploma you were talking about, he told the man. You do, do you? the editor grumbled. Get on a train to Denver and send me back some of those Wild West stories. A year later he returned, half-owner of a Colorado silver mine, to collect his wife and daughter.

Your mother was nothing but a Tennessee hillbilly when I first met her, Colonel Coates would tell his children at the dinner table in the years ahead. When the children, and then the grandchildren, grew old enough to hear what lay behind the words, they each marvelled at the implicit sensuality in Dippy's familiar response. *That's right, Taylor bought me my first pair of shoes.* Everybody knew it wasn't true, at least not the substance, but in tone it was a seduction replayed, an old skit to show the strategies of a love that could not be unmade.

Since turning eighty, Dippy slept more during the day, catnaps on the sofa in the den, a quilt pulled over her legs, not because she was tired but because her dreams were more vivid and interesting than they had ever been before, and nothing she witnessed in them frightened her. She hadn't slept so much in daylight since 1942 when she was always tired. Awaking from those naps she was miserable. The extreme loneliness of the dead seemed in her as if she had been spinning in solitude through the blackness of outer space. That ended though when she left the house to become a nurse. After the war Taylor came home. It took some time for him to become her friend again, to settle in his own mind that he wasn't going anywhere without her the rest of his life. The migrations began again, so many places, so many homes she created only to dismantle them a year or two later.

None of the years though were as hard to endure as the three before the last. Taylor, infirm but alert, first his prostate and then the shingles which left extensive scars across his shoulders and chest, issuing orders from bed: I want this, I want that, I want the goddamn pain to let off for sixty blasted seconds. You're a nurse, do something. Dippy, have you fed the dogs? Has the *Post* been delivered yet? Did you hire a boy to pick the apples? Dippy, come up here and tell me what's happened to your ability to fix a simple egg.

The house and lands were too much for her to manage alone. She had secretly put herself and the Colonel on the waiting list at Vincent Hall up in Fairfax. There were days she wished to God He would make Taylor vanish into history, which was what the man had always wanted anyway. Just as she became acclimated to the regimen of his illness and moods, he popped out of bed one day fifteen months ago, announcing he would occupy his last days touring the fields of battle in the area. He recharged the battery in the Ford pick-up and motored down the cedar-lined drive on his mission, to be grounded semi-voluntarily three months later after what seemed like, but wasn't, a premeditated string of collisions, mad acts against authority. He plowed into a Prince George's County Sheriff's patrol car, a state park maintenance vehicle, a welded pyramid of cannonballs at New Market. None of these accidents injured more than vanity and metal. Each occurred during a low speed drift, the Colonel mesmerized by the oblique and mystical harmonies played for him by Fredericksburg, by Bull Run, by New Market where the cadets had fought.

The truck was sold rather than repaired. Taylor sulked and groused for several weeks, the pace of his recuperation slackening to a plateau. He entered a year of book reading, map gazing, talking back to the anchormen on the television news, typing letters to the editors of papers in Washington, Richmond, and Charlottesville, disavowing the new conservatism because its steam was religious jumpabout, lacking in dignity and too hot-blooded for an Episcopalian whose virtue had never faltered to begin with. *Are we cowards?* one letter inquired after a terrorist attack on an embassy. *Many Americans today seem to think so. We are afraid we are but I tell you we are not. What the true citizens and families of this nation have learned is not to abide by courage wasted.* For his grandchildren he penned accounts of the clan, the Coates and the Barringtons and Tylers and Holts and Hucksteps, hoping to seduce them into a fascination with their heritage, that precious ancestral silt deposited in the land. *My grandpa,* he wrote, *was Major Theodore Coates of the Army of Northern Virginia. He was assigned to General Early's staff and fought valiantly for the Confederate cause until the Battle of Antietam where within an hour's carnage he was struck directly in the ear by a cleaner bullet. The wound itself was not fatal but it destroyed the Major's inner ear, denying him his equilibrium and orientation and causing him to ride in front of his own artillery as they discharged a salvo of grapeshot over the lines, so witnesses said.* To a different child Taylor wrote, *When I was a little boy like yourself, my father took me to Richmond to a congress of white-haired veterans of the Confederate Armies. I was introduced to these gallant old warriors but no man impressed me more than Major Henry Kyd Douglas, who had ridden with Stonewall. I recall his blue eyes meeting mine, those same eyes that had looked upon the great General. He shook my hand. You must shake my hand also with this connection in mind.* When one of the grandchildren, a boy at college in New England, wrote back that the rebellion, not to mention the family's participation in it, was too disgraceful and produced in him a guilt by association, Taylor responded, *You might reasonably suppose that your ancestors were on the wrong side in this conflict, but I assure you they were not wrong-minded, no more so than the nation itself was. White men weren't slaughtering each other because of black men, that was clear from the start. Read about the city of New York during those years. When you go into Boston on your weekends, what is it that you see? Do you really mean to tell me that Northerners died to save the Negro from us?*

What do you think of communism? he had asked a married granddaughter last Christmas. It's foo foo, she answered, and afterwards he decided he had communicated enough with the new generation.

Writing in his study on the second floor of the antebellum brick farmhouse, Taylor could look out across hayfields and orchards to the Blue Ridge. He found the gentility of the view very satisfying. On stormy days the mountains were purple. Dramatic shafts of light would pierce the clouds and the Colonel was reminded of the colors of the Passion and Golgotha. When he was tired of sitting he would walk the dogs around the property since they were too lazy to do it by themselves. It was a serene year and neither Dippy nor Taylor had much desire to go beyond their own land. When once a week she took the station wagon into Culpeper to shop, Taylor went along, and he did not protest being demoted to the status of a passenger.

Last night had been a restless one, troubled by a vague insomnia. He slipped out of bed three or four times to listen to the radio, stare out the window at the silhouettes of the outbuildings in the Appalachian moonshine. When he urinated it felt as though the wrong stuff was streaming out, not liquid waste but vital fluid. Nights such as this he felt were nothing more than waiting to kick off into eternity, to blink and gasp and be a corpse. At breakfast his shingles burned again and his breathing was more constricted. He had difficulty concentrating on the morning paper. His tongue seemed coated with an aftertaste of medicine that even Dippy's coffee couldn't penetrate.

After lunch Dippy snoozed on the couch, the afghan she was knitting bunched on her chest. When she awoke she went right to the kitchen door, knowing he was gone. It was wrong of Taylor to do this to her. Trusting him had never been much of an issue in the course of their marriage except when the children were growing up, and only then because he played too rough with them, wanted them to learn reckless skills and showed no patience for the slow art of child-rearing. He had once knocked out Grover when the boy was twelve years old, demonstrating how to defend himself. Throughout his life the Colonel had been a good enough man to admit his shortcomings, by and by, but now he had even survived his ability to do that.

She walked nervously around the house, emptying the foul nubs of tobacco he had crammed into ashtrays, thinking about what she might do. Nothing. Phone the sheriff and have the old mule arrested before he banged into someone and hurt them. That would serve him right and placate the annoyance she felt at Taylor's dwindling competence, three-quarters self-indulgence and willful whimsy anyway, she thought, the man trespassing everywhere, scattering his mind over too much ground. It was as though the Colonel had decided to refuse to pay attention. If he hadn't returned within the hour she would call Taylor's nephew in Warrenton for advice. In the meantime she couldn't stay in the house alone, marking his absence.

She put on her black rubber boots, cotton work gloves from out of a kitchen drawer, a blue serge coat over her dress, wrapped a red chiffon scarf around her tidy hair and knotted it under her chin. On her way out she turned the heat to low beneath the tea kettle. In the yard the dogs ran up to her and she shooed them away as she always did, afraid their clumsy affection would knock her down.

Behind the house the pasture was sprayed with wildflowers for the first time she could remember, the result of a Christmas gift called *Meadow in a Can* from one of the grandchildren. She walked out into it and the air smelled like sun-hot fresh linen. She went as far down as the swale, sniffed at its cool stone dampness and headed back, the dogs leaping in front of her, whirlybirds for tails. She didn't like toolsheds, perhaps because she had despised outhouses, stepping in with the bugs and reptiles that haunted perpetual shadow. In Mexico as a girl she had placed her bare bottom right smack on a scorpion, burst back out into the sunlight with her drawers around her ankles, hysterical, the Mexican stable boys getting a good laugh. She reached into the shed just far enough to get the rake and pruning clippers, thinking she'd pull what remained of last autumn's leaves out of the ivy beds, and cut jonquils to take inside. Below the front porch, where the boxwoods swelled with an aroma that Dippy associated with what was colonial and southern, she tugged at the ivy with the tines of the rake, accomplishing little. Then the Colonel came home.

The station wagon bounced over the cattle bars sunk into the entrance of the drive and lurched ahead, slicing gravel. She looked back toward the road, wondering if Taylor was being chased but certainly he wasn't. Dippy reached the turnaround as he pulled in, swerving and skidding, making white dust. One of the front fenders was puckered from the headlight to the wheel well. She stamped over and rapped with the handle of the rake on this new damage Taylor had dared to bring home.

He remained in the car, veiled behind the glare on the windshield, his hands clawed to the steering wheel, reluctant to drop them shaking to his lap while he suffered his pride. The dogs barked and hopped into the air outside his door as if they sprang off trampolines. Dippy kept rapping on the fender with the rake, harder and harder, drumming shame. His jaw slackened and his shoulders seemed no longer able to endure the gravity of the spinning world. He prayed for a composure, for the muscle of his feckless heart to beat fiercely against their damn devilish luck, the fate that had made them two living fossils, clinging to the earth with no more strength than moths in a rising breeze.

The Colonel rolled down his window. "Stop that," he said.

"You are a hazard, old man."

"Stop that. I won't stand for this Baptist behavior."

"Come out of there."

"Stop that. Stop doing that."

Well, Dippy did cease her banging on the fender but then she didn't know what to do next to emancipate the sickness that came when she had realized Taylor had launched himself back onto the highways where he was likely to murder himself. She jabbed at the fender with the rake once more.

"I expect you must've run over somebody this time out, old fool."

"I won't be mocked, Dippy," the Colonel proclaimed. "Why, I never killed anyone in my life."

He quivered with the temporary health of rage, and he wouldn't say another word to her though he kept going on to himself. Ah, he said bitterly, look. I can't say one thing without being reminded of another I don't want. There was the curse of age for you, a life darting behind itself to pick through the droppings. When the war had ended he was visited by the most distasteful melancholy imaginable, so profane that he had never spoken of it to anyone, and never would. It continued through the year of 1946 as he rebuilt roads and airstrips in Germany. At the time it didn't seem right to go through what he had in the Corps of Engineers without being able to kill somebody for it as a sort of metaphysical payment. A high form of earthly enlightenment had been denied him, he had thought then. You were supposed to bring that bloody knowledge home from war and make good use of it somehow. The irony of the recollection cast a wild imbalance into his gray eyes. He poked his head out the window, infested by memory.

"What was so important that you had to sneak off like a hoodlum?"

"Bones," he said too loudly, "bones," followed by a sigh. He had jumped ahead and had to backtrack to his explanation.

"Dog food," he corrected himself. She knew better and he had to tell the truth. "I went to see where Major Pelham fell, that's all."

Taylor coaxed his limbs out of the car and she listened to him tell the story of what he had been up to. "Noisy bones?" she said skeptically. He brushed past her to open the tailgate on the wagon. She frowned, though, because inside she felt herself straining to hear the muddled end of an echo ringing across the boundlessness. Was a message being delivered or not? Her longevity had made her comfortable with the patterns of coincidence and happenstance that life enjoyed stitching, cosmic embroidery on a simple chemical design of flesh. She tried to make herself extra-receptive to this peculiar sensation of contrivance but nothing clear came through.

"I think you've finally gone cuckoo, Taylor Coates," she said.

"None of that. These are heroes." He patted the sacks. "Gallant boys."

Dippy was bewildered. Goodness, she thought, what sort of

intrusion was this? Who's to say how she knew, or what sense was to be made out of it? A bridge formed between somewhere and somewhere else and Dippy understood that the man who had given the Colonel the bones was right—they were *noisy* bones, not the first she had met either. Oh, you could call those invisible places by so many names: intuition, spirit and ether, witchery and limbo. Don't think that she didn't reflect endlessly about the meaning of each word that could be attached to the force of the unknown. Even as a child her life had been visited by startling moments of clairvoyance and fusion. Each instance felt as if she had just awakened at night to someone calling through a door.

"Look," the Colonel invited, and peeled back the lip of the burlap to reveal the clean dome of a skull.

There were occasions in Dippy's life, each with its own pitch and resonance, chilling seconds when she attracted information from the atmosphere that translated into impulsive behavior: refusing to allow children out of the house, once persuading Taylor not to buy a horse because she sensed evil in the presence of the animal, sending money to a Buddhist temple she had entered briefly when they lived in Indonesia. She avoided riding in cars with Connecticut license plates if she could. As a nurse at Bethesda Naval Hospital during the war, she watched a sailor die on the operating table after hearing her son's voice say, *He's a goner, Ma*. You're dead too, aren't you, she heard herself say back to him, and then held her tears while still another dying patient was wheeled in.

—There are a few things you don't know about me, she said to the Colonel in February when he saw her mailing a letter to a scientist she had read about in the paper, a man at Duke University who researched these phenomena.

—That's not right. After all this time.

—Yes it is, she said. Secrets are what crones and children thrive on.

The Colonel pawed through the bones, exhibiting a look of sanctified pleasure. Warriors in a sack, seasoned messengers of glory. Conscripts from the republic of death. Dippy cursed them like any mother or wife. Dog food indeed. Why else were the bones here but to seduce the Colonel with their chatter.

"I suppose we better call the police."

"The police!" the Colonel said. "Never. I'm going to find out where these poor boys belong."

"There's only one place bones belong," she said.

"They'll take their seat in history first," Taylor insisted, shuffling the bones he had pulled out back into their sacks. He straightened up, frail and indignant.

"God wants those souls placed to rest."

"No he don't, Dippy. Not yet he don't. Not till I find out who they were."

Rally them, Colonel, rally the boys.

Major John Pelham commanded Stuart's Horse Artillery until he fell at the Battle of Kelly's Ford, mortally wounded by shrapnel that ribboned his flesh and broke the forelegs of his sorrel mount. The skirmish was between cavalry charging blindly through a terrain of deep woods and dense scrub along the banks of the Rappahannock, the riders cantering through trackless forest, squads of men blundering into tangled thickets, the legs of their coarse pants cut by lead and briar thorns. Down went Pelham as he inspired his men forward, and the event was memorialized many years later by a roadside marker at a junction on Route 29, a sign erected near Elkwood by the United Daughters of the Confederacy informing the curious that four miles to the southeast the young Major had been martyred to the rebel cause.

Brandy Station, two miles south of Elkwood, was where Colonel Coates really headed when he deserted his slumbering wife to replenish the supply of dog food, a legitimate errand that he automatically forgot in favor of cruising Fleetwood Hill. The hill was the field of war that engaged him most thoroughly, for there was fought the greatest cavalry battle ever on American soil. The site, virtually unchanged since the mayhem of 1863, had the smell of clover and apple blossoms at this time of year, a nostalgic blend that floated a man's thoughts through the decades of Aprils he had survived. The Colonel studied accounts of the conflict, knew its opposing strategies, its advances and countercharges, flankings and retreats. He preferred to sit atop a granite outcropping on the knob of the rise and, with an exhilarating rush of details, play out the eleven-hour struggle for himself, the thunder of the enfilades, the agonizing percussion of hooves, swords, musketry. Here the sons of America had devoured each other as if they were Moors and Christians. Here slaughter was an exquisite legend. History could be scratched by the imagination and made to bleed on a few hundred acres of green farmland magnificently fouled by violence.

A year without independence had made Colonel Coates lust for a prowl at Brandy Station. After the war between the north and the south, that was all the aristocracy had left, the right to remembrance. Taylor had claimed this right and felt obliged to it, his vigil registered in the bloody heart of the land as if he himself —his existence—was the true outcome of the fray: a florid, half-bald man alone in a rolling pasture, hitching his loose pants up repeatedly to keep them above the horns of his failing hips, stricken by the deep blue plunge of loss for those things he wanted but now knew he would not have; for those things he had possessed and loved but whose time was past; for myth and now time itself, for what was, for the impossibility of ever being there.

And yet he would return from the battlefield uplifted.

Out on the road, however, the Colonel was distracted by the withdrawal of federal troops back across the river and he bypassed Brandy Station, not realizing his mistake until he spotted the marker post commemorating Pelham on the east side of the highway. Abruptly and without signalling, he veered onto the shoulder and turned on the country road, grim but unrepentant of the nuisance he made for the traffic behind him. Before the privilege of mobility had been taken from him, he had spent an afternoon in aggravated search for the location of Pelham's slaying. The direction of the marker was vague—four miles to the southeast—and the road that supposedly went there split, forked, crossed and looped through pine and pasture without bringing Taylor to the ford of the river. Sixteen miles later he threw up his hands and jogged west, eventually arriving at a surfaced pike that returned him to Route 29.

It was now or never again, the Colonel rationalized. From the diaries of the Generals he had learned that an opportunity renewed by destiny could not be prevented. The soldiers themselves often hastened forth under the influence of such patterns through the same geography, wandering here and there until suddenly foes met and clashed. The paths they followed were subject to mortifying change. What was right yesterday might be wrong today. But that was the nature of rebel territory—a free-for-all. The Colonel, in slow reconnaissance, took the road to a tee intersection, craning to see the houses at the end of their lanes, under guard of oaks, evergreens, rail fences. Virginia, he thought, was the abattoir of the south, mother of the destruction. These were the

estates that sent their young men to war, the houses where the
lucky wounded returned to expire in their own beds, where the
enemy plundered, where the secessionist ladies wept through the
night as the armies marched by. What did people in the north know
of the residue of terror that had settled in the stones and beams
of these estates? Where in America were there such noble structures,
one after another, each a silent record of strife? It was not an
exaggeration to say that the Colonel adored these houses.

At the intersection the pavement ended and an orangish gravel
lane cut left and right. Taylor calculated a southwest direction by
examining the sun. The odometer had advanced three miles. He
swung left, pleased that the road soon curved auspiciously by his
reckoning to the south over swampy ground created, he was sure,
by its proximity to the river. For four miles more the road
wormed through this low wet countryside reeking of bog rot,
switched its designation twice and then ascended to higher land,
no river in sight, no water crossing, no defunct mill-house, no
aura of hostility. Nothing but the warm hum of springtime.

By God, I'm missing in action, the Colonel joked to himself,
confused as to his whereabouts. And that was how he ended up
in possession of the bones.

Cresting a ridge he sighted the glint of running water a half
mile in the distance. The road he was on went off away from it
but there was a narrower track burrowing through a stand of
hardwood that appeared as though it might drop in the right
direction. On the opposite fringe of the grove, the Colonel saw he
had blundered onto private property—and a trash haven at that.
The track wasn't a road at all but a drive dead-ending in ruts
around an unpainted frame house, the center of a cluster of
shanty-like outbuildings and rusted junk. An ancient pink refrigerator stood sentry on a swayback porch, the only color in a
monotony of gray and weathered, hammered boards. A hound
scrambled from under the foundation and barked an alarm. Colonel Coates tried to reverse back through the woods but he wasn't
up to it. The rear wheels went off the packed dirt into a spongy
muck at the same time the front fender debarked the trunk of a
hickory tree. The wagon lodged across the track, the Colonel
demoralized and flustered.

It must be understood that the Colonel was not a man who was
unaware, who had no insight into his behavior. He realized he
was becoming more spellbound by both the sacred and the profane
than ever before. Contact with the world at hand was lost or
revived on an inscrutable schedule. So distressed was he by this

condition he had devised a plan for its rougher moments: If you get confused, sit down, stay put, until the mind brightens.

He remained where he was, smoking Chesterfields with pointless determination, the ashes collecting in his lap. Picket lines formed in the underbrush under the skirt of trees. Then the guns played on him, and an ineffective hail of grapeshot bounced off the hood of the car. The Colonel withstood the onslaught, battling against the failure of the vision. Then came his capture and subsequent imprisonment at Fort Delaware, the parole and at last the shameful journey home.

President Trass was a man preoccupied with his own thoughts, but eventually he noticed that his bird dog was baying itself hoarse. When he came out on the porch of the house he was born into, the Colonel spotted his advance and ducked down onto the car seat, felt immediately foolish in doing so and rose back into view. He cranked open the window, shouting out with as much vigor as was left to his voice:

"I'm unarmed."

President Trass halted in front of the station wagon, wary of tricks. No telling what was up when a white man blockaded your drive. "Yeah?" he said suspiciously. "That's good news. What y'all want 'round here?"

The Colonel admitted his mission. "I'm looking for Kelly's Ford, where Pelham fell."

"That a fact," President Trass said. He slowly pointed in the direction the Colonel had come from. "You way off. You about two miles east of the crossing."

"Is that so," said the Colonel. "Much obliged." He stepped on the gas. A volley of mud kicked into the air over President Trass's head. The rear wheels spun in place.

Colonel Coates was invited into the house to wait for President Trass's neighbor to bring a tractor over for the car. They sat in the parlor, the Colonel on a threadbare sofa, President Trass in an overstuffed wingback chair. Neatly framed pictures were tacked in a well-sighted line across one wall: four tintypes of nineteenth-century Negroes, a sepia-toned group portrait with a twentyish look, an array of black-and-white snapshots, some of the subjects in the caps and gowns of graduation—President Trass's ancestors and offspring.

To Colonel Coates's eye, President Trass looked like an old salamander dressed in bib overalls, a slick lymphatic edgelessness to the black man's features. President Trass thought that the Colonel, removed of the hat squashed onto his skull like a bottlecap, resembled a newly hatched chicken hawk, hot-skinned, old-ugly, and fierce at birth. They faced each other without exchanging a word. The longer President Trass considered the Colonel's *there*ness in the room, the more he began to believe that it was no coincidence, that something providential had happened, that Jesus had sent him a chicken hawk to relieve the Trass clan of the macabre burden they had accepted as their own for more than a hundred years, the remains of the soldiers President's granddaddy had plowed up on the first piece of land he cleared as a free man, a sharecropper in the year 1867. President Trass licked the dry swell of his lips, looked down at his own hands as if they were a miracle he was beginning to understand.

"What you spect to see at ol' Kelly's Ford anyway? Ain't nuthin there worth a look."

"Eh?" said the Colonel.

"Say there ain't much there."

"That so."

President Trass kept his head bowed and prayed himself clean: Shared a lot of jokes, Jesus, me and You, a lot of jokes. First white man I ever *invite* through my door and You lettin' me think he some kinda damn cracker angel. Well, Lord, I ain't afraid no more somebody goin' take this all wrong, leastwise this ol' chicken hawk.

"What's worth seein', I got," said President Trass.

The Colonel coughed abruptly and squinted. "I'm not the man who would know," he said.

"You come here lookin' for soldiers, you must be the man. They's yo' boys, ain't they?" said President, and he led the Colonel out back to one of the cold sheds and gave him the bones that four generations of Trass family couldn't quite decide what to do with.

As Dippy expected he would, given his interests, the Colonel became obsessed with the bones, the necroscopic opportunities they presented, and she readjusted her daily life to accept the company of both the living and the dead. Because she had forbidden Taylor to bring the two burlap sacks inside the house, he spent his time in the workshop that adjoined the garage, paying little attention to much else than his mounds of dusty relics. Every two hours she brought the Colonel his medication. At noon she brought him lunch and tea, and at four each afternoon for the five full days he spent in the workshop, she took him a shot of brandy to tire him out so he'd come willingly back to the house, complaining of the heaviness in his arms. Between trips to the workshop she'd fuss with needless cleaning, cook, or nap, instantly dreaming. She dreamed of her first daughter's elopement in 1939 with a German immigrant who later abandoned her. Once she dreamed of the good-looking doctor who had plunged his hand into her drawers when she worked at Bethesda—she woke up smoothing her skirt, saying, Woo, that's enough of that. And she dreamed of the two of her children in their graves, a little girl from influenza, the boy who died during the liberation of France. They would stay in her mind all day after she dreamed them. Even a long life was daunted by its feeling of brevity and compression. Not so great a distance seemed to separate them now and she took comfort in that sensation of a togetherness restored.

And Taylor out there in the garage, history's vulture, pecking through the remains. She dreamed him too, atop a horse, leading his skeletons toward the fray into which they cheered. They cheered, and the extent of her sadness awakened her.

How do we teach our souls to love death? he had asked her in bed the evening of the second day, the fumes of wintergreen ointment rising off his skin.

Who says you have to bother, she said. Leave those bones alone.

They'll be placed with their own, he said. I'm working on it.

What do you remember of your life, the Colonel had asked President Trass in the shed. It ain't over yet, President said. But I remember everything—the gals, the dances, the weather. What about white men? the Colonel was eager to know. President answered, They was around. Then he told the Colonel about his nigger notion and said take the bones because there wasn't a Trass alive or dead who was willing to put them to rest and he was tired of the noise.

The Colonel cleared his worktable of under-used tools and scattered the contents of the sacks across the length of its gummy surface. He turned on the radio, lit a Chesterfield and surveyed what he had. He counted twelve pelvic cradles but only ten skulls and nine jawbones. One of the jaws had gold fillings in several of the bare teeth, evidence attesting to the integrity of the hate passing through generations of Trass caretakers.

Well, twelve men then, a squad, a lost patrol, eighteen complete though fractured legs between them sharing twenty feet, one still in its boot. The first and second day the Colonel reconstructed what he could of twenty-three hands from two hundred and sixteen finger joints. He divided the ribs up, thirteen to a soldier.

Something curious happened but he didn't speak of it to Dippy. Metal objects in the workshop began to spark him, fluttering his heart when he touched them so he put on sheepskin gloves and wore them whenever he was out there. His hands became inept and the pace of his work slowed. He started the third day aligning vertabrae into spines but gave it up by lunch. His interest transferred to those material objects that fell from the sacks: the boot with its rattle of tiny bones, a cartridge box with mini-balls intact, a flattened canteen, six belt buckles, five stamped *CSA*, a coffee can he filled the first day with copper and tin buttons, indeterminate fragments of leather and scraps of delicate gray wool. On the fourth day he brought to the workshop a wheelbarrow load of books and reprinted documents from his study in the house, prepared to concentrate on the forensic clues that would send the boys home. The weather changed, bringing a frost, and his legs cramped violently. Dippy helped him carry a space heater up from the cellar to supplement the one already glowing in the shop. When she delivered his lunch on the fifth day, she found him on a stool bent over the table, an open book balanced on his thighs, lost in abstraction as he regarded the buttons arranged in groups of threes. He appeared not to notice when she set down the tray. The radio was louder than usual. Easter was a week away and the announcer preached irritatingly about the sacrifices Christ had made. Dippy turned the sound off. Taylor looked up at her as if she had somehow thwarted his right to sovereignty.

"I'm close, Goddamn it all," he said, scowling and yet with a fatigued look, the remoteness quickly returning. "These are General Extra Billy Smith's Boys. The Warren Blues, maybe. The Sperryville Sharpshooters." His voice became unsure. "I don't know for a fact."

"You don't have to tell me," she said. "I can hear the racket they're making."

The Colonel waved her away and she left. Dippy did not think his devotion to the bones morbid or absurd, only unnecessary, wasted time for a man with nothing more to spend. She could have told Taylor, if he believed in what couldn't be properly understood, the nature of the noise the bones were making. The bones were preparing to march. She hated the clamor they made, a frightening, crazed exuberance. She went back to the house and suffered the grief of its emptiness.

That night a thunderstorm moved in from the west, blowing down the eastern slope of the mountains. The Colonel couldn't sleep. He stood at the bedroom window and peered out, seeing atomic sabers strike the land. He slipped back under the covers with his wife and felt himself growing backwards. His muscles surged with youth and confidence. Here too was Dippy, ripe in motherhood, squirting milk at his touch. And here were his schoolchums, the roster of names so familiar, Extra Billy's Boys one and all. *Company D. Company K.* Fellows he grew up with. Well I'll be, he said to himself in wonder. I went to school with them damn bones.

On the sixth day Dippy went to the workshop shortly after Taylor, disturbed by the extreme volume of the radio music coming across the drive. Pushing open the door she was assaulted by a duet from Handel's *Messiah,* the words and music distorted by loudness. The Colonel was on his feet, at attention, singing with abandon although his lyrics were out of sequence with the broadcast of the performance for Holy Week:

O death where is thy sting? O grave, where is thy victory?

His face turned red and waxy as she watched in anguish. His shirttails flagged out between his sweater and belt, the laces of one shoe were untied. His gloved hands quivered at his side. The Colonel seemed caught between turmoil and euphoria, singing to his audience of skulls propped along the table. His voice became cracked and tormented as he repeated the lines again and again, faster each time and with increasing passion. Dippy, thinking the Colonel had gone mad, was scared to death. She hurried to the radio and pulled its plug from the wall. Taylor gradually became aware that his wife had joined him. He felt a funny pressure throughout his body, funny because its effect was a joyous feeling of weightlessness. He tried to smile lovingly but knew he failed in his expression. Dippy stared back at him, mournful, one hand to her mouth, as if he were insane. Then a calmness came to him.

"Dippy," he bargained feebly. "I don't wish to be buried in my blue suit."

She helped him back to the house, insisted he take a sleeping pill, undressed his dissipating body and put him to bed. She couldn't raise him for his supper, nor did he stir when she herself retired later in the evening. She woke the following morning startled by the sound of the station wagon leaving the garage. By the time she reached the window there was nothing to see. She telephoned the police to bring him back, covered herself with a houserobe and went to the kitchen to wait.

Two hours later the curator at the Warren Rifles Confederate Museum in Fort Royal observed an old man enter the building and perform a stiff-legged inspection of the display cases. Afterward, the same man approached the curator with a request to view the muster rolls of the 49th regiment. There was nothing unusual about the old man's desire and the curator agreed. He offered the gentleman a seat while he excused himself and went into the archives, but when he returned to the public area of the museum with the lists the old man had left.

As he waited for the curator, the Colonel was overwhelmed by a sense of severe desolation. The room seemed all at once to be crowded beyond capacity. He felt constricted and began to choke. The noise was deafening, unintelligible, and he was stunned to think how Dippy and President Trass could tolerate it.

In the car again he felt better; yet when the road ascended out of the valley to crest the Blue Ridge, suddenly the Colonel couldn't breathe the air for all the souls that thickened it. He died at the wheel, his hands grasping toward his heart, the station wagon rolling off the road into a meadow bright with black-eyed Susans, crashing just enough for Dippy to justify a closed coffin. The undertaker was a childhood friend of Taylor's, loyal to the military caste and the dignity of southern families, understanding of the privacy they required when burying their own. With discretion he gave her the large coffin she asked for, assisted her in carrying the two heavy satchels into the mourning parlor and then left, closing the doors behind him without so much as a glance over his shoulder to witness her final act as a wife, the act of sealing the Colonel's coffin after she had heaped the bones in there with him.

She was dry-eyed and efficient throughout the service and burial in the Coates's family plot outside Warrenton. Children and grandchildren worried that she was holding up too well, that she had separated from the reality of the event, that when the impact arrived she would die too. She could have told them not to concern themselves. She could have told them how relieved she was to be the last southern woman, the last of the last to lower the men who had broke from the Union into their graves, how relieved she was to hear the Colonel exhorting the bones, *Keep in ranks, boys, hold the line, be brave,* until the terrible cheering grew more and more distant and their voices diminished and she was finally alone, free of glory.

—*for Paul Peterson*

ABLE, BAKER, CHARLIE, DOG

by Stephanie Vaughn

When I was twelve years old, my father was tall and awesome. I
can see him walking across the parade ground behind our quarters. The wind blew snow into the folds of his coat and made the
hem swoop around his legs. He did not lower his head, he did
not jam his hands into the pockets. He was coming home along a
diagonal that would cut the parade ground into perfect triangles,
and he was not going to be stopped by any snowstorm. I stood at
the kitchen door and watched him through a hole I had rubbed
in the steamy glass.

My grandmother and mother fidgeted with pans of food that
had been kept warm too long. It was one o'clock on Saturday and
he had been expected home at noon.

"You want to know what this chicken looks like?" said my
grandmother. "It looks like it died last year."

My mother looked into the pan but didn't say anything.

My grandmother believed my mother should have married a
minister, not an Army officer. Once my mother had gone out
with a minister, and now he was on the radio every Sunday in
Ohio. My grandmother thought my father had misrepresented
himself as a religious man. There was a story my mother told about
their first date. They went to a restaurant and my father told
her that he was going to have twelve sons and name them
Peter, James, John, et cetera. "And I thought, Twelve sons!"
said my mother. "Boy, do I pity your poor wife." My mother
had two miscarriages and then she had me. My father named me
Gemma, which my grandmother believed was not even a Christian
name.

"You want to know what this squash looks like?" said my grandmother.

"It'll be fine," said my mother.

Just then the wind gusted on the parade ground, and my father veered to the left. He stopped and looked up. How is it possible you have caught me off guard, he seemed to ask. Exactly where have I miscalculated the velocities, how have I misjudged the vectors?

"It looks like somebody peed in it," my grandmother said.

"Keep your voice low," my father told me that day as we ate the ruined squash and chicken. "Keep your voice low and you can win any point."

We were living in Fort Niagara, a little Army post at the juncture of the Niagara River and Lake Ontario. We had been there through the fall and into the winter, as my father, who was second in command, waited for his next promotion. It began to snow in October. The arctic winds swept across the lake from Canada and shook the windows of our house. Snow drifted across the parade ground, and floes of ice piled up against each other in the river, so that if a person were courageous enough, or fool-hardy enough, and also lucky, he could walk the mile across the river to Canada.

"And always speak in sentences," he told me. "You have developed a junior-high habit of speaking in fragments. Learn to come to a full stop when you complete an idea. Use semicolons and periods in your speech."

My mother put down her fork and knife. Her hands were so thin and light they seemed to pass through the table as she dropped them in her lap. "Zachary, perhaps we could save some of the lecture for dessert?" she said.

My grandmother leaned back into her own heaviness. "The poor kid never gets to eat a hot meal," she said. She was referring to the rule that said I could not cut my food or eat while I was speaking or being spoken to, and I was always being spoken to. My father used mealtimes to lecture on the mechanics of life, the how-tos of a civilized world. Normally, I was receptive to his advice, but that day I was angry with him.

"You know, Dad," I said, "I don't think my friends are going to notice a missing semicolon."

I thought he would give me a fierce look, but instead he winked. "And don't say 'you know,' " he said.

He never said "you know," never spoke in fragments, never

slurred his speech, even years later when he had just put away a fifth of Scotch and was trying to describe the Eskimo custom of chewing up the meat before it was given to the elders who had no teeth. He spoke with such calculation and precision that his sentences hung over us like high vaulted ceilings, or rolled across the table like ornaments sculptured from stone. It was a huge cathedral of a voice, full of volume and complexity.

He taught me the alphabet. Able, Baker, Charlie, Dog. It was the alphabet the military used to keep "B"s separate from "V"s and "I"s separate from "Y"s. He liked the music of it, the way it sounded on his fine voice. I was four years old and my grand-mother had not come to live with us yet. We were stationed in Manila, and living in a house the Army had built on squat stilts to protect us from the insects. There was a typhoon sweeping in-land, and we could hear the hoarse sound of metal scraping across the Army's paved street. It was the corrugated roof of the house next door.

"Don't you think it's time we went under the house?" my mother said. She was sitting on a duffel bag that contained our tarps and food rations. The house had a loose plank in the living-room floor, so that if the roof blew away, or the walls caved in, we could escape through the opening and sit in the low space between the reinforced floor and the ground until the military rescue bus came.

My father looked at me and said, "Able, Baker, Charlie, Dog. Can you say it, Gemma?"

I looked up at the dark slope of our own metal roof.

"Can you say it?"

"Able, Baker, Charlie, Dog," I said.

The metal rumbled on the road outside. My mother lifted the plank.

"We will be all right," he said. "Easy, Fox, George, How."

"Anybody want to join me?" said my mother.

"Easy," I said.

"Rachel, please put that plank back."

"Easy, Fox, George, How," I said.

My mother replaced the plank and sat on the floor beside me. The storm grew louder, the rain fell against the roof like handfuls of gravel.

"Item, Jig, King." My father's voice grew lower, fuller. We sat under the sound of it and felt safe. "Love, Mike, Nan."

But then we heard another sound—something that went *whap-*

whap, softly, between the gusts of rain. We tilted our heads toward the shuttered windows.

"Well," said my father, standing up to stretch. "I think we are losing a board or two off the side of the house."

"Where are you going?" said my mother. "Just where do you think you're going?"

He put on his rain slicker and went into the next room. When he returned, he was carrying a bucket of nails and a hammer. "Obviously," he said, "I am going fishing."

We moved back to the States when I was six, and he taught me how to play parcheesi, checkers, chess, cribbage, dominoes, and twenty questions. "When you lose," he told me, "don't cry. When you win, don't gloat."

He taught me how to plant tomatoes and load a shotgun shell. He showed me how to gut a dove, turning it inside out as the Europeans do, using the flexible breastbone for a pivot. He read a great many books and never forgot a fact or a technical description. He explained the principles of crop rotation and the flying buttress. He discussed the Defenestration of Prague.

When I was in elementary school, he was sent abroad twice on year-long tours—once to Turkey and once to Greenland, both strategic outposts for America's Early Warning System. I wanted to, but could not write him letters. His came to me every week, but without the rhythms of his voice the words seemed pale and flat, like the transparent shapes of cells under a microscope. He did not write about his work, because his work was secret. He did not send advice, because that he left to my mother and grandmother in his absence. He wrote about small things—the smooth white rocks he found on a mountainside in Turkey, the first fresh egg he ate in Greenland. When I reread the letters after he died, I was struck by their grace and invention. But when I read them as a child, I looked through the words—"eggs . . . shipment . . . frozen"—and there was nothing on the other side but the great vacuum of his missing voice.

"I can't think of anything to say," I told my mother the first time she urged me to write to him. He had already been in Turkey for three months. She stood behind me at the heavy library table and smoothed my hair, touched my shoulders. "Tell him about your tap lessons," she said. "Tell him about ballet."

"Dear Dad," I wrote. "I am taking tap lessons. I am also taking ballet." I tried to imagine what he looked like. I tried to put a face before my face, but it was gray and featureless, like the face of a statue worn flat by wind and rain. "And I hope you have a Happy Birthday next month," I concluded, hoping to evade the necessity of writing him again in three weeks.

The autumn I turned twelve, we moved to Fort Niagara, which was the administrative base for the missile sites strung along the Canadian border between Lake Erie and Lake Ontario. It was a handsome post, full of oak trees, brick buildings, and history. The French had taken the land from the Indians and built the original fort. The British took the fort from the French, and the Americans took it from the British. My father recounted the battles for us as we drove there along the wide sweep of the Niagara River, past apple orchards and thick pastures. My grandmother sat in the back seat and made a note of each red convertible that passed. I was supposed to be counting the white ones. When we drove through the gate and saw the post for the first time—the expanses of clipped grass, the tall trees, the row of Colonial houses overlooking the river—my grandmother put down her tablet and said, "This is some post." She looked at my father admiringly, the first indication she had ever given that he might be a good match for my mother after all. She asked to be taken to the far end of the post, where the Old Fort was. It sat on a point of land at the juncture of the lake and river, and looked appropriately warlike, with its moat and tiny gun windows, but it was surprisingly small—a simple square of yellow stone. "Is this all there is?" I said as my grandmother and I posed for pictures on the drawbridge near two soldiers dressed in Revolutionary War costumes. It was hard to imagine that chunks of a vast continent had been won and lost within the confines of a fortress hardly bigger than Sleeping Beauty's castle at Disneyland. Later, as we drove back along the river, my father said in his aphoristic way, "Sometimes the biggest battles are the smallest ones."

The week after we settled in our quarters, we made the obligatory trip to the Falls. It was a sultry day—Indian summer—and our eyes began to water as we neared the chemical factories that surround the city of Niagara Falls. We stopped for iced tea and my father explained how the glaciers had formed the escarpment through which the Falls had cut a deep gorge. "Escarpment" —that was the term he used, instead of "cliff." It skidded along the roof of his mouth and entered the conversation with a soft explosion.

We went to the Niagara Falls Museum and examined the containers people had used successfully to go over the Falls early in the century, when there was a thousand-dollar prize given to survivors. Two were wooden barrels strapped with metal bands. One was a giant rubber ball reinforced with a steel cage. A fourth was a long steel capsule. On the walls were photographs of each survivor and plaques explaining who had been injured and how. The steel capsule was used by a man who had broken almost every bone in his body. The plaque said that he was in the hospital for twenty-three weeks and then took his capsule around the world on a speaking tour. One day when he was in New Zealand, he slipped on an orange peel, broke his leg, and later died of complications.

We went next to Goat Island and stood on the open bank to watch the leap and dive of the white water. My mother held her handbag close to her breasts. She had a habit of always holding things this way—a stack of dinner plates, the dish towel, some mail she had brought in from the porch; she hunched over slightly, so that her body seemed at once to be protective and protected. "I don't like the river," she said. "I think it wants to hypnotize you." My father put his hands in his pockets to show how at ease he was, and my grandmother went off to buy an ice-cream cone.

At the observation point, we stood at a metal fence and looked into the frothing water at the bottom of the gorge. We watched bits and pieces of rainbows appear and vanish in the sunlight that was refracted off the water through the mist. My father pointed to a black shape in the rapids above the Horseshoe Falls. "That's a river barge," he said. He lowered his voice so that he could be heard under the roar of the water. "A long time ago, there were two men standing on that barge waiting to see whether in the next moment of their lives they would go over."

He told us the story of the barge then—how it had broken loose from a tug near Buffalo and floated down-river, gathering speed. The two men tore at the air, waved and shouted to people on shore, but the barge entered the rapids. They bumped around over the rocks, and the white water rose in the air. One man—"He was the thinking man," said my father—thought they might be able to wedge the barge among the rocks if they allowed the hull to fill with water. They came closer to the Falls—four hundred yards, three hundred—before the barge jerked broadside and stopped. They were there all afternoon and night, listening to the sound of the water pounding into the boulders at the bottom of the gorge. The next morning, they were rescued, and one of the men, the thinking man, told the newspapers that he had spent the night playing poker in his head. He played all the hands, and he bluffed himself. He drew to inside straights. If the barge had torn loose from the rocks in the night, he was going to go over the Falls saying, "Five-card draw, jacks or better to open." The other man had sat on the barge, his arms clasped around his knees, and watched the mist blow back from the edge of the Falls in the moonlight. He could not speak.

"The scream of the water entered his body," said my father. He paused to let us think about that.

"Well, what does that mean?" my grandmother said at last.

My father rested his arms on the fence and gazed pleasantly at the Falls. "He went insane."

The river fascinated me. I often stood between the yellow curtains of my bedroom and looked down upon it and thought about how deep and swift it was, how black under the glittering surface. The newspaper carried stories about people who jumped over the Falls, fourteen miles upriver from our house. I thought of their bodies pushed along the soft silt of the bottom, tumbling silently, huddled in upon themselves like fetuses—jilted brides, unemployed factory workers, old people who did not want to go to rest homes, teen-agers who got bad grades, young women who fell in love with married men. They floated invisibly past my bedroom window, out into the lake.

That winter, I thought I was going to die. I thought I had cancer of the breasts. My mother had explained to me about menstruation, she had given me a book about the reproductive systems of men and women, but she had not told me about breasts and how they begin as invisible lumps which become tender and sore.

I thought the soreness had begun in a Phys. Ed. class one day in December when I was hit in the chest with a basketball. I didn't worry about it, and it went away by New Year's. In January, I found a pamphlet at the bus stop. I was stamping my feet in the cold, looking down at my boots, when I saw the headline—"CANCER: SEVEN WARNING SIGNALS." When I got home, I went into the bathroom and undressed. I examined myself for enlarged moles and small wounds that wouldn't heal. I was systematic. I sat on the edge of the tub with the pamphlet by my side and began with my toenails, looking under the tips of them. I felt my soles, arches, ankles. I worked my way up my body and then I felt the soreness again, around both nipples. At dinner that night I didn't say anything all through the meal. In bed I slept on my back, with my arms stiff against my sides.

The next Saturday was the day my father came home late for lunch. The squash sat on the back of the stove and turned to ochre soup. The chicken fell away from the bones. After lunch he went into the living room and drank Scotch and read a book. When I came down for supper, he was still sitting there, and he told my mother he would eat later. My grandmother, my mother, and I ate silently at the kitchen table. I took a long bath. I scrubbed my chest hard.

I went straight to my bedroom, and after a while my mother came upstairs and said, "What's wrong?"

I didn't say anything.

She stood in front of me with her hands clasped in front of her. She seemed to lean toward her own hands. "But you've been acting, you know"—and here she laughed self-consciously, as she used the forbidden phrase—"you know, you've been acting different. You were so quiet today."

I went to my chest of drawers and took the pamphlet out from under a stack of folded underpants and gave it to her.

"What's this?"

"I think I have No. 4," I said.

She must have known immediately what the problem was, but she didn't smile. She asked me to raise my nightgown and she examined my chest, pressing firmly, as if she were a doctor. I told her about the soreness. "Here?" she said. "And here? What about here, too?" She told me I was beginning to "develop." I knew what she meant, but I wanted her to be precise.

"You're getting breasts," she said.

"But I don't *see* anything."

"You will."

"You never told me it would hurt."

"Oh, dear. I just forgot. When you're grown up you just forget what it was like."

I asked her whether, just to be safe, I could see a doctor. She said that of course I could, and I felt better, as if I had had a disease and already been cured. As she was leaving the room, I said, "Do you think I need a bra?" She smiled. I went to sleep watching the snow fall past the window. I had my hands cupped over my new breasts.

When I awoke, I did not recognize the window. The snow had stopped and moonlight slanted through the glass. I could not make out the words, but I heard my father's voice filling up the house. I tiptoed down the back staircase that led to the kitchen and stood in the slice of shadow near the doorjamb. My grandmother was telling my mother to pack her bags. He was a degenerate, she said—she had always seen that in him. My mother said, "Why, Zachary? Why are you doing this?"

"Just go pack your bags," my grandmother said. "I'll get the child."

My father said conversationally, tensely, "Do I have to break your arms?"

I leaned into the light. He was holding on to a bottle of Scotch with one hand, and my mother was trying to pull it away with both of hers. He jerked his arm back and forth, so that she was drawn into a little dance, back and forth across the linoleum in front of him.

"The Lord knows the way of righteousness," said my grandmother.

"Please," said my mother. "Please, please."

"And the way of the ungodly shall perish," said my grandmother.

"Whose house is this?" said my father. His voice exploded. He snapped his arm back, trying to take the bottle from my mother in one powerful gesture. It smashed against the wall, and I stepped into the kitchen. The white light from the ceiling fixture burned across the smooth surfaces of the refrigerator, the stove, the white Formica counter tops. It was as if an atom had been smashed somewhere and a wave of radiation was rolling through the kitchen. I looked him in the eye and waited for him to speak. I sensed my mother and grandmother on either side of me, in petrified postures. At last, he said, "Well." His voice cracked. The word split in two. "Wel-el." He said it again. His face took on a flatness.

"I am going back to bed," I said. I went up the narrow steps, and he followed me. My mother and grandmother came along behind, whispering. He tucked in the covers, and sat on the edge of the bed, watching me. My mother and grandmother stood stiff against the door. "I am sorry I woke you up," he said finally, and his voice was deep and soothing. The two women watched him go down the hall, and when I heard his steps on the front staircase I rolled over and put my face in the pillow. I heard them turn off the lights and say good night to me. I heard them go to their bedrooms. I lay there for a long time, listening for a sound downstairs, and then it came—the sound of the front door closing.

I went downstairs and put on my hat, coat, boots. I followed his footsteps in the snow, down the front walk and across the road to the riverbank. He did not seem surprised to see me next to him. We stood side by side, hands in our pockets, breathing frost into the air. The river was filled from shore to shore with white heaps of ice, which cast blue shadows in the moonlight.

"This is the edge of America," he said, in a tone that seemed to answer a question I had just asked. There was a creak and crunch of ice as two floes below us scraped each other and jammed against the bank.

"You knew all week, didn't you? Your mother and your grandmother didn't know, but I knew that you could be counted on to know."

I hadn't known until just then, but I guessed the unspeakable thing—that his career was falling apart—and I knew. I nodded. Years later, my mother told me what she had learned about the incident, not from him but from another Army wife. He had called a general a son of a bitch. That was all. I never knew what the issue was or whether he had been right or wrong. Whether the defense of the United States of America had been at stake, or merely the pot in a card game. I didn't even know whether he had called the general a son of a bitch to his face or simply been overheard in an unguarded moment. I only knew that he had been given a "7" instead of a "9" on his Efficiency Report and then passed over for promotion. But that night I nodded, not knowing the cause but knowing the consequences, as we stood on the riverbank above the moonlit ice. "I am looking at that thin beautiful line of Canada," he said. "I think I will go for a walk."

"No," I said. I said it again. "No." I wanted to remember later that I had told him not to go.

"How long do you think it would take to go over and back?" he said.

"Two hours."

He rocked back and forth in his boots, looked up at the moon, then down at the river. I did not say anything.

He started down the bank, sideways, taking long graceful sliding steps, which threw little puffs of snow in the air. He took his hands from his pockets and hopped from the bank to the ice. He tested his weight against the weight of the ice, flexing his knees. I watched him walk a few yards from the shore and then I saw him rise in the air, his long legs scissoring the moonlight, as he crossed from the edge of one floe to the next. He turned and waved to me, one hand making a slow arc.

I could have said anything. I could have said "Come back" or "I love you." Instead, I called after him, "Be sure and write!"

The last thing I heard, long after I had lost sight of him far out on the river, was the sound of his laugh splitting the cold air.

In the spring he resigned his commission and we went back to Ohio. He used his savings to invest in a chain of hardware stores with my uncle. My uncle arranged the contracts with the builders and plumbers, and supervised the employees. My father controlled the inventory and handled the books. He had been a logistics officer, and all the skills he might have used in supervising the movement of land, air, and sea cargoes, or in calculating the disposition of several billion dollars' worth of military supplies, were instead brought to bear on the deployment of nuts and bolts, plumbers' joints and nipples, No. 2 pine, Con-Tact paper, acrylic paint, caulking guns, and rubber dishpans. He learned a new vocabulary—traffic builders, margins, end-cap displays, perfboard merchandisers, seasonal impulse items—and spoke it with the ostentation and faint amusement of a man who has just mastered a foreign language.

"But what I really want to know, Mr. Jenkins," I heard him tell a man on the telephone one day, "is why you think the Triple Gripper Vegetable Ripper would make a good loss-leader item in midwinter." He had been in the hardlines industry, as it was called, for six months, and I was making my first visit to his office, and then only because my mother had sent me there on the pretext of taking him a mid-morning snack during a busy Saturday. I was reluctant to confront him in his civilian role, afraid I would find him somehow diminished. In fact, although he looked incongruous among the reds, yellows, and blues which the previous owner had used to decorate the office, he sounded much like the man who had taught me to speak in complete sentences.

"Mr. Jenkins, I am not asking for a discourse on coleslaw."

When he hung up, he winked at me and said, "Your father is about to become the emperor of the building and housewares trade in Killbuck, Ohio."

I nodded and took a seat in a red-and-blue chair.

Then he looked at his hands spread upon the spotless ink blotter and said, "Of course, you know that I do not give a damn about the Triple Gripper Vegetable Ripper."

I had skipped a grade and entered high school. I saw less and less of him, because I ate dinner early, so that I could go to play rehearsals, basketball games, dances. In the evenings he sat in a green chair and smoked cigarettes, drank Scotch, read books— the same kinds of books, year after year. They were all about

Eskimos and Arctic explorations—an interest he had developed during his tour in Greenland. Sometimes, when I came in late and was in the kitchen making a snack, I watched him through the doorway. Often he looked away from the book and gazed toward the window. He would strike a match and let it burn to his thumb and fingertip, then wave it out. He would raise the glass but not drink from it. I think he must have imagined himself to be in the Arctic during those moments, a warrior tracking across the ice for bear or seal. Sometimes he was waiting for me to join him. He wanted to tell me about the techniques the Eskimos had developed for survival, the way they stitched up skins to make them water-tight vessels. He became obsessive on the subject of meat. The Eskimo diet was nearly all protein. "Eat meat," he said. Two professors at Columbia had tested the value of the Eskimo diet by eating nothing but caribou for a year and claimed they were healthier at the end of the experiment than they had been before.

Later, when I went to college, he developed the habit of calling me long distance when my mother and grandmother had gone to bed and he was alone downstairs with a drink. "Are you getting enough protein?" he asked me once at three in the morning. It was against dorm rules to put through calls after midnight except in cases of emergency, but his deep, commanding voice was so authoritative ("This is Gemma Jackson's father, and I must speak with her immediately") that it was for some time believed on my corridor that the people in my family were either accident-prone or suffering from long terminal illnesses.

He died the summer I received my master's degree. I had accepted a teaching position at a high school in Chicago, and I went home for a month before school began. He was over-weight and short of breath. He drank too much, smoked too many cigarettes. The doctor told him to stop, my mother told him, my grandmother told him.

My grandmother was upstairs watching television and my mother and I were sitting on the front porch. He was asleep in the green chair, with a book in his lap. I left the porch to go to the kitchen to make a sandwich, and as I passed by the chair I heard him say, "Ahhhh. Ahhhhhh." I saw his fist rise to his chest. I saw his eyes open and dilate in the lamplight. I knelt beside him.

"Are you okay?" I said. "Are you dreaming?"

We buried him in a small cemetery near the farm where he was born. In the eulogy he was remembered for having survived the first wave of the invasion of Normandy. He was admired for having been the proprietor of a chain of excellent hardware stores.

"He didn't have to do this," my mother said after the funeral. "He did this to himself."

"He was a good man," said my grandmother. "He put a nice roof over our heads. He sent us to Europe twice."

Afterward I went alone to the cemetery. I knelt beside the heaps of wilted flowers—mostly roses and gladiolas, and one wreath of red, white, and blue carnations. Above me, the maple pods spun through the sunlight like wings, and in the distance the corn trumpeted green across the hillsides. I touched the loose black soil at the edge of the flowers. Able, Baker, Charlie, Dog. I could remember the beginning of the alphabet, up through Mike and Nan. I could remember the end. X-Ray, Yoke, Zebra. I was his only child, and he taught me what he knew. I wept then, but not because he had gone back to Ohio to read about the Eskimos and to sell the artifacts of civilized life to homeowners and builders. I wept because when I was twelve years old I had stood on a snowy riverbank as he became a shadow on the ice, and waited to see whether he would slip between the cracking floes into the water.

UNDER THE WHEAT
by Rick DeMarinis

Down in D-3 I watch the sky gunning through the aperture ninety-odd feet above my head. The missiles are ten months away, and I am lying on my back, listening to the sump. From the bottom of a hole, where the weather is always the same cool sixty-four degrees, plus or minus two, I like to relax and watch the clouds slide through the circle of blue light. I have plenty of time to kill. The aperture is about fifteen feet wide. About the size of a silver dollar from here. A hawk just drifted by. Eagle. Crow. Small cumulus. Nothing. Nothing. Wrapper.

Hot again today, and the sky is drifting across the hole, left to right, a slow thick wind that doesn't gust. When it gusts, it's usually from Canada. Fierce, with hail the size of eyeballs. I've seen wheat go down. Acres and acres of useless straw.

But sometimes it comes out of the southeast, from Bismarck, bringing ten-mile high anvils with it, and you find yourself looking for funnels. This is not tornado country to speak of. The tornado path is to the south and west of here. They walk up from Bismarck and farther south and peter out on the Montana border, rarely touching ground anywhere near this latitude. Still, you keep an eye peeled. I've seen them put down gray fingers to the west, not quite touching but close enough to make you want to find a hole. They say it sounds like freight trains in your yard. I wouldn't know. We are from the coast, where the weather is stable and always predictable because of the ocean. We are trying to adjust.

*　　*　　*

I make five hundred a week doing this, driving a company pick up from hole to hole, checking out the sump pumps. I've found only one failure in two months. Twenty feet of black water in the hole and rising. It's the company's biggest headache. The high water table of North Dakota. You can dig twelve feet in any field and have yourself a well. You can dig yourself a shallow hole, come back in a few days and drink. That's why the farmers here have it made. Except for hail. Mostly they are Russians, these farmers.

Karen wants to go back. I have to remind her it's only for one year. Ten more months. Five hundred a week for a year. But she misses things. The city, her music lessons, movies, the beach, excitement. We live fairly close to a town, but it's one you will never hear of, unless a local goes wild and chainsaws all six members of his family. The movie theater has shown *Bush Pilot, Red Skies of Montana, Ice Palace,* and *Kon Tiki,* so far. These are movies we would not ordinarily pay money to see. She has taken to long walks in the evenings to work out her moods, which are getting harder and harder for me to pretend aren't there. I get time-and-a-half on Saturdays, double-time Sundays and holidays, and thirteen dollars per diem for the inconvenience of relocating all the way from Oxnard, California. That comes to a lot. You don't walk away from a gold mine like that. I try to tell Karen she has to make the effort, adjust. North Dakota isn't all that bad. As a matter of fact, I sort of enjoy the area. Maybe I am more adaptable. We live close to a large brown lake, an earthfill dam loaded with northern pike. I bought myself a little boat and often go out to troll a bit before the carpool comes by. The freezer is crammed with fish, not one under five pounds.

There's a ghost town on the other side of the lake. The houses were built for the men who worked on the dam. That was years ago. They are paintless now, weeds up to the rotten sills. No glass in the windows, but here and there a rag of drape. Sometimes I take my boat across the lake to the ghost town. I walk the over-grown streets and look into the windows. Sometimes something moves. Rats. Gophers. Wind. Loose boards. Sometimes nothing.

When the weather is out of Canada you can watch it move south, coming like a giant roll of silver dough on the horizon. It gets bigger fast and then you'd better find cover. If the cloud is curdled underneath, you know it means hail. The wind can gust to one-hundred knots. It scares Karen. I tell her there's nothing to worry about. Our trailer is on a good foundation and tied down tight. But she has this dream of being uprooted and of flying away in such a wind. She sees her broken body caught in a tree, magpies picking at it. I tell her the trailer will definitely not budge. Still, she gets wild-eyed and can't light a cigarette.

We're sitting at the dinette table looking out the window, watching the front arrive. You can feel the trailer bucking like a boat at its moorings. Lightning is stroking the blond fields a mile away. To the southeast, I can see a gray finger reaching down. This is unusual, I admit. But I say nothing to Karen. It looks like the two fronts are going to butt heads straight over the trailer park. It's getting dark fast. Something splits the sky behind the trailer and big hail pours out. The streets of the park are white and jumping under the black sky. Karen has her hands up to her ears. There's a stampede on our tin roof. Two TV antennas fold at the same time in a dead faint. A jagged Y of lightning strikes so close you can smell it. Electric steam. Karen is wild, screaming. I can't hear her. Our garbage cans are rising. They are floating past the windows into a flattened wheat field. This is something. Karen's face is closed. She doesn't enjoy it at all, not at all.

I'm tooling around in third on the usual bad road, enjoying the lurches, rolls, and twists. I would not do this to my own truck. The fields I'm driving through are wasted. Head-on with the sky and the sky never loses. I've passed a few unhappy-looking farmers standing in their fields with their hands in their pockets, faces frozen in an expression of disgust, spitting. Toward D-8, just over a rise and down into a narrow gulch, I found a true glacier. It was made out of hail stones welded together by their own impact. It hadn't begun to melt yet. Four feet thick and maybe thirty feet long. You can stand on it and shade your eyes from the white glare. You could tell yourself you are inside the arctic circle. What is this, the return of the Ice Age?

Karen did not cook tonight. Another "mood." I poke around the fridge. I don't know what to say to her anymore. I know it's hard. I can understand that. This is not Oxnard. I'll give her that. I'm the first to admit it. I pop a beer and sit down at the table opposite her. Our eyes don't meet. They haven't for weeks. We are like two magnetic north poles, repelling each other for invisible reasons. Last night in bed I touched her. She went stiff. She

didn't have to say a word. I took my hand back. I got the
message. There was the hum of the air conditioner and nothing
else. The world could have been filled with dead bodies. I turned
on the lights. She got up and lit a cigarette after two tries. Nerves.
"I'm going for a walk, Lloyd," she said, checking the sky. "Maybe
we should have a baby?" I said. "I'm making plenty of money."
But she looked at me as if I had picked up an ax.

I would like to know where she finds to go and what she finds
to do there. She hates the town worse than the trailer park. The
trailer park has a rec hall and a social club for the wives. But she
won't take advantage of that. I know the neighbors are talking.
They think she's a snob. They think I spoil her. After she left I
went out on the porch and drank eleven beers. Let them talk.

Three farm kids. Just standing outside the locked gate of D-4.
"What do you kids want?" I know what they want. A "look-see."
Security measures are in effect, but what the hell. There is nothing here yet but a ninety-foot hole with a tarp on it and a sump
pump in the bottom. They are excited. They want to know what
ICBM stands for. What is a warhead? How fast is it? How do you
know if it's really going to smear the right town? What if it went
straight up and came straight down? Can you hit the moon?
"Look at the sky up there, kids," I tell them. "Lie on your backs,
like this, and after a while you sort of get the feeling you're
looking *down,* from on top of it." The kids lie down on the
concrete. Kids have a way of giving all their attention to something interesting. I swear them to secrecy, not for my protection,
because who cares, but because it will make their day. They will
run home, busting with secret info. I drive off to D-9, where the
sump trouble was.

Caught three lunkers this morning. All over twenty-four inches.
It's seven A.M. now and I'm on Ruby Street, the ghost town. The
streets are all named after stones. Why I don't know. This is nothing
like anything we have on the coast. Karen doesn't like the climate
or the people and the flat sky presses down on her from all sides
and gives her bad dreams, sleeping and awake. But what can I *do?*
I'm on Onyx Street, number 49, a two-bedroom bungalow with
a few pieces of furniture left in it. There is a chest of drawers in
the bedroom, a bed with a rotten gray mattress. There is a closet
with a raggedy slip in it. The slip has brown water stains on it. In
the bottom of the chest is a magazine, yellow with age. *Secret*

Confessions. I can imagine the woman who lived here with her husband. Not much like Karen at all. But what did she do while her husband was off working on the dam? Did she stand at this window in her slip and wish she were back in Oxnard? Did she cry her eyes out on this bed and think crazy thoughts? Where is she now? Does she think, "This is July 15, 1962, and I am glad I am not in North Dakota anymore"? Did she take long walks at night and not cook? I have an impulse to do something odd, and do it.

When a thunderhead passes over a cyclone fence that surrounds a site, such as the one passing over D-6 now, you can hear the wire hiss with nervous electrons. It scares me because the fence is a perfect lightning rod, a good conductor. But I stay on my toes. Sometimes, when a big cumulus is overhead stroking the area and roaring, I'll just stay put in my truck until it's had its fun.

Because this is Sunday, I am making better than twelve dollars an hour. I'm driving through a small farming community called Spacebow. A Russian word, I think, because you're supposed to pronounce the *e.* No one I know does. Shade trees on every street. A Russian church here, grain elevator there. No wind. Hot for nine A.M. Men dressed in Sunday black. Ladies in their best. Kids looking uncomfortable and controlled. Even the dogs are behaving. There is a woman, manless I think, because I've seen her before, always alone on her porch, eyes on something far away. A "thinker." Before today I've only waved hello. First one finger off the wheel, nod, then around the block once again and the whole hand out the window and a smile. That was last week. After the first turn past her place today she waves back. A weak hand at first, as if she's not sure that's what I meant. But after a few times around the block she knows that's what I meant. And so I'm stopping. I'm going to ask for a cup of cold water. I'm thirsty anyway. Maybe all this sounds hokey to you if you are from some big town like Oxnard, but this is not a big town like Oxnard.

Her name is Myrna Dan. That last name must be a pruned-down version of Danielovitch or something because the people here are mostly Russians. She is thirty-two, a widow, one brat. A two-year-old named "Piper," crusty with food. She owns a small farm here but there is no one to work it. She has a decent allotment from the U.S. Government and a vegetable garden. If

you are from the coast you would not stop what you were doing
to look at her. Her hands are square and the fingers stubby, made
for rough wooden handles. Hips like gateposts.

No supper again. Karen left a note. "Lloyd, I am going for a
walk. There are some cold cuts in the fridge." It wasn't even
signed. Just like that. One of these days on one of her walks she is
going to get caught by the sky which can change on you in a
minute.

Bill Finkel made a remark on the way in to the dispatch center.
It was a little personal and coming from anybody else I would
have called him on it. But he is the lead engineer, the boss. A few
of the other guys grinned behind their hands. How do I know
where she goes or why? I am not a swami. If it settles her nerves,
why should I push it? I've thought of sending her to Ventura to
live with her mother for a while, but her mother is getting senile
and has taken to writing mean letters. I tell Karen the old lady is
around the bend, don't take those letters too seriously. But what's
the use when the letters come in like clockwork, once a week,
page after page of nasty accusations in a big, inch-high scrawl,
like a kid's, naming things that never happened. Karen takes it
hard, no matter what I say, as if what the old lady says is true.

Spacebow looks deserted. It isn't. The men are off in the fields,
the women are inside working toward evening. Too hot outside
even for the dogs who are sleeping under the porches. Ninety-
nine. I stopped for water at Myrna's. Do you want to see a missile
silo? Sure, she said, goddamn rights, just like that. I have an extra
hardhat in the truck but she doesn't have to wear it if she doesn't
want to. Regulations at this stage of the program are a little
pointless. Just a hole with a sump in it. Of course you can fall into
it and get yourself killed. That's about the only danger. But there
are no regulations that can save you from your own stupidity.
Last winter when these holes were being dug, a kid walked out on
a tarp. The tarp was covered with light snow and he couldn't tell
where the ground ended and the hole began. He dropped the
whole ninety feet and his hardhat did not save his ass. Myrna is
impressed with this story. She is very anxious to see one. D-7 is
closest to Spacebow, only a mile out of town. It isn't on my
schedule today, but so what. I hand her the orange hat. She has
trouble with the chin strap. I help her cinch it. Piper wants to

wear it too and grabs at the straps, whining. Myrna has big jaws. Strong. But not in an ugly way.

I tell her the story about Jack Stern, the Jewish quality control man from St. Louis who took flying lessons because he wanted to be able to get to a decent size city in a hurry whenever he felt the need. This flat empty farmland made his ulcer flare. He didn't know how to drive a car, and yet there he was, tearing around the sky in a Bonanza. One day he flew into a giant hammerhead—thinking, I guess, that a cloud like that is nothing but a lot of water vapor, no matter what shape it has or how big—and was never heard from again. That cloud ate him and the Bonanza. At the airport up in Minot they picked up two words on the emergency frequency, *Oh no,* then static.

I tell her the story about the motor-pool secretary who shot her husband once in the neck and twice in the foot with a target pistol while he slept. Both of them pulling down good money, too. I tell her the one about the one that got away. A northern as big as a shark. Pulled me and my boat a mile before my twelve-pound test monofilament snapped. She gives me a sidelong glance and makes a buzzing sound as if to say, *That* one takes the cake, Mister! We are on the bottom of D-7, watching the circle of sky, lying on our backs.

The trailer *stinks.* I could smell it from the street as soon as I got out of Bill Finkel's car. Fish heads. *Heads!* I guess they've been sitting there like that most of the afternoon. Just the big alligator jaws of my big beautiful pikes, but not the bodies. A platter of them, uncooked, drying out, and getting high. Knife fork napkin glass. I'd like to know what goes on inside her head, what passes for thinking in there. The note: "Lloyd, Eat your fill." Not signed. Is this supposed to be humor? I fail to get the point of it. I have to carry the mess to the garbage cans without breathing. A wind has come up. From the southeast. A big white fire is blazing in the sky over my shoulder. You can hear the far-off rumble, like a whale grunting. I squint west, checking for funnels.

Trouble in D-7. Busted sump. I pick up Myrna and Piper and head for the hole. It's a nice day for a drive. It could be a bearing seizure, but that's only a percentage guess. I unlock the gate and we drive to the edge of it. Space age artillery, I explain, as we stand on the lip of D-7, feeling the vertigo. The tarp is off for maintenance and the hole is solid black. If you let your imagination run, you might see it as bottomless. The "Pit" itself. Myrna is holding Piper back. Piper is whining, she wants to see the hole. Myrna has to slap her away, scolding. I drain my beer and let the can drop. I don't hear it hit. Not even a splash. I grab the fussing kid and hold her out over the hole. "Have yourself a *good* look, brat," I say. I hold her by the ankle with one hand. She is paralyzed. Myrna goes so white I have to smile. "Oh wait," she says. "Please, Lloyd. No." As if I ever would.

Myrna wants to see the D-flight control center. I ask her if she has claustrophobia. She laughs, but it's no joke. That far below the surface inside that capsule behind an eight-ton door can be upsetting if you're susceptible to confinement. The elevator is slow and heavy, designed to haul equipment. The door opens on a dimly-lit room. Spooky. There's crated gear scattered around. And there is the door, one yard thick to withstand the shock waves from the Bomb. I wheel it open. Piper whines, her big eyes distrustful. There is a musty smell in the dank air. The lights and blower are on now, but it will take a while for the air to freshen itself up. I wheel the big door shut. It can't latch yet, but Myrna is impressed. I explain to her what goes on in here. We sit down at the console. I show her where the launch "enabling" switches will be and why it will take two people together to launch an attack, the chairs fifteen feet apart and both switches turned for a several second count before the firing sequence can start, in case one guy goes berserk and decides to end the world because his old lady has been holding out on him, or just for the hell of it, given human nature. I show her the escape hole. It's loaded with ordinary sand. You pull this chain and the sand dumps into the capsule. Then you climb up the tube that held the sand into someone's wheat field. I show her the toilet and the little kitchen. I can see there is something on her mind. Isolated places make you think of weird things. It's happened to me more than once. Not here, but in the ghost town on the other side of the lake.

Topside the weather has changed. The sky is the color of pikebelly, wind rising from the southeast. To the west I can see stubby funnels pushing down from the overcast, but only so far. It looks like the clouds are growing roots. We have to run back to the truck in the rain, Piper screaming on Myrna's hip. A heavy bolt strikes less than a mile away. A blue fireball sizzles where it hits. Smell the ozone. It makes me sneeze.

This is the second day she's been gone. I don't know where or how. All her clothes are here. She doesn't have any money. I don't know what to do. There is no police station. Do I call her mother? Do I notify the FBI? The highway patrol? Bill Finkel?

Everybody in the carpool knows but won't say a word, out of respect for my feelings. Bill Finkel has other things on his mind. He is worried about rumored economy measures in the Assembly and Check-Out program next year. It has nothing to do with me. My job ends before the phase begins. I guess she went back to Oxnard, or maybe Ventura. But how?

We are in the D-flight control center. Myrna, with her hardhat cocked to one side, wants to fool around with the incomplete equipment. Piper is with her grandma. We are seated at the control console and she is pretending to work her switch. She has me pretend to work my switch. She wants to launch the entire flight of missiles, D-1 through D-10, at Cuba or Panama. Why Cuba and Panama? I ask. What about Russia? Why not Cuba or Panama? she says. Besides, I have Russian blood. Everyone around here has Russian blood. No, it's Cuba and Panama. Just think of the looks on their faces. All those people lying in the sun on the decks of those big white holiday boats, the coolies out in the cane fields, the tinhorn generals, and the whole shiteree. They'll look up trying to shade their eyes but they won't be able to. What in hell is this all about, they'll say, then *zap,* poof, *gone.*

I feel it too, craziness like hers. What if I couldn't get that eight-ton door open, Myrna? I see her hardhat wobble, her lip drop. What if? Just what *if?* She puts her arms around me and our hardhats click. She is one strong woman.

Lloyd, Lloyd, she says.

Yo, I say.

Jesus.

Easy.

Lloyd!

Bingo.

It's good down here—no *rules*—and she goes berserk. But later she is calm and up to mischief again. I recognize the look now. Okay, I tell her. What *next,* Myrna? She wants to do something halfway nasty. This, believe me, doesn't surprise me at all.

I'm sitting on the steel floor listening to the blower and waiting for Myrna to finish her business. I'm trying hard to picture what the weather is doing topside. It's not easy to do. It could be clear and calm and blue or it could be wild. There could be a high thin overcast or there could be nothing. You just can't know when you're this far under the wheat. I can hear her trying to work the little chrome lever, even though I told her there's no plumbing yet. Some maintenance yokel is going to find Myrna's "surprise." She comes out, pretending to be sheepish, but I can see that the little joke tickles her.

Something takes my hook and strips off ten yards of line then stops dead. Snag. I reel in. The pole is bent double and the line is singing. Then something lets go but it isn't the line because I'm still snagged. It breaks the surface, a lady's shoe. It's brown and white with a short heel. I toss it into the bottom of the boat. The water is shallow here, and clear. There's something dark and wide under me like a shadow on the water. An old farmhouse, submerged when the dam filled. There's a deep current around the structure. I can see fence, tires, an old truck, feed pens. There is a fat farmer in the yard staring up at me, checking the weather, and I jump away from him, almost tipping the boat. My heart feels tangled in my ribs. But it's only a stump with arms.

The current takes my boat in easy circles. A swimmer would be in serious trouble. I crank up the engine and head back. No fish today. So be it. Sometimes you come home empty-handed. The shoe is new, stylish, and was made in Spain.

I'm standing on the buckled porch of 49 Onyx Street. Myrna is inside reading *Secret Confessions:* "What My Don Must Never Know." The sky is bad. The lake is bad. It will be a while before we can cross back. I knock on the door, as we planned. Myrna is on the bed in the stained, raggedy slip, giggling. "Listen to this dogshit, Lloyd," she says. But I'm not in the mood for weird stories. "I brought you something, honey," I say. She looks at the soggy shoe. "That?" But she agrees to try it on, anyway. I feel like my own ghost, bumping into the familiar but run-down walls of my old house in the middle of nowhere, and I remember my hatred of it. "Hurry up," I say, my voice true as a razor.

A thick tube hairy with rain is snaking out of the sky less than a mile away. Is it going to touch? "They never do, Lloyd. This isn't Kansas. Will you please listen to this dogshit?" Something about a pregnant high-school girl, Dee, locked in a toilet with a knitting needle. Something about this Don who believes in purity. Something about bright red blood. Something about ministers and mothers and old-fashioned shame. I'm not listening, even when Dee slides the big needle in. I have to keep watch on the sky, because there is a first time for everything, even if this is not Kansas. The wind is stripping shingles from every roof I see. A long board is spinning like a slow propeller. The funnel is behind a bluff, holding back. But I can hear it, the freight trains. Myrna is standing behind me, running a knuckle up and down my back. "Hi, darling," she says. "Want to know what I did while you were out working on the dam today?" The dark tube has begun to move out from behind the bluff, but I'm not sure which way. "Tell me," I say. "Tell me."

ON FOR THE LONG HAUL

by T. Coraghessan Boyle

There was nothing wrong with his appendix—no stitch in the side, no inflammation, no pain—but Bayard was having it out. For safety's sake. He'd read an article once about an anthropologist who'd gone to Malaysia to study the social habits of the orangutan and died horribly when her appendix had burst three hundred miles from the nearest hospital; as she lay writhing in her death agony the distraught apes had hauled her halfway up a jackfruit tree, where she was found several days later by a photographer from *Life* magazine. The picture—splayed limbs, gouty face, leaves like a mouthful of teeth—was indelible with him, a shoulder harness to his permanent mental baggage. She'd been unprepared, that anthropologist, inattentive to the little details that can make or break you. Bayard was taking no such chances.

At their first meeting, the surgeon had been skeptical. "You're going to Montana, Mr. Wenk, not Borneo. There are hospitals there, all the modern facilities."

"It's got to go, Doctor," Bayard had quietly insisted, looking up with perfect composure from the knot of his folded hands.

"Listen, Mr. Wenk. I've got to tell you that every surgical procedure, however routine, involves risk"—the doctor paused to let this sink in—"and I really feel the risks outweigh the gains in this case. All the tests are negative—we have no indication of a potential problem here."

"But, Doctor—" Bayard felt himself at a loss for words. How to explain to this earnest, assured man with the suntanned wife, the Mercedes, and the house in Malibu that all of Los Angeles, San Francisco, New York—civilization itself—was on the brink of a catastrophe that would make the Dark Ages look like a Sunday afternoon softball game? How intimate the horrors that lay ahead, the privation, the suffering? He remembered Aesop's fable about the ant and the grasshopper. Some would be prepared, others would not. "You just don't understand how isolated I'm going to be," he said finally.

Isolated, yes. Thirty-five acres in Bounceback, Montana, population thirty-seven. The closest town with a hospital, bank, or restaurant was Missoula, a two-and-a-half-hour drive, an hour of it on washboard dirt. Bayard would have his own well, a cleared acre for vegetable farming, and a four-room cabin with wood stove, electrical generator, and a radiation-proof cellar stocked with a five-year supply of canned and freeze-dried foodstuffs. The whole thing was the brainchild of Sam Arkson, a real-estate developer who specialized in subsistence plots, bomb shelters, and survival homes. Bayard's firm had done some PR work for one of Arkson's companies—Thrive Inc.—and as he looked into the literature of catastrophe, Bayard had found himself growing ever more uncertain about the direction of his own life. *Remember the gas crisis?* asked one of Arkson's pamphlets. *An inconvenience, right? The have-nots stepping on the haves. But what about the food crisis around the corner? Have you thought about what you'd do when they close up the supermarkets with a sign that says* SORRY, TEMPORARILY OUT OF FOOD?

Bayard would never forget the day he'd come across that pamphlet. His palms had begun to sweat as he read on, gauging the effect of nuclear war on the food and water supply, thinking of life without toilet paper, toothpaste, or condiments, summoning images of the imminent economic depression, the starving masses, the dark-skinned marauding hordes pouring across our borders from the south to take, take, take with their greedy desperate clutching hands. That night he'd gone home in a cold sweat, visions of apocalypse dancing in his head. Fran made him a drink, but he couldn't taste it. The girls showed him their schoolwork—the sweet ingenuous loops of their penmanship, the pale watercolors and gold stars—and he felt the tears start up in his eyes. They were doomed, he was doomed, the world sinking like a stone. After they'd gone to bed he slipped out to the kitchen and silently pulled back the refrigerator door. Inside he found a head of deliquescing lettuce, half a gallon of milk, mayonnaise, mustard, chutney, a jar of capers so ancient it might have been unearthed in a tomb, a pint of butter brickle ice cream, and a single Mexicali Belle TV dinner. The larder yielded two cans of pickled Chinese mushrooms, half a dozen packages of artificial rice pudding, and a lone box of Yodo Crunch cereal, three quarters empty. He felt sick. Talk about a prolonged siege; they didn't even have breakfast.

That night his dreams had tentacles. He woke feeling strangled. The coffee was poisonous, the newspaper rife with innuendo, each story, each detail cutting into him with the sharp edge of doom. A major quake was on the way, the hills were on fire, there was murder and mayhem in Hollywood, AIDS was spreading to the heterosexual population, Qaddafi had the bomb. Outside was the traffic. Three million cars, creeping, spitting, killing the atmosphere, inching toward gridlock. The faces of the drivers were impassive. Shift, lurch, advance, stop, shift, lurch. Didn't they know the whole world had gone hollow, rotten like a tooth? Didn't they know they were dead? He looked into their eyes and saw empty sockets, looked into their faces and saw the death's-head. At work it was no better. The secretaries greeted him as if money mattered, as if there was time to breathe, to go out to Chan Dara for lunch and get felt up in the Xerox room; his colleagues were as bland as cue balls, nattering on about baseball, stocks, VCRs, and food processors. He staggered down the hallway as if he'd been hit in the vitals, slamming into the sanctuary of his office like a hunted beast. And there, on his desk, like the bony pointed finger of the Grim Reaper himself, was Arkson's pamphlet.

By two-thirty that afternoon he was perched on a chair in Sam Arkson's San Diego office, talking hard-core survival with the impresario himself. Arkson sat behind a desk the size of a trampoline, looking alternately youthful and fissured with age—he could have been anywhere from thirty-five to sixty. Aggressively tanned and conscientiously muscled, his hair cut so close to the scalp it might have been painted on, he resembled nothing so much as a professional sweatmeister, Vic Tanny fighting the waistline bulge, Jack LaLanne with a mohawk. He was dressed in fatigues and wore a khaki tie. "So," he said, leaning back in his chair and sizing up Bayard with a shrewd, unforgiving gaze, "are you on for the long haul or do you just need a security blanket?"

Bayard was acutely conscious of his paunch, the whiteness of his skin, the hair that trailed down his neck in soft frivolous coils. He felt like a green recruit under the burning gaze of the drill instructor, like an awkward dancer trying out for the wrong role. He coughed into his fist. "The long haul."

Arkson seemed pleased. "Good," he said, a faint smile playing across his lips. "I thought at first you might be one of these halfway types that wants a bomb shelter under the patio or something." He gave Bayard a knowing glance. "They might last a month or two after the blast," he said, "but what then? And what if it's not war we're facing but worldwide economic collapse? Are they going to eat their radiation detectors?"

This was a joke. Bayard laughed nervously. Arkson cut him off with a contemptuous snort and a wave of his hand that consigned all the timid slipshod Halfway Harrys of the world to an early grave. "No," he said, "I can see you're the real thing, a 100 percenter, no finger in the dike for you." He paused. "You're a serious person, Bayard, am I right?'

Bayard nodded.

"And you've got a family you want to protect?"

Bayard nodded again.

"Okay," Arkson was on his feet, a packet of brochures in his hand, "we're going to want to talk hidden location with the space, seeds, fertilizer, and tools to grow food and the means to hunt it, and we're going to talk a five-year renewable stockpile of survival rations, medical supplies, and specie . . . and of course weaponry."

"Weaponry?"

Arkson had looked at him as if he'd just put a bag over his head. "Tell me," he said, folding his arms so that the biceps swelled beneath the balled fists, "when the bust comes and you're sitting on the only food supply in the county, you don't really think your neighbors are going to breeze over for tea and polite chitchat, do you?"

Though Bayard had never handled a gun in his life, he knew the answer: there was a sickness on the earth and he'd have to harden himself to deal with it.

Suddenly Arkson was pointing at the ceiling, as if appealing to a higher authority to back him up. "You know what I've got up there on the roof?" he said, looming over Bayard like an inquisitor. Bayard hadn't the faintest idea.

"A Brantly B2B."

Bayard gave him a blank look.

"A chopper. Whirlybird. You know: upski-downski. And guess who flies it?" Arkson spread the brochure out on the desk in front of him, tapping a forefinger against the glossy photograph of a helicopter floating in a clear blue sky beneath the rubric ESCAPE CRAFT. "That's right, friend: me. I fly it. Leave nothing to

chance, that's my motto." Bayard thumbed through the brochure,
saw minijets, hovercraft, Cessnas, seaplanes, and ultralights.

"I can be out of town in ten minutes. Half an hour later I'm in
my compound—two hundred fenced acres, three security men,
goats, cows, chickens, pigs, corn as high as your chin, wheat,
barley, rye, artesian wells, underground gas and water tanks—and
an arsenal that could blow away the PLO. Listen," he said, and
his eyes were like a stalking cat's, "when the shit hits the fan
they'll be eating each other out there."

Bayard had been impressed. He was also terrified, sick with the
knowledge of his own impotence and vulnerability. The blade was
poised. It could fall today, tonight, tomorrow. They had to get
out. "Fran," he called as he hurried through the front door,
arms laden with glossy brochures, dire broadsides, and assorted
survival tomes from Arkson Publications Ltd. "Fran!"

Fran had always been high-strung—neurotic, actually—and the
sort of pure unrefined paranoia that had suddenly infested Bayard
was second nature to her. Still, she would take some persuading—
he was talking about uprooting their entire life, after all—and it
was up to Bayard to focus that paranoia and bring it to bear on
the issue at hand. She came out of the sun-room in a tentlike
swimsuit, a large, solid, plain-faced woman in her late thirties,
trailing children. She gave him a questioning look while the girls,
chanting "Daddy, Daddy," foamed around his legs. "We've got
to talk," was all he could say.

Later, after the children had been put to bed, he began his
campaign. "We're sitting on a powder keg," he said as he bent
over the dishwasher, stacking plates. She looked up, blinking
behind the big rectangular frames of her glasses like a frogman
coming up for air. "Pardon?"

"L. A., the whole West Coast. It's the first place the Russians'll
hit—if the quake doesn't drop us into the ocean first. Or the
banks go under. You've read about the S and L's, right?"

She looked alarmed. But then she alarmed easily. Chronically
overprotected as a child, cloistered in a parochial school run
along the lines of a medieval nunnery, and then consigned to a
Catholic girls' college that made the earlier school look liberal,
she believed with all her heart in the venality of man and the
perfidy and rottenness of the world. On the rare occasions when
she left the house she clutched her purse like a fullback going
through a gap in the line, saw all pedestrians—even white-haired
grandmothers—as potential muggers, and dodged Asians, Latinos,

Pakistanis, and Iranians as if they were the hordes of Genghis Khan. "What in God's name are you talking about?" she said.

"I'm talking about Montana."

"Montana?"

At this point Bayard had simply fetched his trove of doom literature and spread it across the table. "Read," he said, knowing full well the books and pamphlets could speak far more eloquently than he. In the morning he'd found her hunched over the table still, the ashtray full beside her, a copy of *Doom Newsletter* in her hand, *Panic in the Streets* and *How to Kill, Volumes I–IV* face down beside a steaming coffee mug. "But what about the girls?" she said. "What about school, ballet lessons, tennis, swimming?"

Melissa was nine, Marcia seven. The move to the hinterlands would be disruptive for them, maybe traumatic—Bayard didn't deny it—but then so would nuclear holocaust. "Ballet lessons?" he echoed. "What good do you think ballet lessons are going to be when maniacs are breaking down the door?" And then, more gently: "Look, Fran, it's going to be hard for all of us, but I just don't see how we can stay here now that our eyes have been opened—it's like sitting on the edge of a volcano or something."

She was weakening, he could feel it. When he got home from the office she was sunk into the sofa, her eyes darting across the page before her like frightened animals. Arkson had called. Four times. "Mrs. Wenk, Fran," he'd shouted over the wire as if the barbarians were at the gate, "you've got to listen to me. I have a place for you. Nobody'll find you. You'll live forever. Sell that deathtrap and get out now before it's too late!" Toward the end of the week she went through an entire day without changing out of her nightgown. Bayard pressed his advantage. He sent the girls to the babysitter and took the day off from work to ply her with pamphlets, rhetoric and incontrovertible truths, and statistics on everything from the rising crime rate to nuclear kill ratios. As dusk fell that evening, the last choked rays of sunlight irradiating the smog till it looked like mustard gas coming in over the trenches, she capitulated. In a voice weak with terror and exhaustion, she called him into the bedroom, where she lay still as a corpse. "All right," she croaked. "Let's get out."

After Fran, the surgeon was easy. For fifteen minutes Bayard had quietly persisted while the doctor demurred. Finally, throwing his trump card, the surgeon leaned forward and said, "You're aware your insurance won't cover this, Mr. Wenk?"

Bayard had smiled. "No problem," he said. "I'll pay cash."

*   *   *

Two months later he and Fran sported matching abdominal scars, wore new flannel shirts and down vests, talked knowledgeably of seed sets, fertilizer, and weed killer, and resided in the distant rugged reaches of the glorious Treasure State, some four hundred miles from ground zero of the nearest likely site of atomic devastation. The cabin was a good deal smaller than what they were used to, but then they were used to luxury condominiums, and the cabin sacrificed luxury—comfort, even—for utility. Its exterior was simulated log, designed to make the place look like a trapper's cabin to the average marauder, but the walls were reinforced with steel plates to a thickness that would withstand bazooka or antitank gun. In the basement, which featured four-foot-thick concrete walls and lead shielding, was the larder. Ranks of hermetically sealed canisters mounted the right-hand wall, each with a reassuring shelf life of ten years or more: bulk grains, wild rice, textured vegetable protein, yogurt powder, matzo meal, hardtack, lentils, bran, Metamucil. Lining the opposite wall, precisely stacked, labeled, and alphabetized, were the freeze-dried entrées, from abbacchio alla cacciatora and beef Bourguignon to shrimp creole, turkey tetrazzini, and ziti alla romana. Bayard took comfort in their very names, as a novice might take comfort in the names of the saints: Just-in-Case freeze-dried linguine with white clam sauce, tomato crystals from Lazarus Foods, canned truffles from Gourmets for Tomorrow, and Arkson's own Stash Brand generic foodstuffs, big plain-labeled cans that read CATSUP, SAUER-KRAUT, DETERGENT, LARD. In the evenings, when the house was as quiet as the far side of the moon, Bayard would slip down into the shelter, pull the airtight door closed behind him and spend hours contemplating the breadth, variety, and nutritional range of his cache. Sinking back in a padded armchair, his heartbeat decelerating, breathing slowed to a whisper, he would feel the calm of the womb descend on him. Then he knew the pleasures of the miser, the hoarder, the burrowing squirrel, and he felt as free from care as if he were wafting to and fro in the dark amniotic sea whence he sprang.

Of course, such contentment doesn't come cheap. The whole package—land, cabin, four-wheel-drive vehicle, arms and munitions, foodstuffs, and silver bars, De Beers diamonds, and cowrie shells for barter—had cost nearly half a million. Arkson, whose corporate diversity put him in a league with Gulf & Western, had been able to provide everything, lock, stock, and barrel, right down to the church-key opener in the kitchen drawer and the reusable toilet paper in the bathroom. There were radiation suits, flannels, and thermal underwear from Arkson Outfitters, and weapons—including a pair of Russian-made AK-47s smuggled out of Afghanistan and an Israeli grenade launcher—from Arkson Munitions. In the driveway, from Arkson Motors, Domestic and Import, was the four-wheel-drive, Norwegian-made Olfputt TC-17, which would run on anything handy, from paint thinner to rubbing alcohol, climb the north face of the Eiger in an ice storm, and pull a plow through frame-deep mud. The cabin's bookshelves were mostly given over to the how-to, survival, and Self-help tomes in which Arkson Publications specialized, but there were reprints of selected classics—*A Journal of the Plague Year, Hiroshima,* and *Down and Out in Paris and London*—as well. Arkson made an itemized list, tallied the whole thing up, and presented the bill to Bayard and Fran in the San Diego office.

Fran was so wrought up at this point, she barely gave it a glance. She kept looking over her shoulder at the door, as if in expectation of the first frenzied pillagers, and then she would glance down at the open neck of her purse and the .22-caliber Beretta that Arkson had just handed her. ("My gift to you, Fran," he'd said. "Learn to use it.") Bayard was distracted himself. He tried to look judicious, tried to focus on the sheet of paper before him with the knowing look one puts on for garage mechanics presenting the bill for arcane mechanical procedures and labor at the rate of $120 an hour, but he couldn't. What did it matter? Until he was ensconced in his cabin he was like a crab without a shell. "Seems fair," he muttered.

Arkson had come round the desk to perch on the near edge and take his hand. "No bargain rate for survival, Bayard," he said, "no fire sales. If the price seems steep, just think of it this way: Would you put a price on your life? Or the lives of your wife and children?" He'd paused to give Bayard a saintly look, the look of the young Redeemer stepping through the doors of the temple. "Just be thankful that you two had the financial resources—and the foresight—to protect yourselves."

Bayard had looked down at the big veiny tanned hand clutching his own and had shaken mechanically. He felt numb. The past few weeks had been hellish, what with packing up, supervising the movers, and making last-minute trips to the mall for things like thread, Band-Aids, and dental floss—not to mention agonizing over the sale of the house, anticipating Fran's starts and rushes of panic, and turning in his resignation at the Hooper-Munson Company, where he'd put in fourteen years and worked himself up to Senior Vice-president in Charge of Reversing Negative Corporate Image. Without Arkson it would have been impossible. He'd soothed Fran, driven the children to school, called the movers, cleaners, and painters, and then gone to work on Bayard's assets with the single-mindedness of a general marshaling troops. Arkson Realty had put the condo on the market and found a buyer for the summer place in Big Bear, and Arkson, Arkson, and Arkson, Brokers, had unloaded Bayard's holdings on the stock exchange with a barely significant loss. When combined with Fran's inheritance and the money Bayard had put away for the girls' education, the amount realized would meet Thrive, Inc.'s price and then some. It was all for the best, Arkson kept telling him, all for the best. If Bayard had second thoughts about leaving his job and dropping out of society, he could put them out of his mind: society, as he'd known it, wouldn't last out the year. And as far as money was concerned, well, they'd be living cheaply from here on out.

"Fran," Arkson was saying, taking her hand now, too, and linking the three of them as if he were a revivalist leading them forward to the purifying waters, "Bayard . . ." he paused again, overcome with emotion: "Feel lucky."

Now, two months later, Bayard could stand on the front porch of his cabin, survey the solitary expanse of his property, with its budding aspen and cottonwood and glossy conifers, and take Arkson's parting benediction to heart. He did feel lucky. Oh, perhaps on reflection he could see that Arkson had shaved him on one item or another, and that the doom merchant had kindled a blaze under him and Fran that put them right in the palm of his hand, but Bayard had no regrets. He felt secure, truly secure, for the first time in his adult life, and he bent contentedly to ax or hoe, glad to have escaped the Gomorrah of the city. For her part, Fran seemed to have adjusted well, too. The physical environment beyond the walls of her domain had never much interested her, and so it was principally a matter of adjusting to one set of rooms as opposed to another. Most important though, she seemed more relaxed. In the morning she would lead the girls through their geography or arithmetic, then read, sew, or nap in the early afternoon. Later she would walk round the yard—something she rarely did in Los Angeles—or work in the flower garden she'd planted outside the front door. At night there was television, the signals called down to earth from the heavens by means of the satellite dish Arkson had providently included in the package.

The one problem was the girls. At first they'd been excited, the

whole thing a lark, a vacation in the woods, but as the weeks
wore on they became increasingly withdrawn, secretive, and, as
Bayard suspected, depressed. Marcia missed Mrs. Sturdivant, her
second-grade teacher; Melissa missed her best friend Nicole,
Disneyland, Baskin-Robbins, and the beach, in that order. Bayard
saw the pale sad ovals of their faces framed in the gloom of the
back bedroom as they hovered over twice-used coloring books,
and he felt as if a stake had been driven through his heart. "Don't
worry," Fran said, "give them time. They'll make the adjust-
ment." Bayard hoped so. Because there was no way they were
going back to the city.

One afternoon—it was mid-June, already hot, a light breeze
discovering dust and tossing it on the hoods and windshields of
the cars parked along the street—Bayard was in the lot outside
Chuck's Wagon in downtown Bounceback, loading groceries into
the back of the Olfputt, when he glanced up to see two men
stepping out of a white Mercedes with California plates. One of
them was Arkson, in his business khakis and tie. The other—tall
and red-faced, skinny as a refugee in faded green jumpsuit and
work boots—Bayard had never seen before. Both men stretched
themselves, and then the stranger put his hands on his hips and
slowly revolved a full 360 degrees, his steady expressionless gaze
taking in the gas station, saloon, feedstore, and half-deserted
streets as if he'd come to seize them for nonpayment of taxes.
Bayard could hardly contain himself. "Sam!" he called. "Sam
Arkson!" And then he was in motion, taking the lot in six
animated strides, his hand outstretched in greeting.

At first Arkson didn't seem to recognize him. He'd taken the
stranger's arm and was pointing toward the mountains like a tour
guide when Bayard called out his name. Half-turning, as if at
some minor disturbance, Arkson gave him a preoccupied look,
then swung back to say something under his breath to his com-
panion. By then Bayard was on him, pumping his hand. "Good to
see you, Sam."

Arkson shook numbly. "You too," he murmured, avoiding
Bayard's eyes.

There was an awkward silence. Arkson looked constipated. The
stranger—his face was so red he could have been apoplectic,
terminally sunburned, drunk—glared at Bayard as if they'd just
exchanged insults. Bayard's gaze shifted uneasily from the stranger's eyes to the soiled yellow beret that lay across his head like a
cheese omelet and then back again to Arkson. "I just wanted to

tell you how well we're doing, Sam," he stammered, "and, and to thank you—I mean it, really—for everything you've done for us."

Arkson brightened immediately. If a moment earlier he'd looked like a prisoner in the dock, hangdog and tentative, now he seemed his old self. He smiled, ducked his head, and held up his palm in humble acknowledgment. Then, running his fingers over the stubble of his crown, he stepped back a pace and introduced the ectomorphic stranger. "Rayfield Cullum," he said, "Bayard Wenk."

"Glad to meet you," Bayard said, extending his hand.

The stranger's hands never left his pockets. He stared at Bayard a moment out of his deep-set yellow eyes, then turned his head to spit in the dirt. Bayard's hand dropped like a stone.

"I'd say you two have something in common," Arkson said mysteriously. And then, leaning forward and dropping his voice: "Rayfield and I are just ironing out the details on the plot next to yours. He wants in this week—tomorrow, if not sooner." Arkson laughed. The stranger's eyes lifted to engage Bayard's; his face remained expressionless.

Bayard was taken by surprise. "Plot?" he repeated.

"East and south," Arkson said, nodding. "You'll be neighbors. I've got a retired couple coming in the end of the month from Saratoga Springs—they'll be purchasing the same package as yours directly to the north of you, by that little lake?"

"Package?" Bayard was incredulous. "What is this, Levittown, Montana, or something?"

"Heh-heh, very funny, Bayard." Arkson had put on his serious look, life-and-death, the world's a jungle, LaLanne admonishing his audience over the perils of flab. "The crunch comes, Bayard," he said, "you could support fifty people on those thirty-five acres, what with the game in those woods and the fertility of that soil. You know it as well as I do."

Now Cullum spoke for the first time, his voice a high nagging rasp, like static. "Arkson," he said, driving nails into the first syllable, "I ain't got all day."

It was then that Melissa, giggling like a machine and with a pair of ice-cream cones thrust up like torches over her head, came tearing around the side of the building, her sister in pursuit. Marcia was not giggling. She was crying in frustration, wailing as if her heart had been torn out, and cutting the air with a stick. "Melissa!" Bayard shouted, but it was too late. Her skinny brown legs got tangled and she pitched forward into Cullum, who was just then swiveling his head around at the commotion. There was the scrape of sneakers on gravel, the glare of the sun poised motionless overhead, and then the wet rich fecal smear of chocolate fudge ice cream—four scoops—on the seat of Cullum's jumpsuit. Cullum's knee buckled under the impact, and he jumped back as if bitten by a snake. "Goddammit!" he roared, and Bayard could see that his hands were shaking. "Goddammit to hell!"

Melissa lay sprawled in the dirt. Stricken face, a thin wash of red on her scraped knee. Bayard was already bending roughly for her, angry, an apology on his lips, when Cullum took a step forward and kicked her twice in the ribs. "Little shit," he hissed, his face twisted with lunatic fury, and then Arkson had his broad arms around him, pulling him back like a handler with an attack dog.

Melissa's mouth was working in shock, the first hurt breathless shriek caught in her throat, Marcia stood white-faced behind them, Cullum was spitting out curses and dancing in Arkson's arms. Bayard might have lifted his daughter from the dirt and pressed her to him, he might have protested, threatened, waved his fist at this rabid dog with the red face, but he didn't. No. Before he could think, he was on Cullum, catching him in the center of that flaming face with a fist like a knob of bone. Once, twice, zeroing in on the wicked little dog's eyes and the fleshy dollop of the nose, butter, margarine, wet clay, something giving with a crack, and then a glancing blow off the side of the head. He felt Cullum's work boots flailing for his groin as he stumbled forward under his own momentum, and then Arkson was driving him up against the Mercedes and shouting something in his face. Suddenly freed, Cullum came at him, beret askew, blood bright in his nostrils, but Arkson was there, pinning Bayard to the car and shooting out an arm to catch hold of the skinny man's shirt. "Daddy!" Melissa shrieked, the syllables broken with shock and hurt.

"You son of a bitch!" Bayard shouted.

"All right now, knock it off, will you?" Arkson held them at arm's length like a pair of fighting cocks. "It's just a misunderstanding, that's all."

Bleeding, shrunk into his jumpsuit like a withered tortoise, Cullum held Bayard's gaze and dropped his voice to a hiss. "I'll kill you," he said.

Fran was aghast. "Is he dangerous?" she said, turning to peer over her spectacles at Bayard and the girls as they sat at the kitchen table. She was pouring wine vinegar from a three-gallon jug into a bowl of cucumber spears. Awkwardly. "I mean, he sounds like he escaped from a mental ward or something."

Bayard shrugged. He could still taste the tinny aftershock the incident had left in the back of his throat. A fight. He'd been involved in a fight. Though he hadn't struck anyone in anger since elementary school, hadn't even come close, he'd reacted instinctively in defense of his children. He sipped his gimlet and felt a glow of satisfaction.

"This is the man we're going to have next door to us?" Fran set the bowl on the table beside a platter of reconstituted stir-fried vegetables and defrosted tofu. The girls were subdued, staring down their straws into glasses of chocolate milk. "Well?" Fran's eyes searched him as she sat down across the table. "Do you think I can have any peace of mind with this sort of . . . of violence and lawlessness on my doorstep? Is this what we left the city for?"

Bayard speared a square of tofu and fed it into his mouth. "It's hardly on our doorstep, Fran," he said, gesturing with his fork. "Besides, I can handle him, no problem."

A week passed. Then two. Bayard saw no more of Arkson, nor of Cullum, and the incident began to fade from his mind. Perhaps Cullum had soured on the deal and gone off somewhere else—or back to the hole he'd crawled out of. And what if he did move in? Arkson was right: there was so much land between them they might never lay eyes on each other, let alone compete for resources. At any rate, Bayard was too busy to worry about it. Mornings, it was second-grade geography and fourth-grade history, which meant relearning his state capitals and trying to keep his de Sotos, Coronados, and Cabeza de Vacas straight. Afternoons, he kept busy with various improvement projects—constructing a lopsided playhouse for the girls, fencing his vegetable garden against the mysterious agent that masticated everything he planted right down to the root, splitting and stacking wood, fumbling over the instructions for the prefab aluminum tool shed he'd mail-ordered from the Arkson Outfitters catalog. Every third day he drove in to Bounceback for groceries (he and Fran had decided to go easy on the self-subsistence business until such time as society collapsed and made it imperative), and on weekends the family would make the long trek down to Missoula for a restaurant meal and a movie. It was on one of these occasions that they bought the rabbits.

Bayard was coming out of the hardware store with a box of

two-penny nails, a set of socket wrenches, and a hacksaw when he spotted Fran and the girls across the street, huddled over a man who seemed to be part of the sidewalk. The man, Bayard saw as he crossed the street to join them, was long-haired, bearded, and dirty. He had a burlap sack beside him, and the sack was moving. "Here, here," said the man, grinning up at them, and then he plunged his hand into the bag and drew out a rabbit by the ears. The animal's paws were bound with rubber bands, its fur was rat-colored. "This one here's named Duke," the man said, grinning. "He's trained."

Long-whiskered, long-eared, and long-legged, it looked more like a newborn mule than a rabbit. As the man dangled it before the girls, its paws futilely kicking and eyes big with terror, Bayard almost expected it to bray. "Good eatin', friend," the man said, giving Bayard a shrewd look.

"Daddy," Melissa gasped, "can we buy him? Can we?"

The man was down on his knees, fumbling in the sack. A moment later he extracted a second rabbit, as lanky, brown, and sickly looking as the first. "This one's Lennie. He's trained, too."

"Can we, Daddy?" Marcia chimed in, tugging at his pant leg.

Bayard looked at Fran. The girls held their breath. "Five bucks," the man said.

Down the street sat the Olfputt, gleaming like a gigantic toaster oven. Two women, a man in a cowboy hat, and a boy Melissa's age stood staring at it in awe and bewilderment. Bayard jingled the change in his pocket, hesitating. "For both," the man said.

Initially, the rabbits seemed a good idea. Bayard was no psychologist, but he could see that these gangling, flat-footed rodents, with their multiplicity of needs, with their twitching noses and grateful mouths, might help draw the girls out of themselves. He was right. From the moment they'd hustled the rabbits into the car, cut their bonds, and pressed them to their scrawny chests while Fran fretted over ticks, tularemia, and relapsing fever, the girls were absorbed with them. They fed them grass, lettuce, and the neat little pellets of rabbit food that so much resembled the neat little pellets that the animals excreted. They cuddled, dressed, and brushed them. They helped Bayard construct a pair of interlocking chicken-wire cages and selected the tree from which they would hang, the girls' thin, serious faces compressed with concern over weasels, foxes, coons, coyotes. Melissa devoted less time to tormenting her sister and bemoaning the absence of her school friends; Marcia seemed less withdrawn.

For his part, Bayard, too, found the new pets compelling. They thumped their feet joyously when he approached their cages with lettuce or parsley, and as they nuzzled his fingers he gazed out over his cleared acre to the trees beyond and thought how this was only the beginning. He would have goats, chickens, pigs, maybe even a cow or horse. The way he saw it, a pet today was meat on the hoof tomorrow. Hadn't they eaten horses during the First World War? Mules, oxen, dogs? Not to mention rabbits. Of course, these particular rabbits were an exception. Though in theory they were to be skinned, stewed, and eaten in time of distress, though they represented a hedge against hard times and a life-sustaining stock of protein, Bayard looked into their quiet moist eyes and knew he would eat lentils first.

The following week Bayard took the family into Missoula for a double sci-fi/horror feature (which only helped confirm him in his conviction that the world was disintegrating) and dinner at the local Chinese restaurant. It was after dark when they got home and the Olfputt's headlights swung into the yard to illuminate two tiny figures hanging like wash from the simulated beam that ran the length of the front porch. Melissa spotted them first. "What's that?" she said.

"Where?"

"There, up on the porch."

By the time Bayard saw them it was too late. Fran had seen them too—disheveled ears and limp paws, the puny little carcasses twisting slowly round their monofilament nooses—and, worse, the seven-year-old, rousing from her sleep, had caught a nightmarish glimpse of them before he could flick off the lights. "My God," Fran whispered. They sat there a moment, the dark suffocating, no gleam of light for miles. Then Marcia began to whimper and Melissa called out his name sharply, as if in accusation, as if he alone were responsible for all the hurts and perversions of the world.

Bayard felt he was sinking. Pork fried rice and duck sauce tore at the pit of his stomach with a hellish insistence, Fran was hyperventilating, and the girls' lamentations rose in intensity from piteous bewildered bleats to the caterwauling of demons. Frightened, angry, uncomprehending, he sat there in utter blackness, his hands trembling on the wheel. When finally he flicked on the parking lights and pushed open the door, Fran clutched his arm with the grip of a madwoman. "Don't go out there," she hissed.

"Don't be silly," Bayard said.

"No," she sobbed, clawing at him as if she were drowning. Her eyes raged at him in the dim light, the girls were weeping and moaning, and then she was pressing something into his hand, heavy, cold, instrument of death. "Take this."

Six or seven pickups were parked outside the T&T Cocktail Bar when Bayard rolled in to downtown Bounceback. It was half past eleven, still hot, the town's solitary streetlight glowing like a myopic eye. As he crossed the street to the telephone outside Chuck's Wagon, Bayard could make out a number of shadowy figures in broad-brimmed hats milling around in front of the bar. There was a murmur of disembodied voices, the nagging whine of a country fiddle, stars overhead, the glow of cigarettes below. Drunks, he thought, hurrying past them. Their lives wouldn't be worth a carton of crushed eggs when the ax fell.

Bayard stalked up to the phone, tore the receiver from its cradle, and savagely dialed a number he'd scribbled across a paper napkin. He was angry, keyed up, hot with outrage. He listened to the phone ring once, twice, three times, as he cursed under his breath. This was too much. His wife was sick with fear, his children traumatized, and all he'd worked for—security, self-sufficiency, peace of mind—was threatened. He'd had to prowl round his own home like a criminal, clutching a gun he didn't know how to use, jumping at his own shadow. Each bush was an assassin, each pocket of shadow a crouching adversary, the very trees turned against him. Finally, while Fran and the girls huddled in the locked car, he'd cut down Lennie and Duke, bundled the lifeless bodies in a towel, and hid them out back. Then Fran, her face like a sack of flour, had made him turn on all the lights till the house blazed like a stage set, insisting that he search the closets, poke the muzzle of the gun under the beds, and throw back the doors of the kitchen cabinets like an undercover cop busting drug peddlers. When he'd balked at this last precaution— the cabinets couldn't have concealed anything bigger than a basset hound—she'd reminded him of how they found Charlie Manson under the kitchen sink. "All right," he'd said after searching the basement, "there's nobody here. It's okay."

"It was that maniac, wasn't it?" Fran whispered, as if afraid she'd be overheard.

"Daddy," Melissa cried, "where's Lennie . . . and . . . and Duke?" The last word trailed off in a broken lamentation for the dead, and Bayard felt the anger like a hot nugget inside him.

"I don't know," he said, pressing Melissa to him and massaging her thin quaking little shoulders. "I don't know." Through the doorway he could see Marcia sitting in the big armchair, sucking her thumb. Suddenly he became aware of the gun in his hand. He stared down at it for a long moment, and then almost unconsciously, as if it were a cigarette lighter or nail clipper, he slipped it into his pocket.

Now he stood outside Chuck's Wagon, the night breathing down his neck, the telephone receiver pressed to his ear. Four rings, five, six. Suddenly the line engaged and Arkson, his voice shrunk round a kernel of suspicion, answered with a quick tentative "Yeah?"

"Sam? It's me, Bayard."

"Who?"

"Bayard Wenk."

There was a pause. "Oh yeah," Arkson said finally, "Bayard. What can I do for you? You need anything?"

"No, I just wanted to ask you—"

"Because I know you're going to be short of hardware for harvesting, canning, and all that, and I've got a new line of meat smokers you might want to take a look at—"

"Sam!" Bayard's voice had gone shrill, and he fought to control it. "I just wanted to ask you about the guy in the beret, you know, the one you had with you up here last month—Cullum?"

There was another pause. Bayard could picture his mentor in a flame-retardant bathrobe, getting ready to turn in on a bed that converted to a life raft in the event a second flood came over the earth while he lay sleeping. "Uh-huh. Yeah. What about him?"

"Well, did he ever buy the place? I mean, is he up here now?"

"Listen, Bayard, why not let bygones be bygones, huh? Rayfield is no different than you are—except maybe he doesn't like children, is all. He's a 100 percenter, Bayard, on for the long haul like you. I'm sure he's forgot all about that little incident—and so should you."

Bayard drew a long breath. "I've got to know, Sam."

"It takes all kinds, Bayard."

"I don't need advice, Sam. Just information. Look, I can go down to the county assessor's office in the morning and get what I want."

Arkson sighed. "All right," he said finally. "Yes. He moved in yesterday."

When he turned away from the phone, Bayard felt his face go hot. Survival. It was a joke. He owned thirty-five acres of untrammeled wild-west backwoods wilderness land, and his only neighbor was a psychopath who kicked children in the stomach and mutilated helpless animals. Well, he wasn't going to allow it.

Society might be heading for collapse, but there were still laws on the books. He'd call the sheriff, take Cullum to court, have him locked up.

He was halfway to his car, just drawing even with the open door of the T&T, when he became aware of a familiar sound off to his left—he turned, recognizing the distinctive high whine of an Olfputt engine. There, sitting at the curb, was an Olfputt pickup, looking like half an MX missile with a raised bed grafted to the rear end. He stopped, puzzled. This was no Ford, no Chevy, no Dodge. The Olfputt was as rare in these parts as a palanquin—he'd never seen one himself till Arkson. . . . Suddenly he began to understand.

The door swung open. Cullum's face was dark—purple as a birth stain in the faint light. The engine ticked, raced, and then fell back as the car idled. The headlights seemed to clutch at the street. "Hey, hey," Cullum said. "Mr. Rocky Marciano. Mr. Streetfight."

Bayard became aware of movement in the shadows around him. The barflies, the cowboys, had gathered silently, watching him. Cullum stood twenty feet away, a rifle dangling at his side. Bayard knew that rifle, just as he'd known the Olfputt. Russian-made, he thought. AK-47. Smuggled out of Afghanistan. He felt Fran's little pistol against his thigh, weighing him down like a pocketful of change. His teeth were good, his heartbeat strong. He had a five-year supply of food in his basement and a gun in his pocket. Cullum was waiting.

Bayard took a step forward. Cullum spat in the dirt and raised the rifle. There was a muffled cough from the shadows, and out of the corner of his eye Bayard saw the flare of a match, the implacable dark figures of the spectators, and then the faces of Fran and the children passing in quick review.

He could have gone for his gun, but he didn't even know how to release the safety catch, let alone aim and fire the thing, and it came to him that even if he did know how to handle it, even if he'd fired it a thousand times at cans, bottles, rocks, and junkyard rats, he would never use it, not if all of the hungry hordes of the earth were at his door.

But Cullum would. Oh yes, Cullum would. Cullum was on for the long haul.

HUMAN MOMENTS
IN WORLD WAR III
by Don DeLillo

A note about Vollmer. He no longer describes the earth as a
library globe or a map that has come alive, as a cosmic eye staring
into deep space. This last was his most ambitious fling at imagery.
The war has changed the way he sees the earth. The earth is land
and water, the dwelling place of mortal men, in elevated dictionary terms. He doesn't see it anymore (storm-spiraled, sea-bright,
breathing heat and haze and color) as an occasion for picturesque
language, for easeful play or speculation.

At two hundred and twenty kilometers we see ship wakes and
the larger airports. Icebergs, lightning bolts, sand dunes. I point
out lava flows and cold-core eddies. That silver ribbon off the
Irish coast, I tell him, is an oil slick.

This is my third orbital mission, Vollmer's first. He is an
engineering genius, a communications and weapons genius, and
maybe other kinds of genius as well. As mission specialist I'm
content to be in charge. (The word "specialist," in the peculiar
usage of Colorado Command, refers here to someone who does
not specialize.) Our spacecraft is designed primarily to gather
intelligence. The refinement of the quantum burn technique enables us to make frequent adjustments of orbit without firing
rockets every time. We swing out into high wide trajectories, the
whole earth as our psychic light, to inspect unmanned and possibly hostile satellites. We orbit tightly, snugly, take intimate looks
at surface activities in untraveled places.

The banning of nuclear weapons has made the world safe for
war.

I try not to think big thoughts or submit to rambling abstractions. But the urge sometimes comes over me. Earth orbit puts men into philosophical temper. How can we help it? We see the planet complete, we have a privileged vista. In our attempts to be equal to the experience, we tend to meditate importantly on subjects like the human condition. It makes a man feel *universal,* floating over the continents, seeing the rim of the world, a line as clear as a compass arc, knowing it is just a turning of the bend to Atlantic twilight, to sediment plumes and kelp beds, an island chain glowing in the dusky sea.

I tell myself it is only scenery. I want to think of our life here as ordinary, as a housekeeping arrangement, an unlikely but workable setup caused by a housing shortage or spring floods in the valley.

Vollmer does the systems checklist and goes to his hammock to rest. He is twenty-three years old, a boy with a longish head and close-cropped hair. He talks about northern Minnesota as he removes the objects in his personal preference kit, placing them on an adjacent Velcro surface for tender inspection. I have a 1901 silver dollar in my personal preference kit. Little else of note. Vollmer has graduation pictures, bottle caps, small stones from his backyard. I don't know whether he chose these items himself or whether they were pressed on him by parents who feared that his life in space would be lacking in human moments.

Our hammocks are human moments, I suppose, although I don't know whether Colorado Command planned it that way. We eat hot dogs and almond crunch bars and apply lip balm as part of the presleep checklist. We wear slippers at the firing panel. Vollmer's football jersey is a human moment. Outsized, purple and white, of polyester mesh, bearing the number 79, a big man's number, a prime of no particular distinction, it makes him look stoop-shouldered, abnormally long-framed.

"I still get depressed on Sundays," he says.

"Do we have Sundays here?"

"No, but they have them there and I still feel them. I always know when it's Sunday."

"Why do you get depressed?"

"The slowness of Sundays. Something about the glare, the smell of warm grass, the church service, the relatives visiting in nice clothes. The whole day kind of lasts forever."

"I didn't like Sundays either."

"They were slow but not lazy-slow. They were long and hot, or long and cold. In summer my grandmother made lemonade.

There was a routine. The whole day was kind of set up before-hand and the routine almost never changed. Orbital routine is different. It's satisfying. It gives our time a shape and substance. Those Sundays were shapeless despite the fact you knew what was coming, who was coming, what we'd all say. You knew the first words out of the mouth of each person before anyone spoke. I was the only kid in the group. People were happy to see me. I used to want to hide."

"What's wrong with lemonade?" I ask.

A battle management satellite, unmanned, reports high-energy laser activity in orbital sector Dolores. We take out our laser kits and study them for half an hour. The beaming procedure is complex and because the panel operates on joint control only we must rehearse the sets of established measures with the utmost care.

A note about the earth. The earth is the preserve of day and night. It contains a sane and balanced variation, a natural waking and sleeping, or so it seems to someone deprived of this tidal effect.

This is why Vollmer's remark about Sundays in Minnesota struck me as interesting. He still feels, or claims he feels, or thinks he feels, that inherently earthbound rhythm.

To men at this remove, it is as though things exist in their particular physical form in order to reveal the hidden simplicity of some powerful mathematical truth. The earth reveals to us the simple awesome beauty of day and night. It is there to contain and incorporate these conceptual events.

Vollmer in his shorts and suction clogs resembles a high-school swimmer, all but hairless, an unfinished man not aware he is open to cruel scrutiny, not aware he is without devices, standing with arms folded in a place of echoing voices and chlorine fumes. There is something stupid in the sound of his voice. It is too direct, a deep voice from high in the mouth, well back in the mouth, slightly insistent, a little loud. Vollmer has never said a stupid thing in my presence. It is just his voice that is stupid, a grave and naked bass, a voice without inflection or breath.

We are not cramped here. The flight deck and crew quarters are thoughtfully designed. Food is fair to good. There are books, videocassettes, news and music. We do the manual checklists, the oral checklists, the simulated firings with no sign of boredom or carelessness. If anything, we are getting better at our tasks all the time. The only danger is conversation.

I try to keep our conversations on an everyday plane. I make it a point to talk about small things, routine things. This makes sense to me. It seems a sound tactic, under the circumstances, to restrict our talk to familiar topics, minor matters. I want to build a structure of the commonplace. But Vollmer has a tendency to bring up enormous subjects. He wants to talk about war and the weapons of war. He wants to discuss global strategies, global aggressions. I tell him now that he has stopped describing the earth as a cosmic eye, he wants to see it as a game board or computer model. He looks at me plain-faced and tries to get me in a theoretical argument: selected space-based attacks versus long drawn-out well-modulated land-sea-air engagements. He quotes experts, mentions sources. What am I supposed to say? He will suggest that people are disappointed in the war. The war is dragging into its third week. There is a sense in which it is worn out, played out. He gathers this from the news broadcasts we periodically receive. Something in the announcer's voice hints at a let-down, a fatigue, a faint bitterness about—*something*. Vollmer is probably right about this. I've heard it myself in the tone of the broadcaster's voice, in the voice of Colorado Command, despite the fact that our news is censored, that they are not telling us things they feel we shouldn't know, in our special situation, our exposed and sensitive position. In his direct and stupid-sounding and uncannily perceptive way, young Vollmer says that people are not enjoying this war to the same extent that people have always enjoyed and nourished themselves on war, as a heightening, a periodic intensity. What I object to in Vollmer is that he often shares my deep-reaching and most reluctantly held convictions. Coming from that mild face, in that earnest resonant run-on voice, these ideas unnerve and worry me as they never do when they remain unspoken. Vollmer's candor exposes something painful.

It is not too early in the war to discern nostalgic references to earlier wars. All wars refer back. Ships, planes, entire operations are named after ancient battles, simpler weapons, what we perceive as conflicts of nobler intent. This recon-interceptor is called Tomahawk II. When I sit at the firing panel I look at a photograph of Vollmer's granddad when he was a young man in sagging khakis and a shallow helmet, standing in a bare field, a rifle strapped to his shoulder. This is a human moment and it reminds me that war, among other things, is a form of longing.

*   *   *

We dock with the command station, take on food, exchange videocassettes. The war is going well, they tell us, although it isn't likely they know much more than we do.

Then we separate.

The maneuver is flawless and I am feeling happy and satisfied, having resumed human contact with the nearest form of the outside world, having traded quips and manly insults, traded voices, traded news and rumors—buzzes, rumbles, scuttlebutt. We stow our supplies of broccoli and apple cider and fruit cocktail and butterscotch pudding. I feel a homey emotion, putting away the colorfully packaged goods, a sensation of prosperous well-being, the consumer's solid comfort.

Volmer's T-shirt bears the word *Inscription.*

"People had hoped to be caught up in something bigger than themselves," he says. "They thought it would be a shared crisis. They would feel a sense of shared purpose, shared destiny. Like a snowstorm that blankets a large city—but lasting months, lasting years, carrying everyone along, creating fellow-feeling where there was only suspicion and fear. Strangers talking to each other, meals by candlelight when the power fails. The war would ennoble everything we say and do. What was impersonal would become personal. What was solitary would be shared. But what happens when the sense of shared crisis begins to dwindle much sooner than anyone expected? We begin to think the feeling lasts longer in snowstorms."

A note about selective noise. Forty-eight hours ago I was monitoring data on the mission console when a voice broke in on my report to Colorado Command. The voice was unenhanced, heavy with static. I checked my headset, checked the switches and lights. Seconds later the command signal resumed and I heard our flight dynamics officer ask me to switch to the redundant sense frequencer. I did this but it only caused the weak voice to return, a voice that carried with it a strange and unspecifiable poignancy. I seemed somehow to recognize it. I don't mean I knew who was speaking. It was the tone I recognized, the touching quality of some half-remembered and tender event, even through the static, the sonic mist.

In any case, Colorado Command resumed transmission in a matter of seconds.

"We have a deviate, Tomahawk."

"We copy. There's a voice."

"We have gross oscillation here."

"There's some interference. I have gone redundant but I'm not sure it's helping."

"We are clearing an outframe to locate source."

"Thank you, Colorado."

"It is probably just selective noise. You are negative red on the step-function quad."

"It was a voice," I told them.

"We have just received an affirm on selective noise."

"I could hear words, in English."

"We copy selective noise."

"Someone was talking, Colorado."

"What do you think selective noise is?"

"I don't know what it is."

"You are getting a spill from one of the unmanneds."

"If it's an unmanned, how could it be sending a voice?"

"It is not a voice as such, Tomahawk. It is selective noise. We have some real firm telemetry on that."

"It sounded like a voice."

"It is supposed to sound like a voice. But it is not a voice as such. It is enhanced."

"It sounded unenhanced. It sounded human in all sorts of ways."

"It is signals and they are spilling from geosynchronous orbit. This is your deviate. You are getting voice codes from twenty-two thousand miles. It is basically a weather report. We will correct, Tomahawk. In the meantime, advise you stay redundant."

About ten hours later Vollmer heard the voice. Then he heard two or three other voices. They were people speaking, people in conversation. He gestured to me as he listened, pointed to the headset, then raised his shoulders, held his hands apart to indicate surprise and bafflement. In the swarming noise (as he said later), it wasn't easy to get the drift of what people were saying. The static was frequent, the references were somewhat elusive, but Vollmer mentioned how intensely affecting these voices were, even when the signals were at their weakest. One thing he did know: it wasn't selective noise. A quality of purest, sweetest sadness issued from remote space. He wasn't sure but he thought there was also a background noise integral to the conversation. Laughter. The sound of people laughing.

In other transmissions we've been able to recognize theme music, an announcer's introduction, wisecracks and bursts of applause, commercials for products whose long-lost brand names evoke the golden antiquity of great cities buried in sand and river silt.

Somehow we are picking up signals from radio programs of forty, fifty, sixty years ago.

Our current task is to collect imagery data on troop deployment. Vollmer surrounds his Hasselblad, engrossed in some microadjustment. There is a seaward bulge of stratocumulus. Sunglint and littoral drift. I see blooms of plankton in a blue of such Persian richness it seems an animal rapture, a color-change to express some form of intuitive delight. As the surface features unfurl, I list them aloud by name. It is the only game I play in space, reciting the earth-names, the nomenclature of contour and structure. Glacial scour, moraine debris. Shatter-coning at the edge of a multi-ring impact site. A resurgent caldera, a mass of castellated rimrock. Over the sand seas now. Parabolic dunes, star dunes, straight dunes with radial crests. The emptier the land, the more luminous and precise the names for its features. Vollmer says the thing science does best is name the features of the world.

He has degrees in science and technology. He was a scholarship winner, an honors student, a research assistant. He ran science projects, read technical papers in the deep-pitched earnest voice that rolls off the roof of his mouth. As mission specialist (generalist), I sometimes resent his nonscientific perceptions, the glimmerings of maturity and balanced judgment. I am beginning to feel slightly preempted. I want him to stick to systems, onboard guidance, data parameters. His human insights make me nervous.

"I'm happy," he says.

These words are delivered with matter-of-fact finality and the simple statement affects me powerfully. It frightens me in fact. What does he mean he's happy? Isn't happiness totally outside our frame of reference? How can he think it is possible to be happy here? I want to say to him, "This is just a housekeeping arrangement, a series of more or less routine tasks. Attend to your tasks, do your testing, run through your checklists." I want to say, "Forget the measure of our vision, the sweep of things, the war itself, the terrible death. Forget the overarching night, the stars as static points, as mathematical fields. Forget the cosmic solitude, the upwelling awe and dread."

I want to say, "Happiness is not a fact of this experience, at least not to the extent that one is bold enough to speak of it."

*   *   *

Laser technology contains a core of foreboding and myth. It is a clean sort of lethal package we are dealing with, a well-behaved beam of photons, an engineered coherence, but we approach the weapon with our minds full of ancient warnings and fears. (There ought to be a term for this ironic condition: primitive fear of the weapons we are advanced enough to design and produce.) Maybe this is why the project managers were ordered to work out a firing procedure that depends on the coordinated actions of two men—two temperaments, two souls—operating the controls together. Fear of the power of light, the pure stuff of the universe.

A single dark mind in a moment of inspiration might think it liberating to fling a concentrated beam at some lumbering hump-backed Boeing making its commercial rounds at thirty thousand feet.

Vollmer and I approach the firing panel. The panel is designed in such a way that the joint operators must sit back to back. The reason for this, although Colorado Command never specifically said so, is to keep us from seeing each other's face. Colorado wants to be sure that weapons personnel in particular are not influenced by each other's tics and perturbations. We are back to back, therefore, harnessed in our seats, ready to begin. Vollmer in his purple and white jersey, his fleeced pad-abouts.

This is only a test.

I start the playback. At the sound of a prerecorded voice command, we each insert a modal key in its proper slot. Together we count down from five and then turn the keys one-quarter left. This puts the system in what is called an open-minded mode. We count down from three. The enhanced voice says, *You are open-minded now.*

Vollmer speaks into his voiceprint analyzer.

"This is code B for bluegrass. Request voice identity clearance."

We count down from five and then speak into our voiceprint analyzers. We say whatever comes into our heads. The point is simply to produce a voiceprint that matches the print in the memory bank. This ensures that the men at the panel are the same men authorized to be there when the system is in an open-minded mode.

This is what comes into my head: "I am standing at the corner of Fourth and Main, where thousands are dead of unknown causes, their scorched bodies piled in the street."

We count down from three. The enhanced voice says, *You are cleared to proceed to lock-in position.*

We turn our modal keys half right. I activate the logic chip and study the numbers on my screen. Vollmer disengages voiceprint and puts us in voice circuit rapport with the onboard computer's sensing mesh. We count down from five. The enhanced voice says, *You are locked in now.*

"Random factor seven," I say. "Problem seven. Solution seven."

Vollmer says, "Give me an acronym."

"BROWN, for Bearing Radius Oh White Nine."

My color-spec lights up brown. The numbers on my display screen read 2, 18, 15, 23, 14. These are the alphanumeric values of the letters in the acronym BROWN as they appear in unit succession.

The logic-gate opens. The enhanced voice says, *You are logical now.*

As we move from one step to the next, as the colors, numbers, characters, lights and auditory signals indicate that we are proceeding correctly, a growing satisfaction passes through me—the pleasure of elite and secret skills, a life in which every breath is governed by specific rules, by patterns, codes, controls. I try to keep the results of the operation out of my mind, the whole point of it, the outcome of these sequences of precise and esoteric steps. But often I fail. I let the image in, I think the thought, I even say the word at times. This is confusing, of course. I feel tricked. My pleasure feels betrayed, as if it had a life of its own, a childlike or intelligent-animal existence independent of the man at the firing panel.

We count down from five. Vollmer releases the lever that unwinds the systems-purging disc. My pulse marker shows green at three-second intervals. We count down from three. We turn the modal keys three-quarters right. I activate the beam sequencer. We turn the keys one-quarter right. We count down from three. Bluegrass music plays over the squawk box. The enhanced voice says, *You are moded to fire now.*

We study our world map kits.

"Don't you sometimes feel a power in you?" Vollmer says. "An extreme state of good health, sort of. An *arrogant* healthiness. That's it. You are feeling so good you begin thinking you're a little superior to other people. A kind of life-strength. An optimism about yourself that you generate almost at the expense of others. Don't you sometimes feel this?"

(Yes, as a matter of fact.)

"There's probably a German word for it. But the point I want

to make is that this powerful feeling is so—I don't know—
delicate. That's it. One day you feel it, the next day you are
suddenly puny and doomed. A single little thing goes wrong, you
feel doomed, you feel utterly weak and defeated and unable to act
powerfully or even sensibly. Everyone else is lucky, you are
unlucky, hapless, sad, ineffectual and doomed."

(Yes, yes.)

By chance we are over the Missouri River now, looking toward
the Red Lakes of Minnesota. I watch Vollmer go through his map
kit, trying to match the two worlds. This is a deep and mysterious
happiness, to confirm the accuracy of a map. He seems im-
mensely satisfied. He keeps saying, *"That's it, that's it."*

Vollmer talks about childhood. In orbit he has begun to think
about his early years for the first time. He is surprised at the
power of these memories. As he speaks he keeps his head turned
to the window. Minnesota is a human moment. Upper Red Lake,
Lower Red Lake. He clearly feels he can see himself there.

"Kids don't take walks," he says. "They don't sunbathe or sit
on the porch."

He seems to be saying that children's lives are too well-supplied
to accommodate the spells of reinforced being that the rest of us
depend on. A deft enough thought but not to be pursued. It is
time to prepare for a quantum burn.

We listen to the old radio shows. Light flares and spreads across
the blue-banded edge, sunrise, sunset, the urban grids in shadow.
A man and woman trade well-timed remarks, light, pointed,
bantering. There is a sweetness in the tenor voice of the young
man singing, a simple vigor that time and distance and random
noise have enveloped in eloquence and yearning. Every sound,
every lilt of strings has this veneer of age. Vollmer says he
remembers these programs, although of course he has never
heard them before. What odd happenstance, what flourish or
grace of the laws of physics, enables us to pick up these signals?
Traveled voices, chambered and dense. At times they have the
detached and surreal quality of aural hallucination, voices in attic
rooms, the complaints of dead relatives. But the sound effects are
full of urgency and verve. Cars turn dangerous corners, crisp
gunfire fills the night. It was, it is, wartime. Wartime for Duz and
Grape-Nuts Flakes. Comedians make fun of the way the enemy
talks. We hear hysterical mock German, moonshine Japanese.
The cities are in light, the listening millions, fed, met comfortably
in drowsy rooms, at war, as the night comes softly down. Vollmer

says he recalls specific moments, the comic inflections, the announcer's fat-man laughter. He recalls individual voices rising from the laughter of the studio audience, the cackle of a St. Louis businessman, the brassy wail of a high-shouldered blonde, just arrived in California, where women wear their hair this year in aromatic bales.

Vollmer drifts across the wardroom, upside-down, eating an almond crunch.

He sometimes floats free of his hammock, sleeping in a fetal crouch, bumping into walls, adhering to a corner of the ceiling grid.

"Give me a minute to think of the name," he says in his sleep.

He says he dreams of vertical spaces from which he looks, as a boy, at—*something*. My dreams are the heavy kind, the kind that are hard to wake from, to rise out of. They are strong enough to pull me back down, dense enough to leave me with a heavy head, a drugged and bloated feeling. There are episodes of faceless gratification, vaguely disturbing.

"It's almost unbelievable when you think of it, how they live there in all that ice and sand and mountainous wilderness. Look at it," he says. "Huge barren deserts, huge oceans. How do they endure all those terrible things? The floods alone. The earthquakes alone make it crazy to live there. Look at those fault systems. They're so big, there's so many of them. The volcanic eruptions alone. What could be more frightening than a volcanic eruption? How do they endure avalanches, year after year, with numbing regularity? It's hard to believe people live there. The floods alone. You can see whole huge discolored areas, all flooded out, washed out. How do they survive, where do they go? Look at the cloud buildups. Look at that swirling storm center. What about the people who live in the path of a storm like that? It must be packing incredible winds. The lightning alone. People exposed on beaches, near trees and telephone poles. Look at the cities with their spangled lights spreading in all directions. Try to imagine the crime and violence. Look at the smoke pall hanging low. What does that mean in terms of respiratory disorders? It's crazy. Who would live there? The deserts, how they encroach. Every year they claim more and more arable land. How enormous those snowfields are. Look at the massive storm fronts over the ocean. There are ships down there, small craft some of them. Try to imagine the waves, the rocking. The hurricanes alone. The tidal waves. Look at those coastal communities exposed to tidal waves. What could be more frightening than a tidal wave? But they live there, they stay there. Where could they go?"

I want to talk to him about calorie intake, the effectiveness of the earplugs and nasal decongestants. The earplugs are human moments. The apple cider and the broccoli are human moments. Vollmer himself is a human moment, never more so than when he forgets there is a war.

The close-cropped hair and longish head. The mild blue eyes that bulge slightly. The protuberant eyes of long-bodied people with stooped shoulders. The long hands and wrists. The mild face. The easy face of a handyman in a panel truck that has an extension ladder fixed to the roof and a scuffed license plate, green and white, with the state motto beneath the digits. That kind of face.

He offers to give me a haircut. What an interesting thing a haircut is, when you think of it. Before the war there were time slots reserved for such activities. Houston not only had everything scheduled well in advance but constantly monitored us for whatever meager feedback might result. We were wired, taped, scanned, diagnosed and metered. We were men in space, objects worthy of the most scrupulous care, the deepest sentiments and anxieties.

Now there is a war. Nobody cares about my hair, what I eat, how I feel about the spacecraft's decor, and it is not Houston but Colorado we are in touch with. We are no longer delicate biological specimens adrift in an alien environment. The enemy can kill us with its photons, its mesons, its charged particles faster than any calcium deficiency or trouble of the inner ear, faster than any dusting of micrometeoroids. The emotions have changed. We've stopped being candidates for an embarrassing demise, the kind of mistake or unforeseen event that tends to make a nation grope for the appropriate response. As men in war we can be certain, dying, that we will arouse uncomplicated sorrows, the open and dependable feelings that grateful nations count on to embellish the simplest ceremony.

A note about the universe. Vollmer is on the verge of deciding that our planet is alone in harboring intelligent life. We are an accident and we happened only once. (What a remark to make, in egg-shaped orbit, to someone who doesn't want to discuss the larger questions.) He feels this way because of the war.

The war, he says, will bring about an end to the idea that the universe swarms, as they say, with life. Other astronauts have looked past the star-points and imagined infinite possibility, grape-clustered worlds teeming with higher forms. But this was before the war. Our view is changing even now, his and mine, he says, as we drift across the firmament.

Is Vollmer saying that cosmic optimism is a luxury reserved for periods between world wars? Do we project our current failure and despair out toward the star clouds, the endless night? After all, he says, where are they? If they exist, why has there been no sign, not one, not any, not a single indication that serious people might cling to, not a whisper, a radio pulse, a shadow? The war tells us it is foolish to believe.

Our dialogues with Colorado Command are beginning to sound like computer-generated tea-time chat. Vollmer tolerates Colorado's jargon only to a point. He is critical of their more debased locutions and doesn't mind letting them know. Why, then, if I agree with his views on this matter, am I becoming irritated by his complaints? Is he too young to champion the language? Does he have the experience, the professional standing to scold our flight dynamics officer, our conceptual paradigm officer, our status consultants on waste-management systems and evasion-related zonal options? Or is it something else completely, something unrelated to Colorado Command and our communications with them? Is it the sound of his voice? Is it just his *voice* that is driving me crazy?

Vollmer has entered a strange phase. He spends all his time at the window now, looking down at the earth. He says little or nothing. He simply wants to look, do nothing but look. The oceans, the continents, the archipelagos. We are configured in what is called a cross-orbit series and there is no repetition from one swing around the earth to the next. He sits there looking. He takes meals at the window, does checklists at the window, barely glancing at the instruction sheets as we pass over tropical storms, over grass fires and major ranges. I keep waiting for him to return to his prewar habit of using quaint phrases to describe the earth. It's a beach ball, a sun-ripened fruit. But he simply looks out the window, eating almond crunches, the wrappers floating away. The view clearly fills his consciousness. It is powerful enough to silence him, to still the voice that rolls off the roof of his mouth, to leave him turned in the seat, twisted uncomfortably for hours at a time.

The view is endlessly fulfilling. It is like the answer to a lifetime of questions and vague cravings. It satisfies every childlike curiosity, every muted desire, whatever there is in him of the scientist, the poet, the primitive seer, the watcher of fire and shooting stars, whatever obsessions eat at the night side of his mind, whatever sweet and dreamy yearning he has ever felt for nameless places faraway, whatever earth-sense he possesses, the neural pulse of some wilder awareness, a sympathy for beasts, whatever belief in an immanent vital force, the Lord of Creation, whatever secret harboring of the idea of human oneness, whatever wishfulness and simplehearted hope, whatever of too much and not enough, all at once and little by little, whatever burning urge to escape responsibility and routine, escape his own overspecialization, the circumscribed and inward-spiraling self, whatever remnants of his boyish longing to fly, his dreams of strange spaces and eerie heights, his fantasies of happy death, whatever indolent and sybaritic leanings, lotus-eater, smoker of grasses and herbs, blue-eyed gazer into space—all these are satisfied, all collected and massed in that living body, the sight he sees from the window.

"It is just so interesting," he says at last. "The colors and all."

The colors and all.